WHO
CAT^{WILL}CH
US _{AS}
^{WE} FALL

DEC 1 6

*To all the strong Kenyans in my life and four
in particular: Winnie, Stella, John and Joseph.
This story was inspired by you.*

*As always, to my family – without you, I would still
be a young girl in love with the idea of writing big
stories. Because of you, I write them.*

WHO WILL CATCH US AS WE FALL

Iman

Verjee

ONEWORLD

A Oneworld Book

First published in North America, Great Britain &
Australia by Oneworld Publications, 2016

ISBN 978-1-78074-936-5
ISBN 978-1-78074-937-2 (eBook)

Text designed and typeset by Tetragon, London
Printed and bound in Great Britain by Clays Ltd, St Ives plc

Oneworld Publications
10 Bloomsbury Street
London WC1B 3SR
England

Acknowledgments

When I first began writing this novel, I knew exactly why I was writing it but I was too ashamed to say the reason out loud. The truth is, I felt disconnected from a place I was meant to call home. Yes, its smells, colors and noises thrilled me. It felt familiar in a way that a child's blanket is comforting – a warm memory to shrug on and off whenever I needed it. But like a memory, it had no distinguishable roots, nothing firm to anchor me to it. And it wasn't until I was almost halfway through the novel that I suddenly realized, I had discarded Kenya, not the other way around. Writing gave me something living in my birth country for over twenty-two years could not – a clear perspective.

For that, I have many people to thank. My father, whose passion inspires me and is the driving force behind this story. My mother, who is so inexplicably compassionate that it makes me strive to be a kinder writer and a better human being. Safia, you are the bravest sister I have ever known. Thank you for teaching me how to stand on my own two feet. Mishal, without you by my side, I would (most certainly) go mad. Your quiet yet absolute confidence makes me aspire to better things. Rahim, until I met you, I'd never met anyone so ready to give love. You remind me of everything that is good in this world.

To my grandparents – your histories and struggles are worth remembering and fighting for. I doubt I will ever know two such loving and inspiring people.

Calvin, I wrote this novel before I even knew you and yet you seem to be in every sentence.

To my wonderful friends – Mihir, as always, you were the first person I dared show this novel to and whose advice I have always inexplicably trusted. Zahra, I will always be grateful for your belief and enthusiasm every step of the way and to my girls – Tamiza, Shaloo and Rehana – without even knowing it, you made me who I am today. To Vicky, Devanshi, Amit, Adil, Nina, Meera, Sandhya and all my other Kenyan friends – may you find a little part of yourselves in this story.

Janelle Andrews – my astute agent – thank you for always believing in my ability to write stories, even when I had my doubts, and for making this process so easy and enjoyable.

Rosalind Porter – I will never understand how you saw potential in this novel beneath those first 800 pages of complete rambling and I will be forever thankful for your expertise, friendship and patience.

Jonathan Myerson – I will continue to thank you in every single book I write because every single book I write will be thanks to you.

To Juliet Mabey, James Magniac, Paul Nash, Amanda Dackcombe and the rest of the Oneworld team, thank you for your hard work, dedication and the valuable time you spent bringing this novel to life.

PART ONE

2007

1

Leena watches as the massive, thundering engines of the Kenya Airways Boeing 747 airplane pushes out streams of straw-colored jet fuel, breaking the thinning cover of clouds below to reveal the dreary buildings that form Jomo Kenyatta International Airport. She has always enjoyed looking at the city from such a great height – so structured that it reminds her of a dollhouse she used to own. Today, however, she feels cheated by the neat, seemingly harmless, aerial view.

The flight attendant crackles over the loudspeaker in her practiced voice that she has expertly hammered down so that it is as smooth as velvet. *Kuwakaribisha kwa Nairobi.* Then, in English, *Welcome to Nairobi.*

'First time in Kenya?' The smartly dressed man beside her is holding a Kenyan passport and raises his eyebrows at her hands. She loosens her fingers on the seat handles and doesn't answer.

They land with a swooping bump and skid; the cabin fills with smattering applause and the clicking sound of people already undoing their seatbelts. She keeps hers on in a vain attempt to prolong the moment, apprehensive of the inevitable next step.

A group of teenage girls in the row ahead are taking pictures of each other, tailoring their memories to peace signs and fish-mouths, weaves of colorful bracelets catching the morning light – faint wisps of hair on skin like fairy-tale gold. They are wearing identical blue cotton T-shirts that have the name of a school stamped across the front. Printed in bold, white letters across the back they say, *Global Love: Kenya 2007*. Leena resists the urge to ask them who they are planning on saving.

In their hands she sees their passports – the exclusive maroon and gold of Britain that has shaped most of her teenage dreams. They move and speak in a manner born from the freedom it allows them, to be welcomed wherever they go but, more than that, the liberty it gives them to leave whenever they choose.

She follows their gaze out of the window, her expression reflecting theirs: a curious bewilderment at this frenzied world where the images are brighter, the smells overpowering – the noise settling like a thick blanket across her skull. Her eyes track the dark-skinned, rowdy people of this country as they shove and jostle each other in their fight to disembark first, unbothered by the rules and boundaries that have characterized her life elsewhere. But unlike those girls, she does it without excitement, her stomach pressed with dreadful finality.

The man beside her rises. 'Enjoy your visit. I hope you will find us to be very hospitable.'

And his open expression, his unquestioned assumption that she is a foreigner, strikes a deep chord in her already irritated disposition and she holds up her passport – royal blue emblazoned with the Kenyan coat of arms. 'I'm sure I will.'

His hand freezes at the breast pocket of his blazer, where he has reached in and half-pulled out his phone: an old model Nokia. 'You don't sound Kenyan.' The friendliness in his voice recedes. She is something entirely different to him now. 'That is why I was mistaken.'

She doesn't tell him that his statement is impossible since she hasn't said a word to him the whole flight. She doesn't accuse him of making hasty conjectures based on their multiple and obvious differences, because it is something she understands. Just because you happen to be born in a certain place doesn't mean you belong to it.

'Excuse me, miss?'

The next time Leena opens her eyes, the plane is empty. The air hostess is leaning over her, as lovely in her shapely red uniform and silk necktie as her voice implied her to be. 'We need to get this plane ready for the next set of passengers. Perhaps I can guide you on to where you want to go?'

Unbuckling her seatbelt, Leena struggles upward. Her movements feel too heavy, sluggish and slow and she drags her luggage behind her as she tells the air hostess, 'I know my way around.'

Walking down the slanting corridor of the arrivals section, the airport appears more modern than she remembers it, though there are still the brown linoleum floors that squeak underfoot and the stained stucco walls, the entire building clouded in the musty stench of urine. The duty-free shops are still selling the same overpriced African curios such as soap-stone chess sets and beaded traditional jewelry. She used to have a drawer full of such memorabilia, which she had collected with an irrational hunger during her first holiday back from university – a time when she had been homesick for this place.

'Next.' At the customs booth, a man gestures her forward. He is sweetly rounded with billowing, silk-like cheeks and a visible dampness spreading from under the armpits of his yellow shirt. 'Where from?' he barks.

'London.'

'*Univasaty?*' he asks, used to the likes of her. Wealthy Asians dressed up like Westerners, noses in the air and an excessive amount of degrees in their pockets.

'Yes.'

'When are you going back?'

'I'm not.'

He is used to this also. An apartment there can buy you a home, two housemaids and a brand new Range Rover here. 'So you are returning to Kenya, to home?'

'Yes.' So quietly that he has to lean forward to hear her.

'Passport.' Trying to soften the growl in his throat because, unlike what he is used to, she looks sad, terrified almost, to be standing before him. He stamps the pages of her book without glancing at it and hands it back, shouting out, 'Next!'

'*Asante.*' She thanks him in Swahili and then stops, wondering where it came from – that sneaky bit of herself, startled at the ease with which she has already begun settling into her past.

'*Karibu.*' He waves her impatiently away.

When she eventually exits the building, the early morning mist has condensed into a thick humidity and the sky is bright blue and windless – a typical Nairobi morning. Jai is standing at the entrance and she catches the scent of his cologne, *Cool Water*, which she brought back for him on that last, never-to-be-mentioned-again visit. As always, he speaks first.

'Hello, monkey.'

Finally. The tension in her chest relents, the air cool in her lungs. *Some semblance of coming home.*

Jai steers the cart out of the terminal and toward his old, canvas-green Land Cruiser. She climbs into the passenger seat while he tosses her suitcases into the trunk.

'Nice flight?'

'Long. I had to wait seven hours in Dubai.'

'I told Ma you would hate that.' He hops into the driver's seat and turns the ignition, rolling down his window as the car jumps awake. 'The traffic is insane these days so it might take a couple of hours before we're home. I bought you an omelette sandwich – they're still your favorite right?'

'Come on, Jai, it hasn't been that long.'

'You're right. Four years is nothing when you're running away.'

It is difficult to quell the guilty upsurge his words spark and Leena reminds herself that she had not left Nairobi out of choice. It had forced her out on a rainy night, the only promise of solace being the flickering of taxi lights on the runway, blurred in the storm as the plane had lifted her away.

Jai ruffles her hair. 'I'm glad you're back.'

The smile comes on its own. 'I missed you too.'

Jai turns the car out of the car park and onto the main street with an easy twist of his wrist. 'Maybe you'll realize that this place is better than you remember it.' He cocks his head at her. 'Give us people who stayed some hope.'

The open, trimmed spaces of the airport fall away as they enter the main city, picking up speed amongst cargo trucks rattling dangerously under their loads and the smaller public service vehicles, *matatus*, which duck recklessly in and out of cars. The peeling street signs are bright, momentary flashes before they are thrown back out of vision.

'You don't need me to give you hope – you do enough of that for the whole of Nairobi.'

Jai grins. 'No arguing with that.'

Above them, screeching vultures patiently circle the carcass of a dead dog, repeatedly flattened by careless cars. At intervals, one bird at a time will swoop down and snatch up whatever it can of the animal's remains until the dog is not a dog any more but just a stain and some teeth on the tarmac.

As they go deeper into the city center, Jai closes his window and turns up the air conditioning. He hits the side of the radio twice with his fist until it yelps to life; Kiss FM – a local station – is playing and the two presenters are discussing the upcoming December elections.

'It's all everyone can talk about these days,' the first presenter says, 'and I get the feeling that the public mood is quite upbeat. A lot of Kenyans seem to be optimistic about the direction in which our nation is heading. Of course, the worry of tribal conflict is always there but we can only have faith in our leaders that the elections will be conducted fairly.'

'You know, Maina, tribal problems have always trumped the confidence Kenyans hold in their electoral system and democratic institutions.' The other presenter has taken over. 'And this year, I fear it won't be any different. The election period has always been and will always remain a worrisome time for Kenyans.'

'What do you think?' the first presenter asks, and Leena imagines him leaning into the microphone, pointing outward accusingly at her. 'Are you satisfied with the state of democracy in our country? What are your views on ethnic conflict? Are we going to have a safe and fair election this year? Call in with your thoughts on 0722-K-I-S-S-F-M.'

'Do you think we should be worried?'

Jai shrugs. 'With our politicians, you never know. We can only try to raise awareness of the issues and pray for the best, as we always have.'

Street vendors move in and out of traffic, holding up magazines, newspapers, some of which are two days old, counterfeit DVDs and car fresheners shaped like pine trees.

'Good price.' She hears their voices through the closed windows. 'You buy and I give you good price.' They knock on the glass and make rolling motions with their hands. *Kunisaidia, Mama*, they implore. *Tu kitu kidogo.*

Leena keeps her gaze fixed ahead into the sea of vehicles while Jai leans forward, waving them away. '*Sitaki*,' he says. 'We don't want anything. *Sitaki.*'

She makes sure the doors are locked and, closing her eyes, she does the breathing technique she learned on the internet. One hand on chest, the other lightly placed on her abdomen. Deep breath through the nose, stomach rising. She can hear the woman's infomercial-like drone from the YouTube video. *Phhooof*, a whistled, hard breath out, counting a slow release. *1-2-3-4.*

Jai looks over. 'What are you doing?'

'Nothing, I'm fine.'

The car inches forward and her brother gestures at the thermos of tea. 'Eat. Drink. You must be starving.'

She takes a bite of the sandwich and smiles, even though the bread is too dry. 'You put green chilies in it.'

'Just the way you like it.'

'Do you remember how Angela used to make them for us?' The memory is unexpected, slithering out of her unconscious.

'I have to tell you something.' He cannot hold the words back any more. He has been trying to say this to her ever since it was decided she was coming home. Even before then.

His confession is interrupted by a shout, followed by a quick succession of loud orders. Four bodies dash by their car, slamming the sides of it with their elbows and hands. Leena sees a boy who cannot be more than twelve, running and clutching the two side mirrors of a car, tucked into the torn armpits of his shirt. He stops momentarily as he makes contact with her side of the Land Cruiser and their eyes catch.

She drops her sandwich and grabs onto Jai, craning her neck as she watches the boy go. 'What's happening?'

'I'll go check.' Jai makes a move to climb out.

'Please don't leave me.' The words squeeze from her throat and she doesn't care if they make her sound desperate.

'Stop them! *Mwizi*!' A man is chasing the boys and he pauses by their car, bending over to catch his breath. Jai rolls down the passenger window before Leena can stop him.

'What's going on?'

The man pants. 'Those bloody *chokoras*. They came out of nowhere! Grabbed my side mirrors and when I opened my window to see what was going on, one of the little fuckers snatched the phone right out of my hand!'

He is a thirty-something African man dressed in pants made from a shiny cotton, slightly too short and too tight for him, creasing at the crotch. His sunglasses have been pushed up to his forehead. 'Do you know how hard it is to find Audi parts in this country?'

'Can't catch them now,' Jai says apologetically.

'This country is too much. Full of thieves from up to down.' The man heads back toward his car, letting his sunglasses fall back into position. The traffic resumes and Leena leans her head against the window, trying to slow her heart. Hand on chest and stomach, clutching this time. Breathe in. *Phhooof.* Jai doesn't say anything but she senses him watching.

She should have known that this technique would have no power on this side of the world, where there is nothing to separate her memories from her life.

2

Pooja Kohli stands in her sun-soaked living room and watches a bee settle on the white hibiscus tree under which Kidha, the gardener, crouches in his overalls, pulling weeds from the grass. The sleeves of his uniform have been deliberately shorn off, revealing ball-like muscles which stretch and compress in compliance with his movements. Luna, the family's German shepherd, sniffs around his sandaled feet, her heavy tail thwacking Kidha's thighs as she buries her face in his chest with a delighted whimper. He pauses. Strokes her just-washed fur.

There is a voice behind her. 'They should be here soon.'

'Does the rock garden look dead to you?' She doesn't turn around as her husband puts his arms around her and rests his chin on her head.

'You told Kidha to water it just yesterday.'

She holds onto Raj's forearms, so wide that her ringed fingers span only a part of them. 'She's angry with us.'

'It'll be okay,' he says and she wonders why she always believes him.

Kidha is trimming the impressive bougainvillea tree, a bright magenta bush that has outgrown the clay pot Pooja planted it in, causing small fissures to run out like mean, little rivers – traveling so deep that they've broken off a piece of the urn. It has been sitting sadly on the water drain for days now and she must remind Kidha to fix it before the whole thing comes apart.

Staring out, she wonders how big a part she had to play in her daughter's childishness, her seemingly stubborn refusal to grow up fully. Pooja also knows that there are other reasons. *Certain events can stunt growth, especially at crucial points in one's development.* She had read it in a recently purchased book from Text Book Center; plucked it from one of the shelves entitled 'Self-Help' and hidden it under her cardigan as she sped to the cashier. It had been risky to go to Sarit Center, the main shopping mall in Westlands, where she was bound to run into someone she knew and she had left without waiting for her change. *We live in the past because we are afraid of our future. Trauma and Recovery* – the first title she had spotted.

A few days later, she had walked in on Jai in her room, holding the book and shaking his head at her.

'Don't look at your mother that way.'

'Better hide it before she comes home, Ma.'

She had fussed with her pillow. 'Well, if you weren't so busy-busy and taught me how to use the Google, I could just erase the history.'

And he had put the book down and come to hug her – 'It's Google, Ma, not "the" Google and it's going to be okay,' sounding exactly like his father.

Now, leaning against the pristinely polished Yamaha piano in which she can see a vague and shimmering reflection of herself, they hear the grumble of their son's car, almost three hours since he left that morning. Pooja knocks on the glass door to catch Kidha's attention. When he doesn't turn around, she slides it open to shout.

'Kidha! Gate!'

He drops the garden shears and clicks his tongue at Luna. Pooja watches as the two of them trot around the garden to the front of the house.

Her husband's soft laughter tickles her earlobe. He kisses her cheek in a rare display of affection. Taps her lightly on the backside. Says in his best Amitabh Bachchan voice, 'It's show time, baby.'

They are the first thing she sees, full of impatient excitement, holding up a hastily drawn WELCOME HOME LEENA banner, and her chest tightens.

'Come here, don't stroll!' Her mother is reaching out in a hug. 'I can't wait to get my arms around you.'

When Pooja embraces her, Leena doesn't cry or sigh with relief the way she hoped she would. Her mother's arms have always been a source of great comfort, the kind that soothed and placated all of Leena's childhood demons, but today they are not enough. They cannot subdue the growing, panicked resentment hardening her gut, the longing she feels for another place. If anything, they intensify it. Leena thinks of her small, boxy apartment on the Edgware Road, tucked within its own Middle Eastern pocket of London, the twenty-four-hour kebab shops, shisha cafés and Arabic-themed nightclubs. She used to marvel at the busyness of it all, especially in the summertime when there would be people packed tightly on every patio, leaning against street walls and spending their time appeasing a temperamental sun.

She would go for lone walks in the height of the season, spending the extended hours exploring every part of the city, unhindered. Never once did she glance over her shoulder or feel the prick of suspicious sweat forming in the cusps of her armpits at the thought of walking down side streets alone. She moved faster, lighter over there as the color of her skin became less meaningful.

One time, she was conned by a dreadlocked Caucasian who had followed her to an ATM and told her that he had lost his house keys and left his wallet at his apartment; that he needed money to get to a friend's house. So different from the Europeans back home, who stuck out like shiny gods in her mind, and she had given him ten pounds, slightly bewildered but unafraid. He had been lacking the anger – the desperation – that made the thieves back home so much more dangerous. While this man on Edgware Road had been polite, courteous almost as he carried out his con, smiling and thanking her as he backed down the street, the men she held in her memory were much greedier, wanting something more than just money, seeking revenge for unknown, unspoken betrayals.

Pooja feels her daughter's back and arms clench up and she lets go, afraid of smothering her with desperate hope. She looks to her husband for help. He cups his daughter's cheek in his large palm and feels her inhale against it: the faint scent of tobacco and spices. It is dry and comforting and reminds her of a simpler time.

'You still haven't quit smoking.'

'I didn't have my Leena here to boss me around,' he teases.

Pooja rolls her eyes and pokes her husband with her elbow. 'Maybe he'll listen to you, now that he's tired of me.'

They are being overly nice, awkwardly careful around each other as one would to a distant relative, trying to make up for time's eroding effect on their relationships. Pooja ushers her daughter into the house.

'Why don't we have some breakfast? You must be hungry.'

The marble tiles are cold under Leena's feet – she has slid off her shoes, released her swollen toes. The curtains are drawn and block out the morning heat, making her shiver pleasantly.

After the incident four years ago, she had kept them open for days, had been comforted by the expansive view of the garden and gate it had allowed her. Even at night, the outside lights had been kept on at her insistence, bathing the house in a cheap, citron glow so that everyone except for herself had had trouble sleeping. 'You just never know what sorts of things fill the darkness,' she had said to her family, feeling far away from them for the first time. Now, that sense of isolation is no longer strange to her.

From the corner of her eye, she sees her parents glance at each other and she steps away from the window, sighing in annoyance. 'You know that I'm okay, right?'

'Yes, we know.'

'So please, no tiptoeing. It makes everything worse.'

'You must be tired,' Pooja says. 'Why don't you go and freshen up? Come down whenever you're ready, I'm here all day.'

Leena walks up the winding staircase, the laminate wood slippery under her feet, craning her neck back to see the three of them standing at the bottom, side by side. She wonders if they feel guilty for being relieved, watching her go.

3

Raj Kohli, or *Mzee* Kohli as he is known by his employees at Artisan Furniture Wholesalers Inc., the furniture store he owns, sits on the cold ceramic toilet and lights up a cigarette. His wife has forbidden him to smoke anywhere else in the house, thinking that this will serve as a deterrent, but he enjoys the solitude.

There is a long window to his right, the sill extending downward to the toilet and he leaves it open, exhaling curls of smoke into the rose bushes below. Ever since he has been relegated to the downstairs bathroom, those flowers have been in constant bloom – playful pinks and yellows with a smell that encompasses every other beautiful smell.

He spreads the *Daily Nation* on his lap and leans back, careful to avoid the poking edge of the flush lever. He shifts and settles, trying to locate the exact flat spot of the seat before starting to read, flipping over to the back page first.

In the past month, the sports section has shrunk significantly with the election news taking precedence, but he is glad to see that they haven't scrapped it altogether. He skims over the football – *Bunch of babies* – flies through the recent and expected victory of the Kenyan rugby team – *Drunk hooligans* – dives straight for the cricket. *Fine gentlemen.*

He frowns when he sees that his team has experienced another embarrassing loss in two months of successive losses. Caught out for ninety-eight runs! Travesty! And to Canada – *Ha*! he cries, shaking the paper. Canada of all countries, full of toothless rednecks who smack and fight and skate, devoid of the finesse that is the foundation of his beloved sport. Raj Kohli experiences a rare burst of nostalgia, thinking back to a time when he had been a crucial member of the Kenyan cricket team – one of only two Indians – an all-rounder, opening batsman and spinner. Back then it had been about sportsmanship, teamwork and passion, focusing on making your country proud; none of this desiring after celebrity status, fighting like dogs over who deserved the highest salary. He is upset to find that corruption and match fixing have finally sneaked a chokehold around his most cherished memory. *Idiots!* he exclaims to himself. *A bunch of chubby idiots running this country, ruining everything.* As if to prove a point, he turns to the front of the paper and lands on an article. *Ah!* he says to no one and everyone, jabbing his finger at the page. *Ah!*

ELECTORAL MISCONDUCT, the headline reads and he clucks his tongue. *Who would have thought otherwise?* He lets his eyes roam.

The campaign period has begun and already it is marked by increased cases of violence targeting female candidates. The attacks, aimed at instilling fear and intimidating the candidates and their supporters, have been condemned both locally and internationally but no arrests have been made.

Of course not, scoffs Raj and continues reading.

Campaigns of widespread election irregularities, including the sale of voter identification cards, voter relocation and the use of state machinery in campaigns, are now staining what most Kenyans have been hoping will be a peaceful and fair pre-election period. The Kenya National Human Rights Commission released details earlier of certain instances in which state resources were used to conduct party business. Although authorities have launched investigations into such corrupt activities, the investigations have not resulted in any official reporting or prosecutions and have been tacitly accepted by the ECK and the government.

Raj pauses to look out of the window. Luna is hunting in the daisies for a lizard, head down sniffing, her tail cutting through his wife's strategically placed flowers. He thinks of what a magnificent country this is. Where else can you get sunny weather all year round? In what other city can you go on a safari just forty minutes from your house? To be surrounded by unspoiled ground, you were reminded of the world – you could never lose your sense of humanity here, your respect for Mother Nature and God.

He also has everything he needs for his business: an open, willing market, cheap – albeit regularly dishonest – labor, and customers with money coming out of their ears. *If only*, he thinks, looking down at the newspaper with a shaking head. *If only.*

In the early seventies, the Kenyan East-Indian community was thrown into turmoil following Idi Amin's order for the expulsion of all Asians from Uganda, giving them just ninety days to pack up whatever they could and leave. The crisis had swept into the adjoining East African countries such as Kenya and Tanzania and, although they weren't under any direct political threat, many Asians began to flee these countries as well in search of protection under Her Majesty's Crown, either in England or Canada. This included his mother, sister, cousins and countless friends. But Raj had kept his heels in the fertile, red Kenyan soil and refused to go with them.

'This is my home,' he had told them. 'My family is here, our business that we built from the ground up is here. I'll be damned if I let some greedy politician take it over.'

They had cajoled, manipulated and finally begged but he had ignored them.

'I have as much a right to be here as anyone,' he had insisted over and over again and they had put it down to the infamous Kohli pride and left him. He had been full of blind, patriotic trust in his country and the new government, heady off the numerous possibilities of their recently acquired independence. They would achieve greatness, he had been sure of it. With the right amount of dedication and the correct assignment of leadership, Kenya would thrive and his sacrifices would be richly rewarded by the knowledge that he had been a part of that process.

But now, his certainty is beginning to wane. He thinks of the generation that came after him – ruined by an incredible ease of life and blinded by greed, lavish parties and too much drink. Spending, spending, spending – using the country as a money-well and nothing more. Boys who have grown more reckless in their adulthood than they were in their youth.

He'd made sure that didn't happen to his son. Had caught a whiff of something special in him early on and grabbed a hold of it. Raj was too old for fighting now – he had a family to think about, but Jai didn't.

'Countries aren't built on ideas, son,' he had told Jai. 'They come from action – the actions of strong men such as yourself.' He had taken the book from his son's hands and said, 'You think something is amiss? Go and fix it. What good does it do, memorizing a text book and talking to me about it?'

Three days before Jai was to start his managerial position at Artisan Furnitures, he had told his father that he had accepted a job with PeaceNet Kenya. Despite his wife's pleading looks, her toe kicks, forceful coming from someone so delicate, *Mzee* Kohli had bobbed his head with pride, pumped his closed fist in the air and said, 'Go and build yourself a country.'

In bed that night, he had soothed his crying wife. 'Those ideas, that boy's head,' she said, 'it's going to get him killed one day.'

And Raj had rolled his eyes and hugged her close, patted her back. *It's okay, it's okay*, putting it down to nothing more than a mother's worry and a woman's tendency to over-exaggerate.

He looks at the picture of Pio Gama Pinto which, like him, has been forcibly removed from the living room and placed in isolation in the guest bathroom. He searches the face of the man in the picture and is once again satisfied that he made the correct decision when it came to his future and his son's.

But Leena's. He sighs, taps the bottom of the cigarette packet until one shakes loose. Cups a wide palm around its tip and lights it, leaning back to inhale. He is beginning to question his decision to have her come back, at least right now.

As is the case every five years, most of his friends have taken their families abroad to avoid the possible messy outcome of a rigged election. *Better to stay safe*, they all reasoned. *Business will still be here when we get back.*

'Maybe we should go and visit your mother,' Pooja had suggested. 'Now is as good a time as any. And then we can bring Leena back with us.'

Raj had shaken his head. 'What kind of Kenyan would I be if I left now? I still have to cast my vote.' And so he had bought his daughter a plane ticket and ordered her home.

He sees his wife outside, shooing away the dog and instructing Kidha about some or other overgrown tree and he can't help but smile. Thinks that she is still as lovely and bossy as the day he married her. *But Leena.* He sighs. *Too emotional. Too fragile and broken now.* He turns to the mirror, is met with a strong face partially covered by a well-maintained salt-and-pepper beard. Unable to hide from himself, he throws away the cigarette and worries about his daughter.

4

Grace walks silently into the living room, the silver-plated tray completely still in her hands despite it being overloaded with a full teapot, three sets of cups and five different kinds of *House of Manji* biscuits. The chocolate-layered ones are her favorite and she'd slipped one into the pocket of her apron before bringing it out to the Kohlis.

Draped across the sectional couch with her small feet in her husband's lap, Pooja gestures for Grace to place the tray on the table. Jai stands to take it from her and Grace blushes. He is good looking for a *muhindi* boy. Big and strong, more like an African.

'What shall I make for dinner?' she asks Pooja.

'What's in the freezer? I bought some meat last week.'

'Chicken, beef, mince.' Grace turns her eyes upward, searching the mental image she has of the fridge. Scratches her head, hot beneath her scarf; pounds it slightly.

'We had chicken last night. How about spaghetti?'

'Don't feel like anything so heavy.' Raj pats his stomach. 'I've had too many *karogas* this week.'

Pooja stifles a snap. She has never liked the fact that Raj goes to these outdoor meals with his friends, hiring out a table at the back of the restaurant, all the men gathered around huge silver pots on coal stoves, their faces steaming from the chicken masalas and fish tikkas, and drinking bottles of whiskey until midnight or sometimes later. 'If you stayed at home with your family instead of gallivanting with your drinking buddies…' she reprimands him as Grace waits at the edge of the carpet, wondering what it feels like to have so many choices. *Too confusing.*

'There's fish.' She offers help. *'Teelapia.'* Before she had come to work for the Kohlis, she hadn't known that there were so many different kinds of fish. *Teelapia. Red Snapper. Toona.*

Pooja nods. 'I think Leena still likes fish.'

Grace grunts her acknowledgment, desperate to get out of the room and rip off her scarf; the new girl at the salon had tied the braids too tight. When Pooja waves her away, Grace tiptoe-flies out in the direction of the garden. Kidha is there. She might go and share her biscuit with him.

The three Kohlis look at each other. Look down. Look away. They each wait for one of them to speak, not wanting to be the first. Raj lifts his wife's feet from his lap and reaches out toward the tea. But she is too quick for him, slapping his hand away. 'Since when have you poured tea? You talk and I'll do it. Come on,' Pooja prods chirpily, lifting the pot. 'Talk, talk.'

'She seems happy to be home,' he says, and is met with two sets of lifted, dubious eyebrows. A twitch of his son's mouth. *Just wait until you're married.*

'Not really, Dad.'

'She's just tired from her trip.' Raj accepts the tea from his wife. She leaves the tea bag in the cup, no milk. Three teaspoons of sugar.

'You want diabetes?' she often says to their friends. 'Ask Raj. He has the *pur*-fect recipe.'

Jai speaks hesitantly, guilty for talking about his sister while she is in the house, and he lowers his voice. 'Does she seem a little fragile to you?' He considers telling them about the odd breathing she was doing in the car, blowing up her cheeks and vibrating her lips, clutching her stomach so tight that her fingernails turned white. *No need to worry them.*

'If she says she's okay then we should believe her.' Pooja is firm. 'We have enough problems, no need to go searching, digging for more.' She dips her biscuit into the tea, watches as the crust of the chocolate turns soft and catches it in her mouth just as it begins to fall apart. Her skin breaks out into a shiver, as it always does when she is forced to think about what happened. 'It's been four years now. Why bring back the ghosts?'

Later that night, Leena raps lightly on her brother's partially opened bedroom door. 'Knock, knock.'

He looks up from his laptop, sliding off his headphones. 'It's you.' He is pleased to see her and pushes back his chair to stand, rolling out the stiffness in his ankles.

She looks around as she steps into the room. Gone is the baby blue she remembers, the haphazardly stuck Rocky and Arsenal posters and clothes-strewn floor. Now the room is simple and clean, with gray-tinged green walls and elegant beige bedcovers. Above the bed are hung black-and-white photos in different-sized frames: the hands of an elderly farmer cupping kernels of corn, the hardships of his life dug permanently into his skin; the keen yellow eyes of a lioness peering through blades of grass, caught mid-breath as she readies herself for a hunt; downtown Nairobi stilled at peak hour, when the streets are jammed with lights and music. Kenya – a whole country watching down on him as he sleeps.

She points at them. 'These are beautiful. Where did you get them?'

'A friend.' Jai recalls the moment in the car that morning when he was eager to explain everything. He wants to tell her again but she looks exhausted, fearful almost, and he decides to keep it for another day.

She traces her hand absently over the walls. His window is wide open and a breeze of pollen rustles the pile of papers at his elbow. 'You look busy.'

'There was a fire in a Kikuyu church in Nakuru a few days ago and I was just writing up the report.' He falls back onto the bed and presses the heels of his palms to his closed eyelids. 'It's not a very hopeful sign for these elections.'

She lies down beside him. 'Why not?'

'The men who set the fire were Luos,' he explains, referring to a different tribe. 'All this rivalry between the candidates is seeping down into the villages, causing a lot of tension and violence.'

'Do you ever run into trouble when you're out in the field?'

'Sometimes,' he admits. 'Though I would never tell Ma about it. You meet a lot of angry people, most of it stemming from the fact that they have been forgotten by the government, left to live and die in the worst conditions imaginable, and there comes a point when they just need someone to blame.' His eyes turn to her. 'I look different, I speak differently, so it's easy for them to hate me. But most people I meet are just welcoming and ordinary, glad for the help. It's not like how everyone imagines it to be.'

At times like these, she wonders if her family has forgotten what happened four years ago. It's as if they packed up the memory of it within her full suitcase and sent it off on that midnight flight, waving from the glass doors and shivering in the cold.

Outside, the day is receding into a burning horizon. On the equator, night falls upon you without warning – one minute, everything is speckled in gold and possibility and the next, becomes harrowing, charcoal shadows. Engulfing, she used to think, after what happened. This is what it means to be lost.

She makes a cradle for her head with interlocked fingers. 'Where are the parents?'

'Out for a walk. Ma says Dad is getting old.'

Leena smiles. 'Have you eaten?'

'Grace made some fish.'

'I didn't see her when I came in.'

Jai checks his watch. 'She's probably in her room. It's later than I thought.'

'She's staying in the outhouse?'

'Yes.'

'Is it safe?'

Jai blows out a breath. Tries to understand that it is natural for her to feel that way after everything. 'She's been with us for two and a half years. Don't do that.'

'Do what?'

'Judge her based on what happened. Mistrust is the rotting limb of this country and we have to cut it away if we want to heal and move on.' He throws his arms wide open.

She makes a face. 'Nice imagery.'

He grins like a little boy, only half-kidding. 'I find it effective.'

While he attempts to get comfortable, she notices how large the muscles of his arms have become, the size of his body, which dwarfs everything around him – there is a heaviness to his movements that implies stability rather than slowness. Skin covered in dark, coarse hair. She blinks, and when she opens her eyes she sees a handsome man. Not unlike her father but different in many ways.

She puts a hand gently on his. 'You shouldn't kill yourself for Dad's ideas.'

'I'm not.'

And then she tells him what's on her mind. The pleasant demeanor of the ATM con man. The incident that happened four years ago, the traces of which linger in everything around her, sickening her stomach. *It's no use*, she wants to tell him. *You'll be dead without making a dent.*

5

The next morning she runs into Grace in the corridor between the kitchen and the dining room. They side-step each other awkwardly, colliding and fussing before Leena stops.

'Hello,' she says, too cheerfully.

The other woman stares back at her, balancing a tray full of dirty dishes on her hip – remnants of pink papaya and crusts of buttered toast. 'Fine, fine,' Grace replies, trying to move away. *Shrunken, quiet, stayed in her room all day yesterday, this one is strange. Not like her brother.* 'Do you want toast?' Grace asks. '*Ceerio?*'

'What kind of cereal is there?' Leena asks.

'Weetabix, cornflakes.' Grace tries to remember the name of the fancy honey-coated one that Raj sometimes makes her sneak past his wife, but it's lost on her. 'I'll bring it for you.'

'I can do it, thank you.'

She follows Grace into the cramped kitchen, her eyes wandering over the room. A small stove, colonial-rose cabinets above and below it. A single window casts a hazy dimness so that she has to squint to see anything properly. Searching for the light, Leena finds it behind the refrigerator.

Startled, Grace shuts her eyes against the bald glare and feels a spark of irritation. She always works with the light turned off, has grown comfortable in the dark and now this invasion of her territory makes her bang the dishes down in the sink.

Leena rifles through the cupboards. The kitchen was designed to fit one person comfortably, but now Grace has to press herself into a corner and wait for the girl to finish before she can start her work.

'What are you doing?' A voice at the door makes Grace quickly rearrange her face into a smile. Jai is looking into the kitchen, amused.

Leena stands. 'I can't find the cereal.'

'Grace will get it for you. She doesn't mind.'

Grace nods her head enthusiastically. 'Indian tea?' she asks.

With both their eyes on her, Leena feels like a stranger, disturbing the normality that has been established in her absence. She closes the cabinet door with a sigh. 'Kettle tea is fine. No sugar.'

In the dining room, they sit at the marble-top island and Leena plays with a leftover crust of toast.

'How did you sleep?' Jai asks.

'Fine.' She won't tell him about the nightmares, so common now that she even has them when she is awake. But there is something more menacing about her dreams when she is here – a realness to them that causes her muscles to spasm and lock, weak groans leaking out of her as she sleeps.

Jai turns away. He won't remind her of the thinness of the walls, the close proximity in which they all sleep, so that last night the whole family had been invited into her terror.

She breaks the silence. 'I was thinking of taking the Nissan for a drive.'

'It's not an automatic.'

'You taught me how to drive stick, remember?'

'That was four years ago.'

She throws his own words back at him. 'It's just like riding a bike.'

Jai approaches cautiously, hoisting his bag onto his shoulder. 'Why don't you wait until Ma is back from the temple? She can take you wherever you want to go.'

'It's like being in jail.' Leena crushes a breadcrumb into many smaller pieces.

He feels the sting of annoyance mingled with pity. 'You just got here – be patient and give it some time. It might surprise you.'

When Kidha tells her what happened to the girl, Grace feels a little sorry for putting two teaspoons of sugar in her tea.

They are sitting outside on the low concrete partition just near the back door. It has an inbuilt sink that she uses during the day for washing and cutting vegetables or for wiping the dirt from Jai's shoes. He often comes back from his work trips upcountry with them encrusted in a solid layer of mud so that she has to pick away at them before using a garden pipe to hose them down.

In the mornings, however, she takes the two old mugs and plates that Mrs Kohli has set aside for her and brings them out with a thermos of tea and a full loaf of white bread. Sometimes, if she can manage without anyone noticing, she'll pocket the margarine tub. Then she and Kidha will sit under the cool shade, using it as a place to do some gossiping before Mrs Kohli returns from her meetings.

Grace pushes a large piece of bread into her mouth after generously layering it with Blue Band margarine and slurps her sweet tea. The handle of the cup has broken off and she has to hold the hot ceramic, the heat stinging her palms.

'How do you know this?' she asks Kidha in Kikamba, the dialect of the Kamba tribe to which they both belong.

'I hear them talking sometimes.' He strokes Luna's head with his toe. The dog looks up at him adoringly. 'Pooja is always *ca-crying* about it.'

'That's why she's so strange,' Grace muses. 'This morning in my kitchen, she was *ja-jumping* around me like she'd seen a ghost.'

He throws a piece of bread to a whimpering Luna, who snatches it up mid-air and then bangs her tail down for some more. He tears off another piece but Grace stops him.

'They didn't see it coming,' he tells her.

'Yes, sad.' Grace chews down on the loaf. Feeling some pity for the dog, she gives Luna a dollop of margarine and watches as the animal flicks her tongue around it to get used to the texture. 'But these things happen all the time to us. Why should it be something big when it happens to one of them?'

They hear footsteps and immediately fall silent. A new sound in the house, clicking of small heels, and the girl appears at the door. She stops when she sees them, hadn't expected anyone to be there. Kidha jumps down from the partition.

Leena glances from them to the dog, who is still chewing on the butter. 'Can you please open the gate for me? I'm going out and I'll be back soon, if my mother asks.'

6

The old Nissan lurches forward. Stops. Turns off. Her skin dampens with a premature sweat and she shrugs off her cardigan. Despite the earliness of the morning, the sun has fully ascended, chasing away the clouds and filling the city with a lethargic stillness. She can't even roll down the window – Westlands is full of wandering, opportunistic street boys. She twists the key in the ignition, and is filled with a fleeting second of hope as the car gives a struggling whirr but then falls quiet. She pounds her fist on the dashboard and it spits out dust, choking her. Eyes itching with dryness, she moans and lets her head fall onto the steering wheel. Car horns, a string of curse words, shaking fists – all directed at her and the old car that has decided to break down right in the middle of Westlands roundabout.

Further down the road, a policeman is supposed to be directing traffic coming through Waiyaki Way, a major highway, but instead he is leaning against a giant Samsung billboard as he speaks into his mobile phone. Eyes and ears that are blind and deaf to anything that cannot be milked for *kitu kidogo*.

With no other option, Leena calls Jai and tells him where she is. After an hour spent in traffic, he has almost reached the office. He keeps his voice calm, tells her, 'Don't get out of the car or let anyone in,' trying not to be angry, trying to understand. But he can't help but snap, 'Why would you go for a drive during rush hour?'

Cars move around her, forming lanes between lanes, squeezing into minute spaces and bumping up onto curbs, forcing swarms of pedestrians out onto the road. *Matatus* are blasting reggae and gospel tunes from old, staticky radios and a man hangs out of the door of one, collecting up passengers. When he spots her, he shouts, 'Hey, pretty *muhindi*, let me give you a ride!'

She rests her head once more on the wheel, wondering what she has come back to.

Keep everything locked, her mother would command whenever they were leaving the house. Pooja would twist in her seat and watch as Leena pushed the lock down before she started the car. *Never take any chances.* But Leena's skin is burning and the air in the car is riddled with layers of aged dust, making her cough, so she cracks open a window, slides it downward. She breathes in the air deeply, thick with smog but relieving nonetheless. Her eyes flicker shut as the cool air sweeps against her cheek.

'*Huko! Huko!*' a childish voice shouts.

She hadn't noticed them before, sitting on the island in the center of the roundabout, their faces black from dirt and diesel fumes. Two boys who look to be about fifteen years old, barefoot and quick, race toward her.

A war of reflexes.

Leena reaches to roll up the window but he has done this many times and has already inserted his arm into the car, almost up to the elbow, before she can even begin to close it. Something drips into her lap, oily and wet. In his hand, he is clutching a plastic bottle full of liquid the color of light straw. She draws her knees together, trying to move as far away as possible. The stench of urine is overwhelming.

'Give me the phone or I'll throw it on you.' Wild, throbbing eyes – a mind caught up in a crazed glue-haze. She recognizes the look and it scares her more than the human waste in his hand so she hands him the Blackberry. It's not his fault. His actions are a result of a highly addictive neurotoxin – shoe-repair glue. An escape for many boys just like him, he has probably been sniffing it all night.

The bottle moves a little closer. She squeals and twists further away. Cars keep moving by them; no one stops to help.

'*Kwenda nyuma*!' the boy shouts at his friend. 'The back door better be unlocked,' he growls.

'I'm not opening it.' Her stubbornness surprises her. She had expected to cry, scream, break down. She has been hoping for it for a long time. The liquid quivers above her.

'I'll throw it in your face,' he threatens.

The policeman has finally noticed her, tucking his phone away and starting to run in their direction, shaking the baton in his hand. '*Weh*!' he shouts. '*We-weh*!'

The boy at her side yells at his companion to hurry. The door opens behind her – it must be broken because she is sure she locked it.

'Hey! No!' She grapples with the hand stealing her new purse, which she has hidden under the seat. How many of her mother's rules has she broken today? No opening windows. No fighting back. Something salty hits the side of her cheek and the purse slips from her loosened grip. Her eyes are burning and a bitter sharpness cuts into her tongue, making it jerk unpleasantly. He has dropped the bottle into her lap, spilling the remainder of its contents onto her jeans. She pushes open the door just as the police officer reaches her and the boys sprint off, Blackberry and purse in hand.

She retches, tries to hold it in but it comes up anyway and she throws up beside the officer's shiny black *Bata* shoes, noting with some satisfaction that a few specks have settled on his trouser hem. He wipes it away casually with the back of his hand as if it is a daily occurrence.

Trying not to cry, or breathe in the smell, she kicks the bottle onto the street, a warm wetness gathering beneath the denim of her jeans and soaking into her skin. 'I hate this place.'

The policeman pats her shoulder heavily. 'You're lucky it's just some *chokora* piss,' he says to her. 'The other day, some woman, she had battery acid thrown on her face for one hundred bob.' He draws back his lips, hisses in imagined pain. '*Eh-he!* I tell you. Skin all gone – no more eyes, no more nose, no more anything. Burned, burned, *kabisa*.' Smacking his hands together. 'A shame for such a pretty face.' He leans down and sneers. From the left corner of his mouth a gold-plated tooth shines menacingly beneath the unremitting sunshine.

They make their way over the unpaved ground of the Parklands police station parking lot, an empty space littered with fast-food wrappers, the metal remains of cars that have been written off in accidents and a limping stray cat seeking shelter under one of the overgrown trees. Before they climb out of the car, Jai gives her his water bottle to wash her face. She scrubs hard, gargling and spitting, gratefully accepting the piece of gum he offers.

He looks at her as she opens the door. 'One more thing.'

She turns into a spray of men's deodorant, breathing in the minty scent and coughing as it tickles the back of her throat.

'I'm sorry,' Jai says between bursts of laughter. 'It's not funny, really it isn't...' And she gets out, slamming the door behind her.

The station is a giant prison cell, squat and square with metal barred doors and windows, peeling yellow-red-black stripes painted along the entire length of the structure. Large slabs of broken stone form the haphazard pathway over the muddy ground, lined with bright beds of hydrangea in an attempt to make the building look less run down.

The main room is startlingly bare, the only pieces of furniture being two plastic chairs and a desk in the far left corner. A bald light bulb hangs over the door, turned on despite the earliness of the morning. A chill sticks to the air, rising from the concrete floors.

She hears the clanging of metal and loud voices, muffled by the heavy door behind the counter. Sounds of a struggle, scuffling feet and low groans, but the policeman sitting behind the desk remains unbothered. He is thrown into gloom, writing in a giant logbook, and though he hears them approach he doesn't look up. *First rule of being in charge: make them wait.*

Jai speaks in Kiswahili. 'I want to report stolen property.'

The policeman puts down his pencil. He looks up at the two Asians standing before him: a young, casually dressed man and a girl who is hiding behind him. *These muhindi girls, either fearful or obnoxious, always needing a brother, father or boyfriend to talk for them.*

'You or her?' he asks, pointing. Today, he is feeling humorous.

'Her.'

'*Sawa.* Let her talk then.' He shifts his bored expression to the girl, leaning forward to peer at her. 'Hello, hi,' he calls out in a sing-song manner, waving his hand slightly.

When she steps around the boy, the police officer is unprepared for the shock. He wonders if they see it – the way it seizes the muscles of his face, tightening his stomach. Through the hum in his ears, he hears her say, 'I lost my ID, purse and phone. They were stolen from my car.'

She has not recognized him and that slows the erratic pace of his heart, settling his insides slightly. The snap in her voice offends him, overtakes the twisting panic in his gut, and he takes his time before addressing her, picking up the pencil and drawing four precise columns – tiny lead flakes breaking over the blank page. Lazily, he takes a sip of water from his nearly empty cup and when he is finished, leans back and inhales deeply. '*Sawa*. Tell me.'

'My car broke down on Westlands roundabout and I had my phone, bag and ID stolen by two street children. And I had urine thrown at me!'

He chuckles. '*Chokoras* these days – so inventive. Lucky it wasn't—'

'Battery acid, I know.'

His nostrils flare. 'How long ago?'

'This morning.'

He writes something down in a column; it doesn't matter what, no one checks. 'What was stolen? One thing at a time, please.'

'My phone.'

'What type of phone?'

'A Blackberry. Would you like the exact model?'

Jai's phone rings, interrupting them. 'It's work,' he tells his sister. 'I'll be right back.'

She is left alone with the police officer and again she hears the clanging of doors – jail cells, she realizes – and voices.

'You said you lost your ID,' the policeman addresses her.

'Yes.'

'Do you have your passport with you?'

'Of course not.' She clenches her cheeks. 'I was just out for a drive – I don't carry my passport everywhere.'

He gives her a look. *Perhaps you should.* 'I need to verify your person,' he mutters, though he knows her name already, and then, because it is his nature now, he says, 'unless you have another way.'

He waits for her to offer something else, the way they always do, these Indians. He had never known how easy it could be to bribe until he met one. No respect for money, no understanding of its value because they had so much of it.

'What do you expect me to do?' She throws her hands up.

'Come back with your passport and make sure you are quick, quick. In the afternoon, we are always busy.'

Behind the officer, the door bursts open. Leena steps back, slightly afraid, as a young man is pushed through by a second policeman holding a baton to his back. His wrists are handcuffed in front of him – hands cupped loosely against each other. His gaze falls upon the wet spot on her jeans, his eyes dark-lashed and laughing, strong, large teeth temporarily exposed.

He says to the cop behind the desk, 'Reduced to threatening ladies now?'

The officer growls. 'Move, before I put you back in.' *Boys like this, trouble, trouble all the time.* He thought he had taken care of this one but the *kijana* seems to be enshrouded in some kind of divine luck.

The handcuffed man looks at Leena again with a playful smile. 'The ill-tempered *mzee* here wants some lunch money. Three hundred bob should suffice. What do you say, chief?' He turns back to the officer, whose face has darkened, pencil threatening to crack within his fleshy fist.

With his hands finally free, the man winces as he massages his wrists. He is dressed too neatly for this place – a black turtleneck sweater and beige pants and his hair is cropped in close curls to his head. There is a hint of stubble over his cheeks, running darkest along his full upper lip. He looks at her and sees a bewildered Indian girl, her hair in a loose knot, with a big stain where it shouldn't be.

There is something. He leans in closer to get a better look but is shoved once more. 'Hey!'

The man behind the desk bellows, 'No more drawings, got it?'

'They're not drawings,' he replies. 'It's art.'

'Who cares? It's not allowed.'

'Free speech, my friend.'

'Outside! I'm tired of *kijanas* like you living only to disturb me.'

The young man is at the door, glad to be away from the stench and cold. No matter how many times he comes back here, he will never get used to how lonely and scared it makes him. The girl cranes her neck to watch him leave.

'Don't stay too long,' he warns. 'This place has a tendency of turning victims into suspects.'

They are all quiet after he has gone, looking questioningly at each other. Leena feels as if a shadow has passed over her, partially exposing something.

'You come back with your passport.' The officer slams his book shut.

Jai comes in from the back entrance and sees Leena standing before the cop, her mouth pinched with impatience. 'Is everything okay?'

She shakes her mind clear, relieved that he is back. 'He's telling me that I need ID to process my request even though the request is for a stolen ID.' She is feeling strangely uneasy and her voice grows loud, trembling slightly as she twists the hem of her cardigan between her fingers.

'Why don't you go and wait in the car?' Jai hands her the keys.

She snatches them from him while the policeman tries to hide a smirk, a slightly mocking look on his face as he watches her go.

*

The young man is leaning against a tree, extending his foot outward to play with a stray cat. When he sees her approaching, he pushes himself straight. 'Let you out already?' Something had caused him to linger after seeing her, but he had started to feel silly and almost left.

She fiddles with the keys. 'I couldn't deal with it any more.'

'That's understandable.' His voice is gravelly, rolling with pleasant surprises.

The easiness in his demeanor inspires the same casualness within her and she is able to speak freely. 'Why did they have you in there?'

'Some graffiti I did at City Market – gets them every time.'

'You've been in there before?' She is surprised. He seems too intelligent and, she blushes to think it, too attractive. There is a pleasing symmetry about his features, the way they crowd his narrow face. A low forehead and a wide-bridged nose – a mouth so large that it would look girlish on anyone else but lends him an unabrasive sensuality.

'A true artist always suffers for his craft, a true patriot for his country, is that not so?'

'I don't think I would risk spending one night in that place, let alone one minute, just to write some things on a wall.'

'Not just things,' he corrects her, squinting again. What is it about those sweeping gestures she makes with her hands as she speaks? Each action reveals something new, peeling back the layers of his memory. 'Isn't it my duty as a citizen to question the status quo? To express my opinion?'

'You sound an awful lot like my brother,' she laughs, fiddling with the keys again and trying to ignore the pleasant warmness in her cheeks. The way he looks at her is too direct for a stranger but she doesn't mind it.

'Your brother?' His relaxed manner falters slightly. He peers closer at her. *It can't be.* He would have been told. *But...* He has also learned never to disregard his gut, which is now beginning to churn and ache.

'He's helping me out in there.' She jabs her thumb in the direction of the station. 'He's worried I might blow up or something. Jai is always convinced I'm doing things wrong when I'm not doing them his way.'

A heartbeat pulse at his jaw. 'Jai – that's your brother?'

She looks up from the keys, nodding, and then asks, 'Are you okay?'

He has sagged against the tree and when he hears her voice he gives a violent shake, a stumbling, stammering boy, so drastically changed from the person who stood before her moments ago.

His hand trembles slightly as he rubs his chin. 'I just haven't eaten anything since yesterday.' He moves toward her, shuffles back. For the first time in a long while, his next step eludes him. He looks up and sees Jai at the door – detects a slight shake of his head. *Not yet.*

A person so used to saying what he thinks, he struggles to hold back his feelings. 'I should go.'

She shifts on her feet, wondering if it would be too bold to ask him for a name. What would she do with it anyway? She has lived here long enough to know that even if she wanted to see him again, there are too many lines to cross and too many uncertainties waiting on the other side of them. 'I'll look out for one of your drawings,' she says.

'Art,' he corrects her, the smile deepening the lines of his face once more.

'Right. Art.'

He stumbles backward, filled with an odd sensation that his body and brain are not working together, as if forcing his muscles to move in a direction they don't want to go. Casting one look back at Jai emerging from the station, there is enough trust between them for him to know that it wasn't done out of malice but out of love for a person they both care deeply for, though it doesn't make him any less angry.

'Bye,' she calls out. But he keeps moving, pretending not to hear her.

7

The policeman's pockets are deliciously heavier than this morning. He scratches the long nail of his pinky finger across his aggravated nostril and picks apart the hard layers encrusting the inside wall of his nose. *Too dry, this heat. Too hot.* He watches the Land Cruiser back out of the station, turn with a roar onto the main road. Pats his recently acquired money. Smiles because he no longer feels guilty cheating a system that long ago betrayed him.

Youthful and fresh on the job, his mother had helped him to dress in the sky-blue shirt, the black uniform trousers that had been a size too big. Handing him his baton she'd sat back on her heels, clutching her head and exclaiming loudly, 'Oh, Constable!', weeping and writhing so that he had been late after trying to calm her down.

The first morning as a part of the Kenyan Police, he had joined the ranks of workers walking to one of Kibera's eight exits: men in patched overalls and women in freshly washed blouses, squeezing past one another in pathways so narrow that it was necessary to turn sideways to pass through them. He'd plunged past wheelbarrow porters, twisting his body to avoid the sharp edges of their carts. Strode past the vendors on both sides of the street selling fresh fruit and vegetables, soap, sweets and cigarettes. Past Miss Judy's school, where she was leading her students in morning prayer, chirping like small birds within the *mabati* structure that was painted crayon-yellow, giving it an uncomplicated cheerfulness.

He waved to the tailors hunched over pedal-powered sewing machines, greeted the accountants and lawyers who shared trestle tables in open-air offices, feeling them stare. *Let them look.* He was better than Kimani the houseboy. Better than Njoroge the cook. Better than Wangai the driver. Better than his drunkard, whore-loving father, who had worked for Hatari Security Company as a night guard. He worked for the president now. Forward on, forward on, into the high-rise center of Nairobi.

Already he saw himself outside of this forsaken place, living within the modern joys of the city – in a small house with his mother, where he would one day be able to afford a car and not have to worry about the disease-riddled mud dirtying his shoes or duck the 'flying toilets' – bags of human waste – as they came whirling, carelessly thrown onto the streets.

Constable Jeffery Omondi, fourteen steps closer to becoming commissioner of police, a good friend and confidant of the president—

'*Weh*! Watch where you step, who do you think you are?' Thomas Ngusye, who owned the only cinema in Kibera, complete with seventy plastic chairs, drew his stepped-on foot back and sneered. 'Constable what? Lowest-ranked police officer, that's what.'

'I'm still higher than you,' Jeffery had called back, nothing to stop him.

He had spent all day out on the road, striding in front of cars and directing them with his bare hands – even the *mzungu* his father had worked for listened to him. Officer in Charge of the Smooth Operation of Traffic. He chased away street boys, taught *matatu* touts a lesson. Officer in Charge of Cleaning Up Nairobi Roads. At the end of the day, he rewarded himself by taking a *matatu* home rather than walking because his salary, low in comparison to many others, was still the largest he had ever received.

Meeting his friends at Mama Lucy's, he took a step up from the *chang'aa*, the regular moonshine he drank, and spent his wages sipping on *busaa*, a fermented maize drink served in half-liter cans instead of glasses. By ten o'clock that evening, he lay bleary-eyed on the mud floor beside a plastic sheet filled with roasted maize, having just enough sense to slip some into his pocket before anyone saw.

Jeffery is jolted back to the present by Heba, a trembling old Muslim woman who is a constant visitor to his station. He knows what she is going to say before she says it.

'He stole one of my cats,' she announces in her rusted voice, raising a wobbly finger. 'That man, he owes me money, took my land and stole away one of my cats.'

Same story, same man with no name. Jeffery snaps, 'You have more than a hundred cats. What is one?'

He sees her sometimes on his nightly visits to the city center, wandering the broken and dark alleys with bread in her pocket and a packet of milk, so crazy that even the night thieves leave her alone. She once told him that she was searching for lost kitten souls, those that Allah had bestowed upon her the responsibility of saving.

'I'm an angel,' she tells him, pushing a browning piece of paper in his face. 'In this prophecy, Allah says he has sent down an angel in white,' gesturing to her salwar kameez, permanently stained with dust, 'to do his work. He will reward anyone who helps bountifully.' *Scrawled nothings, jibber-jabber garbage.* He is tempted to tear it up.

'Go away, old woman.'

'We had a business deal,' she shrieks. 'With that man in the tall building – he says there is no money to build but he is hiding it from me.'

'What's his name?'

'Owiti.'

Owiti today. William yesterday. Tomorrow himself, Jeffery.

'One day I will have millions of shillings,' she warns him.

'Then come back when you have it.' He shouts for the junior police officer. Let him deal with this mad, shrunken creature. Jeffery is in charge of this police station; he's above such nonsense. Thirteen years later and three steps up from where he started – but only because one man hanged himself at this very desk and the other left to work at the main airport, tempted by the higher salary and a lower level of resentment from customers.

As the other policeman drags her out, Heba fixes her cataract-stained eyes on him. 'I know what you did.'

'What did you say?' Jeffery holds his hand up to stop them.

'I know how you harmed that poor soul.' Her eyes roll back in her head; her second-hand walker gives a tremendous shake. 'That sad, broken-to-pieces girl. But Allah will forgive you if you help me. *Bismil-lahir-rahmanir-rahim*,' she begins praying.

'Which girl?' Jeffery presses his hands to the desk, rising. Feels a pool of sweat form beneath his collar. *How could she possibly know?*

'Oh that poor, poor thing. She is only a kitten.' Heba groans. 'And you have left her to die.'

His sweat dries up, hands banging down. Ridiculous of him to have indulged her in the first place. He would have shot her with pleasure, then and there, if he hadn't been his mother's son. 'Go home and don't come back!'

Jeffery sits back down, tired of them all, pulling at the waistband of his trousers, now two sizes too small instead of one size too loose. Three steps up in the job but the same ground-floor salary. Then he remembers the cash in his pockets. No need to think of anything else right now – he has found ways to get by. Cheat or be cheated. He'd learned his lesson long ago.

8

The drive home from the station is full of unshared thoughts. Leena picks at her jeans where there is now a crinkled, stiff stain.

'I'll have to throw these away.'

'Just ask Grace to wash them for you,' Jai says.

'I had piss thrown on me.' She finally feels the aggressive stirrings of an undeserving victim. 'Even if she washes them ten times, I'll never wear them again.'

He keeps his eyes on the road. 'If you're going to do that, give them to Grace. I'm sure she'd appreciate a good pair of trousers.' He pauses, considering something. 'After all of this, are you still okay?'

Her fingers drum on the armrest. She is tired of being perceived as the weak one, the fragile, estranged daughter. 'The only thing that is going to make me not okay is if you keep asking me if I'm okay.'

A placating pat to her knee. 'We'll have to get you a new phone but we have Ma's old Samsung, which you can use for now.'

'I'm not using that. It's so old, I might as well not have a phone at all!' Throwing herself back onto the seat with a dramatic flourish, Leena knows that she is being difficult but has found that anger and indignation are the safest responses in times of turmoil. Simple emotions, capable of generating just enough feeling without complicated layers to sift through. Once you push deeper, when you open yourself up to sorrow and fear, it becomes impossible to re-emerge, and even if you do, there is no guarantee you will be the same.

To distract herself, she thinks of the young man at the station, finds something romantic in reimagining his face to suit her preferences. In her mind, his skin is lighter, his accent more polished and, in recreating their meeting, she has set them in a trendy café in London: a petite, modern space.

Sneaking a look at her brother, she thinks that life would be a lot less muddy if there weren't so many variables to consider. If differences weren't like two banks of a roaring river, separated by slippery, moss-covered stones and spiraling riptides. *Possible yet impossible to cross.*

'Who were you talking to at the police station?' Jai asks and she blushes to think that he knows what is happening inside her head.

'Some artist who was jailed for doing graffiti.'

'That doesn't sound so threatening.' He speaks as if indifferent but is watching her closely.

'Sounded political to me.' She fiddles with the radio, bumps it with her fist to steady the sound. 'I didn't get his name, though.' Almost regretful.

'Those kinds of artists never use their real names anyway.'

'How do you know that?'

He fumbles for an explanation. 'I read it somewhere.'

'Have you spotted anything like that around?' She hopes he might be able to tell her who the man is. 'He said something about a wall at City Market.'

'No,' Jai lies, having seen the artwork before it was put up, knowing the exact location because he had helped in designing and tracing most of them under the cover of night, using only a torch to see, while his parents thought he was at a nightclub. Arriving home to scrub away the spray-paint grease from his skin and hiding the stained hoodie at the back of his closet.

They have turned into the paved road leading toward their house, past similar palatial homes. Someone has recently trimmed their lawn and she spots the green shavings scattered over the road; she pulls in the heady scent of it, acute and moist.

While they wait for Kidha to open the gate, Jai watches his sister. She has leaned back and closed her eyes, her skin flushed and bothered. He wonders if, on some level, she knew who she had been talking to. Finds it impossible that she wouldn't.

He knows that he should have told her a long time ago, should tell her now, but he feels he needs more time. He needs to observe her carefully, for just a little while longer, because he wants to make sure that when he tells her, she will be able to understand what he is saying.

9

In the red brick, one-bedroomed Parklands apartment, three stories up from an all-night chemist and an Indian sweet shop, an old painting is uncovered. Other more recent drawings, meaningless now, are pushed aside to reveal the patchy jersey sheet that has been used to hide it for so long. With a slight tug, it falls in gentle waves to the floor. He brushes impatiently at the alarmed silverfish darting for cover, using the edge of his sleeve to wipe away the dense layers of dust that have collected upon the glass, the only work of his that he has ever framed.

He had been deeply involved in graffiti by the time he had begun painting this; when he'd finally had the chance to convert the thoughts in his head to writings on the wall, the only logical starting point had been her. He would begin by tracing an outline of the steep hill of her cheekbone, her sharp lips – continuing on until those features transformed into a scorching sun or an overstuffed belly of some MP; he would forge her almond eye from an anomalous bump in the wall, and when he was done it would have turned into the beak of a vulture – his own personal message to the universe.

He remembers the wild energy that had consumed him the day he had painted this. He had drawn the outline of her in the shape of his emotions; a reclining nude woman with her back to him, left elbow resting in the dip of her waist, fingers of the right hand caught up in black tresses of hair. The rising curve of her buttocks leading to an extended right leg dangling over the edge of the chest she was lying upon, left knee tucked up.

He had started to fill in the body with painstaking strokes of his brush and, finding it lacking an intimacy he was compelled to reach, used his fingers instead. Languid circles, taking his time within all the secret crevices, using his thumb, index finger, even the heel of his palm, reaching where the light could not. Rapid dots, *tak-tak-tak*, forming the humped bones of her spine.

Upon its completion he was faced by magical twists of color – a lithe brown body lolling beneath the arching branches of a magenta bougainvillea tree, its flowers settling upon the old chest she was guarding. Secrets or memories, happiness or gloom. *Which one*? he asked himself before remembering that one could not come without the other.

'*Cuzo!*'

A rapid banging on the door shakes him out of his reverie.

'*Cuzo* – open up, hurry.'

Quickly, he rewraps the painting in the bedsheet, sliding it back behind everything else, a pang of loneliness following him to the door.

Jackie.

In all the confusion, the unexpected blurring of time, he had forgotten about her. With a steadying breath, he pulls open the door and a girl stumbles in smelling of butterscotch body lotion, used generously to cover up the stench of marijuana.

'Where have you been?' she demands. 'I've been coming around here for two days now looking for you.' Jackie fans her face, takes out a tissue from the cup of her bra and dabs her shiny forehead.

'I had to go to Nani's place, Chris's friend, to borrow his phone and I thought I would stop by here and try one last time.'

'I thought you were staying with Otis.'

The girl adjusts her denim skirt and tugs at the red corset top in an effort to cover up her midriff, but it keeps riding up. 'Nah, man, that *jama*! One day he comes home and tells me to leave. No explanation, nothing.' She gestures to her damaged hair, pulled back into a dry, frizzy ponytail. 'Not even enough *doh* to fix some braids.'

'But enough for a bag of *bangi*. I told you to stop smoking that stuff.'

'No judgment here, *cuzo*. We all do what we can to get by.'

'What do you need, Jackie?'

'Just a place to stay for a little while. Three days and then I'll bounce.'

The place is still as bare as she remembers it. The faded pink carpet and a cluster of old pots and pans beside a charcoal stove beneath the window. The box TV and sagging brown couch that she knows he will sleep on today, letting her take the only bed in the small room. 'All that photography not paying as well as it used to?' she asks.

'It pays fine.'

'There's no use hanging onto what's dead,' she says.

'No one has died.'

'There is more than one way to be gone forever, *cuzo*.'

He considers telling her about what happened earlier. It is on the tip of his tongue. Perhaps if he says it, it will feel less like a fragmented dream. Instead, he tells her, 'You can stay as long as you want. This is your home too – take the bed.'

Thanking him, Jackie's eyes flicker to the wall. 'What are you doing over there?' pointing at the paintings.

'Nothing.' He lunges forward but she leaps over the couch and gets to them first, pushing away the first few drawings and spotting the hastily thrown-over sheet. She pulls it away and together they stare down at the sighing woman. Jackie senses a sneer; she remembers that girl alright.

'This is not good, *cuzo*.'

'I was just cleaning up.'

She turns to him. Her powdery eyeshadow has melted in the heat, leaving clownish streaks that make her appear wilder than usual. 'What happened?'

He looks at the painting of Leena, astounded by the similarity it shares with its subject, despite him not having seen her for years before he completed it. He touches it, hovers somewhere between the shoulder blades and says, 'She did.'

PART TWO

1995

10

It was easy to call upon those summer days of her childhood. Full of earth and grit. In the midday heat, the dust contaminated the air and settled on her skin in a hard, reddish layer. Then there followed the cold showers, watching clumps of dirt swirl around the metal drain of the bathtub before disappearing forever.

Afterward, while Jai was sent to watch TV, her mother would sit Leena down on her dresser to tackle her tangles. Comb clutched in one hand, Pooja firmly grasped her daughter's hair in the other and pulled it so far back that Leena's eyes would smart. But she didn't mind. These moments alone with her mother were rare and she thrilled at the cool touch of Pooja's hand, her soft, high humming.

They lived in a compound of identical apartments, stone exteriors with white grilles on the windows that curled at the bottom like the letter S. Low and flat, with three brick steps leading out, the maisonettes sat in a wide circle so that it didn't matter where your house was, you could still push back your curtain, peek through the gap and see everyone's business.

During the day, along with the other children living in the compound, Leena would race around the curving street on her BMX bicycle, remove her feet from the pedals as she turned the corners and take her hands off the brakes if she was feeling brave. The pedals would whirr and scratch her ankles and she would proudly show them off like battle scars.

The mothers used to shout at them – dark and stout Indian women, bright saris pushed over their shoulders as they leaned over stainless steel pots on *jikos*, their knees straddling the charcoal stoves, stirring onions which snapped and crackled in the hot oil.

To Leena, it seemed as if they cooked from the moment they woke up until their husbands returned home from work. Even after she had left the flats, she couldn't think of that place without the memory of a spicy curry burning her eyes or the sweet taste of the *jalebis* that they used to hand out as the children went by, pinching their chins and pushing the sticky orange sweet into every mouth, even if it wasn't wanted. Her mother was always absent from these scenes, with her Bridge games and charity events, leaving for the temple early in the morning after feathery kisses goodbye, making Leena feel like a proud orphan.

'Be careful, Shamit!' Mrs Goyal would shout. 'I don't want a son with a broken head. Of what use will you be to me then?'

'Look at you – thinking you're a hero. You're lucky I don't tell your father what a *besharam* daughter he has. Mannerless girl!' Mrs Shah would scold her daughter, Preeti, giving her a stern tap on the backside.

Although those days were only full of good memories, the ones Leena clung to the most were the ones when Jai was with them. They learned quickly never to ask him. He came when he wanted and even then it was with an air of distraction, as if he always had something more important on his mind. He would pick up a soccer ball and juggle it between his nimble feet and they would play football. If he came out swinging a cricket bat, two teams would automatically form, eagerly awaiting his cue. When he grew tired, he would leave the game and, for the sake of her pride, Leena would force everyone to keep on playing for a few more minutes, but the enjoyment would always slow, dwindle down and eventually stop. This teenage boy who was so much older, smarter and handsome than the rest of them, with his head of tamed black curls and dancing features, whose life was so exciting that they longed and dreaded to be a part of it.

'Ask him to come and play with us. He'll listen to you.'

'He never listens to me,' she would reply, even then, too proud to ask.

So someone else, if they were feeling brave, would speak up. 'What's next, Jai?'

'Jai, do you want some banana crisps? My mother made a fresh batch.'

Sometimes it would work. They would manage to trap his attention and he would stir, raise himself up on his elbows and give them a brilliant grin, biting down into the deep-fried plantain. Other times, he would be too lost within himself and their words would never reach him.

'Sorry, not today, guys,' he would answer, rolling up and balancing on his heels before standing fully.

They would trail back toward their bikes that were strewn over the curb and falling onto the street, or return to the multicolored hopscotch game scrawled hastily in chalk on the pavement, feeling the thrill in the air suddenly collapse. The day would compress without him, turn dull and shrink, the hope unintentionally dragged from it and its magic completely lost.

In the early evening of Leena's twelfth birthday, the Kohlis were driving back from Carnivore, an open-air restaurant situated in the Langata suburb where they had organized a Sunday lunch for her school friends.

Pooja rolled down her window slightly to allow in some cold air, hoping it would help settle the swimming sensation in her head brought on by one too many cocktails. She had spent the day sitting in the dining area, which had led onto the vast playground with its numerous slides, seesaws and a plastic brick castle that consisted of rope ladders, bridges and cargo nets. While the children had played, the parents sat in the shade of overarching palm trees, sipping cold beers and *Dawas* while the waiter moved quickly around them, cleaning away plates and refilling empty glasses. It had been a day full of laughter, the clicking of cameras, cherry-topped Black Forest cake and her husband holding her hand beneath the table, teasing her fingers.

She had been disappointed when the sun started to lose its solidness, as it stretched out across the afternoon sky and people began to leave, pulling on their cardigans and shivering in the slight chill that the evening brought with it.

It had been a successful event and now the family sat in contented silence as Raj tapped his fingers on the wheel and hummed old Hindi film songs. The trunk of the station wagon was full of presents and leftover goodie bags, from which Jai had grabbed a Chupa-Chups lollipop.

'That's not for you,' Leena had protested from the other side of the backseat, lunging toward him.

He dodged her snatching fingers easily, her seatbelt holding her back. He wrapped his tongue around the Coca-Cola flavored lollipop, sucked on it lightly before smacking his lips together. 'I don't know why I had to come to this lame party.'

'It wasn't lame!' It had been Leena's first boy-girl party because her mother had conceded that she was now old enough to invite boys as well as girls. She had worn her new outfit for it: a white, flower-printed T-shirt and a denim skirt that had a pair of shorts stitched into them. *Culottes*, Pooja had called them the night she had returned from visiting her brother in London. *Everyone is wearing them on Oxford Street. See how easy they are? You can sit, stand, jump, run, everything without your panties showing.*

Twelve years old and still a baby. Jai rolled his eyes and reached back into the goodie bags, found her favorite – Strawberry & Cream – and gave it to her. 'Now you have one too so you can stop bugging me.' He inserted the headphones of his new Sony Walkman into his ears and pressed play on his recently made mix tape.

'I want to listen with you.' Leena grabbed his arm. 'Let me listen with you.'

'You have your own Walkman.' She had received hers that morning as a birthday present.

'I didn't have time to make a tape!'

'Stop it.'

'Give me!'

'You'll spoil the whole thing.'

'*Maaa.*'

'*Baas.*' Nothing as loud as their father's quiet voice, telling them he'd had enough. 'Can't you see I'm driving?' He looked back at his children.

'Watch out!' Jai leaned forward with wide eyes, pointing outward, and Raj turned speedily in his seat to see a man lying in the middle of the road. He slammed his brakes, heard the squealing protest of the wheels before the car came to a halt in a haze of rubber fumes.

Parking the car up on the curb, Raj climbed out while instructing his family to lock the doors. He approached the man, whose only movements were the sharp jerks of struggling breath.

Raj hiked up his trousers and knelt down. '*Mzee*,' he spoke gently, not wanting to startle him. '*Makosa ni nini?*' The man rolled, stretched out on his back and looked up at Raj with wet, unseeing eyes. He spoke in single words.

'Sick,' he groaned. 'Diabetes.'

'Where is your medicine?' Raj was calm despite the cars veering narrowly by them, the sound of horns telling him that they considered this a nuisance, keeping their palms pressed down as they passed. *Beeeeeeeeeeeeeeeep.*

'None.' White foam had formed at the corners of his mouth, his eyes rolling and fluttering shut before he lurched back with a gasp. 'And. No. Money.'

Raj glanced back at his car. 'I'll be back,' he told the man, dodging the traffic back to his family, knocking urgently on his wife's window.

'What are you doing?' Her relaxed disposition from the afternoon was slowly fading.

'We have to take him to the hospital.'

'No, we don't,' she replied. 'Just get back in the car. It's getting late.'

Raj didn't have time for an argument. Sticking his hand inside the window he unlocked the door and ushered Pooja out. 'Get in the back, quickly. I'll go and get him.' He gestured for Jai to help him.

Pooja shouted after them, the light-headedness beginning to settle into a throbbing headache. 'You – Raj Kohli, come back here!'

But he was already away with his son, back on the road and lost in the cacophonic noise of the traffic.

They had never had an African in their car before. Skin cracked open with dryness, rubbing his tongue continuously over his lips and along his inner cheeks. His clothes were old strips of dirty cotton and the soles of his shoes were broken – like flapping, dusty mouths every time he moved his feet. Leena wanted to open a window for his smell to escape but she was squeezed tightly between her mother and Jai.

She recalled Pooja's constant warnings. *You must be careful, most of them are thieves – they robbed my friend Bharti, they hijacked your second cousin, Jiten, and tied him up and stuffed him in the boot for three hours!* Those words caused fear to pile up in her because it made it impossible not to see this man as the enemy.

Her father spoke, his soft voice immediately soothing her. 'We're almost there.'

'Where exactly is *there*?' Pooja asked pointedly, speaking in Punjabi.

'We're taking him to M.P. Shah Hospital.'

Pooja shook her head. 'Don't you ever think that other people would also be able to solve these problems if you just let them?'

'Did you see anyone else stopping for him?'

She talked over her husband. 'Always having to be the first, always wanting to be the hero.'

'What would you have me do? Leave him dying in the middle of the road?'

'And when we get to the hospital? If he has no money, they'll just let him die there anyway.'

Raj remained silent, unwilling to reveal his full plan to Pooja. *Constantly wanting to argue*, he thought irritably. *The woman was born with difficulty in her blood.*

When they reached the hospital, Jai helped his father to carry the man across the parking lot, toward the swinging white doors of Emergency Care. It was difficult and took time, given how heavy and limp the man had become. When they placed him in the plastic chair of the crowded waiting room, the man groaned and his head began to pitch and roll.

'Let it kill me.'

'Hush.' Raj patted his shoulder. 'You'll be better soon.'

People in the waiting room had lowered their magazines, watching the scene keenly.

'Go and tell the receptionist he needs immediate help,' Raj instructed his son, and as Jai went to speak to the woman behind the desk, Raj slipped three thousand shillings into the man's limp hand and pressed it shut. 'This should be enough for you right now.'

'Thank you, *mzee*,' his fingers clutched tightly.

As they made their way back to the car, Raj wrapped his arm around his son's shoulders and brought him close, whispering, 'No telling your mother about this, you hear...'

They were watching the nine o'clock news later that night when they were interrupted by the shrill ring of the telephone.

'Mr Kohli? This is Dr Pattni from...'

'Yes, yes. How is he?'

'I'm afraid I don't know.'

Confusion made his words slow. 'What do you mean you don't know?'

'He left just after you dropped him off.'

'But he could barely even stand!' Raj remembered to speak in whispers, gripping the telephone, struggling to understand.

'The nurse at the front desk told me that he waited for five minutes after you left and then stood up and walked out. No one saw where he went.'

'Are you saying that he tricked me into thinking he was sick so that I would give him money?'

'I've seen it happen before. It was very kind of you to bring him in.'

Raj swallowed down his building aggression. 'Thank you for calling.' He put the phone down and turned to his son, who was standing beside him. 'You heard that?'

'Yes.'

'You know, the people with the kindest hearts are often the ones who get trampled on the most. That doesn't mean you stop being generous, understood?' Raj gazed down at the phone, thinking of the man and what Pio might have done and his anger slowly broke apart. He said to Jai, 'One day, you will be called upon to do the right thing and nothing else will matter except that you do it. African, Indian, *Gorah*, it doesn't matter when we are all Kenyans.'

11

The world fell away, shimmered and thinned. The circle of people around her dropped down one by one, folded up like cardboard mannequins to be stashed away. All she could feel was the sturdy, round hardness of the marble pressed against the tip of her index finger, her head filled with the oceanic rush of her breath. *Ready. Set.*

'Hurry up and take your shot.'

Go.

The voice distracted her and the marble slipped from her hand, bounced sadly once and rolled a couple of centimeters ahead.

'You cheated!' Leena pulled herself up off her knees, starting toward Tag. 'Do you know how long it took me to set up that shot? I would have hit you, I know I would have.'

Her circle of friends slowly rippled back into existence.

Tag rolled his eyes. *Girls. Especially this one.* 'Think what you want.'

She grabbed the marble and stepped back, her arms crossed tightly over her chest as he knelt down, eyebrows sinking forward in concentration. 'Fine, take your shot. Just remember—'

'Excuse me?'

It came from behind her, a voice on the wind. One that she didn't recognize, unsettling her because everything in this closely guarded, gated compound was familiar.

A boy was watching them with eyes that were quiet, dark pools and his hands were curled around the thick, worn-out strap of his satchel. Her mother's voice came to her. *You must be very, very careful of these Africans. They can even use their children to trick you.*

'What are you staring at him like that for?' Jai came down the steps of their house to stand beside the boy.

'Didn't know you had African friends, Jai.' Tag had set his marble carefully down and had stood up, sneering. The crowd around him tittered nervously, having been taught, as Leena had, to be suspicious of such people.

'Can I help you?' Jai asked the boy, ignoring Tag.

'I'm looking for Angela.' His English was drawn out and careful, steady despite the whispers around him.

Leena spoke up. 'You mean our Angela?'

At that, the boy looked at her once more, his face crinkling into a question.

'Your Angela?'

Jai interrupted, shooting his sister a warning look. 'Angela Muriuki?'

'Is she here?'

'She's around the back.' Jai gestured for the boy to follow him.

Tag was down on the pavement again, victory within reach and the boy forgotten. When the last marble was knocked out of the fading dust circle, he threw his hands up in celebration. 'I win.'

But Leena wasn't listening. She was too busy staring after her brother, at the boy who walked so lightly beside him – grave and serious, entering into shadows.

Raj heard his daughter come loudly through the door, a shout on her lips. She was so intent on finding Pooja, she failed to see him leaning on the sill of the open window in the living room, out of which he had been smoking leisurely and watching her play.

The sky was sinking into darkness, opening up its pockets of evening stars – tiny blades of metallic light blurring the edges of all the street objects so that they merged into one large, indistinguishable shadow. As if timed, the yellow lights from the neighboring houses sprung on as people sat down for dinner. Several housemaids emerged from around the verandas, out of their uniforms and in long skirts and cotton blouses, clutching plastic bags full of their belongings. They converged at the main gate, ready to walk home or take *matatus* together, speaking in rapid, fading tones. Housewives leaned out of doorways to call for their children, releasing cooking smells so that soon the entire compound was alive in the stink of Indian curry staples: cumin, fried red onions and garlic.

To rid himself of the stench, Raj lit another Embassy Light. He was disappointed at the ending of the game outside. It pleased him to watch the children playing, their unrestrained, boisterous nature that knew how to exist only in extremes. When he had been his daughter's age, all he had known was frenzied joy or the powerful crush of sorrow – anger that moved him to tears or the total stillness of an untroubled mind. There had been no room for a middle ground, no space for those diluted, in-between emotions which, as an adult, he had begun to settle for. *Mock feelings*, he called them, because they weren't real, only poor imitations of something true. Under the guise of maturity he had grown shallow and bland, but when he watched his daughter play – saw the permanent crease of irritation across her forehead or heard the tantrum-stamp of her shoes – it stirred within him a sweet recollection, a longing for a simpler time.

He turned from the window and to the small picture that hung on the right wall, swallowed by the busy, floral wallpaper.

'You never lost that, did you?' Raj said to Pio Gama Pinto.

The modest Goan man stared back at him with that infamous, wide smile and 1950s bushy haircut, his essence perfectly captured in the sepia-toned newspaper clipping.

When Raj had first come across that photo, he had been sixteen and restless. Two years after independence, the country was awash in so many possibilities that one went hunting for a dream the way they did a lion on safari – as mad and hungry men, greedy for a purpose. He had been rifling through the newspaper in the back room of a family friend's *duka* and had paused at the image of a young Asian man hoisted upon the shoulders of his cheering black compatriots; had discovered something within its frozen celebra-tion – a lingering hope that he had struggled to catch hold of before the demanding shop owner barged through the door.

'What are you doing in my things?'

'Who is this?' Raj ignored the man's annoyance and held up the photo.

'*Baap-re-baap!*' The owner smacked his forehead in exclamation. 'What rock have you been living under, boy? That's Pio. *Pee-O.* Doesn't your father teach you anything?'

'What does he do?' His curiosity made him unashamed of his ignorance.

'He's a freedom fighter – helped ship all those dandy-looking white fellows back to Eng-*laand.*'

That evening, Raj sneaked the picture out of the man's storage room, folded lovingly in the breast pocket of his shirt. He spent the night locked up in his room, searching within the photograph for an answer to a need he could not identify. There was an arresting air to the man, dressed in a button-down sweater vest and striped tie, his arms thrown out in modest victory. Pio was the only one looking directly into the camera; the faces of the men upon whose shoulders he sat were all upturned.

The following week, Raj hungrily snatched up any information he could gather about the man, whether it was from the old newspapers his mother kept for cleaning and sorting rice, from his father or uncle or any other adult he managed to corner – and discovered that what the old shopkeeper had told him was true. Raj had accidentally stumbled upon one of Kenya's first freedom fighters, and an Indian one at that.

'Brave man,' Raj's uncle, Dilip, informed him. 'He returned from India to become involved in the local movement here, even supplied them with weapons. And in the middle of the night, he would put up political posters throughout the city, moving like a superhero. No one could catch him.'

'Must have been exciting,' Raj mused.

'But also very dangerous. See, for all his troubles, Pio was detained in 1954. But you wouldn't remember – you were only a young boy.'

Raj gripped the plastic covering of the dining table, steam clouds of heat beneath his fingers. 'For how long?'

'He was released five years later but do you think that stopped him?' Dilip Uncle shook his head. 'Of course not. He continued fighting to set Kenyatta free, and after that was achieved he helped ensure the KANU victory in the 1961 elections.' His uncle scooped up handfuls of white rice and dal, pausing to contemplate. When he spoke again, flecks of yellow lentils hopped out between his words. 'I met him once, you know. Ran into him on the street, just like that. So unassuming he was, but very clever. I could tell he was special straight away, just by looking at him.'

'Take me to meet him.'

At that, Dilip Uncle had howled. Dropped his mouth open so wide that Raj had glimpsed the pinkly quivering tonsils. '*Uh-reh!* He's a very busy man. Why on earth would he want to meet you?'

So after discovering that Pinto lived in Westlands, Raj rode his bike to the bustling district and parked inside the scratchy lantana bushes crowding the gate, hoping to sight the white Saab motor vehicle the man was known for driving.

Blackened with age, Pinto's house ran long and low across a tangle of undergrowth and from the doorway to the gate there weaved a narrow driveway of flattened mud. From his position, Raj caught movements in the window and detected faint outlines of a living room, smelled roasted coffee and eggs and his stomach growled.

He was there every day for the next three weeks, an apple in his pocket or an omelette sandwich wrapped in tin foil. One day he took leftover fish curry along with a piece of thick white bread and ate it cold as he learned the man's routine off by heart, tracked through his scratched toy binoculars.

Breakfast at seven thirty, seated in the kitchen nook surrounded by falling sunlight, Pinto engrossed himself in the newspaper until the sounds of his family distracted him; a wife and three daughters. At their voices, he would fold the paper in his lap and wait as they came up, one by one, for a morning kiss. Pinto would then disappear upstairs and his youngest daughter would come out of the house, bundled up for the chilly morning in a woolen sweater. She would play on the driveway, squat down on her haunches and search for whatever treasure her young mind conjured up, her delighted shouts disturbing the still air.

Some days, Pinto would join her early, dressed for work in an ironed white shirt and pressed trousers, always completed with a button-down sweater vest. His hair would be slicked back and he would pick up his daughter – 'How about we go for a ride today?' – and put her in the front seat of his Saab. They would drive the short, winding distance to the gate and back again. Pinto would repeat this several times – sometimes he would keep going until his wife came out looking for him.

'We're going to be late.'

And his daughter would be plucked from the car by her nanny, still clinging to her father's fingers as Pinto's wife waved goodbye in the rising tire dust, the couple making their way out onto the main street. There Raj would be, huddled behind the itchy leaves of the lantana bush, ducking bees and swatting mosquitoes.

Twenty-one days passed in this manner until, one morning, Raj was digging at an elbow scab and waiting for Pinto to leave at eight thirty, just as he always did, when the car slowed down more than usual. Raj looked up and, to his nervous surprise, saw the driver's window roll down as it approached his hiding spot. He saw the man he had been watching from a distance for so many days now and was taken aback by how large he was – how real – when not viewed in a newspaper clipping or through binoculars.

'Hello there.' The voice was unassuming, bouncing with friendliness. An arm extended outward, gesturing for Raj to come closer. But he stayed fixed to the ground and even the greedy mosquitoes pinching his skin were not enough to force him out onto the road. 'I won't hurt you. I only want to answer your question.'

Intrigued, Raj took a small step forward. 'What question?'

'You must have one,' replied Pinto, pausing mid-sentence as Raj came the full way out, taking fairy-steps toward the Saab, where he saw that the man was alone. 'Otherwise you wouldn't be waiting here every day.'

Pinto was right. The purpose of Raj's visit had been lost in all the excitement at seeing the man in the flesh, but now as he looked upon the wide-browed young man he remembered it again.

He asked, 'How did you do it?'

Smiling as if it were a question he was used to, Pinto returned with, 'What exactly do you mean by *it*?'

'How did you become a hero?'

Eyebrows shooting up; this version of the question was new to him, a strange and uncomfortable thought. 'Who told you I was a hero?'

'Everyone says so. They say that you're brave, that you freed us from the *Wazungu*. That even the Africans trust you.'

Pinto's index finger tapped against the steering wheel, his face clouded. 'Is that what you want? To become a hero?'

Raj's heart picked up its pace as the dream purred inside him. 'Isn't that what you do?'

The car turned off, returning the morning to its previous, bird-filled silence. Pinto pushed open the heavy door and his movements were so agile, so practiced at being invisible, that he was on one knee and face level with Raj before the boy knew what was happening. 'Truth be told,' Pinto started, 'we all want to be heroes. We all want to make that difference in that moment of time, to be admired for our bravery and respected for our actions.'

With every word, Raj nodded. *Admired. Respected.* They were the fingers that plucked at his dream, strumming it awake.

'But as long as you want to be a hero, you will never become one.'

Raj's excitement faltered. 'I don't understand.'

'People think I'm brave for spending all those years in jail, for putting up some posters on walls and helping others, but it's not because I'm courageous or a hero,' Pinto explained. 'It's because I know what is right and I'm willing to fight for it.'

'And what is that?'

Pinto rose, dusted off his cotton-clad knees. He was a slim man, younger than Raj had thought, but there was a peculiar grace about him, an oldness of soul that Raj understood was what made

Dilip Uncle say that the man was special. Back in the car now, the smile once again on his face, Pinto asked, 'Do you know why the Africans trust me?'

A shake of a small head, eager bristles of hair gleaming in the sun.

'Because I trust them. Because we work together as equals and treat each other as such, as Kenyans fighting for the same cause. That is what's right.' As the car revved loudly, Pinto shouted over its sound. 'Next time you want to ask me something, knock on my door.' And he was gone, a cream car in a flurry of dark red dust.

That evening at the dinner table, it emerged that Pinto was in trouble.

Raj's father banged his fist down. '*Eh pagal hogaya?* He'll be killed for it, just wait and see.'

A story was spreading through Nairobi that Pinto and his socialist comrades were plotting a parliamentary coup after their demands for a ceiling distribution of wealth and just rewards for the Mau-Mau freedom fighters was brushed off by the president, swatted away within the gold tassels of his fly whip.

'He discovered that the *mzee* had allocated himself over fifty farms in Central Province and Rift Valley. That he will be displacing all the Kikuyu squatters and other farmers to make room for his fat cronies. No better than the colonialists,' Dilip Uncle had said. 'What else could he have done?'

'Not called our president a bastard, for one,' Raj's father had replied. 'I'm surprised he wasn't killed there and then.'

'Well, the *mzee* did call him one first.'

And then, one misty February morning, Raj's father came to break the news to him. 'Now, *beta*, I don't want you to be too upset...'

Pinto had been killed, shot at the gate of his house, riddled with bullets from those exact bushes Raj used to hide within, his nose irritated by the woody wild flowers.

'Must have been desperate.' He heard his father and uncle speaking in low tones later that day as he lay upstairs in his bed, trying to understand his grief. 'To do it in broad daylight and right outside his house! In front of his daughter and on that busy street.'

'Time to leave this place,' Raj's aunt had warned. ''I told you, they don't want us here.'

Raj had been devastated. He'd mourned as if he had lost a loved one, someone as close to him as his mother or sister, but somehow worse because, without Pinto, that budding dream of his lost direction. It wandered and tripped, became afraid of itself and hid tightly away under a horde of questions that would forever go unanswered.

The picture of Pinto was framed and hung up on his bedroom wall and Raj tucked his dreams behind the glass so that they would always be close to him. Then he did what his father advised and moved on with his life, because it was silly to hang onto the dead and all the doubt that came with them.

He met Pooja when he was nineteen, working as an accountant at the family's fish shop and, over a shared bottle of coke, he told her the story of Pio Gama Pinto and of his aspirations and she fell in love with him and his eyes, which were as quick and bright as his words.

Following the death of his uncle, Raj's father sold the fish shop and started a small used furniture store where their main clientele were local Africans. It was during this time that Raj began to put into practice what little advice he had received from Pinto.

Unlike his father, Raj was friendly with his African customers and employees, reprimanding the older man for calling them 'thieves', 'lazy idiots' and 'monkeys.'

'But they're stealing from us,' his father had protested. 'You should know – you're the one doing the books.'

'Not all of them,' Raj had corrected him. 'And yes, some of them are thieves but there are also Indian thieves – and big ones too.

Stealing millions of shillings from our country... so what can you say about them?'

But the full realization of his dreams remained constantly out of his reach. Raj often blamed it on the fact that he was running a business, had become a husband and a father and that these things occupied enormous spaces in his life, leaving room for little else. He also knew that he was partly responsible – that though his dreams were beautiful, they were also terrifying and he had been slightly frightened to catch up to them.

So, early on in his son's life, when Raj recognized something in Jai that was reminiscent of his own idealism, he took it upon himself to nurture the boy, to teach him the lessons he had learned from Pinto – to mold Jai's rapidly adjusting mind and body into strong, hard shapes so that fear would never fit into him.

Which was why, upon seeing Angela's son approach Leena as she played marbles, Raj had immediately sent Jai out.

'See that boy with your sister? I want you to help him with whatever he needs.'

Now the street was empty and Jai was emerging from the veranda, kicking a small stone ahead of him. At sixteen, his father had been a clueless boy, but Jai carried within him a solid sense of conviction – a steel framework of principle that few men Raj knew possessed – and it made his chest puff out with pride.

It was as if the boy had come to him at just the right time – when Raj was old enough that his dreams were beginning to change, break down and turn cruel, morphing into painful regrets.

'He's Angela's son,' Pooja informed her family once they were all seated at the table. She was hot and bothered, having had to lean over the stove for half an hour, deep-frying the pooris. Normally,

Angela would have made them but Pooja had allowed her to go home early.

She fanned out her loose tunic, blowing down the collar. 'He was living in Eldoret with his grandmother but she passed away from a serious bout of malaria.'

'I didn't know Angela had a son.' Leena pressed her nail down into the balloon-like poori. With a slight whistle it flattened into a yellow heap on her plate.

'Your father and I knew about Michael – that's his name. He's around your age.' Pooja turned to Jai. 'He was going to school there but now he'll be living with Angela so you'll see him around here sometimes.'

Pooja had made it clear to Angela that she would not be paying for the extra set of hands. She was the one doing Angela the favor – so that she wouldn't have to leave her son at home during the school holidays while she came to work.

'Do we have to be friends with him?' Leena chewed down anxiously on her food, imagining all the cruel taunts she might receive if she should befriend this strange, light-stepping boy.

Whilst debating how to answer, Pooja looked over at her husband. She had been worried about bringing the boy here, especially at this *raging-hormone* age and especially around her daughter. 'You just never know with these *kharias*,' she had told Raj, hush-hush in their bed the night Angela had informed them about Michael. 'And yet here you are saying we must agree to let her bring him into our home because that is what Pinto would have done.'

At the table that night, unable to keep the crossness from his voice, Raj told his daughter, 'Of course you'll be his friend.'

Pooja interjected, 'He's coming here to work. Not to play.'

'No matter what you decide, I want you to treat him with respect and kindness, is that understood?' Raj addressed Leena but looked instead at his son. He put his napkin down. 'Jai, come outside with me while these two ladies clean up.'

They left the table together, his daughter's nasal whine following them out onto the street. 'It's not fair that Jai gets to go outside while I have to clear up the table.' Stomping feet could be heard above her mother's harsh reprimanding. 'I hate being a girl.'

The street outside was empty but Raj still led his son to the most secluded area on the compound – behind all the houses, where the communal water tank was situated. He settled on the brick ledge there, crossing one leg over the other knee and pulling a cigarette from his trouser pocket.

'Sit down,' he told his son as the air filled with the fast hiss of a matchstick lighting. The orange flame, captured in the round cup of his father's palm, danced in flickers about his face and Jai immediately went to him. He tucked his hands beneath his thighs, zipping up his hooded sweatshirt right beneath his chin. He was used to the seriousness of his father's tone, understood already what was coming next.

'Your sister can do whatever she wants but you will become friends with that boy.'

Jai scuffed his feet against the loose gravel. He dragged the heel of his sneaker slowly toward the ledge, opening up a valley of tiny, gray stones. He said through gritted teeth, 'Okay.'

Arguing with his father was impossible. Jai had recognized early on the burden that had been placed upon him but was now old enough to reach the conclusion that while having your own hopes could be thrilling, being forced to carry someone else's was exhausting. And yet, he always found himself relenting, always agreeing.

Raj exhaled – a dragon puff of smoke. 'I knew you would understand. You're a special boy. You're going to do great things when you're older.'

'I wish you would stop telling me what I am.' The words sneaked out. Perhaps it was the darkness, the fact that he could not make out the details of his father's face so was unable to detect the gathering up of his features, the set lips and tight brow.

'I'm reminding you because I know how easy it is to forget.' Raj dropped the cigarette to the ground, let it smolder. 'When I was younger, I asked a great man what it takes to be a hero. He told me that it wasn't about being the bravest person – it was about being a good one. About sacrificing your happiness for the right thing.' He searched the straight-edged nose and apple cheeks of his son. A mirror image of himself. 'I couldn't understand him then but now that I do, I want to teach you.'

'I just want to be normal.' There it was again, his feelings made bolder by the night.

'But you aren't normal, don't you see? None of us are until we allow ourselves to be.' Raj was facing his son fully now. 'It is the greatest injustice you can do to yourself – to settle for ordinary.'

Jai took his hand out from under his father's and slipped it into the pocket of his jacket. As always, the words his father spoke affected him in a way no one else's did. Perhaps it was the weight of them; they carried a thrill, which despite his annoyance, always had a way of exciting him, pushing him into action, and he said, in the final spark of his father's dying cigarette, 'I'll talk to Michael tomorrow.'

It was after lunchtime the next day when Jai went out onto the veranda. There was a back door leading onto it from the kitchen – a congested space cut off from the rest of the street by a low iron fence. A clothes line swung across the width of it, the concrete floor permanently wet from drying garments. There was a narrow bench that ran along the perimeter, though no space existed upon it to sit. It was overrun by potted plants, ponytail palms, blooming white-flowered cacti and Leena's favorite, a purple-tinged flower, puffed out like soft cotton. A *touch-me-not*, it shrunk and closed up at the slightest touch. Slowly, she placed the tip of her pinky along the slim, ridged leaf and allowed it to curl, drawing up its edges into a spiky barrier.

'Why do you like to scare the *prrant?*' Angela asked in her comforting Kikuyu accent, the absence of '*l*' replaced by a heavy, rolling '*r*' making everything sound like a shout, even the most loving murmur.

'I want to know why it does that.' Leena touched another leaf, giggling as it compressed and folded into itself.

'I've told you a hundred times, it's for protection. So they won't get eaten by insects or other animals.' Jai turned to Angela impatiently. 'I'm looking for Michael.'

'He stayed home today. He's feeling tired after his journey and wanted to rest.'

That morning, his father's words having slept within him, Jai had risen full of childish excitement. He felt it deflate slightly now, curdle in disappointment. 'When he does decide to come, please let me know.'

Angela picked up a wet shirt and began scrubbing it hard, *slap-slap*, against her knuckles. She wondered whether that was a good idea. Two or three days of playing and they'll be done with each other, she decided.

'Okay.' She waved them away, her arms buried in foam. 'Go now and let me finish my work.'

12

Eldoret. The town of hills – training grounds for Kipchoge Keino, the famous long-distance running champion who was also the hero of Michael's childhood. A place of wholesale *dukas* and manufacturing companies such as Ken-Knit, Lochab Brothers and Raiplywoods, set up and developed by the oldest East-Indian families living in the Rift Valley Region. A city of few museums and too many nightclubs, with a vast night sky that hung low like a canopy, traversed by *Ngai* himself, the creator and giver of all things.

Michael had never been close with his grandmother – had in fact lived in terror of the heavy-set, lumbering woman upon whose doorstep he had been dropped when he was three years old, after his mother had found some casual labor working for an Indian family in the capital city.

'Nairobi is no place for a child to grow up,' his grandmother had said to him when he began asking questions. 'Drugs, sex, thieves – it's a city where everything that can be stolen will be stolen, including yourself.'

Known to most people as simply Madam, his grandmother made a living trading anything that her hands came upon. Potatoes, *sukuma-wiki*, maize, all of which she grew in the communal shamba running along the edges of her home, closing off the half-acre plot with a wire fence and keeping such close guard of it that no one dared steal a single cob or pull one leaf of the collard greens.

She took Michael out to plow, dig, water and hoe as soon as he was old enough for proper hand-eye co-ordination. Chickens, a few short-haired cows, some goats; whether it was the gift of the gab or the ability to terrorize, his grandmother sold back to people the things they already had at a grossly inflated price and garnered a reputation as a cunning and ruthless businesswoman.

As Michael grew up she began to accept books and magazines instead of money for her goods, but only those written in English. She had forced them upon him as his friends played outside on the street, saying, 'Your father, *mjinga*, stupid man, thought he could win without knowing a single thing! You are going to learn their language, speak it properly, become as clever as they are – it's the only way to send them back and return this country to the people it rightfully belongs to.'

A gossiper, a maker of sordid stories, Madam went about systematically destroying the reputations of all those who crossed or angered her, or those she felt to be a threat. Michael heard her talking about his mother once, when he was supposed to be asleep but had instead crawled up behind the door of the bedroom they shared.

She was sitting opposite another woman, Mama Itanya, and they were slowly sipping on Jack Daniels from small glass mugs. Michael had no idea how she had managed to get her hands on something so decadent, but he wasn't surprised. His grandmother was as wily and devious as a magician and just as selfish with her tricks. He watched them swirl, suckle and gulp in the light of a quarter moon and devised a plan on how he would sneak some. Little did he know that two weeks later the old woman would be dead and he would be the sole inheritor of that half-full bottle of whiskey. He couldn't have envisioned the night he sat beside her bed and looked over her still body, finding it impossible that someone so fearsome could succumb to something as inconsequential as a mosquito. A peculiar sadness would pick away at him and, although he would be eager to see his mother again, he would also be reluctant to leave that town, those people, and the only memories he had.

But that night he listened to her with growing rage, any insult against his mother feeling like a personal slight against himself.

'I *wouldi* never work for anyone!' she was burping, the drink making her louder than usual, her Kikuyu-laced English more difficult to understand.

Mama Itanya had hushed her. 'The boy will hear you.'

Madam drank again, ignoring her companion. 'I told his mother, you come *andi* work for me and we make good money together. We get there *sirowry buti surery.* None of *thisi* working for criminals. *Ngai!* Ten thousand shillings a month – how *cani* anyone live off that over there?'

The day following her death, Michael had left Mama Itanya, who was also his grandmother's second cousin, in charge of the house and *shamba* and had boarded the Eldoret Express at eight thirty in the morning. On the torn and rickety seat, pressed beside a student of Chepkoilel Campus, Michael had listened to her babble excitedly about her boyfriend in Nairobi.

'City boys are different. So sophisticated,' she had told him, describing the fancy, European-style restaurants, the shopping malls and hotels, the Phoenix Theater where one could go and watch a local play, and coffee shops – 'Can you imagine sipping coffee for one whole hour? Absurd.' Trying but failing to communicate fully the intangible energy of the capital, the dreams it infected you with so that, even if you wanted to leave, once you set foot in Nairobi you were changed forever and there was no going back.

Still, Michael had no idea what to expect when he arrived in the congested city. He saw all manners of people – cheeky, African pedestrians; sour-mouthed Indian shop owners; *mzungus* in all their khaki glory, pink-faced and friendly, as if they had been plucked straight from a romance novel. He even spotted a Chinese man haggling at an electronics store and stopped to gape at the unusual sight. The sounds of the evening traffic mixed with gospel music from bus radios and people setting up shop wherever there was space on the bumpy, unpaved roadside – selling sweets, hot peanuts and magazines. Above his head ran lines of wire mannequins dressed up in the latest Western fashions.

Michael leaped across an overflowing, festering sewer filled with rainwater, fast-food wrappers, plastic bottles and cigarette butts, aghast to see some boys washing themselves in it. The 'city of possibilities' the girl on the bus had promised him, but to Michael it was ugly and disturbing.

When he reached the apartment building his mother worked at, he gave Angela's name to the askari as instructed. But when he stepped inside he was even more terrified of this neat, tiny oasis than he had been outside on the darkening street, because it was full of the very people his grandmother had warned him about – *muhindis*. Those loud, expressive people who spat on sidewalks and spoke with swinging hands and bobbing necks.

'That's how you can tell they're lying,' his grandmother had said. 'Too dramatic – they are trying too hard to make you believe them.'

Walking amongst the cluster of houses, the occupants peering down at him suspiciously, Michael worried about how he would find his mother without an apartment number. He had to stop behind a group of children engaged in a game of glass balls and ask for her.

He had never experienced looks of that kind before. Not fear or hatred, but something that lay in the muddy, indeterminate space between the two, making them glance suspiciously at each other but never at him. Shifting from foot to foot, he stared back at the small Indian girl who watched him like a jumpy animal, when a boy emerged from a house and gave him the first smile he had received all afternoon.

'Come with me,' he had said and Michael followed, looking up at the sky of a city where night-time smelled of smoke, the stars were not as close and God was missing.

Michael waited for the *muhindi* boy to leave before running straight into his mother's arms. Bony but gentle, unlike his grandmother, not that the old woman had ever embraced him. Angela's arms fit perfectly around him, holding him to her chest just the way, as a child, he had longed to be held. *So happy you are here, sorry I never visited, expensive bus fare, saving it all up for you.* Excuses he didn't care to hear because he had forgiven her a long time ago.

They left soon after and walked to the Parklands district, reaching the unpainted, brick building where Angela lived with her sister and niece, Jackie, who was two years younger than Michael but acted like she was much older. A city girl with wild energy in her veins.

She asked him if he wanted to go to school with her but he refused, telling his mother that it made more sense to wait until the beginning of the new term and so, a few days later, Angela insisted that he start going to work with her.

'Your auntie will be at her job all day and I don't want to leave you at home alone, at least not until you are properly settled in. Nairobi can be dangerous.'

He hadn't wanted to argue, to fuss, to remind her that he was almost sixteen now and not the young boy she had left, because he didn't want to make her upset or regret bringing him back. Despite the Eldoret-shaped hole in his chest, Michael couldn't imagine being without her any more. So he listened when she said, 'You stay with me and no going inside the house!' He had no choice but to trudge along, keeping Madam's words close, like the old blanket she had given him, along with the books he had carried when he left her house.

He used the blanket to cover his ears whenever he lay down on the bumpy mattress in the evenings. There were too many night noises and he had trouble sleeping. The living room floor was hard against his hip, the scratching of rat claws and murmurs of cockroaches throwing him back awake every time he started to fall into slumber. Oftentimes, he would give up and sit by the windowsill, feeling homesick and watching the city run chaotically beneath him, well into the mist-covered hours of the morning.

13

Soon after he arrived, Michael was at their house every day. Most of the time he kept to himself, staying with Angela out on the veranda and Leena wouldn't see him until dusk, at his mother's side, quiet and fluid in the darkness with his trusted satchel. Angela would shout out a goodbye and Leena would wave from the window but his eyes stayed trained ahead, a face that was serious but never guarded. When she and Jai attempted to speak to him, Michael would answer in that measured, intelligent way of his, as if he considered each word a thousand times before stringing them together – a perfectly constructed necklace of thought.

'A city is a city,' he said to them once, shrugging his shoulders when Jai asked how he was settling into Nairobi. 'There's noise, pollution and too many people everywhere. It's the same wherever you go, just on a bigger or smaller scale.' He felt their watchful eyes, wondering if they knew he had picked the phrase directly from a copy of *Time* magazine that their father had thrown out.

To Leena, he spoke like a grown up and in perfect English, declining to join their games no matter how many times Jai asked him. When he wasn't helping Angela with the dishes or folding clothes, he sat cross-legged on the veranda floor with a book spread neatly over his knees.

But there were times she caught him watching them as they played, his hands slung in his pockets. The immobility of his features made him appear bored, as if he was there because he needed a break from whatever chore he was doing. But on closer inspection, she saw his eyes moving quickly, following their movements. His body was held tightly, on edge, as if he was the one taking the penalty shot or fielding the cricket ball rolling toward the boundary. He watched with careful intent, as if calculating the precise force needed to swing a bat in order to smash six runs or the exact angle at which one had to flick the marble if they wanted to knock everyone else out of the circle.

Whenever he saw her watching him, Michael would straighten up and respond with a quick nod of acknowledgment, disappearing around the back. She would turn away and he would fall onto a stool, missing the games he played and the people he used to play them with back home in Eldoret.

But he found it intriguing, the rules that they followed so carefully here, the discipline with which they played. The football he had engaged in had been carefree – composed of rough teenagers running around and smashing into each other, pulling T-shirts and shorts, simply with the goal of getting the ball past the keeper – it didn't really matter how it got there in the first place. But here, they were always shouting, always accusing, picking up the ball and kicking it from odd corners, edges, a few meters from the net – and it seemed more exciting that way. And what was that game they played with the thick bats? Smashing the small, red ball around like lunatics, screaming *Six, Four, Ooooooouuuuuut*, the *muhindi* boy his mother worked for zoom-zooming in and out of the other children, arms spread out like a low-flying plane.

The boy who would not leave him alone. His first full day at the compound, Jai had jumped over the low fence of the veranda, landing so smoothly that Michael didn't hear or see him until he turned around and came face to face with a wide smile. Valley-like dimples and small teeth, made whiter by his sun-browned skin.

'Oh!' Michael almost dropped the bucket of wet clothes his mother had given him to hang up on the clothes line.

'I'm Jai.' A hand stretching out in greeting.

Michael recognized him as the one who had helped him on his very first evening in Nairobi, his first encounter of kindness in the frenzied city, but his grandmother's words stuck, invisible and stubborn, between them. *You can't trust these people,* she had told him. *A muhindi is worse than a snake in the grass – they don't care if you spot them or not, they'll sting you with their poison in broad daylight if it means getting ahead.*

And so Michael had pulled up the plastic bucket, creating a shield between his chest and Jai's hand.

'Michael,' he said.

'I know – I've been waiting for you for almost a week now!' Jai's words were impatient as he took the bucket from Michael, sliding it across the cement floor with a quick swipe of his arm.

A prick of anxious sweat. 'Why?'

'Do you want to play football with us?'

The offer was tempting but his grandmother's warnings were stronger, his anxiety heightened by the remembrance of all those circling eyes, trapping him in their suspiciousness. He felt safe on the veranda, hidden, and wasn't ready to risk coming out.

'I have work to do.'

Unused to being refused, Jai was surprised. Michael had seen the way the other children responded to his invitations – exploding into talkative pleasure, eager and quick to do whatever he said, his sister included. Still, Jai accepted Michael's refusal graciously.

'If you change your mind, you know where I live. But don't worry, I'll find you again tomorrow.'

And true to his word, the boy was back on the veranda in the morning, a half-eaten tangerine in one hand and a cricket ball in the other. He held it up to Michael, who paused from peeling carrots, bright orange skin around his bare feet. Jai cocked his eyebrow. 'How about it?'

'I can't.' A mumble, his hand moving aggressively against the thin vegetable. The game looked like a lot of fun and Michael was annoyed at himself for refusing, cross at his grandmother for her words, but even more so at Jai for tempting him.

'Next time,' Jai called over his shoulder as he hopped over the fence.

The next day, a soccer ball stopped at his stool, tapping his foot in a dare. Michael picked it up, its rough rubber taut beneath his hands. It was a lot firmer than the half-deflated one he used to play with and he bounced it over his knees.

'You're pretty good at that.' Jai was leaning against the wall, watching.

Michael let the ball fall to the tip of his toe, flicking it in a wide arch toward Jai. 'I used to play all the time.'

'We're just about to start a game,' Jai offered.

The eager smile was pushing him off the stool, weakening his resolve. Michael almost agreed but was interrupted by shouts from the other children. 'Come on, Jai, what's taking so long? We have enough people to play already.'

'Maybe next time,' he said to Jai, retreating slowly back to his chair.

It was a Saturday morning and Michael sat sulking and peeling potatoes. He dropped the skinned ones into a green bucket and tossed the remains onto a sheet of newspaper. He had always hated the smell of spuds, like old water and mud, and now he ripped the skin off with fast strokes of the small knife. He hadn't minded doing it for his grandmother because at least he had been the one eating them. But these were for the Kohlis; once dipped into a pot brimming with spices, black seeds and bay leaves, he would never see them again.

Angela put her hand on his. 'Watch you don't cut your finger.'

He jerked away, keeping up the same frantic speed. For the first time since he had moved to Nairobi, he was irked by his mother. That morning, he had begged to stay home with Jackie, having grown tired of washing clothes, scraping food residue off the bottoms of plates and brushing dirt from the veranda floor – especially when it was so warm out and the day was made for playing.

A noise from within the house caused him to look up. He saw Mrs Kohli at her bedroom window, drawing back the lace drapes. It was ten o'clock and she had just woken up, sleepy and pleased, welcoming in the weekend light. Several minutes later, the shower turned on and the pipes groaned to life and he envied the unhurried way with which she was treating the day.

Now that Jackie was home for the school holidays, she often invited her friends over and Michael realized how much he had missed the company of children he felt comfortable with – who spoke his language, understood his jokes and looked at him without any sort of meaning. His cousin had offered to show him all the wonderful things about Nairobi that he had missed out on, having been raised in a 'small and boring town with goats instead of people.'

Last week, Jackie had returned from a day spent at Uhuru Park, her face painted in the design of a butterfly – blue glitter wings expanding outward over her cheeks – and a balloon hat wrapped around her braids. She carried with her the smell of charcoaled meat and freshly cut grass and told him of the cold glass bottle of coke she had drunk from and the one ride she had spent ten shillings on – offering to take him the following weekend. But his mother had refused, telling him that she needed his help at work.

'I don't know why they can't peel their own potatoes,' he said now.

Angela's eyes darted quickly to the back door. 'Hush. Someone will hear you.'

He lowered his voice and switched to Swahili. 'Why do we have to sit here and do all the work while they're in there, watching TV or sleeping until late? Don't they also have hands?'

Angela was concentrating on stitching a loose button onto one of Raj's work shirts. The slim silver needle glinted between her fingers, the white thread invisible between her teeth. Without a pause, she said, 'I know what your grandmother must have told you about me.'

Michael focused on the potato, the slimy juice stinging a never-noticed-before cut in his skin. His mother continued speaking.

'She used to tell me all the time what a coward I was. How I had betrayed her and everyone else in this country when I decided to work as a housegirl and, even worse, for an Indian family. *Encouraging subordination*, she used to tell me. *Letting them believe that they're better than us.*' Angela jutted out her jaw. 'But I'm grateful for this job because it allows me to live here, in the city, with your aunt, and I was also able to send you to a good school.'

'Why didn't you just stay in Eldoret with my grandmother?' he asked. 'You wouldn't have had to work for anyone.'

Angela scoffed. 'I would have had to work for her and that would have been worse than anything. She hated me, blamed me for what happened to your father and would have taken any opportunity to torture me. Besides, I want a life for you here.' She pushed the needle back through the shirt. 'The Kohlis aren't such a bad family. They pay me on time, they treat us kindly – I can think of a lot worse jobs for someone to have.'

Rebuked, Michael turned back to peeling and they continued to work in silence, his gaze fixed downward. Eventually, Pooja began shouting for Angela as she came down the stairs and his mother rose, folding the shirt and taking it with her as she went.

The knife dragged along the potato, jerky and removing most of the vegetable along with the skin. He slowed his hand.

'I agree with you. I don't know why we can't do anything for ourselves.'

Startled, Michael looked up to see Jai at the doorway, bouncing a yo-yo. He placed it in his pocket and dragged a chair out of the kitchen. 'Let me help.'

'I can do it.' Michael's voice was stiff with embarrassment. But the boy ignored him, picking up the largest vegetable he could find. Michael asked, 'How did you understand what I was saying?'

'I speak some Swahili,' Jai told him. 'Enough to understand that you're upset.'

'I was wrong to say those things.'

They kept peeling. Jai was singing a galloping tune, pausing to unclip a boxy-looking device from his belt. It was similar to a mini radio but without the speakers and he snapped open the contraption, flipping over the tape inside.

'What's that?' Michael asked.

'A Walkman. It plays tapes of my favorite music.' Jai handed Michael one of the headphones – 'We can listen together while we work' – dragging the chair closer so that the headphones could sit comfortably in both their ears.

Intrigued, Michael slipped it into his ear, felt the uncomfortable newness of its pressure and then a loud bass flooded his head, tickling his teeth. He laughed giddily. 'This is great!'

Jai was still peeling. 'I go through so many battery packs a week.'

Michael didn't know the song that was playing – it was in English. But he reveled in the way the music seemed to surround him; at the same time within and outside of him, making his feet tap involuntarily.

Jai turned down the music. 'If you ever get bored helping out your mother, you can always join in our games. It would be nice to have some actual competition.'

'What's the one you play with the bats?' Michael felt more comfortable now, after sharing the music.

'It's cricket.' Jai tossed down some potato peels on the newspaper below their feet.

'It looks complicated.'

'Like all things, until you understand it. I could teach it to you.'

Michael was beginning to believe that his grandmother might have been wrong about these *muhindis* – there was nothing slippery about Jai's manner.

Angela emerged from the kitchen and the two boys sat up quickly, pushing apart. Michael handed Jai back his headphones. Under his mother's quizzical gaze, he felt like a burglar caught in the act of sneaking out of a house that wasn't his. 'Breakfast is ready,' she informed Jai.

Jai dropped the peeled potato into the bucket and rose, wiping his hands on his trousers. 'Remember,' he craned his neck back to Michael as he stepped into the house. 'Whenever you want.'

A few minutes later, Angela looked up from the dishes she was washing to see Michael hunched over the bucket of vegetables, his shoulders moving, tapping his foot and, under his breath, humming a song she didn't recognize.

*

He hadn't tried to catch the ball. It just smacked into his open, waiting palm held straight up like he was about to ask a question in class. It was a natural reflex, a smooth impulse that required no effort or strain. Just a neat swinging back of the elbow, hand cupped like a net.

'Whoa.' Jai dropped his cricket bat. 'Whoa! That was amazing, you made it look so easy,' he said, reaching Michael and holding up his palm for a congratulatory high five. Michael handed him the ball instead.

'Right place at the right time,' he said, but the adrenaline was pumping through him in jolts, warming his cheeks.

'Do you want to join us?'

They were out on the street, their backs to the houses on either side. To the left was the gate and to the right of them, beyond the walls, a crowded line of kiosks – small, locally owned shops that sold everything from cigarettes to soda bottles and *sukuma-wiki*. Past that, there were the slums: clustered, make-shift shelters whose corrugated metal roofs made tinkling music in the rain, like steel drums. They had been forced to play that way after Ricky Singh smacked a huge one into Nishit Patel's house, past the front yard and into the back one, narrowly missing his wife's head.

The wickets were created from fallen branches and placed four meters apart. Tag was at one end, Jai's bat at the other and Leena stood in the middle, impatiently gesturing for the ball.

'It'll be fun,' Jai prodded.

The sting of the ball still sat in Michael's palm, temptingly heavy. Combined with the fact that he had actually begun to like this *muhindi* boy, Michael was compelled to answer the same question differently that day.

'Come on, Jai!' Leena called out to her brother's back. She was tired of his repeated, inexplicable attempts to draw Michael into their games, their lives, when he so clearly didn't want to be a part of them. She was surprised then, and a little nervous, when Michael started to walk toward them. Tag spoke up loudly.

'There's no room for anyone else. We have full teams already – sorry!' And then, soft enough so that it could pretend to be a whisper, 'Who wants to play with a maid's son?'

Jai shouted back, 'Your mother was calling you in for lunch, Tag. You can go now – Michael will take your place.'

Tag's voice died in his throat. He turned to Leena for support but she scuffed the ground with her toe, arms folded behind her back.

'She was calling you in fifteen minutes ago.' As always, she sided with her brother.

Tag dropped the bat, kicked it away. 'Whatever. I'm tired of this game anyway.'

Jai pulled on Michael's arm. 'You can't say no now.'

As they approached, Leena refused to meet her brother's eye. She was angry at him for ruining the game, thought he was selfish for sending Tag away just so Michael could join in. He wasn't like the rest of them and it created a level of discomfort that made playing the game less fun.

But Leena was also jealous of the way her brother looked at the boy with a keen interest he never seemed to regard any of them with. Jai spoke freely with Michael, his smile a permanent white, as he pointed out which position to stand in, where to hit the ball. Watching them stand close together, their movements so similar, as if they intrinsically knew what one was about to say to the other, she realized that Michael would never have to ache or beg for Jai's company – and that was what hurt her the most.

'Do you know how to play?' Jai asked.

The bat was heavier than he had anticipated and as Michael went to pick it up, his arm dropped with the weight. Leena was glaring at him, tapping her foot in annoyance. He seemed to be grinning at her, as if they shared something secret, and she remembered those days he'd stood by the veranda fence and watched them.

Jai jogged to the opposite wicket. 'Leena, you're up.' He tossed the ball to her and she rolled it in her palm, letting the worn-out red leather leak into her fingertips as she took her position a few steps behind Jai.

At his cue, she took off – a skipping run just as he had taught her. Keeping the ball loosely between her fingers, she released it as her arm came down, a satisfying clockwork motion that rushed and settled in the hinge of her shoulder. The ball bounced once, racing toward Michael – a blurry, red dot. He wouldn't be able to hit that. It was her best bowling performance. She almost began cheering.

Smack. The ball fell to the center of the bat, sending hard vibrations through the wood and up to his palms, his skin erupting into tingles. They all watched it sail through the air.

'Whoa,' Jai said again once Michael had lowered his bat. Leena stood at the line, panting and furious as her brother rushed to Michael. 'That's what we call a six – see how it went flying over the boundary without bouncing?'

Once Jai had returned to his position, Michael shrugged at Leena. Something about the flashing annoyance in her eyes made him want to tease her, the excitement making him bold.

'It's not my fault you bowl like a girl.'

Jai turned to his sister and burst into laughter, his fist thrown up in a delighted cheer.

From then on, Michael joined in their games and they discovered that he was good at all of them. That he could run barefoot and never miss a step, or swing a cricket bat as if it were an extension of his own limb and send the ball flying over the compound wall with a loud *crack*.

'I suppose it's nice to be with someone your own age,' Pooja told her complaining daughter, watching out the window and worrying herself.

But Leena knew it had nothing to do with age. Tag was only a year younger than Jai but she had never seen her brother sprint out to Tag the way he did to Michael, searching for him as soon as breakfast was over, leaving her lonely at the table. He never discussed the winning tactics of football with the other boys the way he did with Michael, huddled together under the wide shade of the bougainvillea tree, drawing diagrams in the dirt with a twig, their faces serious until one of them cracked a joke and the air broke with their unstoppable laughter.

Jai refused to participate in any of the games that Michael wasn't included in and so he quickly became a fixture in their lives, a constant member of their group, unlike them in so many ways but too talented for it to make much of a difference.

But outside of those games, Michael remained a ghost to them. It was as if they didn't see him when they invited the other boys in for snacks or to watch the highlights from the previous day's Manchester United or Arsenal football match. It was more than intentional, this act of leaving Michael out. It occurred to them naturally, as a thing never to be questioned or thought about.

Leena knew that Michael was affected by this. She could see it in the dulling of his eyes, the almost undetectable clench of his fist, which he quickly hid in the pocket of his shorts. But he never complained. Michael moved through life the way he did through the games they played – gracefully and seemingly without effort yet with a firm and unshakeable confidence that turned everything the right way.

'He's your maid's son,' Tag said to Leena once as she followed him in for his mother's chocolate milkshake. Jai and Michael were lying on the grass outside and their sounds petered out behind her. 'Of course I wouldn't invite him into my home. What if he stole something? What if he wanted to use my toilet?'

And although she took the cold drink outside, holding it up to them after checking that Tag wasn't in sight, they both refused.

'Why would he want to drink from Tag's glass when he wasn't even allowed inside his house?' Jai asked in a way that made her feel at fault.

She had always enjoyed Tag's mother's milkshake – sprinkled with pistachio flakes that crunched down between her teeth as she drank it. But that day, it wouldn't move past the middle of her throat and she poured most of it out behind the bougainvillea tree.

14

Traffic officer Jeffery Omondi pulled out a handkerchief from his pocket and wiped the back of his neck, which was tickling with sweat. He brought the cloth forward, frowning at the brown residual streaks left there. Dust and fumes laced the humid air, made it thick and impossibly heavy, unavoidable while standing in the middle of afternoon traffic.

He had strategically placed himself at the junction of Ngong Road and Haile Selassie Avenue, his preferred spot to teach the more junior officers the most important lesson of all – how to mint money – because it never failed to provide him with the necessary opportunity.

'*Eh-he*, are you watching?' he snapped at the spindly, alarmed boy beside him. Barely a man, younger than Jeffery had been when he first joined the police force and he had only been twenty-two. '*Mjinga*,' he cursed under his breath. *Fool*. Not for the first time, Jeffery contemplated what had become of his beloved Kenyan Police Force, in whose motto, *Utamishi Kwa Wote*, he had truly believed. Service to All – a phrase that suggested justice, equality and an unshakeable sense of patriotism, but what he had discovered instead was greed, conspiracy and a different, truer motto: *Utamishi Kwa Mimi* – Service to Myself.

It wasn't that he hadn't been aware that corruption within the police force was endemic, aggravated by the low wages and appallingly poor housing, along with a general sense of mistrust from the public – he may have been naive but he hadn't been disillusioned. However, he had been profoundly dejected to discover just how deep the infection really ran. From the lowest police officer to the highest-ranking government official, it was rare that Jeffery met a clean man anywhere in the force. Corruption was rampant at every level – a carefully thought-out process of abusing public resources that required a chain of willing participants from down to up, each parting with their own share of the money once the deal was done. He had found it difficult to navigate the institution, which was a messy maze of bribery, canvassing and influence peddling, but he had been let know early on that if he wasn't willing to play the game, he would be transferred, or even worse, fired.

So when he had started to get his hands dirty, he told himself that it was for a bigger cause. That one day, when he was the top man, sitting in the spacious government office surrounded by a three hundred and sixty degree view of the city, well versed in all malpractices, he would turn the force into a pristine beacon of hope, where a 'Good Day's Work' didn't involve a police officer allowing himself to be bribed by a criminal in custody, soiling Nairobi's streets for nothing more than five thousand shillings.

But somewhere along the line, that dream had rotted under his ever-loosening morals. He had been blinded by how easy bribery was and bowled over by the rewards one was able to reap. He could afford three large meals a day and could dine in restaurants, which as a younger man had been beyond his reach. He spent years ignoring his wife, leaving her at home while he wandered the enchanting nightlife of the city, which fell easily under his command like a desperate prostitute recognizing how his trouser pockets puffed out with wealth.

And because people offered it themselves, because so many Kenyans were willing to pay their way out of the law – to take the shortest route – it never felt like stealing.

'There.' Jeffery pointed to a car heading toward them, grabbing the boy roughly. The car weaved from the left lane to the right, overtaking a slower-moving vehicle before switching back to the left. He tried not to say, *Ah-ha!* because it happened all the time. He lifted his hand and flagged down the driver as she approached Nairobi Club. 'Come on,' he told the junior officer. 'You want me to leave you here?' and stopped because the words were not his, but someone else's.

Same road, similar car pulling to a stop before a younger version of himself. His fellow officer, David, knocking on the driver's window – a twenty-something African woman – asking her to open the rear door so that he could climb in. She had done as instructed and David had shouted over the hood of the Toyota to Jeffery, 'Omondi, what are you staring at? You want me to leave you here?'

And Jeffery had disappeared into the cool interior of the car, sneaking a look back at the traffic they were meant to be directing and then casting his eyes upon the rearview mirror, where the driver was watching them uneasily. She was chewing down on her lipsticked mouth and getting doll-pink dye all over her teeth. *It's your right to refuse us entry into your car*, he wanted to tell her, but was certain that David would disapprove. After all, this was being done for Jeffery.

'Driver's license, ID.' David held out his hand as she shuffled through her glove compartment and handed him the documents.

She pulled on her afro, which was so large it could have been a violation of traffic laws itself. Jeffery appreciated it; he didn't see many young women with their natural hair any more. Always braids or mermaid-like weaves, dressed for an affluent future, pretending to be independent but hunting for a rich man and never a Kenyan – mostly *mzungus* in bars and Nigerian tycoons.

He had read an article in the *Standard* newspaper about how Kenyan men could learn the art of romance from these flashy *ogas* from the west. How his fellow men here refused to go that extra mile to sweep their women off their feet and then acted insulted when these pretty ladies trotted off to some Nigerian businessman in a handmade suit, holding a big bouquet of roses. *Things cost money*, he had wanted to write back to the editor. *It's not that we don't want to, but how can I spend five thousand shillings on dinner and flowers if it costs me more than a quarter of my monthly salary?*

'Drive,' David had commanded, shaking Jeffery out of his thinking. They were back in traffic, moving in silence except for David occasionally slapping the license against his thigh. Eventually he asked the girl, 'Do you know why I pulled you over?'

She tightened her trembling grip on the wheel. 'I didn't do anything wrong.'

'That is incorrect.' David was pleased with himself. 'In fact, you wrongly changed lanes. You moved from the left lane to the right and then back again, which is an offense. Perhaps you should have stayed in the right one, it would have taken you back into town.'

The woman treaded carefully in an effort not to aggravate him. 'It was a broken white line, which means that I was allowed to change lanes as long as it was safe to do so, which it was. So you see, I haven't broken any laws.'

'Surely you have.' David's manner was infuriatingly slow but beneath his smile, Jeffery had sensed a warning. '*Sisi-haturuhusu-watu-wabadilishe-lanes-hapo.*'

She spoke again, this time a buoyed confidence in her tone thanks to his lack of any sound argument. 'I was perfectly within the law to change lanes and overtake a slower moving car and get back into my lane twenty meters before the intersection.'

His smile completely gone, David scooted forward. He spoke in an agonizingly sing-song manner, as if addressing a child. 'Wedonot-allow-forchangeson-that-road,' he had repeated, glancing in Jeffery's direction but Jeffery had chosen to keep staring out of the window. He would hear about it later, no doubt, but in that moment, his first participation in breaking the very thing he had sworn to uphold, Jeffery was humiliated. Betrayed by the system and a government that forced him and so many others like him to so easily degrade themselves, to become starving vultures, beaking and grasping at whatever they could get their claws around.

'*Sawa.*' David heaved a sigh and fell back against the seat once more. 'Just drive to the traffic headquarters.'

'Why?' Her voice had turned querulous.

David sneered. 'I have to book you and ground your car until your case can be heard in front of a judge. We are the Kenyan Police – we don't allow for law breakers to get away so easily as that.'

'I haven't done anything wrong.' The anger in her voice was replaced by a resigned helplessness. David snuck Jeffery a knowing look. Easy as that – threaten them with the staggering inefficiency of certain institutions of the country and they would be willing to pay an arm and a leg to get out of it.

'*Shuari yako.*' David had inspected the dirt beneath his fingernails. 'It's your problem now. Continue driving, please.'

Her eyes darted from the road to the rearview mirror, where she looked at the two officers in disbelief. 'You're stopping me for some rule you just made up so you can get some money!'

'Also another reason,' David's lips had twitched. 'Visual pollution. This car is dirty! *Aieesh!*'

'What kind of people are you?' The woman was muttering to herself. 'Supposed to stop thieves but instead you are too busy stealing yourselves.'

'Madam, please watch your tone.' David was beginning to enjoy himself. 'Or will I have to put you in jail for harassing a police officer?'

'But I've done nothing!'

'*Nipe* five thousand.' David was suddenly impatient with this silly game they were playing. 'Five thousand and I will allow you to pass, *sawa*?'

'You must be joking.' Her indignation was unconvincing. 'I don't have that kind of money.' She was planning on what to do next – Jeffery saw it in the quick scurrying of her eyes back and forth from her purse – she was wondering how low she could take him.

'*Ninasikia njaa*,' David had told her, then addressing Jeffery, 'Aren't you hungry also?'

His mouth remained a vacuum for words, his lips stiff. With a yelping sigh, the woman pulled into the next petrol station she saw. As she dug through her wallet, David nudged his friend.

'I only have one thousand.'

David took it. 'Come on, *Mama*. I know you have some little bit more.' Despite the wink, the mischievous smile, she knew he was serious.

'Here's five hundred more. But really, that's all I have.'

It was blind robbery, done in the manner of a simple transaction – she was a willing participant so Jeffery could not feel sorry for her. He knew that if she had agreed to follow the law, to take them to the traffic headquarters, David would have told her to drop them off. He refused to waste his time with paperwork when he could be out on the road making money. It was people like her, Jeffery concluded with a bone-deep resentment, who kept corruption going.

She pushed the remaining shillings into David's hand. 'Get out now. I'm late for a meeting.'

'*Asante*, madam.' David thanked her, pushing Jeffery out of the door. Once both policemen were back on the road, David tapped on the window and said cheerfully, 'Have a good day.'

She was gone in a squeal of tires and David let out a low sigh. 'Too bad she wasn't a *muhindi* or a *mzungu*, that's where the money is to be made. Though sometimes the Americans cause too much trouble. They become offended very quickly.' He stretched out the five hundred shilling note, its metallic stink rising up to their nostrils. 'Remember that – always a woman because they're more scared and it's the *muhindis* who keep lots of cash in their pockets.'

'What about my share?' Jeffery had asked.

David had folded up the money into the breast pocket of his uniform. 'For what? Sitting there like a *mjinga*? *Sikia*, I did that to teach you a lesson. Eat or be eaten – this is no place for your conscience.'

He told the boy the same thing that day, having climbed out of the car pocketing two thousand shillings. *Prices are going up, have to adjust*, not wanting to admit that he had become extremely adept at recognizing how much people were willing or able to spend and extracting just a little more from them. 'If you want a job that values honesty and integrity then go somewhere else,' he said, a threat-covered warning. *It's not too late*, is what he really wanted to say.

This is no place for young Kenyans. How many new officers had he seen joining the force, suddenly infected with the extortion and bribery vice? He was a prime example. It was too late for him, but if he could help others Jeffery took it as an opportunity to balance out his multiple sins, hoping that in some way it might restore his old faith, his naivety. Yes, the money had raised him from the muddy, shit-stained slums of his childhood, away from depravity and death, but had filled him with something infinitely worse.

A year in as a junior constable, Jeffery's senior officer had called him into his office.

'Omondi, Omondi,' his voice loud and gruff, petering into a *tsk-tsk* note of dissatisfaction. 'You wanted to speak with me.'

Standing at attention – with everything at stake, Jeffery moved and spoke with the greatest detail. 'Yes, sir.'

The man leaned back in his chair, which groaned as a complaint of his weight. 'You are asking for a raise?'

That morning, Jeffery had left his mother on a pile of maize leaves beside her bed. She was heaving, unable to move and slicked in her own sweat, urine and feces. He had taken off all her clothes and covered her with a thin blanket, leaving a plastic bag beside her in case she found the strength to use it. She whimpered after him as he left, 'Help me, Constable. Help me, my son.'

Seventeen thousand shillings a month was enough to buy him drinks at Mama Lucy's and the occasional sandwich from Uchumi but it wasn't enough to save a life. Not enough to save the only life he cared about.

On the *matatu*, Jeffery had scrawled down his request, listing his credentials and merits, which he was sure entitled him to better pay. Clean to the bone – no bribes or misdemeanors, bringing in violators of traffic including drivers of public vehicles that were all well below the safety requirements for transporting Kenyan citizens. It hadn't been easy, considering how inclined they were to pay him off.

'I've been working here for almost a year. In that time, I've made the roads better and safer for Kenyans,' he said, trying not to beg but finding his body arching over the desk, hands clasped desperately.

A loud laugh ensued, papers scuffling as the senior officer rubbed his belly in amusement. 'I will give you a raise,' he conceded, and Jeffery bolted upright. *He knew it.* Wait until he told the other officers, thieves all of them, who laughed in the face of his steadfast values. *Goodness always wins. Patriots are richly rewarded.* 'I will give you a raise but only if you bring in six *vayhacles*.'

'Yes, sir.'

'Allow me to finish. Six *vayhacles* at five thousand shillings per car.'

Jeffery's confidence waned, terror and grief climbing up into his chest. 'You want me to bribe someone?'

The officer expertly avoided the question. 'Six *vayhacles* for five thousand each makes it thirty thousand. Try for ten thousand for one and I will give you ten percent.'

'But we're supposed to be fighting—'

'Listen here carefully, *kijana*. I am not in the business of self-lessly helping you. You give me something, I give in return. *Sawa*?'

Jeffery protested weakly, 'You remember the motto, *Utamishi…*'

'Values cannot give you food. They cannot buy you a house or look after your wife and children.' The officer heaved as if in pain. 'Or in your case, your mother.'

'How did you know?'

'They talk.' The large man waved his hand in the direction of his door. 'Everybody here talks except for you.'

As the officer ushered him out, Jeffery tried one last time. 'I need the money today. If you loan it to me, I will bring you six cars, even seven! I won't take anything. You can keep it all.'

'Do you think I am a bank?' barked the man. 'Go find someone else to help you – six cars in one day is easy.' He waved Jeffery away, no room for discussion. 'You heard me, *sindiyo*? Six and no less.'

Jeffery got up from the chair and moved toward the door, confused and hurt because all of his hard work had amounted to nothing. He left the senior officer's desk angry, determined and goaded on by the only option he had and went straight to the man he knew could help him – David.

Already on his way out for the afternoon's work, the man hopped down the stairs of the station, smiling. 'Don't worry, brother,' he had said, with menace in his voice. 'I know the place exactly.'

15

One afternoon, the rain was so relentless it forced everyone indoors and the drain that ran along the side of the street overflowed. Leena left her brother and Michael sitting at the small table in the muggy shadows of the kitchen, where the heat of the downpour collected like steam and caused her T-shirt to stick to her skin. She dashed the short distance to Tag's house, the rainwater rippling out onto the tarmac like a shallow river and wetting her socks.

'My mother won't like it if you dirty our carpet,' he told her, standing guard at his door.

So she flipped her hair over one shoulder and squeezed the water from it, roping it around her palm. Before she stepped in, while removing her shoes and socks, she squinted back at her house. She heard her brother laugh and the sound pricked her chest. She had said goodbye when leaving but he was so engrossed in his conversation he had barely glanced back at her. But Michael had paused, flicked his eyes above Jai's head and she had tried not to scowl while he struggled to keep his grin hidden.

'Do you have extra socks?' she asked Tag.

After he came down with a pair of old superhero socks, he led her into the living room, where she was immediately overcome by the smell of sandalwood and rose, scratching her throat and disturbing her vision. Her feet slipped on the polished, laminate floor and she slid-skidded over to the sofa, as far away as possible from the incense sticks. She focused on the framed picture of his deceased grandmother, the garland of marigolds strung over her photo in accordance with the Hindu funeral tradition. The standing lamp at the side of the room cast a low light into the endless layers of flame-colored petals, making them appear as if platelets of gold – the expensive steps to a next life.

'I have an idea that I'm sure will work.' Tag snapped his fingers. 'Earth to Leena. You're going to be very important in all of this.'

Leena dragged her eyes away from the fiery frame and attempted to pay attention. She was beginning to regret having approached Tag last week, storming out of the house after finding that Jai and Michael had gone to the fruit market without telling her. It was her favorite place – Jai knew that – and he'd never failed to ask her to go.

'I hate him,' she had told Tag when he discovered her kicking stones at the wall. She had picked one up and threw it with such force that it cracked into gray shrapnel. 'I just want him to go away.'

It wasn't a secret that Tag disliked Michael. The boy wasn't one of them. 'Have you seen his shorts?' he had asked Leena, coming to stand beside her. 'Full of holes. His sandals too.'

At this image Leena had felt a little sorry for Michael, though she had told Tag she had never noticed. It was something about the way Michael carried himself, so assuredly, as if none of what the other children were interested in mattered. It had the effect of making her feel slightly silly, more infuriated with him than she already was.

'Jai says you shouldn't hate people just because they don't have as much money as you.'

It was true, you couldn't blame someone for being poor, but that didn't mean you had to be kind to them out of pity either. Tag was tired of being humiliated, beaten in soccer, thrashed in cricket and marbles – his blood had fumed the last time they played. Not even Jai had managed to outsmart Michael at games.

Now, on his couch, he finished telling Leena his plan and she played nervously with the print on the socks he had given her. It came away in her hands – blue and red flakes – broken pieces of Superman. 'Maybe there's another way?' she suggested. 'I can talk to Jai and tell him how upset we are.'

Tag shook his head firmly. 'This is perfect. Perfectly believable.'

That was what made her so uneasy: the certainty that it would work. 'It seems a little mean.'

'I'll find someone else to help if you don't want to.'

Outside, the rain had slowed to a light drizzle. The sun pushed through the clouds, fire-lighting their edges. Leena watched Jai emerge from the house with Michael. They were laughing about something, struggling with each other – pulling at T-shirts and shoving shoulders. One of them dropped a soccer ball and it was bounced back and forth as they trotted to the center of the street to begin a game. She willed Jai to look up, to give her that familiar smile and wave, gesture for her to join them. When he didn't, she turned back to Tag, sighing in relent. 'Just tell me what I have to do.'

A few days afterward, Michael caught up with her on the street.

'You're doing it wrong, you know.' He had come up behind her as she was practicing a hands-free technique on her bicycle. She ignored him, spreading her arms out as the bike quivered so violently beneath her that even reaching out to grab the handlebars didn't stop it from spilling her onto the sidewalk.

It was early and the street was deserted. Only the hushed voices of women whispering goodbye to their husbands and the high-pitched calls of morning birds interrupted her activity. Although it was not yet eight o'clock her parents had already left the house. Jai was still asleep so she had slipped out into the cold daylight, bumping her bike down the front stairs.

From her position on the ground, she glared up at Michael and thought she detected his mouth twitching. He always seemed to be laughing at her.

'What do you know about it?' she snapped. 'I've never seen you ride a bike.'

Unperturbed by her rudeness, he held out his hand. 'Let me help you up.'

Though moody and unpredictable, permanently glowering at him, Leena intrigued Michael. He felt sorry for her, the way she constantly followed her brother around, eager to be allowed into their games, their conversations, and felt guilty for having come between them.

'I don't think your sister likes me very much,' he had told Jai once, watching as she stormed into the house after he had beaten her at a game of marbles.

Jai had brushed it off. 'She's just competitive – she'll get over it.'

But Michael noticed the way she whispered with the other children, the narrowed eyes and stiff shoulders he received whenever he tried to talk to her. That morning, as he pulled her up easily from the ground, he asked, 'Are you okay?'

His hand was dry and pleasantly coarse and her voice softened, despite her irritation. 'Yes, thanks.'

'What are you doing?'

'I'm practicing riding without hands.' As she answered, her eyes went carefully from window to window, saw that most curtains were still drawn.

'I can help you if you want,' he offered, seizing this opportunity to win her over. 'It's all about physics.' Spotting her confusion, he pointed at the bike he had lifted from the ground. 'Do you mind?'

She hesitated a slight second, which stopped his breath, causing his cheeks to burn with hope. She shook her head. 'Go ahead.'

He settled on the bike while adjusting the height of the seat. 'You're quite short.'

He bit down guiltily on his words, but it was difficult not to tease her.

'I'm only twelve and I'm a girl,' she defended herself.

With a tug of the metal chain, he began to pedal. 'Walk with me.'

Michael's grandmother had once traded her best chicken for a rundown silver and red BMX. He had come back from school to see it leaning against the fever tree that grew close to the shamba – a bright and beautiful image – and he had asked her, breathless, what it was for.

'It's a tool,' she had barked, forcing him upon it. 'You are going to learn how to be just like them, understood? Even silly things like riding this machine.'

He had left it in Eldoret with a heavy heart, lending it to a boy down the street, who promised safe-keeping, although Michael knew he would never see it again.

'Everyone thinks they have to start off slow,' he told Leena, picking up speed. 'But the truth is, it's much easier when you're moving faster and have more momentum.'

She was forced to break into a jog to keep up. He straightened his back, lifted his hands smoothly from the handlebars, stretching them out until his fingertips grazed her shoulder. The bike never veered and eventually he brought it to a slow halt.

'Why don't you try it now?' He readjusted the seat, knowing exactly what height to slide it back into.

She did as she had watched him do and he walked with her – his strides matching her pace exactly as he instructed her. 'Put more weight on the back of your seat. Good, now take your hands off but leave two fingers on each bar.' He started to jog, pushing her into a faster speed. As she moved past him, she heard him call out, 'Now take them off.'

Stretching out her arms, she pulled up her back and let the wind fuss her hair. She was distracted by it, the low, sweet whistle in her ears and the tarmac speeding by, and almost didn't hear him shout, 'Stop!'

It was too late. By the time she had reached the bend, her bike had already tipped over the curb and sent her somersaulting onto the grass.

Michael sprinted after her, falling to his knees when he reached the bike. 'Are you okay?' His voice was urgent, eyebrows furrowed with worry. 'Leena, answer me.'

To hear him say her name was jarring. Up until then, they had been strangers, hardly speaking a word to each other. He was the boy she despised without knowing why, the one she scowled at suspiciously at every chance she got. He was also the boy who had taught her a new trick and made it seem easy. Who laughed and teased her as if it were the most natural thing to do, and when he said her name it was in a way that made it sound not like how it was but as it should be.

'Answer me,' he was saying.

She took his offering fingers once more, grinning hugely and throwing her leg back over the bike. 'Let's do it again.'

He relaxed under her untroubled manner, pleased with the way she was looking at him. But before they could begin again, Angela was calling out for him.

'I have to go.' He waited for a moment, giving her the chance to say something and she almost asked him to stay. But then her feet were pedaling once more, the racing power back in her thighs. He kicked away a stone, his gaze trailing her until she turned the corner. Then he spun around and headed back toward his mother.

The next morning she was woken early by a stomach knotted with excitement. Her parents were downstairs, filling the house with the opening and closing of kitchen cabinets, the kettle's steamy whistle, their low conversation. When she heard Angela's voice through all the commotion, her anticipation grew until her body couldn't contain it and her knees began to jerk impatiently. Finally, both the front and back door sounded, followed by the revving of the Nissan. She threw off her blanket and leaped out of bed. She was half-way across the room when Jai woke up.

'Where are you going?' he murmured sleepily.

'To the washroom.'

The fib came swiftly, confusing her because she had never been deliberately untruthful with her brother. She waited, frozen mid-step until the muscle in her calf began to pulse and protest, but she refused to move until she was sure he had fallen back asleep. Yanking the bicycle from the cupboard where it was stored, she sped down the stairs and into the thin morning light.

But the street was empty.

He wasn't there.

As the realization hit her, she was overcome by a feeling of foolishness. Hearing Angela's voice downstairs, there had been no doubt in her mind that Michael would be waiting for her, as eager as she was, but there was no sign of him, no sound or activity – just a lonely, wide circle of houses.

She climbed onto her bike and began a slow ride around the compound.

She thought of all the things she would say to him. *Traitor. Deceiver. Liar.* He had never outwardly promised her anything and yet she felt betrayed by him. Perhaps she wouldn't say anything at all. She set her mouth and nodded to herself. Yes, she would never speak to him again.

'Good morning.'

The voice pulled her bike to a bumpy halt.

'What are you doing here?' She kept her back turned to him, trying to swallow down her relief.

'I thought you might want to practice some more.'

She wrung her fingers around the handlebars, flicked the pedals and let them *whirr* manically as he came around to stand in front of her. 'You're late,' she pouted, and when she lifted her eyes, saw that he was regarding her seriously.

'I know. I'm sorry.'

At his apology, her anger faltered. 'Come on,' she said, pushing past him, a smile on her face.

For the rest of the week, he waited for her as she slipped out onto the quiet street with her bike. And when she saw him leaning against the veranda gate, kicking a small football between his feet, she admitted to herself that she was glad to see him. She tried not to acknowledge the rush of pleasure when he looked up and seemed equally happy, waiting patiently as she cycled toward him.

He would walk beside her, run as she went faster, eventually having to stop and catch his breath, no longer able to keep up as her delighted shrieks rid the morning of its peacefulness.

But then the sun would rise up from behind the misty cover of clouds and, slowly, the other children would emerge from their houses and the two of them would lose each other. But every morning as he watched her riding toward him, Michael would quickly forget that he had been forced to watch her leave the previous day – how she had disappeared into her own circle of friends as he had turned back to the pile of dirty dishes and vegetables ready to be peeled and boiled, his heart tightening at the reminder of why he was really there.

16

Following the unjust refusal of his request for a raise, Constable Jeffery Omondi discovered a dance called Bribery. It involved several intricate steps, a willing participant, a lead and a mutual whirling, spinning and climax, which left both partners with a satisfied outcome of relief.

David stayed with him for the first day on the promise that he would receive some part of whatever exchange happened. They stationed themselves at the very same roundabout and instantly Jeffery felt his temperature rise, a hotness spreading through his body. His mother would have been disappointed to discover what he was doing, and under normal circumstances he would have been ashamed, but death had a way of putting things into perspective. Still, his arm remained paralyzed by his side; every time he tried to lift it to stop a car, it stayed stubbornly immobile.

'If you don't stop one soon, I'll stop it for you,' David snapped, growing impatient.

The next car was a trundling old Subaru, wheezing its way toward them, and Jeffery stepped out onto the road and raised a palm, having to chase the vehicle for several steps before it came to a jerking halt. He rapped on the passenger window and motioned for the driver to open the back door. As they climbed in, David rolled his eyes.

'What's the matter?' Jeffery asked.

'Wait and see. We are here for you to learn, what else?'

The driver was a Kikuyu man who seemed too young for his face. Graying hair and teeth, which though intact were stained and chipped, making him appear toothless. His clothes seemed to swallow him up and each time he moved it was with a tremble and a shake. The car had the pervasive stink of cheap alcohol and the driver constantly smacked his lips together, fiddling for a sweet in his pocket with a quivering wrist.

It was easy for Jeffery to recognize the side effects of prolonged addiction to *chang'aa*. A popular alcohol amongst his friends, the memories of Jeffery's father had kept him from succumbing to its lures. It cost only ten shillings per glass and was very potent, distilled from millet, maize and sorghum. The place his father used to frequent tended to add other substances such as jet-fuel, embalming fluid or battery acid to give the drink an extra kick, and although many who enjoyed it suffered from blindness or death, the only horrific consequence of his father's habit had been his temper.

'Have you been drinking?' Jeffery demanded in the car.

'No.'

The next step was lost on the police officer. His instincts told him to pull the driver over and take the wheel. But then he remembered his mother who was getting weaker every second and he looked to David for help. The other man was looking out of the window, covering his mouth with his hand. Either he was disgusted by the stench or amused at the situation, Jeffery couldn't tell.

'It's against the law to drink and drive,' Jeffery announced to the car in general. 'Where are you going?'

'To pick up my employer at City Market,' replied the driver. He, like David, seemed bored.

Jeffery tried once more. 'We are going to take this car to the station and put you in a jail cell. You'll have to get your employer to pay the fine. Ten thousand shillings for drunk driving.'

The driver stayed silent and turned on the ignition. He knew how to play this game, while Jeffery was still stumbling, still stammering. 'Give me five hundred bob and I'll let you go.'

'I only have fifty.' The man reached into his pocket and brought out a note that had been folded multiple times into a neat, little square. 'For my lunch and bus fare.'

David heaved. 'Enough of this – what do you think you're going to get from this *mzee*? Look at him, seriously, Jeff, *wewe ni mjinga*.' Jeffery began to climb out but David grabbed him back. 'At least take the money.'

But his fingers were too loose – *what would the man eat? How would he return home?* So David took it for him, clapped the driver on the shoulder and said, 'Thank you for chai. Move on.'

They stood in uncomfortable silence and watched the man rattle away. All Jeffery could think about was the fifty shilling note now nestled against David's chest.

'Rule number one,' David said, 'choose your car wisely. Why waste time with someone who has nothing to give you? Fifty bob can't even buy you a hand-job from the most diseased whore on K-Street, *sawa*?' He was looking at Jeffery as if he were sharing a vital piece of information, too valuable to part with. 'What did I tell you last time? Women. And *muhindi* women if you can. Those ones with the fancy sunglasses and lots of jewelry. They'll give you anything just so you'll leave them alone.'

'Why did you take his money?' Jeffery asked.

'*Pesa ni pesa,* no matter how little. Do you think I'm here just to pass time and become poor like you?'

They waited for the next car and as they did, David said to him, 'Stand up straight. Who will be scared of you when you are like so? Hunched *kama* a hundred-year-old tortoise.'

He squinted past Jeffery. 'Stop this one,' he said, pointing to a navy-blue Range Rover that was speeding in and out of traffic. 'Tell him that he's driving too fast, acting like he owns the road, as if the president is his father and we all have to make way for him.'

This time it was easier to raise his arm to signal the car to stop. 'Open your back door, sir,' Jeffery shouted in order to be heard through the glass. The driver, a Kenyan boy, still in his late-teens, rolled down the passenger window and pushed his sunglasses up onto his forehead.

'What for?' he demanded. 'You think this is a taxi?'

Words formed but were quickly lost, drowned in Jeffery's timidity. 'You're going too fast?' he said, speaking as if it were a question.

'So is everyone else on this road. Stop wasting my time, thinking you can intimidate me into giving you some lunch money.'

Jeffery's mouth opened and closed like a dying fish. He tried to think only of his mother and not of his own humiliation.

'ID,' said David sternly, stepping in and holding out his hand. 'And driver's license.'

The driver exhaled noisily through his nose, indicating his annoyance but compliant nonetheless. He handed David the documents while Jeffery watched his fellow officer. He tried to push up his spine and stick out his gut, but unlike David he was missing the paunch. David spent a couple of minutes looking at the documents before sliding the ID card into the license booklet and closing it.

'All in order?' the driver smirked.

The documents in hand, David moved around the car leisurely, thumbs hooked into his belt loops. As he approached the windshield he stopped, leaned in closer to read the insurance sticker. The driver squirmed. Satisfied, David pocketed the license.

He came back to Jeffery. 'Insurance is expired,' he announced.

'Not until tomorrow.'

'*Sawa*, come have a look for yourself.'

'I have my new one in the glove compartment.'

'And yet you have not put it up.' David held up his hand as the driver reached across to open it. 'Too late, we are going to the police station. Let us in,' he said, tapping at his breast pocket where he had placed the documents. Reluctantly, the driver opened the door and Jeffery followed his friend meekly, his body burning with humiliation.

As they drove, the young boy seemed to slowly shrink so that, eventually, he appeared more and more like an obnoxious teenager who had bitten off more than he could chew. As they approached Kilimani police station, David instructed him to keep going.

'Comfortable?' he said to Jeffery, and then to the boy, 'Your father will be upset to know that his car is going to be impounded.'

'What do you want?'

How could it be their fault – how could they be accused of stealing, bribing, when it was offered so easily as that?

'Since you asked, *nipe* ten K.'

'I only have two hundred bob.'

A roar in David's throat followed by an expressive glance at the lavish watch, the gold-link bracelet. '*Kijana wacha maneno.* Five thousand and we'll let you go and see your girlfriend. Otherwise, you go to court to face charges – perhaps tomorrow, or the day after. Perhaps after several weeks, who knows?'

The boy swerved onto the side of the road, jerking to a halt. He dug his wallet from his trouser pocket. Jeffery watched as he counted out five thousand shillings, less than half of the wad he had in the case. There it was – the solution sat right in front of him in that fold-up wallet. His mother's life tangled up in that immature boy's hands and how easily he parted with it, as if it meant nothing – as if it were only a few pieces of old paper to get rid of an inconvenience. Jeffery was close to snatching the entire pouch but David moved before him, replaced the driver's documents with the money.

'Get out, get out, why are you staring?' David growled at Jeffery, who was finding it impossible to move.

Once the car had gone, David patted his pocket and looked happy. 'Turning out to be a good day,' he burped with pleasure. Then glared at Jeffery. 'See how easy it can be?'

Back to preying on cars, pockets still empty. The sun had traveled to the middle of the sky, a spotlight burning directly downward. Soon it would set and everything would be obscured.

'Ready for lesson number two?'

Jeffery remained silent. David had refused to give any of the money from the boy to him. 'Why should I?' he had asked when Jeffery had requested his share. 'You did nothing to help. In fact, you only made it harder.'

'I'm ready,' Jeffery muttered.

'Who will listen to you when you speak that way? Quiet and high, like a woman?'

'I'm ready.' The shout scratched his throat. Today, he wouldn't go home empty-handed.

'You must be on the lookout for any and all opportunities. A driver talking on the phone, a vehicle with tinted windows, speeding – when you stop the driver, always ask for the license first. You see how I did it? I kept everything in my pocket and if he wanted it back, he had to let me into his vehicle, *sawa*? Much easier to talk when you're inside the car.'

'What if he refuses to listen to me?'

'You go around the car and you look. You check the insurance, you *gonga-gonga* the tires and tell him that they're worn out. If all else fails, tell him that it looks like he has a lot of money and that the Kenyan police salary is very, very bad.' Using his tongue to pry out a two-day-old piece of chicken, David chewed down on it thoughtfully. 'That one works very well.'

Another car was coming toward them – a sleek, forest-green convertible – behind the wheel an impressively groomed Indian woman adorned in jewelry, shiny pinpoints of light at her ears and fingers.

'See that one?' David pointed.

'Yes.'

'I told you, you are the one leading, *sindiyo*?'

'Yes.'

'Now this lady here.' David flicked up his eyebrows. 'Let's watch her shake, shake. These *muhindis* really know how to dance.'

17

Tag put his plan into motion following a soccer game. Leena was lying in the shade of a tree, broken rays of sunlight playing behind her eyelids. The muscles in her thighs and shoulders were just beginning to ease and her soles burned – the effort she had used in running gathered at their centers, causing her toes to twitch and spasm pleasantly. Kicking off her sneakers, she used them as a pillow. Jai and Michael were discussing the validity of the last goal in the game – low, serious tones that lent a soothing background to her tired musings.

When the commotion began in one of the houses, an occasional bursting shout followed by a door slamming, she was too drained to think anything of it. It was only when Michael and Jai fell quiet and the voices came closer that she raised herself up and forced her eyes to focus.

'Hey, *kharia*!' Tag marched toward them, followed by a group of boys. 'I want my money back.' He was such a skillful actor that for a moment, in her distraction, even Leena believed him.

'What money?' Despite the unpleasant shock that Tag's fury had thrown upon them, Michael's voice remained calm and steady.

'I had two hundred shillings in my pocket this morning and now it's gone.'

'Have you checked the grass? Maybe it fell out while you were playing.'

'I don't have to look. I know you took it.'

'And how do you know that?' Jai stood up. He was taller than Tag, bigger too, and he clenched his hands into fists, advancing on the boy.

'Who else would have taken it?' Tag gestured to the boys surrounding him.

'I could have. Why aren't you accusing me?'

A shadow of irritation crossed Tag's face. 'Because nothing has ever been stolen until he got here!' he said, pointing at Michael and then turning to Leena. 'You saw him do it, didn't you?'

She had told him not to include her. She had promised to remain silent – not tell anyone what he was planning – but that she didn't want a direct part in it. Now, everyone was watching her expectantly, their faces telling her that her answer was far more important than a simple yes or no. It would be a declaration: an act of drawing her line in the hardening mud and choosing a side.

'I don't want to get in the middle of anything,' she mumbled, satisfied with the half-way point she had established.

Tag's voice rose. 'Either you saw him or you didn't.'

Michael came to stand in front of her. He talked slowly, trying to arrange his thoughts. 'I'm sorry you lost your money but I didn't take it.' Being accused in this manner filled Michael with a new kind of resentment – one that was aggressive and all-encompassing, reminiscent of his grandmother's own bitterness.

Tag sneered. 'You must feel really bad when you come here, seeing us live the way we do and then having to go back to your mud hut or slum, where you have no electricity and obviously no water, because you stink like proper shit.' The words hit Michael like a physical assault – squeezing his throat shut. 'So I understand that you saw some money and took it to buy yourself a soda or something but it's mine and I want it back.'

And while the group of boys whom he had just played alongside turned against him one by one, sniggering at his expense, all Michael could do was sniff the air around him and glance quickly at Leena, hoping she didn't feel the same way.

'Go away, Tag,' Jai warned, grabbing the boy's arm and shoving him backward. 'When you find your money, come back and apologize.'

'He's going to give me back my two hundred shillings or else I'll make sure everyone knows what happened.' The damage done, Tag relented, receding back to his house.

The three of them stood in a semicircle and watched him go. Leena dug her toe into the dirt and twisted her ankle, creating a hollow. Michael was the first to speak. His voice was stiffer than she had ever heard it.

'Are you going to ask me if I took it?'

'I know you didn't,' Jai replied.

'What about you?' Michael turned to Leena.

Her foot refused to stop moving, reaching down to a lost root, she had dug so far in her guilt. Picking sides was not as easy as it used to be and she found herself in an unexpected, messy middle. 'He stole my marble once,' she offered, and when the two of them laughed, she did too, pleased to have made them happy.

That evening, Michael and Angela were apprehended at the Kohlis' doorstep by Tag and his mother. A large woman, she wore a mint-green sari with arabesques in yellow and pearl and a low-cut blouse revealing wrinkled breasts. She moved in quick, conquering strides and glared at them through the ashy darkness.

'You wait here,' she ordered, banging on the door with a closed fist. 'Pooja!' she called up at the window. 'It's me, Harinder. *Mane waat karvi che*.'

'Is something the matter?' Angela stepped hesitantly forward.

'Keep quiet.' Harinder spun quickly, shaking her finger. 'Like you don't know what your son did.' As she continued to *rap-rap* against the door, Angela turned to Michael.

'What is she talking about?' She addressed him in Kikuyu.

'No speaking in your funny language! You think I don't understand you?'

Michael ignored Harinder and replied to his mother. 'I didn't do it.' But she was unable to ask him what he was referring to because Pooja had already pulled open the door. She saw the furious woman at her doorstep and, startled, stepped back slightly.

'What's all the banging for?'

At the ruckus, Jai and Leena slipped past their mother and came to stand outside.

'You two, wait inside,' Pooja instructed, but they ignored her. Her daughter had been acting odd all evening. Secretive, unable to sit still, jumping at the slightest noise. Before Raj had left for his *karoga* he had told his wife that she was overreacting but, at the sight of Harinder, Pooja knew something had happened.

'Your servant's boy has stolen Tag's money,' Harinder announced loudly.

'Don't call her that.' Jai stepped forward and Pooja smacked him lightly over the head. *What have I told you about respecting your elders?*

'Harinder, please speak slowly. I can't understand you,' said Pooja.

'The boy stole three hundred shillings from my son.'

'You said it was two hundred this afternoon,' Leena pointed out. They had not agreed on this, bringing their parents into it. When she had first approached Tag, she had only wanted Jai to stop spending so much time with Michael but she had never wanted to embarrass him this way – especially now, when they were just becoming friends.

'I meant three hundred.' Tag was cowering behind his mother. He hadn't wanted such a big scene either, just for the boy to be sent away, but the afternoon hadn't gone as he had planned and he had been forced to improvise.

'You knew about this?' Pooja asked her daughter.

'Tag accused Michael of stealing his money but it's not true,' Jai spoke up.

Michael wanted to step forward and defend himself. He felt the indignation press heavily against his chest, but his mother's grip pinched his skin tightly. While he stood forward in defiance, her body was stooped and hung back.

'Are you sure?' Pooja asked Harinder, trying to calm the woman. *So inconvenient*, she thought. *Why do these things keep happening to us?*

'Are you calling my son a liar?'

'Of course not.' Pooja sighed. *A real drama queen this one.* 'Perhaps it was just a misunderstanding?'

Tag tried to catch Leena's eye. 'I know it was him. We were playing and I had it and now it's gone.'

'Michael?' Pooja turned to the boy. So composed, looking so much older than he ought to – she had never paid much attention to him before this moment and she couldn't be sure what his blank expression meant. She almost felt guilty for so readily believing Tag, but how could she not? Poverty made you desperate, especially as a child. Especially when you saw what it was possible to have.

'I didn't do it.' He faced the people in front of him with a heavy and tightening heart. His head hurt.

Leena watched him with dismay, saw her brother step forward

and knew what he was about to do so she did it first. Not thinking, just wanting to relieve herself and make right what she had encouraged to go wrong.

'I took it.'

'What?' Tag's mouth fell agape as he stared at her, confused.

'What did you say?' Pooja grasped her daughter by the shoulder and waved her finger in Leena's face. 'Now you listen here, Leena Kohli, this isn't a game.'

Leena pulled away and went to stand beside Michael. How long had she been waiting for an opportunity to send him away? And now that it presented itself so readily, she was determined to make it disappear. To tether herself to him, if need be. She repeated, 'I'm sorry. I took it.'

Tag wrung his hands together, hopping from foot to foot. *Girls. What silly things – can't trust them.* But he wasn't going to admit any wrongdoing on his part. If Leena wanted to take the fall for the *kharia* then he would let her. He spoke hurriedly, tugging on his mother's sari. 'Can we go now?'

There are things a mother knows unequivocally about her children and Pooja was certain she hadn't raised a thief. 'Where is the money now?' she demanded.

'I spent it.'

'On what?'

'Sweets.'

The impressed look on Jai's face clenched her gut with excitement and she almost grinned, basking in the heroic feeling of self-sacrifice. Pooja grabbed her chin and twisted it until they were facing each other, her dark, thick eyebrow cocked. *You don't think I know what that look means?*

'Must have been expensive sweets.' Her mother's voice was a low threat.

'Yes.' Suddenly overcome by an urge to cry, Leena just wanted to be let go.

Pooja dropped her grip, turned back to Harinder, who was now *tsk-tsking* under her breath. This was surely going to be around the block by the next morning. Pooja Kohli had a *chokora* for a daughter.

'I'll return the money, of course,' she told Harinder through gritted teeth.

'It's only three hundred bob,' said Tag's mother, suddenly calm, delighted to be getting more than she had bargained for out of the situation. Wait until Mrs Laljee heard the news! 'I'm not angry with you, *beta*. No need to cry.' Harinder glared once more at Michael and Angela before guiding her son back toward their house.

'Ma,' Jai began, but Pooja put out her hand to stop him.

'Not another word from anyone.' She looked at Angela sternly. 'You can go home now.'

'My boy didn't do anything,' Angela said, in a weak defense that came too late.

Pooja didn't reply, distracted by the growing strain in her gut as she looked from her children to Michael, huddled close together in a loose triangle. She called them in quickly, pushing her daughter more forcefully than she had intended and worrying to herself that these sorts of relationships always brought more problems than they were worth.

Once back home, Angela sat her son down on the shapeless couch and paced the small length of the apartment uneasily. Something had been weighing her down for some time now, ever since Michael had started spending more time with Jai, and she was angry with herself for having ignored it for so long – for not having warned him to be more careful. Perhaps a part of her had been hoping she was wrong, that she had been too influenced by what had happened in the country's past. That maybe, in this day and age, things could be different for her son. She had been disappointed, but not surprised, to learn that they were not.

'What is it?' he asked when she finally came to a standstill.

'You're playing too much with them.'

'You're the one who insists I go with you every day.'

His tone surprised her. When he had come back from Eldoret, he had been soundlessly obedient but now he spoke with certainty and she saw that he was no longer a child. She carried on, 'I make you come with me so that you can help with the workload, not so you can kick around a football and cause trouble!'

'They're my friends,' he argued.

'I know you want to think that.'

'But Jai—'

'Is a nice boy, yes. The Kohlis are a very nice family.' *But.*

He waited for her to go on, feeling like the lost and afraid child he had been when he had come to Nairobi for the first time, close to two months ago. But in some ways he was wiser – braver with his thoughts – infused with the city's boldness.

'You weren't brought up here, Mike,' she reminded him. 'You don't know how things work here, what the rules are.' She ran a tired hand across her neck, rubbing at her chin. 'Why do you think I didn't allow you to speak in front of those women today?'

'Because she called you a servant.' The words clenched in his gut.

Angela shook her head. 'That wasn't right; but it also wasn't the reason.'

'Then what was it?'

'It wasn't our place to speak.'

'She was accusing me of something I didn't do,' he half-rose from the couch, protesting. 'I had to make sure everyone knew the truth. I didn't want you to lose your job.' *I don't want to lose them.*

'Do you know what happens to a drinking zebra when it makes too much noise in front of a hungry crocodile?' Angela asked but her son kept silent, watching her with those young, far-too-deep eyes. 'It gets swallowed up.'

'I don't know what you mean.' But despite his stubbornness, she saw that he did.

'When we're at the Kohlis, our job is to work and say little. Our employers should not know about our lives, our troubles, our families. Because one day that information may be used against us.'

'They wouldn't do that to us.'

She went to sit next to him, softening her voice so that her words wouldn't sound so cruel. 'How did Mrs Kohli react when that boy accused you of stealing? Did she defend you? Get angry for you? No, she was suspicious. Even now, she is suspicious. She trusted them straight away, not you.' He was trying to move apart from her but she tightened her grip on his upper arm. 'No matter how nice they can be, they will always consider us different from them.'

After a brief silence, she said, 'I want to make you aware of all this so that one day, when the time comes and you understand it all, you won't be too heartbroken.'

He rose quickly, his words fast. 'Didn't you see them today? They defended me when you refused to. Leena put herself in trouble so that her mother wouldn't think me a thief. And you! You just stood there and let that woman call you a servant.'

His words rendered her mute; his expression, a familiar one, brought up the memory of a rancorous, old woman in a house on a hill in Eldoret, glaring at her in the dark from across a table as she clung to a three-year-old boy. Angela had been tired and hungry but Madam hadn't even offered her a drink of water. She had simply stood up from her seat, strode over in her gigantic way and taken Michael.

'You don't deserve him,' Madam had told her all those years ago. 'Just like my son deserved better, so does yours. He will stay with me but so long as he does, you cannot come back here.'

'He's my son,' she had protested weakly.

'And those are my conditions.' Hard-hearted as always. 'Get out now. You are nothing but a sad, little weakling.'

Now, Angela looked away from her son and chewed down hard on the inside ridges of her cheek. Michael left the house and went into the courtyard outside. Immediately, he was assaulted by the sulfurous leak from the open doorway of the Indian hair salon. His skin prickled at this new substance – he thought he would suffocate on it – and he slid down against the wall, breathing between his knees.

Somewhere to his right, he could hear the gossiping of the traveling market women, three of them pausing beside him for a rest – dropping their seemingly bottomless wicker baskets against their legs, thick as barks. *Mama Mbogas*, they were called. Vegetable women. Every morning he watched them leave from his window, their baskets balanced delicately on the stoops of their backs, belying their heavy load. Tomatoes, carrots, sugar cane – one of them carried only live chickens, clucking forlornly with their legs bound together and their pink beaks peeking out from beneath an old blanket. These women moved slowly throughout the city, calling out in their gravelly voices. *Mama, shillingi kumi, kilo bili. Good price, help me and I will give you good price.* Their voices sounded like ghosts to him, old and wise – a dense lullaby that sat upon the world and always made him wistful.

'*Kijana, wewe ni mgonjwa?*' One of them paused between talking and laid a hand on his forehead, asking if he was sick.

He shook his head, but gratefully accepted a banana before they picked up their baskets once more and left. He tried not to cry, because with their absence he felt an aching loneliness stretch open inside him and, for the first time, agreed with his grandmother fully and thought his mother a coward.

18

It terrified Jeffery, how quickly a living person could be reduced to an animal. He had come home the first evening to find his mother squatting near their house because severe abdominal cramps had prevented her from going any further. Sweating profusely, making noises like an injured hyena, she relieved herself on their doorstep, leaning weakly against the mud wall as people side-stepped or jumped over her.

It was not uncommon to see people crouching on the roadside in Kibera, pulling up their skirts or with their trousers around their ankles, pissing or shitting wherever the space allowed – upon piles of old garbage or in the open trenches that ran freely next to homes, restaurants and even schools. But his mother had never been one of them. Too proud, she had spent even the little money they had to pay the five shillings to use the toilets that were privately owned by landlords.

'Just because we live in hell doesn't mean we're allowed to act sinfully,' she used to say to him. As a boy, he would take the money she gave him to use the bathroom services and pocket it for sweets or save up for a new pair of shoes and hunker down like all the other children, far away from home or while she slept. To see her do it now overwhelmed him with pity and disgust. He knelt and caught her as she fell forward, pulling down her dress and carrying her into the small house, watching as she curled up on the bed they shared.

He left her there, asking a neighbor to check in on her, and made his way to the closest health clinic, its avocado-colored *mabati* structure a sore thumb in the low-lying, gray landscape of Kibera. When he arrived, it was to an ever-growing queue crowding the restricted lanes between buildings and up the unsteady steps to the main entrance. When he looked around, he saw mostly young mothers with children strapped to their backs, straddled in brightly patterned *shukas*, heard the groans and high-pitched screams of babies too young to understand that they were dying.

Despite the angry protests, people blocking him with their shoulders, Jeffery managed to shove his way through the swelling crowd and into the unlit stone corridor where he searched for a doctor, a nurse, anyone who might be able to tell him what was wrong with his mother. But each time, he was either ignored or told to wait like all the others, huddled over the wet cement floor. So he sat impatiently, cradling a young boy whose mother had fallen asleep against Jeffery's shoulder.

'I've been coming here for four days now,' she told him when she eventually roused. 'Always the same, always waiting, always for nothing. Waiting for his suffering to end – what else?'

In Kibera, there were no government clinics or hospitals, just as there were no government schools or other public services – close to two hundred thousand people left to fend for themselves, forgotten by everyone who lived in the nearby city. Most providers of health care were charitable organizations, churches or do-gooding volunteers from abroad, hungry for adventure. And most of these institutions were severely understaffed or provided limited services so that one had to wait for days before receiving care. Often, it came too late.

While he waited, Jeffery considered finding another clinic but he knew that he would only waste time and might be met with an even larger crowd. He debated going to a local kiosk to buy medicine but he had heard about the shopkeepers there being quacks, ready to give you anything for a little money and you only recovered if you were lucky.

After sitting that way for close to five hours, darkness having closed in on him long ago, a nurse came by and told them all to leave. 'The doctor has gone home,' she announced. 'Come back tomorrow.'

He chased after her, begging, 'Please, my mother is sick. If someone could just come and look at her.'

She shrugged him off and repeated, 'The doctor has gone home.'

And so he had returned early the next morning before going to work and then again after, each time finding the same woman with the young boy, who was more of a skeleton than a human being and who had stopped crying and begun to whimper. Then the whimpering gave way to raspy, struggling breaths and finally, those too eventually stopped. His mother held him for a long time after that, pressing her face to his emaciated chest and wailing so profoundly, *no, no, no*, that Jeffery found himself sobbing alongside her. He cried, sticky saliva slipping through his lips and excess fluid running from his nose, but it didn't matter because when he looked around he saw that there was no dignity to be found there.

When he finally calmed down enough to help her wrap the boy carefully in a *shuka* – how wrong those colors seemed now, so mocking and full of life – he asked her what had happened.

'Too much diarrhea and vomiting,' she told him. 'Everything coming out and nothing staying in.' He let her go, recognizing those symptoms in his mother.

'What was it?' Wanting to know, not wanting to know.

'*Kipindupindu.*'

Cholera.

He should have known.

In the past few months, the country had been hit by severe drought, which had led to a shortage of water. The ground had wrinkled like a raisin, reduced to dust beneath his feet. The skies remained stagnant, an unbroken blue, and so hot that the air suffocated you as you breathed it in, a cotton-ball tongue and a throat full of dirt. In Kibera, the landlords who controlled the water points were the same ones who owned the toilets and, adept at recognizing desperation, they hiked up the price of one jerry can of water to thirty shillings. For most people, water became impossible to afford. Jeffery began to steal it from the broken, public mains, crouching down and letting it spray into old plastic bottles that he collected from the roadside. But this water ran alongside alleyways that were polluted with garbage and human waste, and now Jeffery understood what had caused his mother to be so sick.

'How many days?' he asked the woman.

'Less than a week.'

He had left the clinic with another plan in mind: to take his mother to Kenyatta Hospital in Nairobi, where she would receive better and much faster care. It would be expensive, he was told. You need money for transport, for medicine, for a bed. Sometimes there were too many people and so to see a doctor you needed to be able to offer something extra.

'Let it go,' everyone advised him. 'She is dying, why waste your money?'

He ignored them. 'How much? How much will it cost me?'

'More than you can afford,' everyone answered.

This was why he had gone to see his senior officer and why, two days later, he was standing at Westlands roundabout and stopping every car with a vengeance. He had a list of violations in his mind, which he ticked off one by one.

Cracked side mirror.

Almost flat tire. Danger to the road.

Tinted windows.

No seatbelt. Danger to oneself.

Talking on the phone.

So many reasons he could come up with, but it was saying them that proved difficult. Most drivers ignored him, threatened him or, worst of all, gave him no more than fifty shillings and he took it because he was desperate.

Every time that dirt-riddled note was rolled into his palm, the blood-like smell of it hitting his nostrils, a little of his pride was replaced by anger, his values stubbed away by resentment until he forgot to be ashamed and only felt hungry, greedy for some more.

It was close to five o'clock and he counted out less than a thousand shillings in his pocket. He was ready to go home, back to the clinic, back to waiting and praying and doing nothing. And then she came. In a sleek, silver Mercedes, sunglasses so big they grazed the tops of her cheekbones. In this bribery dance, just as he was preparing to quit, Jeffery found his prima ballerina.

Hand held straight out, chest puffed, voice gruffed.

'Stop right there!'

Right in the middle of the traffic, he stepped in front of the car so that she was forced to press down hard on her brakes. The cars behind her shrieked their horns at him, drove around the obstruction, glaring eyes tracking him through closed windows. But he was blind and deaf to them. He saw only her, perfectly polished, like a smoothed down piece of valuable soapstone.

She rolled down her window. 'What is it?' she inquired in a high voice. He detected a slight tremor in her mouth, her worried eyes.

'License.'

'First tell me why you pulled me over.'

Jeffery remained silent, keeping his hand out. Lead the dance and she would have to follow his feet. He repeated himself and she reached into her purse, handing him the red booklet. He slipped it into his shirt pocket, took a slow turn about the car; he glanced at her insurance, poked at her headlights, pounded her bumper with his fist harder than he had intended and saw her grimace in annoyance. Then he gestured at the back seat.

'Open.'

Single words halted any possible arguments and she had no choice but to unlock it for him now that he had her documents. As Jeffery climbed in, the expensive smell of leather submerged him, edged with a pineapple-scented car freshener. The seats were cool despite the heat outside and it excited him because the Mercedes was the most extravagant thing he had ever sat in, ever touched, and he took an appreciative moment to glance around.

High-heeled shoes, forgotten packets of Trident mint-chewing gum and an extra jacket littered the seats around him – everything about their neglect spoke of the value of her life. He saw how easily the world must fall under her hands, was stung by the fact that she had more possessions in her car than he had ever had in his life. He collected that feeling and held it in his voice, used it to push away the shame that threatened to surface at any moment.

'Drive,' he commanded. 'Parklands police station.'

Her thick hair fell across her cheek, olive skin shining with the beginnings of a nervous sweat. Pretty, young *muhindi* girl, just as David had instructed.

'I haven't done anything.'

'Obstruction of traffic!' he barked. 'You cannot just stop in the middle of a roundabout!'

Her mouth opened and closed in disbelieving anger. 'You made me do that!'

He tapped her license to remind her who was in charge. Under normal circumstances, he would have been appalled at himself for playing such a dirty trick, but surrounded by the gross extravagance of her life he was reminded of the hardship of his own and everything was different. 'Come on, let's go. *Twende, twende!*'

'I'm not paying you off, just so you know,' she warned him as she began to move. 'I'll go to the police station, where I will file a complaint against you.'

'*Sawa.*' He feigned indifference, finding that once he lost himself in the pretense threatening her became easier. 'I'll have to keep your car and maybe you in a jail cell until someone can come and pick you up. Maybe they'll be here in twenty minutes, maybe two hours with the traffic. I'm sure you know how dangerous it is in there, especially for someone like you. It's very possible to get HIV.' He pushed himself forward, snickered at her through the rearview mirror and found that his face had taken on a new shape, scowling, loose lines that made him appear aged.

'You can't do this to me. I'm going to call my father.'

'You're welcome to do that once we get to the station.' Sensing her growing unease, he straightened up and spread out his legs to appear larger. He burped and said, 'Please go faster. We're almost there.'

Instead, she slowed down and he knew that his chance had come. Sighing, as if doing her a favor, he said, '*Sawa.* Take out ten thousand shillings and I will let you go.'

She scoffed. 'I don't have that kind of money.'

'Okay, eight thousand.' He saw that she was almost crying, felt bitter and hoped that she would. He wanted to ask her what she could possibly understand about desperation. A part of him wanted to put her in the jail cell, just to teach her a lesson. It was absurd that she should have four half-full bottles of water in the pockets of her back seats – that for those things he considered life, she treated as luxuries she could afford to waste.

'I have four thousand on me and that's it. That's all I'm giving you.'

He tried to stop his hands from shaking as she pulled out the notes from her purse and threw them at him. His breath was ragged, cut short with disbelief, as he shoved them deep into his pocket.

'Just drop me at the station and carry on.' His authority established, he sat back comfortably and enjoyed the short ride. He decided that he wouldn't tell his senior officer about the money – he would use it for his mother today and give the officer back what he made tomorrow.

He instructed the girl to stop at the gate, springing out and smiling – 'Thank you, madam! Have a very good evening' – and slipped one of the water bottles into his back pocket.

When she was gone, he touched the money lightly, felt it flutter as if alive. Altogether he had collected close to five thousand shillings, enough to get his mother to the hospital. Enough to get her the care she needed, at least for now.

He was so lost in his own thoughts that he didn't hear his name being called. A hand stretched out to stop him at the entrance to the station. The senior officer was smoking on the concrete ledge of a small flower garden. 'Jeff,' he called, as if to a friend, rising and flexing the thick muscle in his neck. 'You have something for me.'

Not a question.

Jeffery considered lying but from the raised eyebrow, the way the cigarette drooped warningly from the corner of his mouth, Jeffery knew the officer had seen him climbing out of the car, heard the joy in his voice as he waved the lady away. He wondered if it was too late now to slip most of it into his trouser pocket but the man was already standing before him, hand out waiting.

'Please, sir. I need the money today; it's a matter of life and death.' There were no spaces between his words, just a hurried plea.

'Isn't everything?' The officer's fingers curled in an indication for Jeffery to hand it over. 'Don't worry, don't worry! I will give you your share.' His long fingernails scratched Jeffery's skin as he took the notes, licking his thumb and counting them out.

After he was done, he rolled it into a thick wad, handing Jeffery two hundred shillings. 'See? Did you think I would cheat you?'

'This is only two hundred bob.'

'Are you questioning me?' The voice was no longer friendly.

'But I gave you five thousand!'

'And I asked you for thirty. I'm the one being generous.'

Jeffery turned to leave, anxious to return to his mother. But the officer's heavy hand pulled him back. Something was tugged out of his pocket and his trousers became light. 'Thank you, I'm very thirsty.' The officer opened the bottle. Tossing the cap aside, he took down half the contents in one voracious sip. When the man came back up for air, gasping and sucking on his cigarette, he barked, 'What are you looking at? Go, before I kick you out of here for good.'

There were no streetlights in Kibera to pierce the inky blackness that came with nightfall. He walked as if blindfolded, unable to see two steps ahead of him. There were momentary flickers of yellow from some shacks, illegally obtained electricity, which was dim and buzzed like swarms of insects overhead. Jeffery had none at home because, like everything else here, you had to pay someone else for it – thirty-five shillings a month – and he was saving to take them away from here, to be the first man in generations of his family to move out of the slums and into the city.

He was careful to stay as close to the walls as possible, wanting to avoid the flying toilets. With nightfall came violence and many people chose to stay within the shaky yet safer confines of their houses, relieving themselves in paper bags rather than risk going outside. They then threw these bags out onto the street, as far from their homes as possible. Sometimes, the bags of human waste landed, if you were unfortunate enough, on the roof above your head, bursting open as they hit the sharp corners of galvanized metal and raining down in clumps of sticky wetness. If you were luckier, they would be thrown at your feet and spray only your shoes and the hems of your trousers, which were more easily wiped away.

But despite this, Jeffery had always found night-time in Kibera peaceful. He passed a bar where people were laughing and telling each other stories over a drink, their outlines lit by a gasoline lamp that threw gold beams upon the wooden tables. Further down the road, an old man was grilling goat meat over a small *jiko* and he waved at Jeffery as he passed. A man and woman talking, a TV playing a dubbed-over telenovela and the bleating of goats – sounds of the living, the persevering. Despite it all, losing themselves in the small bits of normalcy they found, whilst clinging to hope. *There is always tomorrow.*

As he approached his home, he heard new noises – people crying, curious onlookers peeling back the curtain he had hung up over their door for privacy, and glancing inside. He began to run, tripped over a bump in the street and had to steady himself by grabbing the low roofs on either side of him. He felt the sharp edge of the metal dig into his skin but was unable to sense the pain as he half-crawled to the door.

'Get out, get out.' He pushed people away with his shoulders and stepped into the dark room, instantly gagging at the smell. It kept him at the entrance, the crushing stench of rot, feces and death. It was so brutally raw, encompassing him as if it were a solid presence – like the Devil himself.

At first he couldn't make out his mother because no light reached in that far, but as he staggered toward the back wall, his eyes adjusting to the shadows, he glimpsed the outline of her still figure. Someone had picked her up from the floor and placed her on the bed, a good Samaritan who had the kind sense to wrap her in a *shuka* before propping her up against the wall of the shamba so that she appeared to be sitting, waiting for him as she usually did. The only thing that gave it away was the way her neck tilted upward, her mouth frozen stiff and her bones marble-cold. He shook her, dragged her forward and slapped her cheeks but as soon as he let her go, she fell back. There wasn't a single thing in her that was moving, that wasn't empty.

A hand on his shoulder. 'She's gone. Be happy for her – she is at peace.'

'I tried, I really tried. Don't, why? Please, don't.' A string of nonsensical words caught on his tongue. 'I'll get the money tomorrow. Please don't leave me.'

How quickly her face, which had always been so young, had sunken. Her body, which had always been so strong, shriveled down to that of a little girl's. He tried to force her eyes closed, not able to bear seeing his reflection in them, to be taunted by a feature belonging to the living, but each time he did, they slowly opened again.

'Jeffery.'

'Leave us alone.'

A warm wetness surrounding him – he climbed into the bed beside her, bringing her close, tucking her head beneath his chin.

Feeling her so close, knowing that soon she would be completely gone from him, he started to cry.

He thought of the woman in the car once again, wondered how it was possible for people to exist here, living on too much – who spent and spent and yet when they reached back into their pockets, found that they were still full, still filling up, while people like him were left to live and die like animals by a government who saw no profit to be made from such a desolate place.

When he next spoke, it was to no one in particular because by that time everyone had left. 'Why have they forgotten us? Is Kibera not also a place? Are we not also human beings, citizens of this country?' He kissed his mother's pointed nose, her once proud forehead. And the next time he pushed her eyes closed, he kept his fingers pressed down against her lids, whispering against her icy cheek, 'We are Kenyans too.'

19

There was an old fruit market opposite their apartment block that sat on a large, abandoned field that was marshy and easily mistaken by most people who drove past it to be a rubbish dump. It was packed full of crude, make-shift stalls created from cardboard boxes and bright, plastic crates. Most of them were covered by thick, polythene roofs designed to protect the goods from the heat and unexpected rains, which came down heavy and without warning. The crates overflowed with colorful rivers, the neon pink flesh of watermelon and the dark yellow of passion fruit, clouds of pure white sugar cane that were impossible not to sink your teeth into, feeling the juice flood into your mouth.

The ground was always muddy and littered with a rainbow of fruit peels, cockroaches and discarded paper bags. Intermingling with the sticky smell of fruit was the charcoal scent of Mary's Kitchen, a family-run establishment that consisted of two plastic tables covered in plaid cloth and four chairs. It was located at the far corner of the market and was always packed with tourists and locals alike, forever with bottles of lukewarm Tusker beer, no matter what time of day it was, scraping up the restaurant's most famous dish of *nyama choma*.

Michael had introduced them to the goat meat, grilled over an open fire. He used his teeth to tug at the crisp, charred edges. He had showed them how to drizzle it with *kachumbari*, a mixture of chili sauce, onions, diced tomatoes and fresh coriander, scooping it up in *ugali*, a type of bread made from maize flour. Pressing it down into soft white baskets, he had placed the meat in the center, rolling it up and pushing it into his eager mouth, then washing everything down with a long swig of coke.

It was nearing the end of their summer vacation, when the days seemed even more precious and difficult to hold onto. They found Michael sitting cross-legged on the floor of the veranda, a stainless steel bowl in his lap, deftly picking apart pea pods and letting the small, hard vegetables roll in his palm before dropping them one by one into the bowl with a soft *ching*.

'Everyone is at the market,' Jai told him.

'I promised my mum I would help her finish this.' Michael's fingers never stopped moving even as he looked up to talk to them. 'You guys can go ahead without me.'

He had been careful to follow Angela's instructions ever since that evening spent arguing on the brown sofa. They had come back to work the next morning to find that Mrs Kohli had locked up most of the drawers and cupboards, leaving open only those that Angela needed to do her work.

'It's just for safety,' she had said, but there had been a quickness to her movements, a suspicious sprint of her eyes, which had made Michael believe that no matter how upset his mother's words made him, they held a heavy truth.

'I hope this doesn't have to do with what Tag said.' Jai sat down beside him.

'We didn't believe him – you know that,' Leena added.

'I know. And thank you for helping me.' He looked up at her and she blushed slightly under the concern of what he said next. 'I hope you didn't get into any trouble because of me.'

'It was fine.' Her voice was higher than usual.

The night it happened, the two of them had received a ranting lecture from their mother after she had demanded to see the sweets they had claimed to buy.

'We finished them,' Leena told her.

'Where are the wrappers or did you eat those as well?'

'I threw them away.'

'And yet I have not found one in any dustbin around the house.' Pooja leaned down to glare at her daughter. 'I hope you aren't taking the blame for what Michael did. Stealing is very serious.'

'Michael didn't do it. He was with us all day.'

'He could have hidden it – these *kharias* are very clever, you know,' she warned them.

'I'm sorry, Ma. It won't happen again.'

'Of course it won't!' her mother had yelled. 'Because you never took it to begin with! Don't let me catch you pulling another stunt like that otherwise I'll never allow you to play with that boy again.'

Now, sitting around Michael as he shelled the peas, Jai gestured to Leena to do the same. She folded her oversized T-shirt in her lap and pushed a handful of green vegetables into its folds. She stared down at the long half-moon shapes. 'What do I do with these?'

Michael dropped his peas into the bowl and came closer to her. As he took one from her lap, she noticed the smooth, wide surface of his hands – the cleanness of his palm. There were no dark, extra lines like the ones that ran through hers; just soft, undisturbed skin and fingers that did everything with meticulous care.

'See this marking here?' He pointed to the division that ran down the entire length of the pod. 'That's the opening. All you have to do is this.' He pressed it softly between his thumb and forefinger and it popped cleanly open.

He showed her the three peas sitting inside – a trio of wrinkled, miniature golf balls. He dropped them into her cupped palm and she closed her fist around them, running their ridges against her skin. 'Easy, isn't it?'

'Yes.'

He went back to his spot closer to her brother; they were racing to see who could clear the most pods the fastest but she stayed as she was, peas in hand. She traced their inflexible, hexagonal pattern and threw two of them into the bowl, allowing the third to linger. It stuck to her skin, refused to let go and she slipped it into her pocket.

'What are you doing?'

The sound of Angela's voice caused her to jump, her cheeks burning with embarrassment. 'I was just—'

But Angela wasn't listening. 'Stand up!'

'We were just helping Mike finish so that we could all go to the market,' Jai told her.

Angela grabbed the bowl from the center of the circle. 'Do you know what your mother would say if she saw you sitting here?' She spoke to them in rapid Swahili.

'We don't mind helping out.'

Angela paused to observe the three children looking up at her. Her son hadn't spoken to her properly since that day, always mumbling or averting his eyes but listening to her nonetheless and spending most of his time helping her with the work. She had caught him, in the past few days, washing the dishes with his eyes on Leena and Jai in the garden, sometimes stopping altogether so that she had to turn off the faucet because the soapy water had started to fill up the sink.

Looking down at the three hopeful faces, Angela was unable to refuse them and reminded herself that it was only one day – no harm could come from it.

'Take Michael with you,' she told Jai. 'I'll finish up here.' She shooed them away, dusting off Leena's T-shirt and calling out to their running backs, 'Jai, don't forget to hold your sister's hand when you're crossing the street!'

After they had gone, she settled down on the concrete floor. Michael was only a young boy and she would allow him this, knowing that it wouldn't last. That eventually, as age wore out their naivety, the three of them would begin to understand the power of their differences, would be unable to resist them. She thought to herself that it was not unlike the story that had been playing in the news recently.

A lioness at Nairobi National Park had adopted a baby antelope after she had killed his mother. For two weeks, she nurtured him, treated him as if he were one of her own. There were pictures on TV, showing her nuzzling it, keeping it warm and hauling it along by the scruff of its neck, as if it were one of her own cubs. But close to three weeks in, the baby had grown into a sleek, chestnut creature, raising itself on prancing legs. The lioness had shivered from her slumber, shaken out her fur and rolled onto her front paws. She saw the lithe animal, now meaty enough to be eaten and, as the unsuspecting youngster danced closer, the lioness yawned open her mouth and wolfed him down for breakfast.

There was a group of boys from the compound already at the market and as they approached the entrance, Tag said, 'I see you brought your pet along with you.'

'Mike beat you five times in a row in cricket and kicked your ass in football last week so show him some respect,' Jai said, stepping forward.

'Show this Kikuyu some respect? Shouldn't he be cleaning your toilet or something?'

The two boys were standing chest to chest, staring at each other for an awful eternity before Tag finally took a step back. He growled at Leena, 'I hope you won't get us into any trouble. Why are you here, anyway? Did your Barbie break?'

'Leave her alone.' It was Michael who said this.

Tag bared his teeth, saying to the boys behind him, 'Come on, let's go.'

It was a game of theirs – who could go through the market and come out with the most stolen fruit. Jai won this every time, and although Leena didn't think it was right, she didn't mind because he always shared it with the street boys lurking outside.

It was the one activity Michael refused to participate in and when she asked him why, he gave her that secretive, all-knowing grin. 'It's much easier to forgive a *muhindi* for stealing than an African.'

The game had started weeks ago and the fruit sellers must have caught on because it wasn't long before a woman let up a cry.

'He's stolen my apples!'

The three of them turned in the direction of the shout and saw one of the boys from the compound struggling to get out of the grip of one of the women sellers.

'We better help him before there's a fight,' Michael said, and took off toward the commotion with Jai.

'Stay here,' her bother called over his shoulder.

But it was too exciting to miss and so she ran after them, stumbling on the uneven, bumpy ground and watching as Jai and Michael attempted to pry the lady's hands away from the boy. From where she was standing, she noticed that some of the men from stalls further down had emerged to see what the noise was about.

She called out, 'Jai, we have to go otherwise we'll be in trouble.'

Her brother bit down hard into the woman's hand, causing her to squeal and release the boy, who dropped a load of tangerines, oranges and mangoes in his rush to get away.

'Hurry up,' Michael said.

They headed toward the exit and Leena followed but their pace was too fast and she tripped and fell, grazing her knee, a deep pounding in her elbow. When she looked up, Jai was already out of sight. Tears stung her eyes when she thought of all the mothers who had stopped to look, who must have recognized her from Flat 15, shaking their heads and tittering. One of them was sure to tell her mother what had happened.

And then there he was. His chest rising in hard breaths, standing above her with his eyebrows creased but still smiling.

'Get on,' he instructed, crouching down half-way.

She climbed onto Michael's back, felt the strange sensation of being too close to a boy who wasn't her brother and her heart raced, although she was too young to fully comprehend why. He began to run easily, never stumbling, away from the shouts, weaving in and out of stalls that passed her in momentary bursts of color. His words rushed in her ears, 'Hold on tight, isn't this fun? Everything is going to be okay,' even though somehow, she already knew it was.

Pooja slammed down the phone, gritting her teeth. *That girl! That boy! Her husband!* Thinking about everyone else except for her. Never considering the embarrassment she had to put up with, the defending she had to do when the ladies at the temple heard these kinds of stories. *Poor Raj, getting cheated by one of them. Aren't you worried about Jai, tossing ball with your maid's son? Oh, your daughter...* Pooja grunted at this last memory, for it was the worst one – *your daughter is a little thief.*

She replayed the conversation she had just had with Harinder on the telephone. How concerned the other woman had pretended to be while informing Pooja, quite delightedly, about Leena's antics.

'I just heard about Leena.'

'What about her?' Pooja had huddled close to the corridor wall, cupping her palm against the receiver so that the words were caught in the basket of her hand, for no one else to hear.

Harinder had tried to sound sorry, but Pooja could detect the joviality rounding her words, making them skip. 'Some of the women were shopping at the market today and they saw Leena stealing apples.'

Pooja had frozen, staring at the phone in disbelief. 'That can't be true.'

'She was with your maid's boy. They were running away together.' A click of a tongue. 'I would be very careful, letting her spend all that time with him – first Tag's money and then this. People are beginning to talk.'

'Thank you for telling me.' Pooja put the phone down. *Her daughter and that boy!* If she was acting this way now, who was going to want to marry her when she was older?

'Isn't she a little young for you to be worrying about that?' Raj looked up from his newspaper as Pooja came shouting into the living room. It was close to five o'clock and the children were upstairs. She could hear Angela in the kitchen, whistling as she cooked dinner. She heard the light pitter-patter of Michael's feet as he helped her.

'People remember such things,' she snapped at him, taking a seat on the opposite couch. 'They'll talk and talk and never forget.'

She saw the way the other women glanced at each other when she was around, nice to her face but whispering behind her back. *Pooja doesn't know how to run her own house, doesn't know how to control her children or her husband.* Soon, she would be the brunt of all their jokes and even worse, so would her daughter.

'Tomorrow, there will be another story occupying their attention.'

'I told you I didn't want him in my house. All this nonsense started when he got here,' she hissed, careful not to be overheard.

'He's just a boy – there's no use blaming him.'

'Doesn't it concern you? Our daughter taking the fall when he was the one who stole Tag's money? Took those apples?' She shook her head. 'She's learning from her father.'

Raj glanced sharply at his wife. 'What do you mean?'

'Always looking out for someone else, no matter what it costs you.' Pooja shook her finger at him. 'I know about the man with diabetes.'

'How?'

'I met Dr Pattni last week. Imagine what a fool I looked like when he told me! A woman with a liar for a husband.'

'I didn't lie to you. I just didn't want you to worry.'

'Of course I would be worried! Giving out our money, just like that. Do you think any of *them* would help you?'

'I thought he was going to die. I had to do something.'

'That's the problem – you didn't. They're all liars,' she whispered to him, her eyes wide. 'Most of them are thieves. They can't help it – it's part of their culture. You know this, yet you haven't taught your children anything! They run around with that boy as if he is their—'

She searched for the word, throwing her arms out. 'As if he is their best friend, but you wait one day. You wait and see what happens.'

'We gave Angela our word.' Her husband's voice was resolute.

'I'll find another maid then. Mrs Laljee says she knows a girl who's looking.'

Raj was firm. 'Angela has been with us for twelve years. We trust her with the house, the children. I'm not asking her to leave just because you're worried about what Mrs Laljee thinks.' He lowered his voice, stealing glances at the door. The activity in the kitchen hadn't slowed or stopped and, satisfied they hadn't been overheard, he tried to pacify his wife. 'School is starting soon so he won't be around as much.'

'I'm going to check on dinner.' She was at the door leading into the corridor, yanking it open. 'You go upstairs and talk to your children. Make sure they know just how angry their mother is.'

Peace and quiet. Raj took his time going up the steep staircase, feeling the old wood strain and stretch beneath his weighty footsteps. On reaching the top of the corridor, he looked down at the cracked linoleum floor, the lime green walls, and heard the high sound of water running in the toilet.

This apartment had been his home for almost fifteen years now; they had rented it six months after they were married. Back then, it had enchanted him. He had been comforted by the way everything was planned to fit neatly together – the dining room running into the living room, leading straight to the kitchen. It had been cozy and warm when he had first entered it but now it appeared old fashioned and tired, sagging under his growing family.

Pooja had been won over by the sense of community it had provided, the close proximity in which they lived to other similar people, because it made her feel safe. But Raj was exhausted by constantly being surrounded by eyes and ears that made it their business to know his, of people who thought it their right to pass judgment on what he chose to do, how he chose to raise his kids.

Artisan Furniture Wholesalers had begun to grow quickly in the past few years and now provided him with enough money to begin dreaming of his own garden, where he would be able to smoke in peace and wander the endless ideas of his mind without some busybody wanting to gossip and disturb him. He wanted high walls and even higher gates, perhaps a dog he could take for long walks in the leafy suburb, tidy streets tucked away from the noise of the city. Unbeknown to his wife, Raj had begun looking at several houses in the newer, wealthier areas of Muthaiga and Runda, had already fallen in love with the repose they promised and was waiting for the right moment to mention it. God knows, the last thing he wanted with that woman was another argument.

He approached the first door on the right and heard his children's voices. 'May I come in?' he called out.

'Yes.'

He pushed open the door to the sight of them sitting side by side on the large desk placed by the window. The table had been split into two; Jai's side was organized and structured, everything in its proper place. But Leena's was bursting with strewn crayons, countless fruit-smelling erasers that he often found in the most unexpected spots – wedged into couch cushions, tucked into a book to mark a page – and several pictures she had drawn were sellotaped to the wall beneath the window frame.

He sat beside them on the old bunk bed. He touched the dark wood, knew where to find the place where the paint had chipped away due to a young boy's carelessness, and when he looked up from this, he was met with his daughter's tawny eyes. She was chewing on her lip, pulling a piece of dry skin between her teeth.

'I'm sorry,' she said before he even spoke.

'Why are you apologizing?' He leaned forward with interest, clasping his hands at his knees.

'Because we stole.'

'No, we didn't,' Jai interrupted, glaring at his sister and then, because his father was watching him sternly, lowered his eyes and mumbled, 'not today, at least.'

'I thought I raised you better than that,' he said to his son.

'It's only a game.' Jai burned under his father's accusation, tired of struggling to reach a higher version of himself, wanting, for once, his father to recognize how young he was.

'Stealing is not a game. Taking from someone while they struggle to survive is not a joke. That's not the kind of person you are, understand?'

'Everyone was doing it.' Leena spoke up in an effort to protect her brother.

'If everyone was jumping off a building, would you join them?'

'That's not the same thing,' Jai protested.

'It's exactly the same thing. Just because everyone else is doing it, doesn't make it right.'

How many friends did he have who had built their businesses off important connections, through bribery, manipulation, sometimes outright stealing? Those who had taken advantage of a weak system that thrived on power and greed, sometimes becoming involved in huge scandals and pocketing public coffers, making themselves sickeningly rich while remaining purposefully blind to those they were stealing from. He could have done it, but how could he claim to be a part of this country, to love it and step upon the backs of its people at the same time?

'Just because we're privileged doesn't mean we should remain oblivious to the hardships of others, do I make myself clear?'

'Yes.' It was barely a whisper from both of them. Jai stopped him as he rose.

'I don't know what Ma told you but Michael had nothing to do with this.'

'I don't want you to protect him if he's done something wrong.'

'He didn't steal anything.'

'He was helping me because I fell,' Leena told her father. 'Because the ground was too bumpy and everyone was running so fast...' Her voice had turned into a whine, close to crying. He patted her cheek roughly.

'I believe you. Why don't you go downstairs and help set the table for dinner?'

She did as he requested, the rapid pace of her tiny footsteps on the creaky steps reverberating through the entire house. After a brief pause, he pulled out Leena's chair and sat beside Jai, putting most of his weight into his thighs so he wouldn't break it. They looked out onto the street together, saw Michael emerge from the veranda with a black garbage bag to throw into the communal bin they shared with five other surrounding apartments.

'You've become good friends with him,' Raj observed.

'Yes.'

'That's good.' He nodded with approval and held his son's shoulder tightly. 'You know, when I was your age, things were very different in this country.'

'I know,' Jai interrupted. 'Things were much harder, the British were here and everyone was killing everyone and Leena and I are lucky to have what we do.' He said it all in one, exasperated breath, having heard this lecture a hundred times before.

Raj fixed his eyes on Michael outside. 'Even though things were ugly, beneath it all we were fighting because we had a love for this country. That's missing now. People have forgotten what we went through, all the struggles that we, Indians and Africans, went through together, to get where we are today. Now we kill each other like cowards. We steal, we cheat, we hate – we were so greedy for a better future that we sucked it dry as soon as it started looking bright.' Raj's eyes fixed onto his son. 'I'm guilty too. I started a business, forgot about everything else that needed working on and now it's too late for me but I want to make sure it isn't for you.' He had picked up a pencil and was drawing idly within the cross-hatched shadings of his daughter's art. 'I know I can be hard on you but it's only because you have a gift which others don't and I don't want you to forget that. I don't want you to waste it.'

He saw the way his son was with Michael – completely oblivious to their differences, to all those things that should have rendered their friendship impossible. They were able to converse, to laugh and be comfortable with each other as if the struggles and anger of a past fraught with accusations and hatred were inconsequential, as if nothing but being young boys mattered. *If the whole country could be this way.*

He watched his son staring out of the window, his usually animated face unmoving. Perhaps he was guilty of trying to redeem his own wasted years through Jai, had found a vessel through which he could put all his unused ideas into practice, but it wasn't a selfish purpose. He was doing it to make the future better for his children.

Finally, Jai spoke. 'It won't happen again.'

They watched Michael disappear back onto the veranda, the metal gate swinging shut behind him from the strong, evening wind. Overcome with emotion, Raj patted his son gruffly on the back and stood. 'Come down for dinner,' he said, heading for the door. 'And tell your mother that you've learned your lesson. God knows, she never listens to me.'

That night, Leena had trouble falling asleep and it had nothing to do with being reprimanded for stealing. Something had started up in her, an invisible army marching through her blood, which kept her tossing and turning, kicking off her blankets in frustration. The day flashed through her mind in small, significant pieces. Silken palms. Three emerald peas sitting close together – one now hidden away in her jewelry case. The reassuring smile warming her and the way he had leaned down to pick her up.

Her cheeks stung at the memory, a bittersweet ache in her chest because she wanted to relive the thrill of that moment, if only once more. *Everything is going to be okay*, he had promised, and she collected up those words, felt as if they were important but was uncertain as to why they were, gathered them up and stored them lovingly in the treasure box of her memories – a shining, perfect diamond amongst so much, now irrelevant, clutter.

20

The stench of roasted meat reminded him of his dead mother. Jeffery sat back on the high bar stool and placed his hand over his mouth, burping down the spreading feeling of nausea. He was perched amongst five other police officers, only here after David had dragged him from the station one evening, insisting that he come along. Jeffery had agreed because it was still too hard to go home to the low-sitting shack, which now seemed overly spacious and empty. The hurt seemed to grow stronger every time he climbed into the bed where his mother had suffered her last humiliation, even though he had stripped it bare. He had thrown away the blanket and sheet and slept uncovered, curled and shivering, with only his loneliness for company.

In the old, cheap bar he watched the other policemen eagerly wet their mouths with beer, the light dipping into the brown-glass bottle and making the lager appear gold. They wiped their lips with the ends of their sleeves, grabbing continuously at the *nyama choma* on the shared platter at the center of the table, caught in a feeding frenzy.

Klub House was a restaurant that had been built to look like a gigantic, sprawling tree house. It was split into three sections: a restaurant, a nightclub and a sports bar. There was also a motel that was semi-detached from it, consistently booked out by the end of every night as swinging-hipped women led eager tourists, exhausted husbands or lonely men, such as himself, into one of the damp-smelling rooms for two or three hours of numbing escape.

Although they might have been more comfortable in the restaurant, Jeffery's colleagues had chosen to settle on a high table in the nightclub, perched like fat vultures under disco lights that shone their aggressive colors into his eyes. They came and went in short, flashing bursts and had the effect of isolating every object from its surroundings – so that the bar appeared to hover slightly above the ground, the waiter's head severed from his shoulders, the short-skirted prostitutes on the dance floor one moment and back at the table, sipping cheap wine, the next.

'What's the matter? Eat, drink and we'll get you a woman later.' David pushed a beer toward Jeffery and he accepted it weakly, twirling it between his thoughtful fingers.

With great difficulty, he dragged his eyes away from the women to hear the conversation back at the table. '*Matatu saccos*, I'm telling you,' one officer was boasting. 'It's the way to go. Every month, upfront cash. In July, I put fifty *thou* in my bank account.'

Fifty thousand shillings. A figure so enormous that even when Jeffery tried to imagine what he could do with it, his mind remained stupidly empty. He put the beer to his mouth and gulped the foamy liquid, filling his chest to the brink of explosion.

'What's a *sacco*?' David asked, scooting forward in his chair.

'*Matatus* have begun organizing themselves into companies per district – just clever businessmen looking for more ways to make money and I thought, why not capitalize? Went to see this *jama* and told him that if he wanted his *matatus* to operate peacefully then he better hand over fifty a month. So he collected from his guys and now,' dusting his hands with a proud smile, 'we're all happy.'

'Are there more of them?'

'All over,' the officer confirmed. 'So I don't mind sharing.' He grinned and looked over at Jeffery, who was now on his second beer and had begun to feel dull-headed. Share for a price – one day, the man would return to collect the debt David would owe him for this information. Nothing was free in Nairobi, not even generosity.

'When you say they can operate peacefully, what do you mean?' Jeffery asked.

'You know how these guys are – they like to break the rules *kidogo*. Pack in passengers until there's no space for even air. I think they would tie them to the roof and tires if they could.' The officer chuckled. 'Sometimes the insurance is missing, sometimes they speed or fail monthly inspections – all these things, I help make go away.'

'And when they crash?' Jeffery asked, the beer and neon lights making his speech hostile. 'What then? What do you give back to the families who have lost someone because of your greed? Or do you drown yourself in money to help you forget?'

The officer laughed, too pleased to be offended. '*Bwana*, what country do you think you are living in? If we don't help ourselves, who will?'

'It's not right,' Jeffery argued, moving onto his third beer for the night. But he was uneasy, because for the first time he felt a sneaky temptation, remembering how easy it had been to collect five thousand shillings from that *muhindi* driver – so quickly she had given it up that it had caused any guilt he might have had to dissipate and left in its place a feverish desperation to feel those crisp notes beneath his fingers once again.

As the officer turned away, his attention caught someplace else, David said to Jeffery, 'When are you going to stop holding onto your values and realize that they are the one thing causing you to sink?'

Jeffery remained silent, letting his eyes wander the nearly empty bar. It was only seven thirty and in a few hours it would be close to impossible to make it even two steps ahead without bumping into another person. His gaze stopped at a shapely silhouette, leaning suggestively against the wall, her elbow resting in the bowl-shaped dip of her waist.

She was cradling a glass of wine between her sharp fingernails, surrounded by an aura of tired elegance, betrayed by the black top cut too low over her breasts, a skirt pulled tight over impressive thighs – the confirmation he needed to let him know exactly what she was. As he stared at her, she straightened and spread her legs slightly, trailing her dark weave over her mouth.

With shallow breath, he turned to his drink and swallowed down most of it in confusion. He instantly regretted the action because the last thing he needed was his morals loosened. Still, his fingers searched for his wallet, flipped it open, counting out the notes. He calculated roughly in his mind the cost of three beers and food, though he hadn't eaten, and came to the dismaying conclusion that he didn't have enough. David was watching him.

'I told you,' he said, and Jeffery saw that he was glad, 'you could have that one and many others better than her if you just climb down from that high mountain you sit on.'

'I don't want her.' His voice was unconvincing. His loneliness was potent; it made him haggard and drawn and even as he lay awake, trying to relieve himself, the enjoyment he drew from his own hand always turned ugly. That was why, after he closed his wallet, his eyes refused to move from the woman at the wall. It was why he could almost taste her salty flesh, smell the cheap sweetness of the perfume she wore and imagine in great detail, the wet insides of her eager mouth.

'I'll lend you some money.' The offer was whispered.

'*Sitaki.*' Jeffery shook his head in stubborn refusal.

'Do you think I'm stupid, Jeff? Come on, there's nothing to be shy about. It's a man's right to sleep beside a beautiful woman.'

'What do you want from me?' He asked it wearily, but was excited at this unexpected prospect, eager to get to her before someone else did.

'I want you to come with me to see this *sacco* leader tomorrow.' David glanced at the police officer who had been telling them about it. 'I don't trust this *jama* and I want someone there to back me up, just in case.'

The woman drained the last of her drink. She looked at him and tipped the glass slightly in his direction. He turned back to David. 'Yes, okay. Give me the money and I'll come with you tomorrow.'

David pressed a wad of notes into Jeffery's hand. When their eyes met, Jeffery was frightened of the smile on the man's face – ever so sinister as he urged, 'Go and have fun.'

The window was stuck closed and the overhead fan refused to work so that the air around him stayed perfectly still and suffocatingly hot. Her tongue trailed the bony expanse of his chest and, in the dim light coming from the bar outside, he saw them, two unlikely figures in the cracked mirror of the dresser. He directed his eyes upward to where flies buzzed, restless in the heat. The *thump-thump* of music was an unrelenting distraction and he tried to push it from his mind and concentrate on the slick feel of her, the sweet heat rising from her belly as she curved down on him, her mouth hovering above his.

He tried not to gag. Her breath felt like steam and smelled of dried alcohol. She removed his belt, slid his trousers down and when her hand went around him, he pulled slightly too hard on her weave so that she scowled. 'You know, it's extra charge after one hour.'

Throwing his head back on the pillow, he allowed her to continue – her touch so delicate in comparison to his hard tugs, the slight scrape of her nails surprisingly erotic. Fingers replaced by mouth and then she was scrambling on top of him, grabbing a hold of the bed frame, reminding Jeffery that she wanted to get this over and done with as quickly as possible. He pressed his hands into her thighs and said, 'Slowly, slowly.'

She ignored him, making ridiculous noises that angered rather than excited him and he extracted himself from the tight grip of her legs. She glanced at him in shock, pushing her hair from her sweaty forehead.

'I said slowly, please.' He twisted her over so that she was pressed beneath him and he bound her with his legs.

She began to struggle, her nails scratching, but it was only when she bit down hard on the fleshiest part of his chin that he remembered where he was and released her.

He rolled over onto his back and lay motionless as she chewed her gum and climbed back on top of him. He lost himself in her rhythm and heat, had to hold onto her knees to keep her from slipping away, and when she stretched out her hips and convulsed slightly, a ripple going up through the center of her breasts and contracting her face, he tried but failed to reach a similar release.

As she dressed, he asked, 'Aren't you supposed to wait until I'm…' searching for the word, 'done?'

With some tissues crumpled in her fist, she wiped between her legs. The action was so crude, it bordered on arousing and he shifted impatiently on the bed.

'If you want me to stay, then it's extra.'

There followed several moments of painful contemplation before he shook his head.

'*Sawa.*' She shrugged, grabbed her purse and left without a backward glance.

He had to finish off the job himself, but this time it wasn't accompanied by its usual heaviness because he held in his memory the weight of her upon him, the feeling of being pressed so close to the hidden parts of her. It had been so comforting that he knew with certainty he would go and meet David tomorrow, that he would agree to whatever partnership the man proposed and then he would come back here and give her whatever she wanted, just to have her tucked into the space of his body where there used to be something.

21

It had been odd, going to bed feeling one way and waking up to a completely different perspective. That was how he had felt it had happened anyway – as if he had been informed by his muddled dreams and hadn't yet had the chance to decipher fully their meaning. Now that school had started he looked forward to the evenings when he would join his mother at the Kohlis' house, but now it was with a new kind of apprehension – a twisted, miserable excitement that often kept him sleepless at night but springing with energy in the morning. He lost control over his eyes, his thoughts and movements, which worked together to seek her out, accompanied by sweaty palms and a host of butterflies warring in his stomach – physical symptoms, which in any other situation would have been unpleasant but which he now enjoyed.

It began one night, after Jai and Leena had gone inside for dinner and he wandered the compound, waiting for his mother to finish. He had been accosted in the small alleyway between two houses by Tag. The boy followed him for several steps before Michael stopped.

'What do you want?'

'You're the intruder here.' Tag was advancing. 'This is where I live. I'll go wherever I want.'

Michael had tried to move past the boy, back into the lit-up street, but heavy fingers were laid on his chest.

'She was in on it, you know,' Tag informed him. 'She came up with the idea because she wanted to get rid of you.'

'Who?'

'Quit playing dumb. You know who. She said you smell funny and dress in ugly, old clothes and that you refuse to leave them alone, even though Jai is only being nice to you because his father told him to be.' Tag was glad that he had caught Leena crying behind the water tank that day. She had been so upset, so ready to spill everything and then begged profusely afterward for him to keep her secrets safe.

Not wanting to hear any more, Michael said, 'Get out of my way.'

Tag pushed himself up off the wall, his large frame blocking the entire path. 'Make me.'

'What do you want?' Michael asked, a little tiredly.

'*She* wants you to stop coming here. Get a hint – you don't belong in this place.'

'Then why did she defend me?' His stomach plummeted in pleasure at this memory.

Silence. They heard Angela calling and he was about to push past Tag when his collar was grabbed and he was shoved up against the grille gate of someone's veranda. The smell of Indian spices and bad breath. Michael turned his head away.

'She was just scared that she was going to get into trouble. It had nothing to do with you.'

'Mike?' His mother stood at the edge of the tunnel-like alleyway, ready to come in. Tag released him and Michael straightened his shirt, starting to smile. He was still grinning when he emerged onto the street and into the graying evening.

He should have been upset. As they made their way home, Michael searched for a sense of betrayal or injustice, thought that he would have been hurt to learn that she had wanted him to leave, but instead found himself walking with a light step beside his mother, unable to stop smiling.

'What was that boy saying to you?' his mother demanded as they carefully navigated the broken, almost non-existent pedestrian pathway, past hordes of other people making their way home. A light drizzle had started and a faint layer of mist built upon his cheeks, caught in his eyelashes, polka-dotting his vision.

'Nothing important. He just doesn't like me, that's all.'

'And that doesn't make you angry?'

He shook his head because he finally understood the reason for Tag's hostility. The boy had threatened him because of her, because he was intimidated by his presence, and the shock of it jolted Michael into his own awareness.

'I don't care about him.'

The world had shrunk into the small, gangly figure of a twelve-year-old girl. Everywhere he looked, he discovered her. Her name housed itself on his tongue, waiting to jump out every time he opened his mouth to speak. It was liberating to be so possessed by another, as if she were living inside his skin.

It didn't matter to him what Leena had thought before, because she had changed her mind. She had protected him, come to the decision that what she had planned was wrong and had wanted him to stay.

Evenings soon became the center of their lives. Those free hours after school they stole to sit together beneath the bougainvillea tree, in the soft chill that carried the scent of wood fires being lit up for the night. Michael watched Leena speak in that charming way, more with her hands than her words. Always gesturing in wide sweeps when she was explaining something, or stabbing the air with frustration – he had come to know all her gestures by now. Sometimes, he even found himself mimicking her.

She was telling him about her school, a private one in the suburbs of Karen, and the way she described it – small classrooms of fifteen children, British expatriate teachers who were strict about manners and cleanliness, the science lab and outdoor swimming pool – burned him up with longing.

'Do you have British teachers also?' she asked.

Embarrassment. It was a new feeling that came with the others – a severe self-consciousness that caused Jackie to yell at him every morning to hurry up: 'I was ready in five minutes and you're still finding your trousers,' pointing at his torn pajamas and raising an eyebrow. He had rushed back up to put on his school pants, her giggles running through his ears, making him laugh until he shook and felt his mind slip away.

Every afternoon before leaving school, he would check his appearance in the bathroom, waiting until all the other students had gone before grabbing the slimy, black bar of soap and running it under his arms, wiping away the foam with a wad of wet toilet paper. He bowed his head under the cool water of the tap before gargling repeatedly.

When he reached the apartments, he worried that it had all been for nothing because the sun was too hot and he had sweated all over again. That was why, despite wanting to always stand close to her, he kept his distance, worried she might catch a whiff of him. So when she asked whether he had British teachers, he wanted to lie but couldn't bring himself to.

'No. They're all Kenyans.'

She stared at him, reflecting on how strange he had become – aloof, without a trace of the easiness that had been there when he had helped with her bike. Gone was the cool, collected boy she had come to know. Nowadays, he couldn't seem to keep still, his eyes forever darting, his feet always stepping away from her – and when she asked him questions, he no longer teased her but regarded her with a seriousness that was out of place in their new friendship.

'I bet they teach you things relevant to our history,' Jai interjected. 'We learn about British prime ministers and American wars, when all I really want to know is how the Mau Mau got our country back.'

He had been this way ever since school had started, disillusioned and frustrated, refusing to back down on his new opinions, even though Pooja often rubbed her temples and groaned, 'Why must we always talk about such things at dinner?'

Finally, concerned about her son's recent interest in Kenya's past, his growing friendship with Michael and the way he shunned all the other boys in the compound and at school, she asked, 'Is there something going on that we should know about?'

'Just because my ideas don't agree with yours doesn't mean there's something wrong.' He looked her boldly in the eye, in his lap a history book she had spotted Michael with, not long before.

'Don't talk to me that way.' Pooja banged her fist down on the table. 'Bringing so much shame onto this family,' she said, pointing at her husband. 'And you aren't doing a thing to stop it.'

'Leave the boy alone.' Raj spoke proudly. 'He's growing up.'

In their room, Leena tried asking him again. 'She's worried about you,' she told her brother. 'And so am I.'

She felt distanced from Jai in a way she never had before; it was as if his readings had created an unshakeable barrier of misunderstanding between them – as if everything she said and did was wrong.

'There's nothing to worry about. I'm fine.'

In truth, Jai's feelings had never been more tangled, more impossible to decipher. He knew that his father was proud of him, could sense it in the way Raj spoke to him, more like an equal – listening to him talk with rapt attention. Sometimes, in the middle of a conversation, Raj would rub Jai's head with his large hand and say, 'You're such a clever boy. You've made us very proud,' gesturing at Pinto's picture, which Jai didn't like to look at any more because it was full of too-big dreams and the disappointments that inevitably came with them. Yet it had pleased him that his father thought of him that way – and he was involuntarily sucked into the heroic, larger-than-life version of himself that lived inside his father's mind.

But he found, after reading the books Michael had lent him, that he was burdened with a phantom despair. The history of his people in Kenya was fraught with racial tension and violence, beginning with the *coolies* brought in by the British to build the Ugandan railway and it seemed that even now, those divisions were there, stronger than ever, and he was overwhelmed by it. Sometimes he wished he could erase all the information he had learned and live with the easiness of an unthinking, empty mind.

Wanting to break the heaviness in his chest, he leaned over the edge of his bunk and said to his sister, 'Michael is our friend.'

'I know.' She tried not to feel as if he were blaming her for something.

'You shouldn't let what anyone else says about him change that.'

The mattress shifted above. She reached up to touch the shafts of wood holding him away from her. 'I won't.'

'It's harder than you think. People can be cruel.' They lay in silence, listening to the night noises before he spoke again. 'I'm not sure what's happening to me, so what do I tell Ma? Sometimes I feel so confused and angry.'

Leena didn't know what to say – was at a loss as to how to comfort him, afraid that her words might drive him further away, might disappoint him on this first time he was looking to her for answers.

'You're the best person I know,' she said finally.

Again, his face came into view and it was more relaxed this time, more like himself. When he smiled, it was a flood of happiness in her chest. 'Thanks, monkey.'

22

There was an old electronics store downtown, situated in the center of Biashara Street, nestled between dozens of small shops, which had been standing there for three generations, selling everything from leather to textiles, live chickens and food. Jeffery passed the many East Indian *dukas*, such as Sunu's Baby & Children and Taj's Fancy Shop, pausing to glance at the bright silks draped in the display windows and the costume jewelry sets that most Indian women wore – and wondered what one would look like on her. He imagined the necklace high up on her neck, falling in stiff waves of gold and ruby and he paused, fingers pressed to the glass, before David kicked his ankles and forced him forward.

'There it is.' David pointed to a large sign that read Abdullah & Sons Electronics and they crossed the street, holding up their hands to pause speeding *matatus* and *boda-bodas*, motorcycle taxis, as they criss-crossed their way to the shop's entrance.

A bell chimed as they went in and the man at the counter paused from what he was doing, placing the phone battery aside as they approached, asking pleasantly, 'Yes, officers? What can I do for you?'

David rested his palms on the glass countertop. 'Is this your shop?'

'It is.'

'You have many things here,' David observed, gesturing at the shelves stacked with radio parts, CD players, TVs in sealed packages. 'Where do you get everything from?'

'Overseas, mostly.' The man's manner was untroubled and he spoke in Swahili. 'I make a few trips to America every year.'

'Business must be doing well then.' David was glowering, his voice packed with envy, and Jeffery found that he was affected by a tightening in his chest as well, a plummeting jealousy. His whole life he had been dreaming of leaving Kibera for Nairobi, only a few kilometers away, but it had never occurred to him to think of traveling any further.

'God willing.' The shopkeeper understood they wanted something and was prepared to make them wait for it. 'If you could give me a few minutes,' he held up the phone battery, 'I have to fix this for a customer.'

They watched him as he worked. He was likely in his early thirties, light-skinned and groomed, dressed in a lavender shirt left open at the collar. Everything about him was extravagant. A thick gold chain was roped around his neck, a matching hoop in his left earlobe. Most of his fingers were adorned with large-stone, imitation rings and whenever he moved, the officers were overwhelmed by a musky scent of cheap deodorant, disguising itself as cologne. Catching the lemony whiff, Jeffery noticed that in every exaggerated action, a small bit of the man's falsity came leaking through, and when he glanced at David he received a nod in confirmation.

After several minutes, David asked, 'Are you finished?'

'Sorry to keep you waiting. As you can see, I was busy.'

David stood, stretched and tilted his body as if to peer into the back of the shop. 'Don't you have any employees to help you?'

'They've gone for lunch.'

The two officers glanced purposefully at the clock overhead, which read ten forty-five. 'So early?'

'I didn't think I would have so many jobs, so I told my man to take the day off.'

'It doesn't do you any good, playing games with a police officer.'

'I'm not lying.'

David folded his hands into his belt. 'Tell me this. You seem like a very successful businessman. You go on trips, you wear lots of necklaces and such things. And yet, when I look around, it seems to me that your shop is in trouble.' He held his hand up to stop the man from interjecting. 'No need, I understand. The black market for electronics is growing and why would anyone come here to buy something when they can get it cheap, cheap from the *chokora* down the street?'

'It's difficult,' the young man admitted. 'But I'm getting by.'

'And how is that?' David leaned in once more.

For the first time, the man looked uncomfortable.

David's voice shaped itself into a steely sternness. 'A *sacco*, *sindiyo*?'

Stubborn quietness filled the shop; the sound of haggling street vendors outside came sneaking through.

Jeffery thought about the necklace again. 'Answer him.' There was a forcefulness in his tone that surprised even David.

'What do you want?' The man's smile was gone.

'To help you.' David stuck his belly out in satisfaction. 'We can come to an arrangement that can benefit both of us.'

'What makes you think I want to help you?'

David strode around the shop. He trailed his fingers through the headphone packages, knocked on the screen of an expensive Sony TV, extracting a whimper from the shop owner. 'As you said, you obtain all of these goods from overseas. And yet, you do not pay tax on them.'

'You don't know that.' A bristling voice.

'Yes, I do. No matter, I shall report you and by the time you're done paying whatever tax you have evaded, plus the hefty fine for avoiding it, your business will be over.' David leered at the shop owner. 'No more trips to America. In the meantime, all the *matatus* in your *sacco* will be subject to inspection and I can say with surety that they won't pass. You'll have to pay for the repairs, of course, before they can operate. Must think of the safety of Kenyan passengers.'

A forced smile. 'Why all this hostility, *bwana*? I never said I wasn't willing to help you out.'

David stopped at the front desk once more. 'Good. Now that we are no longer pretending with each other and you have decided to stop wasting my time, let's discuss.'

As they talked, Jeffery moved outside, the bell chiming loudly above him as he leaned against the closing door, shutting his eyes and listening to the sounds of people and cars playing havoc on the streets.

Two weeks later, in the same bar, this time scooping up meat in heaps of ugali himself, David slipped something into his hand.

'Thirty thousand – your share. Of course, I took what I lent you plus interest.' It didn't matter. Jeffery took the cash, dumbstruck, as if it might be snatched away from him at any moment. *I have to look after my well-being*, he thought, as he slipped the money into his back pocket, wolfing down his food and washing it away with warm beer and a burp.

The following day, Jeffery returned to Biashara Street, to Taj's Fancy Shop, and purchased the gold-plated jewelry set he had seen, adorned with scarlet stones. It came in a set with earrings and a petal-like pedant to drape in her hair and it would fall like a symbol upon her forehead announcing that she was his, or would be soon enough.

He waited for the rest of the day at Klub House and it was late evening by the time he scrambled off his stool toward her, having ordered them drinks.

'I've been waiting all day for you.' His voice close to a snap.

She looked at him quizzically, as if she didn't recognize him. Suddenly embarrassed, he said, as if begging, 'I'm the one who—'

She took the wine, unimpressed. 'I remember you.'

'Where were you?' he asked.

'It's not your business but I have a job as a waitress.'

'At which bar?'

She smiled a little condescendingly. 'I don't mix my businesses. I'm sure you understand that,' she said, looking pointedly at his blue shirt, the telltale silver buttons and stitched-in badge that sat on top of his breast pocket.

'I bought you this.' He removed the velvet box, placed it on the table beside her. 'I very much hope you like it.' He spoke formally, desperate to impress her.

She touched the gift, fingers lingering. 'What is it?'

'Why don't you open it?' Her expression overjoyed him; she was grinning fully, showing off all her teeth, not the sultry smile he knew she reserved for clients.

With a small gasp she lifted the cover, laying a trembling hand on the red cushion inside. She stared at the set for the longest time, pausing only to take a long gulp of her wine. The maroon liquid stained her mouth, darkening it. He saw the pink contrast of her tongue as she licked the droplets away and he touched her hand urgently.

'Do you like it?'

Her throat rippled, her eyes brimming. 'Aqua Bar.'

'Pardon?' His eyebrows came together in a question.

She shut the case and drained the last of her drink, took his hand. She placed it high up on her thigh and leaned forward so that he caught sight of the chocolate slope of her breasts. He stumbled close to her, breathing raspily. She whispered in his ear, 'That's the bar where I work.'

23

Pooja sat in the small armchair and surveyed her family. Raj was lounging on the couch, a half-read newspaper laid over his lap. Leena was resting her head against his shoulder, legs tucked up, playing with the frill of her full skirt. It had rained last night and now the house was filled with the residues of it; humid and stifling. She toyed with her stockings, wondering why her mother had made her wear them. Jai was perched at the edge of the sofa cushion.

'Can I go now? Michael is waiting for me.'

'No you cannot go,' Pooja answered. 'We're all going to the temple.'

Groans. Rolling eyes. Slumping shoulders and pouting mouths. 'But, *Maaa!*'

'No *But, Maaas.*' Pooja pulled her mouth back to imitate her daughter's high-pitched whine. 'I said we're going, so we're going.'

Raj slammed his newspaper shut, a swell of irritation in his chest forcing him upward. His wife was always deciding things without talking about them first. 'Where is all of this coming from?'

Her children had been acting up. Such nonsense, non-stop. Talking back, hiding things from her, lying and fighting – still playing too much with that boy even though school had started.

That was what worried her the most. They needed direction now more than ever.

She had spoken to Mrs Laljee from Flat 39 about this yesterday, when the elderly woman had come to borrow a cup of sugar and vanilla essence for a pound cake. 'I was wondering if I could come in?' She had pushed her way through Pooja's door and into the living room.

'Of course.' She had led the woman to the couch, calling into the kitchen, 'Angela! Bring some tea and biscuits.'

The two women sat side by side, their knees turned toward each other. Mrs Laljee folded her gray salwar kameez between her knees and adjusted her *chuni* to sit more comfortably, hoisting the chiffon scarf upon her head.

'Is everything alright?' Pooja asked.

'Is everything okay with you, *beta*?' Mrs Laljee put a motherly hand on her thigh.

'Why wouldn't it be?' At last, Pooja saw the reason for the woman's visit.

'Oh, Pooja.' Mrs Laljee shook her head. 'I'm so worried about your daughter.'

Putting her fingers on top of the woman's hand in a tight clutch, she felt suddenly grateful that she could finally confide in someone who was willing to listen. 'What have you heard? She's just growing up – that's all.'

'I remember she used to be such a sweet, polite girl. Now all I hear are stories that she's stealing money and running around fruit markets in her skirt, like some kind of hooligan! It doesn't look nice.' She grimaced, as if embarrassed. 'Forgive my intrusion – you know I'm not one to pry.'

The women fell silent when Angela entered the room. They waited for her to put down the tray, and when she picked up the tea pot, Pooja stopped her. 'I'll do it.'

Once the housemaid was gone, Mrs Laljee spoke again. 'Does she have to bring that boy with her every day?'

'There's no one else to look after him.'

'Then get a new maid. Is she really worth all this trouble?'

'I thought about getting a new girl but Raj refused.' Then, more concerned, 'What kind of trouble do you mean?'

'I don't know – these *kharias* can get up to anything, really.' Mrs Laljee didn't bother to lower her voice. 'And if something does happen, people will blame you.' She accepted a tea cup, swirled a chocolate biscuit in the hot liquid. 'My *ayah* has a daughter and I wouldn't even let her in my house.' She sucked the tea out of the cookie, pushing it whole into her mouth. 'I suppose it's okay for Jai to play with him, for now at least, but it's different with girls. You could be getting yourself into some serious hot water if you don't discipline her now.'

'What shall I do?' Pooja asked, out of ideas.

'Start bringing them to the *Gurdwara*,' had been Mrs Laljee's answer. 'They can meet some new friends there – those who share the same values, speak the same language. We should never under-estimate the power of community, especially in this country. It's important we stick together.'

'Raj would never agree. He's not a religious man.' Pooja gestured with an irritated scoff at the picture of Pio Gama Pinto. 'That's who he talks to.'

'Nonsense.' Mrs Laljee picked up another biscuit. 'That's not a divine being. Pio was just a silly man who gave up his life for a silly dream. You must encourage Raj to come along,' she urged. 'A man without God is like a house without a toilet. It's unnatural and doesn't make sense.'

Listening to his wife retell the story, Raj kicked away the footstool in front of him. 'I'll be damned if I let Mrs Laljee run this family!'

She ignored his anger and stated again, 'We're going.'

And true to her word, twenty minutes later, Raj and his son were dressed, the house tightly locked up, and Angela and Michael instructed to stay out on the veranda until the Kohlis returned.

Raj tied a scarf around Jai's head in the shoe room of the *Gurdwara*. Pooja had taken their daughter to the other side; men and women sat separately and, today, Raj was glad for it. He tied his own cloth in an expert knot at his neck. It was compulsory to cover one's head as a sign of respect when entering the temple and, after doing so, Raj led his son into the prayer hall.

The commotion stopped at the entrance; once Raj crossed the carpeted threshold, all he could hear was the gentle whirring of fans overhead and the murmurings of prayer. They walked quietly to the far end of the room and sat by the wall.

Contrary to his wife's thinking, Raj did believe in God. It was the setting that the temple provided for finding and connecting with Him that he found questionable. The *Gurdwara* was composed of two floors. The top floor was the prayer room, where people came in as early as four thirty in the morning to sit in quiet meditation, listening to the songs and scriptures. When Raj was younger, the prayer room had been a neat and simple space where it was easy to lose yourself in the *kirtan*, the singing of hymns.

It had been possible to attach a part of yourself to the melancholic, yearning words and for a little while, at least, escape the confines of your body and catch up with your soul. But recently, the money donated by the community had been used to upgrade the look of the temple and now there were marble floors, gilded frescos and ornate domes, more of a showpiece than a sanctuary, and Raj couldn't help but feel that, for all of this beauty, God was no longer there.

Below the quiet praying room was the *langar*, the canteen where food was served to all visitors for free. It was a place overrun with chaotic shouting and laughing, children dashing between legs. A breeding ground for gossip, politics and falling in love, Raj found that the recent generation of temple-goers came to the *Gurdwara* for nothing more than a hot lunch and a couple of hours of socializing.

Mrs Laljee was a prime example of this. She regularly came to the temple under the pretense of religion but Raj knew she spent most of her time in the canteen, either cooking or wandering from group to group while they were eating, eager to learn new stories or throw around her opinions. *She would have made an expert lawyer*, Raj thought to himself. *Full of bullshit.*

And now she had roped in his wife. He sighed, thought about the countless houses he had seen in Runda and Muthaiga, spacious and wonderfully isolated. It was time to tell his wife that they were moving.

The heat made Leena's eyelids heavy and she struggled to keep them open. Her mother had wrapped a *chuni* around her head and shoulders and together with the weighty velvet dress and black stockings, packed in by swaying women in the throes of God, she felt as if she were slowly dying.

The languid movement of the fans overhead was like a wicked lullaby and she found herself jerking uncomfortably in and out of sleep. She coughed, stretched, even pinched the underside of her arm, all in an effort to keep awake. Pooja continuously glared at her in irritation, raising a finger to her lips indicating Leena to be quiet.

She peeked over at the men's side and saw Jai somewhere near the back. She wondered how he managed to sit so upright, be so attentive, even though the songs were in a language that was foreign to them and the music was wailing and dramatic. Her eyes continued to wander but stopped suddenly when she saw Tag. As if he felt her gaze upon him he turned slightly and gave her a secret grin. Blushing, she quickly snapped back and was suddenly wide awake. Her heart pulsated uncomfortably and her knee refused to stop bouncing. She leaned back out to take another peek but was blocked by the rising figure of her mother and felt Pooja's strong fingers grip her elbow and force her up. 'I have to help in the kitchen and you're coming with me.'

There was no possibility of falling asleep in the *langar*. Leena's ears filled with the banging of pots, the steamy whistles of pressure cookers and the air was thick with spices and heat. Pooja washed her daughter's hands, wrapped the *chuni* tighter around her head and handed her a pot full of *kichri*, a mixture of rice, daal lentils and vegetables, and told her to stand at the table outside.

'People are going to want to eat soon so hurry up.'

Leena was placed behind the long, buffet-style table, serving spoon in hand, along with several other children doing the same with other dishes. It was an impressive spread; there was pea and cauliflower curry, stuffed parathas and *chawal*, fragrant basmati rice. At the end, she spotted the desserts – yellow ladoos and buttery chickpea fudge. At home they ate meat but at the temple it was forbidden and she wondered if Angela had kept the leftovers from last night's roast chicken dinner.

'Hi, Leena.' Tag was standing before her, a plate in his hand. She dropped the spoon into the pot in momentary distraction and had to step up on her tiptoes to retrieve it.

'Hi.' She hoped he thought it was the steam from the food that was making her so flushed.

'I never see you here.'

'My mother made us come today. I would rather be at home watching TV.'

'Me too.' A grinning confession, holding up his Styrofoam plate and she scooped up a ladle-full of food, watching as it fell in sticky, graying clumps. 'After we eat, some of us go to the back field and play football, if you want to join us.'

She tried to contain her excitement. His keen attention, the way his cheeks reddened as he said this, intrigued her and made her feel special. 'I'll be out as soon as I'm finished.'

After he left, she served with gusto, eager to empty the container and join him outside. Once it was finished, she clanged down her spoon with satisfaction.

'Where do you think you're going?' Her mother rushed out of the kitchen, a large pot in her hands.

'It's finished.'

'No, it's not.' She refilled the empty one. 'Keep going – can't you see how long the queue is? And don't give out too much at once, otherwise I'll put you in the kitchen to help cook.'

When Leena was relieved of her station it was almost an hour later and she ran through the back doors, toward the field, not caring if she bumped and elbowed several people on her way there. Past the library, the council building where her mother held all her meetings, picking up speed but then skidding to a halt when she reached the edge of the flattened, dry grass and saw that it was empty.

Raj told his wife as soon as they returned home, took her by the elbow and dragged her up the stairs, even though she protested, 'Mrs Laljee has invited us to her house for tea. She was so happy to see us at the *Gurdwara*.'

'To hell with that woman.' Raj gruffly closed the bedroom door behind him. 'She should find a different hobby – one that doesn't include butting into peoples' lives.'

'She was only trying to be helpful.'

'She was being a busybody,' he corrected her. 'Just like everyone else on this street.'

Pooja sat down at her dresser, began taking off her jewelry. She tilted her head and the mirror caught the light coming in from behind her, like floating dust upon her dark hair, now thrown over one shoulder. He watched her through the glass – such severely beautiful features, all sharpness and points, and for a moment, he reconsidered telling her. He didn't want to upset her, didn't want to spoil this moment when she was sat in front of him, looking that way. 'Please, honey. We have to be at Mrs Laljee's house in twenty minutes.'

That name again. His annoyance flared. 'I'm tired of living this way. I hate that this family has thirty members instead of just the four of us.'

'What are you talking about?' She combed her hair, held it in one hand while the other moved in gentle, downward strokes.

'I'm talking about Mrs Laljee coming over to borrow a cup of sugar but really wanting to tell us how to run our lives.'

Pooja put the comb down and swung around to face him. Her mouth had become tight, pinched lines forming in the dip leading up to her nose. He didn't look at her as he continued talking.

'I want to move.'

'No.' Her answer was instant.

'Pooja—'

She stood in a spritz of rose perfume and came to him. When she spoke, her voice was like a little girl's. 'Don't do this to me. I'm happy here – I feel safe here. I know the children are safe here. I don't want to go anywhere else.'

'But they're getting older now. Soon, they'll want their own rooms. I've been looking at some houses—'

She kept his words at bay with strong shakes of her head and he felt them swell and collapse in his mouth because he knew the steel gates of her mind – knew that she would not alter her decision. She moved toward the door, not looking back. 'You should hurry. We're going to be late.'

24

Mrs Laljee's son, Vickram, returned home unexpectedly from England one weekend.

'He's on holiday,' she told the neighbors when they inquired, though it was only October. She said it with a fight in her voice, challenging them to question her.

'I hear he got into some trouble.'

Leena was lying in the grass outside Tag's house when she heard his mother say this to another neighbor, *hush-hush* because Mrs Laljee had eyes and ears everywhere.

'What kind of trouble?'

'He was caught up in some bad habits – you know how easy it is for our children to become lost over there.'

The second neighbor leaned in closer. 'Someone told me that he's—' here she paused to find the appropriate word. She crossed her eyes and wagged her head. 'Crooked.'

At that, Tag snorted out his vanilla milkshake. Goaded by his reaction, she asked, 'What does that mean?'

He told her with a malicious glint in his eye. 'It means he's a faggot.'

The two women turned to him sharply. His mother lifted her hand in indication of a slap and said, 'Do you want me to give you one?'

The rest of the day was full of whispered anticipation. Everyone was eager to meet Vickram, to discover the real story of his return, so in the late afternoon when he finally emerged, the women bolted upright from their *jikos*, halting their work. Alerting each other to his presence with hissed whistles, they trained their collective gaze upon him – an unsuspecting antelope in the midst of hungry lionesses.

With careful eyes, they tried to gauge from his demeanor what had gone wrong, but if anything was amiss Vickram refused to show it. He smiled pleasantly as he walked down the street, lifting his hand in an occasional wave.

'Good afternoon, Aunty Ji, lovely to see you,' he smiled, even reaching over veranda fences and kissing cheeks. 'I go by Vic now. It *has* been a very long time.'

He was a lanky boy, dressed in a plaid shirt that was buttoned up and pressed, and he squinted behind metallic-rimmed spectacles. Everything from the slight cowlick in his hair down to the carefully rolled-up trouser hems was intentional and meticulous, just as she imagined a British man would be.

'I bet he wears makeup too,' Tag chuckled.

'I think he's handsome.'

Tag rolled his eyes and Leena looked away, upset. His attention flattered her, the way he whispered secrets into her ear and shared his milkshakes, but she couldn't shake the sense of discomfort that came with being around him. The easiness she had shared with her brother and Michael was gone and the excitement she felt with Tag brought with it more anxiety than happiness. She twisted her fingers together and, on impulse, leaned around the tree in the direction of her house.

Jai and Michael were engaged in one of their lengthy conversations, having brought their chairs close together, their knees touching. On his lap, Michael had a book, his hands resting lightly upon the closed leather cover. As if he sensed her watching, Michael paused from his words and glanced up. She waved and held her breath. After a long moment he raised his hand, and when he smiled it set off such a strong burst of relief in her chest, she almost ran to him.

'What's a faggot?' Leena asked at the dinner table that night.

Her father dropped his fork. Her mother dropped her mouth.

'What did you say, young lady?' Pooja demanded.

'What's a fag—'

Her mother held up her hand. 'Where did you hear it?'

'Tag called Vickram that today.'

Shaken, Pooja told her daughter, 'It means nothing. It's a dirty word and I don't want you to use it.' She looked at her husband in disbelief. 'Children these days. We would have never uttered such things.'

'Do you know what it is?' Leena asked Jai, who was hiding a smile behind his hand.

'Yes.'

Pooja looked at her daughter warningly. 'Stop asking. You don't need to know what it means. Finish your dinner.'

They went back to scraping the cutlery against their plates and even though it was Leena's favorite – coconut chicken and egg curry, she couldn't eat it. She kept thinking about the word, how even if one said it in the most gentle, loving tone, it still came out sounding wicked and ugly. How, when Tag had called Vickram that, he was delighted and disgusted in equal measures; how his eyes narrowed and spit formed at the corners of his mouth. She wondered how one word, a single, short word could mean and do so much. All day, it had kept the neighbors at a safe distance from Mrs Laljee's house. Once the hub for gossip and socializing over tea and cake, it now sat alone in the stiff shadow of peoples' turned backs. It sagged under the clucks of pity for the family inside, the relieved whispers that it wasn't them, for poor Mrs Laljee was the victim of the greatest misfortune, the one families on the streets feared the most – a failed son.

The next day, Leena sat cross-legged beneath her favorite tree, tearing apart a bright pink flower. Tag was playing cricket with the other boys and hadn't asked her to join in. She was in part upset, part relieved. Although she enjoyed the game, she was glad for the time alone – it gave her a chance to observe Vickram more closely.

He walked the edges of the game, hands in his pockets and a permanent smile on his face. Unlike his mother, he was unobtrusive and comfortable keeping to himself, indifferent to peoples' reactions as he passed them.

'Do you mind if I join you?'

He had reached her spot, pushing up his glasses and gazing down expectantly. Instantly, Leena glanced toward the field where Tag had paused from his game, shaking his head fervently. *Tell him to keep away.*

She almost did, but Vickram looked so hopeful and unassuming that she couldn't bring herself to. Instead, she shifted slightly to make space and he slid down beside her, stretching out his legs. He looked so delicately clean that she winced to think of his beige chinos stained with dust, the freshness of his cologne disturbed by sweat.

'I'm Vic.' He extended a palm.

'Leena.'

'You were this small when I left,' he grinned, holding his hand up a short distance from the ground. 'It's been, what – three years now? You've grown.'

'I don't remember you.'

'You wouldn't.' He looked out at the cricket game, a shadow of wistfulness obscuring his features. 'I'm very different now.'

There was something absorbing about him; perhaps it was the polished accent, the way it took its time with words, never lazy nor dragging, and she felt a stir of excitement, thinking of the world he came from. There were so many things she wanted to ask him but the questions stuck in her throat as she pulled at the flowers around her nervously. She was acutely aware of everyone staring – mothers and children alike, itching for a story.

'Nothing here has changed though – still as suffocating as ever.' When he detected the ruffle of confusion in her, he explained. 'You see that girl over there?' He pointed at one of the houses, where a girl Leena's age was playing on her swing.

'Yes.'

'Let's say the wicket keeper in this cricket game likes her.' Vickram settled back into the rough bark of the tree, shifting several times before getting comfortable. 'He'll ask his friends about her. His friends will ask their friends, their parents and their relatives.'

'What's your point?'

'We live in such a closed community that someone is bound to know swing-girl. Wicket boy will know her stories, her secrets, before he even meets her. No one here will ever be a stranger.'

'Isn't that a good thing?'

'Sometimes,' he consented. 'Other times, it can smother you. Especially if you're different.'

'Then why did you come back?' She had been holding in the question, but sitting beside him, hearing him talk, her curiosity got the better of her.

He was about to answer when Mrs Laljee interrupted. 'Vickram, come inside now.' She was standing above them, a wool cardigan pulled close over her salwar kameez despite the heat. Leena noticed how pale and drawn she had become; even her voice, which had once been so mountainous, was quiet.

'I'm in the middle of a conversation.' His features had tightened up into something close to a scowl.

'Now.'

They stared at each other for a prolonged moment; mother and son locked in a battle of accusations and guilt. Eventually, Vickram rose. As she dragged him back to their house, Mrs Laljee kept her gaze firmly on the ground, her shoulders huddled up near her ears, as if to keep away her neighbors' sniggers as they watched her go.

Feeling uneasy, Leena made her way back to the house. Mrs Laljee hadn't acknowledged her presence, hadn't even glanced her way while confronting her son. Leena thought about the quick movement of her eyes, the fingers tugging incessantly at the frayed edges of her cardigan, the hidden voice.

'She was embarrassed,' she said aloud.

'Who was?' Michael looked up from his book.

He had heard Leena come onto the veranda and pretended to keep reading, hoping that she would stop by him, and when she spoke, he jumped at the chance to hold her there.

'Mrs Laljee is ashamed of her son.'

He scooted over on the bench and gestured for her to sit. 'Why do you say that?'

As he pressed himself closer to a cactus to make space for her, Leena was touched by his generosity. It was that, and a need to feel close to him once again, that made her ask, 'Michael, what's a faggot?'

He closed the book and placed his palms on top of it. 'Why do you ask?'

'It's what Tag called Vickram.' She sat beside him, pressing the backs of her thighs against her hands.

He had heard his Aunt Fiona use the word. She had returned at three o'clock in the morning from her night excursions, stumbling and bumping into even the few pieces of furniture they had. She had smelled of something strong, like bleach, and her weave was in tangles, her skirt riding up over her long thighs. Throwing off her thick-heeled platforms, she let them land wherever they wanted. The *thud* of the heavy shoe beside his face stirred him to listen to his aunt's conversation with his mother.

'I swear sometimes I think he loves me,' Fiona was saying.

'Isn't that a part of your job?' His mother's words were curt, slightly disgusted.

'This is different, Angie.'

'I don't want to hear about what you do.'

'But you won't believe what I saw today.' Fiona leaned in closer. 'I met him at the bar and afterward, we went to the motel.'

'Fiona...'

'Just listen. It's this dingy place and we got a room where there were two beds and two other people already there.' At her sister's look, Fiona shrugged. 'He hasn't been paid yet and can't afford anything fancier but it didn't bother me at first.' She lit up a cigarette and the traces of smoke carried across the living room, threatening to make Michael cough and reveal himself. 'But then we started hearing these funny sounds from the next bed – I swear, sis, deep grunts and not a woman's either. *Aieesh*. Two men sharing one bed! I got out of there straight away, didn't even finish the job. I know what you think of me but even I still have some values. I would never share a room with faggots.'

'Hush, Fiona – can't you see Mike is sleeping over there?'

'Sorry, sis,' she had giggled. 'Anyway, I don't know how we're going to make the rent. Business is really slow these days, obviously because there are men out there who would rather fuck other men.'

'Why don't you ask for help from the man who's in love with you?'

'I can't do that to him.' Fiona's voice had grown almost tender. 'You should see him – he's so lonely.'

Michael tried to think of a way to say this to Leena. 'I'm not sure how to explain it because I don't really understand it myself. But I don't think it's something you should call other people – it sounds hurtful.'

'Tag says we shouldn't speak to him.'

At the mention of Tag's name, Michael's voice turned hard. 'I think you should make your own decision.'

'I like Vickram,' she admitted. 'But I don't want other people to talk about me. Do you think I'm horrible?' She grew embarrassed under her confession.

'Not at all. But I think you should do what feels right.'

'How do I know what that is?'

Michael played with the old edges of his book. He wished he could follow his own advice – his confession sat at the tip of his tongue. 'Knowing what's right isn't the problem; it's about not being afraid to do it. But once you do,' finally looking up at her, 'you'll see that doing what's right is the easiest thing in the world.'

Sunday afternoons at the compound were unhurried and still. After an indulgent lunch – which included, more often than not, inviting several neighbors over – lethargy stole in and the women left the housework to their maids and gave their children an hour of respite as they climbed into their beds, cocooned between cool sheets and behind drawn curtains, for a two o'clock nap.

It was during this secret hour that Tag came to fetch her. He found her in the high-ceilinged living room, one leg dangling off the couch as she cooled herself with a home-made paper fan. A cartoon was playing on the TV but it was too hot for her to pay attention to it.

'Let's go.' He hovered impatiently at the door.

'Where?' Her feet had already swung to the floor, ready to follow.

'I'll show you.'

She didn't realize where he was leading her until she stood before Mrs Laljee's house, just outside the window, a thick row of green money plant growing downward from a pot set on the sill. Tag picked up the clay urn and handed it to her, leaving the wall beneath exposed.

'Let's do it here,' he said to the other boys, who had been waiting for them, crowded over a cardboard box. Tag left her on the outside of the circle, peering into the window, cupping his hands against the wire netting. 'All clear.'

'What's going on?' She didn't like the feel of all the boys around her, their hissing words and almost hysterical laughter. She was ready to turn back to the boring tranquility of her house before it was too late.

Tag ignored her. 'We better hurry. They could come back at any time.'

'Wait – what are you doing?' Her voice rose in a slight panic as they pulled out cans of black spray paint from the box. She stepped closer but Tag blocked her way, holding out a can.

'Are you going to help or not?'

Michael's words came back to her; she felt sick watching them, heads bowed together, fingers moving swiftly. They guarded their cruelty, hiding it from her. She stepped back, distancing herself from the terrifying scene. 'I won't do it.'

'I knew I couldn't trust you.'

The disappointment on his face made her stomach clench and as she spun around to leave, he caught her arm, twisting it around her back.

His breath was hot in her ear. 'You better not tell anyone.' He shoved her and she stumbled onto the street, her vision blurred.

Michael was folding some bedsheets as she came sprinting toward the house, and on seeing her he quickly dropped what he was doing.

'What happened to you?' he called after her, reaching out to grab her elbow. 'Leena!'

But she ran from his concern – the compassion in his eyes made her feel wretched – and threw herself down onto the couch, the sounds of the cartoon drowning out her tears.

It was a fearful sight. Even in the fading light, it refused to dull, to go away, and people looked on from half-drawn-back curtains, calling each other on the telephone.

'Did you see?'

'Can you believe it?'

'Who would do such a thing?'

'But it *is* the truth… isn't it?'

Leena listened to her mother, the phone cradled close to her ear, and she turned away with a feeling so heavy that each movement was difficult. Though she closed her eyes, tried to fill her mind with happier thoughts, the message still came through, black and jagged and sharp.

Jai was furious when he saw it.

'It's just like them.' He was pacing the small patch of lawn when she emerged from the house, wanting to escape her mother's conversation.

'Who?'

'Tag.' He pointed toward Mrs Laljee's house. 'Who else would be responsible for such a thing?'

'You don't know that it was him.'

There was something in her voice, a crack of fear, that stopped her brother in his tracks. 'Did you have anything to do with this?'

Her eyes filled with tears once more, stinging the already red-rimmed eyelids.

'Jai, come on. Give her a break.'

Remembering the distressed way she had come sprinting into the house, Michael came to stand between the siblings. Jai crossed his arms over his chest, glaring at the two of them, and felt a stirring of jealousy, an unusual emotion for him, seeing the way his friend stood defensively before his sister.

'Have you seen what they've done?' he asked Michael.

Michael had been busy all afternoon helping his mother. Following his friend's pointing finger, he saw it for the first time. His chest dropped, sickening his stomach. Behind him, a sob broke in Leena's throat and though he wanted to comfort her, he was frozen, glued to the words.

GOD HATES FAGZ

'It wasn't me.' She reached out to tug Michael's unresponsive arm. 'You have to believe me – I didn't do it.'

He was still staring at the message, so fixed on the hate that came rushing from it that he barely heard her. She felt him stiffen under her fingers, and fresh tears, this time for letting him down, stung her skin.

'Did you know they were going to do it?' Jai asked.

She had never been able to lie to him. 'Yes.'

'You should have stopped them.'

You should have done what was right.

Michael turned to face her and she could hear his words again; how different the look on his face was now, rigid and angry. He felt the insult more acutely, realizing how easily it could be altered to fit him – another outcast in this small compound.

'I didn't know what to do. It was so hard, Jai.'

'That's not an excuse.' Her brother turned away and repeated, 'This is just like them. With everything that's new and doesn't make sense – all they want to do is make it disappear. Like our friendship with Michael, Dad not going to the temple and now this.' He shook his head. 'You should have stopped them.'

Leena's chin trembled and Michael felt it like a pang in his chest. He wanted to comfort her but she was already backing away, turning to run and out of his reach.

'You shouldn't be so hard on her,' Michael told Jai, after she had gone.

'No one ever is.'

They heard the familiar chugging of his father's Nissan; Raj was returning from an afternoon meeting and the sight of him through the half-open window lifted Jai's spirits. His father would know what to do.

Jai chased his father into the house, waiting impatiently as Raj slipped off his shoes with a satisfied *aah!*

'I need to talk to you.'

'In a minute. Open the window for me, will you?' Raj fell back on the couch.

Jai obeyed, pushing back the white net and swinging it open. His father twisted his body so that it was half-facing the street outside. He searched in his back pocket for his Embassy Lights packet, pulling one out. As his eyes looked up, the cigarette went slack between his fingers. His mouth fell open in shock.

'What the hell is that?'

From across the street, immersed in the dulling blue light of evening, the scrawled words appeared even more malicious and Raj had to pause to steady his breath.

'Someone wrote it this afternoon.' Jai chose to keep the details to himself.

'How come it's still there?'

'They've been too embarrassed to come out.' He turned to his father, who had lit the cigarette and shut his eyes, inhaling slowly. 'I think we should help them clean it up.' He spoke rapidly. 'All it needs is one coat of paint. If we start now, we can finish before it gets too dark.'

Raj glanced at his son in surprise. 'I don't see what this has to do with you.'

Jai stared at his father in confusion. 'It has everything to do with me. You taught me that. Stand up for the little guy, be the hero.' He couldn't help the bitterness that tinged the last word.

'I did but I should also tell you that you have to choose your battles carefully.' Raj chewed down on his lip. 'Mrs Laljee and her son can handle their own fights.'

'Can't Michael handle his?' Jai retorted.

'That's different.' Raj's eyes went involuntarily upward to the photo on his right.

Jai hated that photo more than he ever had in his life. 'Why? Because Pinto only saved Africans?'

His father bristled but kept his voice calm. 'We have to look at the bigger picture,' he tried to explain. 'There are only so many battles you can fight before fighting becomes meaningless.'

'I thought you wanted me to fight for what's right but now I understand what you meant.' Jai was self-righteous and didn't care that, for the first time, he was raising his voice at his father. 'You just want me to fight for what is right for *you*.'

Raj threw out his cigarette. 'You won't go and help and that's final.'

He watched his son leave – long strides to the door and then hurried footsteps echoing throughout the house. Jai's words stuck with him, but more than that, it was the way in which he had said them. He lit up another cigarette, staring at the framed newspaper clipping and losing himself within it. He fought to clear his mind, telling himself that it was absurd to feel reprimanded by your own son.

25

The house was lit up in celebration of her parents' wedding anniversary. The flat was transformed into a wild tapestry of color, from the vermillion roses her father had bought her mother that morning to the orange *jalebis*, the chocolate-covered Indian desserts sprinkled with pistachio shavings and silver trays with intricately engraved handles holding wine glasses and scotch tumblers, pristine under the bright, indoor lamps.

Angela ushered them out of the room. 'I have to get things ready for the party and you're both in my way.'

They stepped out into the growing coolness of the evening. She felt the pinch of smoke in her nose, a charcoal tickle; someone was burning something outside the gate, in the makeshift slums not far off.

Michael was playing with Jai's old yo-yo against the bougainvillea tree, and though Jai bounded toward him, Leena lagged behind. He always went home by six o'clock and to see him here now, close to seven thirty, felt peculiar and thrilling. There was something different about him in the fading daylight, his dark profile sharp against the lurking street shadows, which made her hesitate. She had never noticed that he was taller than her brother, that he had grown into his broad shoulders, the wide and flat span of his upper torso sneaking down into a slim waist. Then she saw the glint of his smile, as gentle as ever.

'Hi, Leena.'

He appeared so much older then and she felt a burst of nervousness, suddenly hating the puffy sleeves of her dress, its childish pink and yellow rosebud pattern. Her hair seemed ridiculous in its curly, wired locks and she pressed it down in vain. His voice cut through her thoughts.

'You look very pretty.'

'She looks like a poodle,' Jai said.

'Not at all.' How heavy his voice was, pushing the world into a spin.

They settled down on the grass, Jai easily and the other two uncomfortably – both conscious of their movements so that they dodged, banged, *sorried* each other on their way down.

Trying to break the awkwardness he felt, Michael said, 'Looks like you're having a huge party.'

'My parents' anniversary. You know how Indians are – you have to invite everyone otherwise someone might be insulted and never invite you to one of their parties ever again,' Jai said.

'It must be nice to know that many people – to feel like you'll never really be alone.'

Having had the chance to observe this *muhindi* culture for many months, Michael had come to appreciate the close-knit community they formed – even, to a certain extent, the sense of obligation and loyalty that bound them to one another.

'My father thinks it's full of busybodies sticking their ears, noses and mouths wherever they don't belong.' Jai looked back at the house where the guests were starting to arrive. 'I'm beginning to agree with him.'

'What about you, Leena?'

She stopped fussing with her dress. Blinked twice. It felt strange to be asked for her opinion, to be looked at with such keen interest.

'What's the point of thinking about it so much? It's just the way it is,' she replied.

'That's exactly the kind of mentality that got us here in the first place,' Jai snapped.

'Come on, Jai.' Michael calmed his friend. 'We're all entitled to our opinions.'

'Not if they're wrong,' he muttered, but Michael ignored him and kept smiling at her. It started a quiver in her chest – a slight but detectable change that thickened the blood in her veins.

A little ruffled, Jai stood, brushing off his trousers. 'I'll bring you out something to eat, if you want,' he said to Michael.

'A few samosas wouldn't hurt, I guess.'

Jai beckoned for Leena to follow him but she stayed rooted to her place. 'You can join us inside,' she said to Michael. He had always been so kind to her and today she wanted to be that for him.

'You know I can't.'

He caught her arm as she stood up to leave. Leaning over, he tucked a flower behind her ear, grazing her neck – the smooth skin behind her hair that she had never paid much attention to before. Now, its presence was a ceaseless vibration. 'Bougainvillea are your favorite, right?'

'Thank you.' The words were insufficient but there was nothing else she could say.

He released her elbow too soon. 'Your mother is waiting for you.'

Her walk back to the house was measured and thoughtful, pausing at the step where her mother had come out. Pooja's gaze was fixed above Leena's head, her eyebrows knitted, the gold-hoop ring in her nose glinting. Then she reached out and snatched the flower from her daughter's hair.

'Hey!' Leena grasped the blank space near her ear, surprised and saddened by what her mother had done.

'I don't want it in your hair.' Pooja pushed her daughter into the doorway, crushing the petals between determined fingers and tossing them, ripped and drained of color, onto the step. 'It's dirty and probably full of ants.'

That night, in bed, Pooja said to her husband, 'Do you still want to move house?'

He turned to her in surprise, pulling off his reading glasses. The party had exhausted him; it was always nice to be around friends but he had reached a stage in his life now where he craved some degree of peace and quiet. 'I do.'

'How long will we have to wait?'

Raj bolted upright, trying to catch up to the implication of his wife's words. When he spoke, his words were fast with excitement. 'There are two houses I've been looking at seriously.'

'Whichever one you want,' she replied absently. 'How long?'

Her haste confused him, stilting his enthusiasm. 'Don't you want to see them first?'

'I trust you.'

'The house in Runda is ready – it's furnished and the current occupants leave for America this coming weekend.' He was cautious, wondering if it was some kind of trick.

'So two weeks?'

'Three at the least – if we do everything quickly. It's only two years old so we wouldn't have to do any renovations.'

Pooja unfurled her pinned hair, letting it span out across her shoulders. 'It's decided then.'

He grabbed her arm, his magazine falling to the floor. 'I'll take you there tomorrow – you're going to love it.'

'I have only one condition.'

His smile turned worried. He didn't like it when she sounded that way, determined as a bulldozer, crushing everything in her path.

'What is it?'

'Angela won't be coming with us.'

Dismayed, Raj felt betrayed by his wife's ulterior motive. She had tricked him and he had fallen blindly into her trap. He tried to reason with her. 'Angela has been with us for twelve years. We can't just let her go without a proper reason.'

'Do you want to move or not?'

He should have pressed her for more information, perhaps tried longer to dissuade her, but he was afraid that she would change her mind, that he would be left to grow old in this compound surrounded by small-minded people, and so he remained silent. Consoling himself with the idea that he would help Angela find another position before they left, he nodded. 'If that's what you think is right.'

'I'll talk to her tomorrow then,' Pooja said, turning away from him so that he wouldn't see the way her face relaxed with relief as she stretched out her hand to flick off the bedside lamp, casting them into darkness.

PART THREE

2002

26

In the middle of the afternoon at a deserted bar situated high up on a busy street in Westlands, Jeffery lounged in the stuffy heat, sipping his whiskey and coke. He watched the road below, lined with rows and rows of nightclubs. Officially known as Mpaka Road, this corner of the city transformed into 'Electric Avenue' after dark, Nairobi's liveliest club district.

During the late afternoon, however, all one could hear was the beginnings of rush-hour traffic, a cacophony of car horns, reggae music and street vendors shouting out prices and knocking on windows. He enjoyed the gaudy colors of the *matatus*, the political and religious messages stamped across their back windows and on the sides of buses; in Nairobi, it was not uncommon to board a bus that carried quotes such as 'Only Jesus can give wholeness to a broken life.'

He watched tiny hurricanes of dust rise beneath the wheels of these chaotic vehicles and drew away from the window in a fit of coughing. Gulping down half his whiskey and coke he released an unsatisfied belch and checked his watch – three o'clock and he was disappointingly sober and annoyed at having been kept waiting.

'*Ingine?*' The damp whisper in his ear, long-ringed fingers accidentally-on-purpose grazing high up on his thigh.

Jeffery's eyes roamed deliberately over the waitress's body. Once upon a time, he would have appreciated the obvious effort she had put into the tight, leopard-print dress, the twisted-up weave. But now, he was only bored as he nodded a yes.

As she moved away to get his drink, he caught her hand roughly. 'No diluting this one, *mnalewa*?'

She sulked off and he downed the dregs of the drink in front of him with satisfaction. No one cheated him, especially not some leggy, aging *malaya* who sometimes waitressed and who was becoming nothing more than an old nuisance.

A fresh glass was placed in front of him and he tugged at her curved waist, pressed her breasts up to his cheek as he leaned down to sniff the whiskey. Catching the pungent whiff he grunted his approval, noting that she had added two shots instead of the one he would be paying for. He pulled out a wad of cash and slipping it into the lace strap of her bra, whispered, '*Baadaye*.'

Happy with this promise to meet her later, she moved away with swinging hips and he said, 'You're playing with fire, *kijana*.'

A young man was hovering behind him and at Jeffery's voice he was goaded into a mild protestation. 'There was jam everywhere, officer.'

'That's not my problem. Where is it?'

A sorrowful face. 'I haven't had a job in a while. If I can come see you next week with the payment, *itakuwa poa sana*.'

Jeffery kept his voice pleasant, his fingers trailing the rim of his glass. He had learned that in matters of money it was necessary to remain polite, no matter how angry one became. 'How will I feed my family now?'

'You know how this job works.' As he spoke, the man, Nick, kept a pleading hand to his chest. 'Sometimes money comes, other times no one is looking to buy. There is so much competition these days.'

Jeffery remained silent and the boy recognized the expectation on his face. He had not come here for nothing. So Nick removed six thousand shillings, more than three-quarters of what he had made that week, and slid it unhappily over the table. But he was partly relieved, having been let off relatively easily. He had been terrified to come here, especially after hearing what this officer had done to his partner.

What was his name again? Nick searched for it as Jeffery counted out the notes in his hand.

'You need to work harder, *sawa*?'

David. That was it.

Nick retreated rapidly, thanking the officer on his way out. Jeffery returned the glass to his lips, muttering under his breath. *Mafala.*

Idiot.

How is it possible to be cheated by your own soul? It was the newest question Jeffery grappled with every night. For thirty years, he had been living one life, so certain of it that even in his poverty he had been content. But one deceptively sunny morning, he had awoken in another man's house, surrounded by a stranger's possessions, including his wife, and found that the life meant for him was something entirely different.

Three years prior to that day, together with David he had been working closely with the *sacco* leader from that unassuming shop on Biashara Street. The first night he had received thirty thousand shillings, Jeffery opened his own bank account upon his friend's advice.

'This is only the beginning, Jeff,' he had been told.

David was quick to monopolize the information he had received about the *saccos*. They latched onto various *matatu* unions springing up around the city before anyone else realized how profitable they were and, within the year, the two of them were receiving payments from ten such companies: a hundred thousand shillings monthly.

Of course, there was the hierarchy to consider and a large percentage of what they collected went to officers in stations above them, including the senior police officer at the Parklands station.

'We forgive and forget, *eh-he*?' the fat man had said. 'Besides, look at how successful you are now. You should be thanking me.'

'He's right,' David had told Jeffery. 'Stop clinging to the past – it's time you moved out of that shack. You have more money now and how much of it can you spend on whores?' A wicked laugh. 'Or should I say whore?'

'We're in love,' Jeffery had informed him.

She called herself Marlyn, and though it wasn't her real name its exoticness suited her perfectly. Mysterious, with a body so perfectly curved, it had an animalistic sway – dark skin that was cool and soft to touch. *Mar-Lynne the mermaid.*

After several months of courtship, which included buying her expensive gifts and staying in luxurious hotels, which back then were still out of his pocket's reach, and dining in fine restaurants, Marlyn stopped seeing other men and Jeffery stopped paying her. She asked to move in with him but he refused, wanting to hold on to his curtained shack, guarding the final remnants of his past.

Despite his moving upward, something held him back from leaving those winding, muddy streets, the outdoor lawyers and Miss Judy reciting the alphabet with singing children. Doing so would be like having his mother die all over again, and he knew that the day he left her house would be the time he was truly lost.

Having grown up in a place where even using the toilet had its price, Jeffery was unsurprised by all the luxuries money could buy.

Alcohol, food, two mobile phones clipped to either side of his belt; soon he became bloated by all of these things. His paunch folded over and his shirt buttons often strained and snapped right off. He could be walking down the street, kissing Marlyn and *pop*! Another button would go flying off, a sad and frightening reminder. His chin sagged and wrinkles sprouted over his forehead and eyes, like flowers in bloom. Marijuana stained his eyes red and tobacco browned his teeth, but still he couldn't bring himself to stop.

And the fatter he grew, the greedier he became for new things, so that eventually even Marlyn became something in want of replacement. He watched her one evening getting dressed for dinner, knotting up her hair so that she could fasten the clasp of her necklace.

'I don't know why you still wear that one when I've bought you so many more expensive things.'

Marlyn studied herself in the mirror, finger traveling over the rusted costume jewelry. Her eyes met his. 'Some things are worth more than just how much they cost, Jeff.'

And he blinked and felt belittled because he had forgotten how that could possibly be true.

That same night, after she had rolled off him, he swung his legs off the bed and reached for the bedside table. Rifling through his wallet, he pulled out a stack of notes. He shoved the money at her, forcing her from her peacefulness. She gave an astonished gasp of laughter as he pried open her fingers and said, 'I need my sleep.'

'I don't understand.' She clenched the notes. He hadn't paid her anything in over a year.

'I'll come and find you when I want.' He adjusted the pillow, closed his eyes.

She had dressed hastily, pausing with one heel dangling from her toes, leaning down to kiss him – her tongue thick and wet between his unresponsive lips. He rolled onto his side and listened to her reluctantly leave and thought how sad it was that she had pocketed the money and felt glad that he was no longer in such a position.

'Thank God!' David had clapped his back at the news. 'Now we can really have some fun.'

A different woman every evening, a new hotel every night – Jeffery became so used to the things in these rooms that had been absent from his previous life – a television, a mirror, his own private bathroom – that going back to Kibera, he saw his home for what it really was: unfit for any living person.

'Yet still you refuse to move into the city.' David had clucked his tongue. 'I don't understand you. Why don't you take a break from all the *malayas* and join me and my wife for dinner?'

Jeffery found himself in the strange position once again, after a very long time, of being jealous. 'That is why you never take a woman.'

'The line has to be drawn somewhere. If it wasn't, imagine all the terrible things we could do to each other.'

David's wife, Esther, was a simple woman with slightly pock-marked skin from a bad bout of chicken pox and who wore her hair natural, a wiry, small afro that framed her angular cheeks and bird-like eyes. She startled him with how she reminded him of his mother, so that the whole first night he clung to her every word.

When David told him that he lived in South C, Jeffery had arrived expecting to stand before a gated house but what he found instead was a block of high-rise apartments – gray and morbid with black grille windows and small balconies. He was embarrassed for his friend as he entered the congested, one-bedroomed flat and saw that it was nothing short of run down. Linoleum floors with cement holes where the tiles had fallen away, the constant running of a leaking toilet and such sparse furniture that the chairs they used for dining were also the ones they dragged to the boxed TV to end the night. Nevertheless, the house smelled homely – yellow corn bubbling in the pot and Mr Sheen wood polish, and Jeffery couldn't help but be desperate for such things, all the more harrowing because they did not come with a price.

It was one such evening when everything changed.

They had just finished dinner and had moved the wooden chairs to the living room, the window thrown open to cool down the house from the heat of the day, and he heard the sounds of three young boys singing and playing the drums from the apartment upstairs.

'Doesn't that disturb you?' Jeffery asked his friend.

'It's entertainment. Sometimes Esther and I go up there to listen to them. One day, they'll be famous – mark my words.'

'Better cash in,' Jeffery grinned.

'I'm working on it.'

The two men sipped on their drinks with slow ease. Jeffery closed his eyes to catch every trill of the cymbals, the dull pounding of drums that seemed to close the walls in around him and he almost felt happy. Then Esther asked, 'Did David tell you the good news?'

An uncomfortable silence fell over them. David puffed his cheeks out in a guilty exhalation. 'I haven't had time yet.'

'Tell me what?' Jeffery paused with the glass at his lips. His friend's expression caused him to return it to his lap without taking a sip.

'It's nothing.' David tweaked his mouth.

'It's big.' Esther prodded her husband, who was glowering at her.

Now that his wife had let the news slip, David had no choice but to continue. 'They offered me the senior officer position at Parklands police station.'

'What happened to Muema?' Jeffery inquired.

'He found a job at the airport. Said it's easier money and much less pressure.'

Jeffery slammed the drink down with much more force than intended, causing Esther to jump. 'It's getting late.'

David called out for him but Jeffery ignored his friend and went staggering down into the dark, claustrophobic evening.

Instead of alighting a *matatu*, he wandered aimlessly down the broken pedestrian walkways, hitting shoulders with drunkards and side-stepping women linked at the elbows, heads bowed close together, sharing secrets. As he passed, he was sure they looked up to snicker. A bicycle swerved by him, the sharp ring of the bell not registering in his mind until someone shouted, '*Mjinga*! Watch where you are going.'

It was past ten o'clock when he boarded the bus. It was empty and he sat toward the back, watching the nightlights of the city grow and shrink behind him, taunting Jeffery with a broken reflection of himself. He was corrupt – a horribly overweight cheat – and he had become this way because of David. Yet he hadn't minded because they had been working together but now he would be alone. His friend was moving up in the ranks and soon Jeffery would have to report to him. He would have to give him a larger share of their profits. In time, David might decide that he no longer needed a partner – and so it was Jeffery's greed and pride that made him do what he did next.

The following morning, instead of heading straight to the station as he always did, Jeffery went to Biashara Street, walking rapidly to the electronics store with his head bowed into the collar of his jacket and shoved open the door so forcefully that the bell continued to shriek after him.

Startled, the man looked up. When he spotted Jeffery, he lifted his hand in a high-five greeting. '*Mambo*.'

'*Poa*.' They clapped hands.

'*David ni wapi*?'

'That's what I've come to talk to you about. We have a problem.'

'What kind of problem?'

'David is going to be announced as the senior officer at Parklands police station,' Jeffery informed him.

'Good for us, *sindiyo*? Always helps to know people in high places.'

'He's going to put you out of business.' A spew of words beyond his control. 'He's been arranging it for some time now with another *sacco* to steal away all your buses.'

'He can't do that.' The man brushed aside the information but Jeffery detected a flicker of worry behind the indifferent façade.

'He will put all your buses under inspection and when they fail, he is going to impound them and sell them off.'

'He can't do that,' the man repeated, looking around his empty shop.

'Who will stop him?' Jeffery asked.

'Why are you telling me this now if he has been planning it for a while? How do I know you are not his accomplice?'

'Your worries are none of my concern. I'm just informing you – if you don't do something *chap chap*, you will be out of business by the end of this month.'

The two men stared at each other for a long moment. The shop-keeper spoke. 'I'll work something out.'

As he left the shop, Jeffery turned back once more. 'I don't want to know what you're planning. I have no part in this – I simply gave you some information and I want you to remember how I have helped you.'

Once outside, he fell against the side of the building, pulling the handkerchief from his pocket to dab his perspiring forehead. He was suffocating on the smoggy, industrial air and pushed himself back up onto the main street. He couldn't imagine what the man might do but his anger had inebriated him, pulled him outside of himself so that he had acted purely on impulse. Two days later, he discovered it was worse than anything he could have imagined.

Too many police officers crowded in the doorway of the station when he came up the driveway that morning, voices climbing over each other; some men pulled out cigarettes with trembling fingers, forgetting about their rations and lighting one after the other, over and over, the air smelling of wet ash.

'What happened?' Jeffery pulled the men out of his way, his large stature forcing its way through. 'Why is everyone standing here like this?' Stopping dead himself when he reached the front of the crowd.

His shock came up all at once, a massive roil, and he had to look away while he swallowed it down. David's body, strung up by thick rope to a hook in the ceiling where an old lampshade used to hang, took a pendulous swing, the tips of his polished black shoes scraping the table eerily. Jeffery noticed that his shoelaces had come undone and he felt an urgency to retie them properly.

'Get him down, *mafalas!*' Jeffery scrambled to get up on the table. 'What are you doing, staring like that? Get him down right now.'

He struggled to hoist himself up, had to pause to catch his breath and found that some men behind him were sniggering, shivering with silent mockery. 'David, David!' He grappled at the dead man's shirt, the mud-flecked hems of his trousers, trying to release him but unable to figure out the first step in doing so, his mind was such a daze. 'This is not what I wanted!' he cried out before realizing he was giving away too much.

A few of the younger officers took Jeffery's place, springing up onto the desk and using a knife to sever the rope around David's thickened, bruised windpipe. He fell, a loud thundering crash, and six men came rushing forward to catch his limp body.

When he was taken from the station half an hour later, wrapped in a black polythene sheet in the back of an ambulance, the image of death lingered in Jeffery's mind.

He believed he had seen the worst of it, witnessing his mother shrink and disappear into her own waste, but this was equally horrifying because though he had been angry with his friend, Jeffery was certain that he would also be lost without him. He put his head in his hands and made a tally: two deaths to his name.

This one was put down to suicide. Too much pressure, the police commissioner had said in front of a host of media. Frenzied, blood-thirsty animals who failed to grasp the dreadful reality of the situation. To them, David had always been dead, whereas Jeffery remembered the gravel rasp of his voice, the brown-stained smile, the softness that fell across his eyes every time someone mentioned his wife.

The commissioner was equally disillusioned. He glorified David as a shining example for all other police officers, adding credentials to his name – a fighter of crime, a patriot in love with his country; he would be sorely missed and had given the commissioner a lot to reflect upon regarding the living standards of the police force, who were the backbone of Kenyan society. And when Jeffery was named the new senior officer later on that very day, he couldn't turn it down, reminding himself that if he did so, his friend's death would have been in vain.

He refused to attend the funeral, instead heading in search of Marlyn after many months, stepping into the dim Westlands bar and, without waiting for her to finish her shift, took her to the Jacaranda Hotel. He was rough and angry with her, and when she cried out he put a hand over her mouth and nose, gripping his fingers tightly together.

'His poor wife. What will she do now?' Marlyn was pressing the sides of her cheeks lightly, where he had bruised her. He hadn't responded but her question had given him an idea of how he could relieve himself of his guilt. After leaving her that night, he went to David's house and walked in to find Esther packing.

'Where are you going?'

'Upcountry, to my family home. How can I stay here alone?'

She looked even smaller and more like his mother. He caught her by both arms and promised, 'I'll look after you.' When she staggered back in confusion, he added, 'It's what David would have wanted.'

He left his house in Kibera and everything that was in it and took his final bus ride into the city a week later, where he moved straight into his friend's South C home. He climbed into bed with his wife and claimed her and that was where, several months later, he was roused and frightened by the obese and greedy stranger smirking back at him from the unformed, shapeless reflection of the exposed windows.

27

Leena walked the empty corridor, turning the lights on as she went. The smooth marble tiles were cold so she raised herself on tiptoes and continued down the stairs. She never noticed how big the house was except for when she was alone in it, staring into the deserted, quiet rooms, some of which they used and a few of which always remained unoccupied.

There was a drawing room her mother had set up in the hopes of entertaining their new neighbors, complete with a colonial-style coffee table and an extravagant divan couch. The plush, ruby carpet blended with the dark, wood-paneled walls and the impressive bookcase, filled almost entirely with Raj's old cricket trophies. The furniture here was now draped in white bedsheets because, as Pooja had come to discover, the neighbors in Runda minded their own business.

'And they're all *gorahs*!' she had exclaimed, dismayed, a week after they had moved in. 'You tricked me, Raj Kohli. What will I do now for company with only white people living here?'

'There is a Punjabi family living three doors up.' Raj tried to placate her. 'Why don't you go and disturb them?'

'How much can I speak to one woman?'

'You mean, how much gossip can one woman give you?' her husband had teased back.

Despite her reservations, Pooja had visited the family anyway, had met Roopa Sharma, and to Raj's relief, it was within this woman's impeccably decorated, three-story house that Pooja found some of the comfort she was seeking.

That night, Leena lay down on the well-worn couch of their family room, looking through the French doors into the garden outside. It was dark and she couldn't make out the shape of things, but heard the wide leaves of the banana trees scratching the glass, bothered by the rain that had just begun to fall.

It was rare that she was left at home by herself, but today her parents had a wedding to attend and Jai was staying late on campus at Nairobi University. She checked the clock on the wall, hoping that he would be home soon.

Every creak and rattle startled her, though she was comforted by the night guard's footsteps patrolling the house at thirty-minute intervals. It reminded her of how she had felt those first few evenings here in Runda, surrounded by too much empty space. All the night sounds that had been so comforting in her old home had spread themselves out here, become bigger and louder and drove her deep into the cushions.

She recalled the first time they had pulled a left turn from the main road, into an emerald side street. How deathly silent it had been, stepping out of the car – disconcerting not to see other children playing in the driveway or hear the shouts of so many women; there was no sign of activity at the new house except for the bustling of insects in flower pots and the rustling leaves of the aging blue gum tree guarding the gate.

Though the house itself was new, it had been built in an old, colonial style – an attempt to recapture a time when life in Kenya had followed a slow and dreamy rhythm – and the flat, wide open garden stretching out behind it was a mosaic of green. Perfectly symmetrical, with a gambrel roof and curved eaves, she had instantly been drawn to the house and, when she stepped inside, sunlight had drowned her on all sides.

Jai had removed his socks and slid along the polished floor, while her mother floated trance-like from room to room. It was so different from the cramped apartment, holding promises of a life where lunches were a lazy, drawn-out affair, complete with pink gin fizzes and evenings that were reserved for high-society parties, where her guests would dance out on the patio until early morning.

'This is not Happy Valley,' her husband had reminded her. 'Where people come to get drunk and swap wives.'

'You take the fun out of everything,' she had pouted, at which he had laughed and kissed her temple.

That day, they had eaten lunch in the garden. Pooja had spread an old tablecloth over the grass, beneath the low branches of a growing, white hibiscus tree and they ate egg sandwiches and drank cold juice from plastic cups.

'Isn't it beautiful?' Pooja had mused, pulling in the air through her nostrils. 'Remember this moment,' she told her children, her thoughts wandering and serene. 'This is what happiness feels like.'

Warmed by the sun, Leena had agreed with her, but then came the inky cover of night and she was alone for the first time in her life. She dreamt of Michael and Angela, saw them crossing the black garden and blending in amongst the flame trees – was certain she heard them slip through the French doors and creep up the stairs to come and stand over her bed. They were frowning and disappointed that she had not thought about them once that day. But then morning came and with it, brazen sunlight, and she had jumped eagerly from her bed to throw open the curtains. The garden was empty, with everything in its place, and she had felt silly and childish for having been so frightened.

'It's because you miss them,' Jai had told her. 'I dream about them too.'

But the dreams stayed only for a few days, though she never admitted it to her brother. Leena became so caught up in the excitement of her new life that she forgot to think of what she had left behind.

She and Pooja spent the first few weeks rearranging the furniture, walking the garden and attempting to identify every tree and flower; they went shopping for new paintings to put up on bare walls, for the divan couch that had golden tassels and looked like something out of a fairy tale. They went from store to store, collecting previously unheard of items that now fit perfectly in their lives. Things such as laundry baskets and potpourri – Pooja even bought a wine rack in the shape of a curvy Maasai woman, made from minuscule beads, and a hand-blown glass vase that was like swirling seas of color.

In these shops, Leena would meet more *gorahs* than she had ever seen. French, German, British – all with the same polite disposition and indifferent attitudes. They didn't stare or stop to make conversation the way she was used to, and though they smiled, it was brief and courteous.

She listened to them converse in magical accents, which she practiced in front of the mirror: 'Isn't that a *lovely* dress. Hello, Mrs *Cow-Lee*, have a nice day!' raising her voice to a singing top note. She transported herself to the cobbled streets of London, as elegant and reserved as these women were in their loose blouses and pressed chinos, their sweatless skin, their clipped speech a refreshing change from the abrasive shouts of the women she remembered from the compound.

These Runda women never ate with their fingers or leaned down to twist her chin, commenting on her many flaws and how she must groom them if she ever wanted to find a husband.

'Boring,' Pooja had told her as they drove home from one such shop. 'They're plain and boring with no taste for life. Just straight, straight faces all the time.'

'They mind their own business,' Leena had argued.

'It's because they're selfish, thinking of themselves only. We *care* about each other.'

Every time they would come home from one of these excursions, Pooja would park the car and lean over the backseat, reaching for every item and removing the price tags, careful to make sure that Betty, the new maid, never saw how much they were spending.

But Jai was different in the new house. Sullen and moody, he spent most of his time locked up in his room. When Leena knocked on his door to ask if she could join him or if he wanted to play with her in the garden, he told her that he was busy and snidely remarked that she should go shopping or meet her friends at the new cinema that had opened up only ten minutes away. He said these things to her with heavy distaste, scowling and turning back to his books, as if her new-found happiness was the greatest insult he had ever received.

Later that night, still on the sofa, Leena was startled awake by a noise. She jerked upright, disorientated and rubbing away her sleep in the two o'clock morning darkness. It took her a moment to realize that it was a woman shouting and her first instinct was to think that it was her mother, that they were being robbed. She perched, frozen, at the end of the couch.

When Jai entered the room, she was flooded with hot relief. 'Who is that?'

'I'm going to check.'

She followed him out to the gate with a hammering chest, where he stopped to speak in Swahili to the guard. Jai had become fluent after Raj had enrolled him in extra classes, and though Leena had begged to go with him, Pooja had refused, asking, 'Why on earth would you need to speak Swahili?'

As the two of them stepped out of the vicinity of their gate, the voices grew louder and Leena now heard a man speaking over the frantic tones of the woman. She was trying to say something but he kept interrupting her with words that were like a sledge hammer, heavy and careless.

'Go back in and go to bed,' Pooja commanded when she saw her daughter emerge, but Leena ignored her because the scene gathering on the street was too intriguing.

A few of the other residents had come out of their houses, dressed in pajamas and wrapping their robes around them, peering up the hill toward the arguing shadows.

'That's the Sharma's daughter,' Pooja whispered loudly. 'She's on holiday from university in England.'

Leena heard the other neighbors snicker at Pooja when she said this, rolling their eyes at her nosy interest. When she turned back to the voices, she saw that the girl was clutching an armload of clothes, pleading, 'Please don't do this. I don't have anywhere to go.'

'You should have thought about that before you touched that—' The man's voice faltered before he spit out words, ripe with disgust. 'That *askari*.'

Pooja's astounded, delighted shock caused her to unashamedly exclaim, '*Uh-reh!*' too loudly, so that Leena had to clap her hand over her mother's mouth.

'People can hear you, Ma,' she hissed, looking apologetically at the German woman who lived opposite them, and who was now shaking her head.

'Well, how can you hang your panties out to dry and then blame people for looking?' Pooja demanded to know, turning to their neighbor and calling out in a sing-song voice, 'Isn't that so, Mrs Schultz?'

'His name is Patrick,' the Sharma girl was saying.

'I don't care. Do you have any idea what people are going to say about you? About us?' The man was tugging at his *langar*, the traditional Indian sarong tucked around his waist.

'He's a human being just like you and me and if people can't understand that then I don't care what they think.'

'Good for her.' Mrs Schultz glared at Pooja, who in turn muttered pointedly.

'These *gorahs*. Really.'

'So go and live with him then.' The man threw a duffle bag at her. 'Pack up your things and go.'

The Sharma girl unzipped the bag slowly, her head tilted up to her father. 'I never meant to hurt you but I won't apologize for it. In London, things like this happen all the time. It's natural, *baba* – it's not a sin.'

'Do they also teach you to run around with a boy behind your family's back? To have a relationship outside of marriage? Outside of your culture? We have our own rules here, our own traditions. Or don't you remember them, have you become so corrupted?'

'It's not that simple.'

The man pointed in the direction of the main road. 'Take your Queen Elizabeth ideas and leave. But when you come to your senses, don't run back here. You don't belong to this family any more.'

The girl panicked. 'Just try to see my side of the story – I don't want to leave you.'

'And I don't want to see you in this house ever again.'

'You know how unsafe it is here at night-time. Where will I go?'

'Go and live with Patrick.' The voice was malicious in its power.

'How can he speak to his daughter that way?' asked a devastated Mrs Schultz.

'He's teaching her a lesson. She must know she cannot shame her family that way,' Pooja told her neighbor.

Mrs Shultz's pale, wrinkled face turned beet. 'And how exactly did she do that, Mrs *Cow-Li*?'

'*Ko-Lee*,' Pooja corrected her, pursing her lips and saying, as if speaking to a child, 'it's *Ko-Lee*.'

Raj stood a little ahead of them, a broad figure on the grass with his legs spread wide, hands tucked together behind him. He watched as the man strode back into his house, the Sharma girl collecting up her clothes, stifled sobs rising occasionally in the cold stillness. Pooja and Jai sneaked a shared look. *I told you so*, his mother's eyes said and Pooja was glad she had taken early precautions to ensure that a similar thing would never happen to her daughter.

'Show time is over,' she announced, ushering Leena back into the house. '*Chalo*, let's go to bed. Goodnight, Mrs Schultz!'

Before Leena stepped into the gate, she saw her father gesture Jai over. He said, 'Go and get her. She'll stay with us tonight.'

Pooja protested but Raj held his hand up to silence her, looking more somber than Leena could ever remember him being.

'This isn't a discussion,' he said, watching as Jai picked up the girl's bags and ushered her down the hill. Leena saw it then, the return of an old glint in Raj's eye, the proud twisting of his lips, and had never been more envious of her brother.

*

'That girl's mother will never speak to me again!' Pooja wailed from upstairs – 'What have you done, Raj? Just like always, only thinking about yourself!' – before her husband closed the bedroom door and made their voices disappear.

Jai and Leena sat opposite the young woman, her muscles jerking occasionally with a shiver, fists clutched between her knees.

'Do you want some tea?' Leena tried to be helpful.

The girl attempted a smile but instead her face contracted and her eyes became wet. 'If you wouldn't mind. I'm so sorry for all of this.' Her words came out in bursts. 'I don't know what I would have done if you hadn't taken me in.'

'We couldn't have let you stay out there.'

'You must think I'm crazy.' She accepted the tea from Leena gratefully, wrapping her long fingers around the cup to keep warm. 'But I couldn't take it any more.'

'Take what?' Leena asked.

'The idea that all I am good for is marrying an Indian man and having babies.'

She was so straightforward, so comfortable with having an opinion of her own, that she reminded Leena of all those European women she had spent such long hours copying. She wondered if going to England did that to you, filled you up with yourself and, if so, she made up her mind that she would go, no matter what.

'You're still shivering,' Jai noted, turning to his sister. 'Leena, can you get—' He waited for a name.

'Simran.'

'Simran, a sweater?'

He waited until he was sure his sister was out of earshot before turning back to Simran. 'Can I ask you a question?'

The girl paused, the lip of the cup to her mouth. She was enjoying the curls of steam rising up around her chin, thawing some of the cold from her bones. 'Considering you just saved my life, sure.'

'It's personal so you don't have to answer if it makes you uncomfortable.'

The way he spoke, with an urgent undercurrent to every word, made her wonder if anyone had ever refused him.

'Ask away.'

'What happened between you and Patrick?'

She liked that he called him Patrick and not the askari or the night guard, the way everyone else she knew would have done. 'My father caught us kissing.' She paused, trying to gauge his reaction. If her confession shocked him, he didn't show it. 'You know, when you leave this place, you think about things in a different way.'

'But you don't love him.'

She let out a dry laugh. 'No. It's just early adulthood rebellion, or that's my father's opinion anyway. I found Patrick attractive and somewhat intriguing but that's it. If I did love him, I would be more worried.'

'What do you mean?'

'Even I can see that a relationship like that would never work.'

'Why not?' There was a force in his voice that made her hesitate – as if he had needed a different answer.

'We're worlds apart. I know it shouldn't matter but it does. When you come from completely different places, when your ideas on life never meet, it's impossible to understand each other on any kind of deep level. Even the language barrier imposes a sort of shallowness.' She took a sip of tea, swirled it thoughtfully in her mouth. 'You'd be fighting your whole life – fighting other people, fighting each other. I don't want that.'

Jai sat back, thinking of the *I-told-you-so* look his mother had given him outside, and recalling a particular incident that had taken place a few weeks after they had moved into the new house.

Leena had been at the mall with her friends that afternoon and he had entered the living room, where his father was reading the newspaper, ignoring his mother as she complained about the Pio Gama Pinto picture he had hung up above the fireplace.

'Why can't you just get a proper painting instead of sticking up this old newspaper, making us look like beggars?'

Jai had stopped at the doorway, taking a preparatory breath. 'I want to go and see Mike.'

'I'll take you,' Raj had offered almost instantly.

'No, you won't,' Pooja interrupted.

'You can't stop me, Ma. He's my friend.'

Pooja's nostrils flared. She had not moved to this lonely house, away from all her friends and into the land of pink-faced, hoity-toity strangers, for nothing. 'Why can't you just listen to me for once? Why does everything have to be a fight?'

'You're the only one fighting,' Raj had told her. 'There's nothing wrong with Jai being the boy's friend.'

'There's everything wrong with it!' But when asked what, Pooja found it difficult to put into words. 'What other children do you know who are friends with such kinds of people?'

'I'm tired of hearing you talk in this closed-minded manner.' Her husband had risen, gone to the door.

'And you!' She hurried to block his path. 'You've stretched your mind so far open, even dirt is getting inside it!'

'Let's go before your mother gets carried away,' Raj had told his son.

'Fine, go. But leave Leena out of it.'

Her ultimatum made them pause. 'What do you mean by that?' Jai asked.

'I don't want her to know that you're meeting him.' Now, more than ever, his mother appeared vulnerable. Shrunken in fright. 'She needs to grow up and find some friends of her own.'

'Michael is her friend.'

Pooja gave a shudder and said to her son, 'You're a clever boy. Think of how people will look at her if anything should happen—' Unable to finish her sentence, she grabbed her husband's hand, the cold metal of her rings digging into his skin.

'If you care about your daughter at least half as much as you do your son, you'll make him see some sense.'

'Do you understand what your mother is saying?'

Jai hadn't liked the thought of lying to Leena or Michael but he had never disobeyed his father so he said, 'Okay, Ma. Whatever you want.'

She had snapped, returning to the couch, 'I wanted them out of our lives but you two are as stubborn as donkeys.'

But she was less aggravated, even close to smiling, as she turned back to the TV.

Now, listening to Simran at the table, Jai wondered if his mother had had a point. 'Would you have fought for him, if you loved him?' he asked.

She hesitated. It was a difficult question and, no matter how much she had changed in her first year abroad, there were some customs she had found impossible to escape, so deeply entrenched were their narratives within her. 'Something like that would take two very brave people.'

When Leena came back down into the kitchen, Jai quickly changed the subject. He told Simran, 'We have a guest room upstairs. You can sleep there.'

She thanked them again as the shouts of a woman dragged their eyes and ears upward.

'I don't know why I married you! You are going to kill me with these thoughts of yours, Raj Kohli – I swear it.'

Simran winced. 'I hope I didn't cause your mother too much trouble.'

'She's always like that,' Jai assured her with a grin to his sister. 'Tomorrow it'll be something else and you'll be old news.'

28

In what he had come to consider a lucky twist of fortune, Jeffery had met Nick a year ago. He had heard from some of the other officers that there were young boys, fresh out of university and unemployed, selling illegally obtained electronics in the back alleys of Mathare slums.

He had been making enough money from the *saccos* by then. Being senior officer meant that he took home the biggest share of the profits and he had the liberty of dipping his fingers into whatever else the juniors were involved in. Normally, it would be difficult for a senior officer to keep track of their activity, but after what had happened with David, they all feared him too much to lie.

'Killed him first and then took his house. And then his wife. Imagine! And he was his *friend*. Now think, what could he do to us?'

This was the kind of conversation Jeffery was used to hearing outside his office when he closed the door and pretended to work, but instead leaned against the window and gathered up the words through the spaces between its sea-green glass slates. Of course, he would always feel guilty but it was more infrequent now, and every time he deposited three hundred thousand shillings into his bank account, David was forgotten completely.

And so Jeffery had made his trip to Mathare slums.

Nick's 'office' was a wooden stool beneath an umbrella, sharing the small lane with glued-up street boys and other drug addicts lying immobile on foul mounds of garbage. Jeffery had worked his way through the mess, disgusted by them and forgetting that he too had once been forced to live that way.

Back then, Nick had been stealing the phones himself – going down busy streets in town and snatching them from peoples' ears and pockets, seeking refuge in back alleys where pedestrians were always reluctant to follow him. More often than not, they never chased him. It was as if they expected to be robbed and so, when it happened, all they did was throw their hands up in the air and yell, 'Shit!'

But as the year passed, and with the help of Jeffery's connections, Nick's business grew and he began to employ those very same drug addicts he had shared a space with, getting them to do the stealing for him in exchange for money.

'You must always cover your tracks,' Jeffery had taught him, 'so that one day, if someone should discover this little shop, they will never be able to trace the stealing back to you.'

The day he had first gone into the slum in search of Nick, he had stopped leisurely at his table and said in his most pleasant voice, '*Kijana, niaje?*' tucking his fingers into his belt loops and letting his belly fall out.

'Officer.' Nick had whipped off his headphones and stared in dismay at his merchandise, which was on full display, and he realized that it was too late to hide it.

Jeffery bent down. '*Sema*, where did you get all of these phones?'

'Some I bought, most are what people threw out and I found.'

Jeffery cocked his head in question, picking up a Nokia that looked almost brand new. 'Now tell me, why would a person throw out such a one?'.

'Maybe they thought it was broken.'

'And maybe you think I'm a *mjinga*,' Jeffery mocked. 'Do you think I'm a fool?'

'No, *mzee*.'

'*Toa* ten K and I won't take you to the station.' Jeffery was impatient to leave that place, which reminded him so much of things he wished to forget.

'Officer, *sikia*—' the boy started.

'Do you want to spend the night in a jail cell?' Jeffery asked. 'I can arrange that, though many things happen there, nothing good.'

The boy unzipped his backpack and reluctantly pulled out cash roped together by a brown elastic band. Counting out ten thousand shillings, he scowled as Jeffery snatched it away. The police officer pushed it into his pocket, felt the wonderful weight of it ground him.

'*Asante*.' As he turned to leave, he spotted a man sitting against the hard wall of garbage, staring up at him accusingly. Jeffery kicked him in the shins. '*Una angalia nini, wewe*?' he snapped, before realizing that the man was blind. Then, agreeably to the boy, 'See you next week.'

As the months went on, Jeffery and Nick agreed on a percentage of seventy to thirty of everything the boy made. They met every Wednesday at the bar in Westlands at three o'clock in the afternoon. It was a brief transaction; the boy would pass him as if going to the toilet, slide the money into Jeffery's lap and the officer would count it, hiding it low under the table.

One day, in the cheap motel he sometimes took her to, Marlyn asked, while buttoning up her blouse, 'How do you know the boy isn't cheating you?'

He lit up a cigarette and allowed the sheets to fall about him as he reached for his empty whiskey glass to use as an ashtray. 'He knows what will happen to him if he does.'

'What?'

Jeffery extended his index and middle finger, placed perpendicular to his thumb, which was raised straight up above his closed fist. He held the finger gun to Marlyn's temple, pulled the imaginary trigger and said, '*Pap.*'

'You need to expand your business,' he told Nick soon after their last meeting at the bar. 'You can't expect to make a decent living selling only phones.'

'How else can I make money like that?'

'*Pale zote,*' Jeffery said. 'That is what is so wonderful about this country! There is a job for every man, you just have to be smart. There's cocaine, booze, pussy, but for you,' glancing disdainfully at the meek boy dressed like a school teacher, 'the easiest would be spare parts.'

'How shall I start?'

Nick hated Jeffery – found him mannerless and so greedy that he was like a whimpering hyena every time you showed him the straight, hexagonal edges of a five shilling coin. But the police officer knew many people, was like a magician, able to pull profits from even the poorest man.

'I know someone – he sells second-hand car parts to people looking for cheap deals. Emblems, side mirrors, headlights, those kinds of things. He's looking for a supplier and he'll pay you a lot more than what you get for those broken *simus.*' He didn't mention that the same man had promised Jeffery a cut of the profits, should Jeffery find him a young, naive supplier.

'Those parts will be hard to get if I'm working alone,' Nick replied. It would require stealing them from cars – those that were parked, stuck in back-to-back traffic – or snatching them from other thieves, and to do so he would need a team.

'Then find someone to help you, that's not my problem.' Jeffery jerked the boy's collar. 'I won't be so kind next time.'

Nick was now working with two other men.

'We've become a gang,' he told Jeffery, as if in warning.

The police officer spat out his drink in a loud snort of amusement. It was humorous to picture the bespectacled former medical student as being a part of something so risky. 'Are you threatening me?' Jeffery leaned in closer to Nick. 'How many times do I have to warn you, *kijana*, before I simply put one in your head and throw you into the river, with the rest of Nairobi's filth?'

Nick, who came from a respectable middle-class family, had only started selling phones on the side for some extra cash to spend in nightclubs and to buy the occasional joint, but now found himself embroiled in a gang who specialized in selling cocaine and a police officer who was even worse than that. 'I'm sorry,' he squeaked.

'As long as I continue being happy with my share, then it's *sawa*. You do whatever you want.' Jeffery accepted the forty thousand shillings placed in his eager palm, more than the boy had ever given him in a single transaction.

After the boy had left, Jeffery leaned out into the smog-filled air and watched the chaos of the city unfurl beneath him. Street vendors selling baby animals – puppies, kittens, rabbits – *chokoras* with their fresh peanuts wrapped in newspaper cones, a woman setting up a hot-dog cart ready for the late-night trade – he could see every kind of *duka* imaginable.

He smiled widely, intrigued by what was happening outside: a young girl leading an old woman down the traffic-blocked street. The elderly lady wore a scarf and in her hand was a broken cane. She walked slowly, pushing out the walking stick to tap and check that she was on the right path. Her eyes were open and she stared blankly ahead, never blinking. It was the one aspect of the trick Jeffery had never understood. How they managed to hold their eyes open for so long, keep them so unseeing, when in fact they were only pretending, because sympathy was a powerful tool. He saw a hand stretch out from behind a car window, could almost hear the sharp cling of coins dropping into the girl's cup and he chuckled, for how could one not love such a city? It was brimming with countless opportunities; one only had to be creative enough.

29

It was during the last month of the first semester at the University of Nairobi that Michael and Jai joined their first student protest.

They discovered the details from a girl in the outdoor cafeteria, as she moved in and out of the narrow aisles between tables, clutching flyers to her chest. She stopped at their table, sliding into the bench seat. Ignoring Jai, she directed her words at Michael, speaking in Swahili.

'There's a demonstration planned three days from now – we're going to protest the proposed fee increment the government is planning.'

'I haven't heard of anything.' Michael tore a sizable chunk from his chapati and dipped it into his beef stew. He rolled it up neatly and tilted his head sideways to take a generous bite.

'They haven't announced it yet but we have a very reliable source who tells us that the fees are going up from fourteen thousand shillings a semester to twenty-two thousand.'

'Where is it taking place?' Jai asked.

'You speak Swahili.' It was a surprised statement, spoken in English.

'You speak English?' His voice was just as skeptical and he spoke with such a straight face that the only thing telling her he was joking was Michael's laughter.

Slightly discomfited by the strange paradox – a *muhindi* who spoke like one of them – she hesitated but told him anyway. 'It's in the city center' – leaving the flyer on the table. 'The details are all in there, got to go!' and she flew off to the next table.

'Do you want to go?' Michael asked as Jai picked up the flyer. It had the date, time and meeting place and, at the bottom, in thick black ink, it said *Comrade Power.*

He tested the words silently and then, to Michael, 'Yes, of course. It's at ten o'clock on Thursday.'

'But what would your mother say!' Michael asked in mock horror.

Ever since Jai had joined the university his mother had not stopped complaining. From his slightly too-wild hair, which hung in mild curls at his neck, to the books he had begun borrowing from the university library, marked up with small scraps of paper, to his absences at the dining table in the evenings, she accused him of being inattentive and selfish, lost in crazy thoughts that none of them had the capacity to understand.

It was in part her anger, her disdain for his actions that drove him further from home and deeper into the small, leather-bound books of history that he found in the libraries and in his classes. Now, excited to have finally been called into action, he shrugged at his friend. 'She'll never find out.'

'These protests are known for becoming violent.' Michael had turned serious. 'It's a breeding ground for looting, stone fights and a war with policemen.'

'Are you saying you don't want to go?'

'I'm saying we ought to be careful.'

'You're afraid I'm going to take charge of the whole thing, aren't you?' Jai accused his friend wryly.

'At least for this one,' Michael said, tilting his plate and wiping up the remainder of his stew with the ends of his chapati, 'let's stick to being spectators.'

They had been hoping for a light rain or even a relieving cover of cloud that Thursday morning, but the sun bore down from the sky, which was as cloudless and blue as ever. The light T-shirt Jai wore already felt heavy and he put a hand over his eyes, squinting.

He had expected it to be more orderly and was slightly disappointed to see that the students were not better organized, or even attentive. They did not seem to share the building excitement that caused his words and muscles to move at an alarming pace. Instead, most of them were spread out across a wide area of the main campus, laughing and conversing amongst themselves, as if it were just an ordinary day. Some were seated at the edges of flower beds, others lounging on the field – though a large circle was slowly being formed around the high steps as one man climbed to the top with a megaphone and threw his fist in the air.

'Comrade Power!' he shouted, stretching out the first word, *Cooom-rade*, and sending out the last with a sharp burst from his mouth.

'Yes!' came the reply.

'*Cooom-rade POWER!*' A swell of noise, a host of closed fists rising in unison. Jai joined in but Michael stayed silent. It was one thing to shout it out alone but to do it amongst so many other voices Jai felt the conviction more strongly, rising up in his chest and warming his cheeks.

'Let's get closer,' he urged Michael, pushing his way to the front of the crowd despite his promise to remain an observer. Michael had no choice but to follow until they were standing on the lowest step, facing the young leader.

'We want peace, we want peace.' He bobbed his palms up and down, encouraging the crowd to chant along with him. 'Peace, peace, peace.' As his voice tapered and the shouting died down, an expectant hush fell over the students. They waited for him to continue.

He addressed them gravely. 'Let us say – we are not going to interfere with any businesses in the CBD.'

'Yes!' the crowd shouted back.

'Let us say – we are not going to vandalize anybody's property.'

'Yes!'

'Let us say – we are *not* going to interfere with *anybody* in the CBD. Everyone in the CBD is safe.'

'Yes!'

'But what do we insist upon?' The man leaned down, repeating it louder. 'What do we insist on? If the government is not going to succumb to our demands, then no rest! No peace!'

'No rest! No peace!'

He turned toward the building behind him, came down as far as the last step and the crowd parted for him. He looked up, where several students were leaning out of the windows to watch the commotion. He shouted at them, 'We're calling upon all of you now – the cowards up there who have not joined us today – we are doing this for you!' Back to facing the group, he sprang theatrically from a flower bed to the grass and out onto the paved street, making his way to the main road. 'It is now, *ama* now!' he yelled through the megaphone and the crowd moved with him, like a slow animal rising from sleep – a furious background to his words.

'*Cooom-rade POWER!*'

That morning, a slow drove of students made their way down University Avenue, two streets long and close to thirty people wide. Occasionally, someone pulled loose from the crowd to pick up stones or discarded tree branches, fanning flags of green leaves as they marched onward.

Five men led the protests, whistles in their mouths and animal-skin drums held close – one even hoisted a radio on to his shoulders and it played a cheerful song that people danced to and sung merrily as they walked, paralyzing the morning commuters. Some drivers honked and shouted and swore but most sat fearfully in their locked cars, searching for alternative routes.

Some students carried hastily made banners drawn up that morning on the university quad, constructed out of manila paper and Sharpies, shouting out slogans as they marched.

'Quality and affordable education for all Kenyans!'

'You cannot condemn a people unheard!'

'*Cooom-rade POWER!*'

'What does that mean?' Jai asked Michael.

He heard a girl's voice. 'It's the motto of the Students of Nairobi Union. Steven, the one who is leading the protest, came up with it during his first riot as chairman, and now it's become our anthem.'

Somehow, the girl from the cafeteria had found them, had fallen back in the crowd and placed herself in the center of the two boys. 'I'm surprised you came.' She spoke as if to both of them but looked at only one.

'I'm a student here too,' Jai reminded her. 'I don't want my fees to be raised for no reason other than to feed some already fat bellies.'

'But don't mummy and daddy pay for you with the profits from the big family business?'

'Just because my parents can afford to pay for my education doesn't mean I don't value money. I'm tired of you making gen-eralizations about the way I am.' Gone was the friendly expression and he lifted his fist to shout with the rest of the students, '*Cooom-rade POWER!*'

She was reproached by his tone. 'It's just that we don't get a lot of *muhindis* interested in joining our protests. I'm Ivy, by the way.'

'Then perhaps you should be friendlier to us *muhindis*, Ivy.'

Smiling, she began to weave her way back to the front, finding it easy, because of her tiny size, to push past the thickly packed rioters. She called over her shoulder, 'Come and find me after this is over and I'll introduce you to Steven.'

They marched throughout the morning as the sun gradually rose to its peak. By the time they reached the Central Business District, it was noon and most students had pulled off their shirts and wrapped them around their heads, shoulders or waists.

It was here that most of the city's stores and restaurants were situated and, as the protesters approached, Jai saw most shop owners frantically turn keys in locks and pull down the metal grilles guarding their doors, keeping their noses pressed to the windows and telephones in their laps, just in case things should start to go wrong.

They had been victims of many crimes during riots such as these, petty thieves looking to take advantage of the chaotic nature of the situation, hiding themselves within the massive crowd and sneaking into shops, helping themselves to whatever they wanted.

The smaller kiosks, which did not have such security measures, were more vulnerable and Jai, caught too far back to help, saw a woman scrambling to close the door of her shop. She was dragged out by four or five boys and thrown to the curb, left to watch as they raided her store – milk packets, coke bottles, bubblegum, some even pushing carrots and *sukuma wiki* into their backpacks – rejoining the group and saying, '*Asante*, Mama, for supporting our cause,' and then shouting out absurdly, as if what they had done in no way contradicted what they were fighting for, 'Justice! Justice! Justice!'

Steven Kimani was a small man with light skin and pleasant features. The broadness of his shoulders was exactly matched by the distance kept between his two feet, so that he looked like a tricky boxer readying himself for a fight.

'New comrades!' He shook their hands firmly and slowly, taking his time to look them in the eye and speaking as if these were words he had rehearsed and repeated countless times before. 'I'm proud of you, thank you for coming. Thank you for fighting. I hope you will be coming with us all the way to Jogo House, where we will be presenting a memorandum to the cabinet secretary.'

It was peaceful as yet. The anti-riot police had not arrived and so they were taking a break in the sweltering heat, lolling about on the traffic islands, on café chairs of now abandoned restaurants, or some simply lying down on the deserted main road. Jai watched as a student picked up two chairs and turned around, heading back in the direction of the campus.

'Many business owners have left the CBD for fear that we are going to be looting,' Steven was saying. 'But all we want is a peaceful demonstration, to fight for our right to affordable education because it is what the government promised us. But they are planning on increasing the fees, which as you know are already very expensive.'

'I saw some students raiding a woman's kiosk,' Jai told him. 'Another one just walked away with outdoor furniture from a coffee shop over there. I think the shop owners have a right to be anxious.'

Steven followed Jai's finger, two metal chairs tucked beneath the man's armpits and scraping along the road. 'There are over two thousand students at this rally and only one of me.' He turned back to Jai. 'It is a shame that some people are so weak in the face of temptation but most of us guys know what we are here for and don't allow ourselves to become distracted.'

It was easy to understand why people would want to follow such a man. He spoke with sturdy fluency and one felt comforted by him, encouraged to be as confident and assured. Steven never allowed his gaze to wander as he spoke, intent on catching every expression, every word, so that one emerged from the conversation feeling special and changed, and with a peculiar feeling that you owed him something back.

'Well, you are their leader,' Michael spoke up, refusing to be sucked into the man's obvious play. 'You should make sure that others don't suffer any violations of their rights while you are fighting for yours.'

A twisted smile bordering on a sneer, but Steven's voice remained courteous. 'I'll keep that in mind,' he said as he shook their hands once more and started to move down the road, shouting into his megaphone, '*Cooom-rade POWER! Cooom-rade POWER!*'

He picked up students as he went, dusting them off and encouraging them to reach for their signs and twigs, to slip rocks into their pockets. Soon, it would be time to face the police.

Jai couldn't be sure which side initiated it. It was difficult to see through the rising clouds of tear gas, difficult to concentrate with the rotten stench from the heated ground below. The crowd, gripped by a sudden hysteria, had begun to scatter and many students ran in a backward direction, seeking the shelter of trees and buildings, some even crawling under parked cars and setting off alarms.

Steven and Ivy, with a group gathering behind them, charged toward the defense line of anti-riot police. Someone shouted, 'They want to draw lines like it's a battlefield? Let's give them a war.'

This elicited a cheer amid the quick *bang!* of warning shots fired into the air by the police, the tear-gas canisters launched upward, largely ignored. One landed beside Michael's foot and he pulled Jai behind the cover of a parked Land Cruiser. Jai pulled off his shirt and wrapped it around his mouth and nose, encouraging Michael to do the same.

'Let's go,' said Jai, overcome with excitement.

'I thought we decided to stay back this time?' It wasn't fear that drove Michael to say this. It was the fact that he didn't believe in violence, in the sudden escalation of forcefulness on both sides – the potential bloodshed and fighting amongst people who knew nothing except that they were meant to be angry.

He watched from his ducked-down position as three men upended a street sign, struggling to bring it down and use part of it as a weapon.

'We didn't come all this way to turn back now,' his friend insisted and took off into the panicked crowd.

'*Cooom-rade POWER! Cooom-rade POWER!*'

It was clear that Steven had been hoping for this exact outcome. His voice carried even without the microphone and his face contracted with determination as he caught retreating students and pulled them forward by their shirt tails or their elbows, encouraging them back – all the while, thrusting his arm repeatedly into the air. 'No Justice! No peace! You cannot condemn a people unheard.'

When they reached Steven's side, he nodded at them with approval. 'Good, you stayed.'

The T-shirts around their faces helped keep the severity of the tear gas at bay, and though it stung the back of Jai's throat, making him cough uncomfortably into the cotton, he shouted, '*Cooom-rade POWER!*' and felt the strength of his voice lift even higher.

His gaze was cut through by the silver spiraling of a canister in the air, the high whistle of its trajectory filling his ears and, for a moment, the protest halted as he watched it come directly for Steven's head. Instinctively, Jai threw an arm around the man's waist and pulled him down so that the canister narrowly missed his cheek and slammed into Jai's upper arm. It ricocheted off him and threw itself further back into the crowd.

Jai brought his forehead to his knees, keeping his eyes shut tightly and his breath even tighter, but the canister never exploded.

'Get up – let me help you.'

As Michael dragged him from the crowd, Jai looked back with sinking horror to see that some students were crowded around the canister.

'Get away!' he shouted in Swahili. 'It's going to explode.'

He wanted to move toward them but his muscles cramped up, closing inward.

Michael left him there, shoving his way through the crowd and toward the canister. When he reached it, he kicked it in a long arc and it landed on a patch of garden, bursting open in three separate clouds of poison.

'You said we'd stay out of this one!' Michael said to his friend as he helped him across the road, away from the crowd. 'What were you thinking? Look at your arm.' As he spoke, he searched around for shelter.

'Over there.' Jai pointed to a small shop where an Indian man was leaning slightly out of the door.

As they approached, the sound of the riots fading into distant cries, Michael called out, 'Please, can you help us?'

The man looked prepared to close them out but then he saw Jai cradling his bloodied left arm and he shoved them inside, shutting the door securely behind them.

'You kids and your fighting,' he muttered, as the two boys fell to their knees at the entrance, coughing and gasping and dragging the T-shirts from their faces. The smoke had filled their throats and every breath was laborious, producing sticky and thick saliva. Their eyes were temporarily blinded by tears; it was as if they were viewing the shop from underwater – a lost city with grimacing masks – and Michael shut his eyes against it. He fought the clawing panic in his chest, pressing his palms to the ground, grateful for something steady and hard beneath him.

The man returned from the back of the shop with two pans of warm water and instructed the boys to wash their eyes with it, constantly returning to his window. As the stinging subsided and the world became solid once more, the shop owner said, 'Let me bring my first aid kit – that looks quite deep,' then, shaking his head, 'What were you thinking, taking your shirts off? Tomorrow, you'll see how much your skin will burn.'

Michael leaned his head in exhaustion against a wooden desk and closed his eyes.

'Are you okay?'

Jai was like an excited boy, still in the grip of his adrenaline. 'That was amazing!'

Michael didn't reply because on the contrary, he had felt like he had been amongst a pack of wild animals who had neither direction nor one defined purpose and, unlike Jai, he was certain that there were other, better ways of doing such things.

The man returned to fix Jai's arm and they stayed in the antique shop well into the evening, after all the students had been chased away and there was nothing but empty streets laden with rocks and the steel tinkles of tear-gas canisters rolling in the wind.

30

Esther had become an annoyance. More than that, she was his personal form of constant punishment. She had been more in love with David than Jeffery had imagined and the shock of his death had loosened something inside of her, leaving her constantly restless and muddled. Jeffery would often awake to noises in the kitchen or living room, the eerie scrape of chair legs as she dragged it to the open window, watching out over the road.

It was not long before this was accompanied by the clinking of a glass bottle as it rolled off the table top, empty. In all those times Jeffery had visited their house, Esther had refused to touch the alcohol her husband had so enjoyed. But now it was possible for her to go through half a bottle of whiskey during the day so that she would come to bed smelling sickly sweet and, on the worst evenings, like vomit.

One night, he heard her incoherent murmurings, louder than usual, and he crept down to see what she was doing, less out of worry than goaded by the desire to shut her up. The house creaked with the *swish swish* of passing cars, the drumming of the boys upstairs, which, when everything was closed, was like the vibrations of a lullaby. But now, they were hard and clear clashes of sound, filling him with sleepy irritation because she had opened all the windows.

Hidden within the shadows, Jeffery saw Esther stumble with the chair, catching herself at the doorway to the living room. She placed the seat beside the window and, grabbing the frame for support, hoisted herself up and steadied her shaking legs beneath her. Five months ago the slight piece of furniture would have held her weight easily, but now it strained and threatened to break beneath her body, which had ballooned with sorrow.

Her nightgown shifted about her body, revealing smooth, unbroken brown shadows and he noticed how, despite her skin having been forced to stretch over her growing size, it remained as taut and perfect as porcelain.

She placed one foot on the windowsill and edged slightly forward, gasping as the chair tilted beneath her, and brought her leg back down. She swallowed in gusts of cold air and clung to her stomach as the foot went back up, toes inching outward.

He should have let her do it. It had become impossible to forget the thing that he had done while she slept so close to him, seeking shelter in his warmth. Often, he would stare at Esther as she dreamed, her mouth slack and salivating, murmuring David's name. *Why, why, why have you left me here this way?* Every why was a fresh accusation, piling upon him like sin after sin until he was unable to breathe under the weight of her grief. He spent less time at home, some days with Marlyn, sometimes with other whores he found in bars, loitering on K-Street or even in the police station, when they came in to report assaults or robberies.

'I was waiting for a taxi and this car came by and the driver threw eggs at me!' one girl complained, holding a dirty tissue to her bleeding forehead. 'Then I dropped my purse in shock and they grabbed it faster than I could see.'

She couldn't have been more than seventeen. A poorly fitted halter top, cat-like red nails and lipstick that smudged higher than the natural curve of her lips. Jeffery scoffed. 'We both know you weren't there waiting for a taxi. But no matter, I'll escort you home personally.' Instead, he had driven her to a motel and taken what he wanted, leaving her no money but with a promise not to arrest her.

He would come home after all of this, haggard and staggering under his many crimes, only to be met with the worst one of all.

Yet something compelled him forward that dark night, as if David was watching, the ringed scars around his neck puckered and ghastly, begging Jeffery to save his wife. And how was it possible to refuse a man after taking his life?

So he grabbed Esther by the collar of her gown and yanked so hard that she fell on top of him, knocking the chair with her heel.

They lay that way for several stunned moments, two fat bellies and a broken chair, with the shouts of *matatus* down below and the thrumming of instruments up above.

'*Aki*, that boy can't even sing!' he had shouted, shoving her off him. 'How is a man supposed to get any sleep in this house?'

Esther stayed pressed to the floor, her skin dampened by drink and sweat, staining her pockmarks darker so that, in the moonlight, she looked truly horrendous.

'Go back to bed,' he had commanded.

Several minutes later, she was crawling in beside him and he was disgusted to find her fingers searching between his thighs. He slapped her hand away. 'Don't touch me.'

'Please, Jeffery.'

With his back to her, she was slim and sweet again and he derived a cruel satisfaction from her attempt to apologize. He took her hand and returned it.

When she was finished, he asked, 'Do you have any family here, Esther?'

'They all live upcountry.'

'Perhaps you should go stay with them for a while.'

He heard her fussing with the sheets, was horrified to discover that she was now touching herself. He had stolen away her husband and then failed to do what was required of one.

'I want to stay here.' She sounded like a small child.

'Then you can't keep acting this way.'

'I have a cousin living in Nairobi – her name is Betty. I will ask her to visit for a while – it might help me get better.'

'I'll go and stay with a friend while she's here,' he said, thinking of Marlyn and of how much he missed those dips and curves of her body, the inner softness of her thighs. A woman who knew how to take care of herself.

Esther didn't reply. He heard her panting, shifting beneath the sheets and it drove him from the bed, down into the living room, refusing to come back up until the next morning.

Two days later, in the lingering afternoon, when the sun tended toward evening, releasing its bright hold on the world, a small lizard climbed the water drain off the east side of the Kohlis' house. Occasionally, it paused to flick out its tongue, scales glowing green, yellow or purple depending on its position in the light.

The only sounds to be heard were the countless blue-jays, stirring up mini-tornadoes in the trees. Inside, infrequent footsteps could be heard in the kitchen as they moved from stove to sink – cooking, washing and drying all at once. Sometimes, Betty could be there until nine o'clock, depending on what time the Kohlis ate their dinner.

Upstairs, in the room at the head of the corridor, the curtains were drawn. Pooja appeared as nothing more than a slight bump under the covers and the only thing that gave her away was a leg jerking in sleep and dream stirrings.

Suddenly, she bolted upright, fighting against the bedsheets. It took her a few moments to reorganize the world and she clutched her pillow tightly. *It was only a nightmare.* She glanced at the telephone, wishing there was a way to contact him. She had to laugh at herself, for what would she say if she could? *Hello, son, are you alive?*

She checked her watch. The darkness in the room made it difficult to tell what time of day it was and when she saw it was closing in on five o'clock, she sprung out of bed. '*Baap-re-baap!* What will happen to dinner?' Searching for her slippers she rushed downstairs, shouting as she went, 'Betty! Betty, where are you?' and came skidding to a halt in the small kitchen, where she found her maid gone.

Just ten minutes before Pooja had woken up, a strange man had knocked on the Kohlis' gate. Betty had sprinted out to it, not bothering to wash away the soap suds on her hands, pulling it open before the noise could disturb Pooja.

She wished she had checked through the gap first, because the man standing at the low step didn't look like someone who might visit the Kohlis. He was breathing too heavily and spat out a thick, brown stream of tobacco, rubbing his tongue across his teeth.

'*Ni nini?*' she demanded.

'Betty?'

'Who are you?'

'My name is Jeffery.'

'What do you want?' She had partially closed the gate so that half of her body was protected.

'Do you know Esther Kipligat?' he asked.

She recognized the name from her mother's side of the family. 'Small?' she couldn't help but ask, curious. 'Short with *funny-funny* marks on her face?' she added, patting her cheeks.

'Yes, that one.'

'She's my cousin. Has something happened?' Immediately, she regretted admitting ties to this woman. If something had happened to Esther Kipligat, it would now be Betty's responsibility.

'Nothing has happened,' the man grimaced. 'Yet.' He stepped forward and took her hand before she could back away. 'We just want you to visit, that's all.'

'Who are you?' she asked again, this time more urgently.

'Her husband.' The word stuck in his throat and he coughed it out. 'She hasn't been feeling well – we've had much to deal with and I thought it might be good to have her family visit.'

Glancing back at the house, Betty saw Pooja's bedroom light flicker on. 'I have work to do.'

'Will you come?' She had never seen a man so desperately hopeful as he pressed down harder upon her fingers. 'I just need you to stay for four days with her. I'm afraid she might do something to herself.'

Betty was certain that Mrs Kohli wouldn't give her that many days off but she asked him anyway, 'Where do you live?'

'Victoria Courts in South C.'

'I'll talk to my employer. If she says yes, you'll see me tomorrow morning.'

'Thank you.' The man shook her hands wildly up and down. '*Asante sana!*'

'I have to go now.' She pushed the gate closed.

'Wait.' He stopped it with his palm, suddenly sounding different, sounding the way he looked – grossly vulgar. As if he no longer noticed her there, the man heaved his way up onto the driveway.

'Please, you must go. I'll lose my job if they see you.'

But he ignored her, too busy staring up at the house. Whitewashed walls and a roof made from brick tiles – it was like something out of a children's fairy tale, creeping out from behind the thick shade of tall trees.

Jeffery had felt powerful before coming here, the top man at the police station, but looking up at the house he was reminded of all the things he still did not have. Of all the people above him, still stomping, still drowning in luxuries bigger than anything he would ever be able to imagine. He stumbled backward as Betty closed the gate on him.

'I hope to see you tomorrow.' He regained his composure before hearing the turning click of the lock.

Betty pocketed the key and hurried back to the house, already hearing Mrs Kohli's shrill voice calling for her. 'Betty! For heaven's sake, where are you?'

Betty thought that perhaps, since she had not taken a holiday yet, this might be as good a reason as any to do so.

Pooja was waiting in the kitchen, tapping her slippered foot.

'I've been calling you,' she said sternly.

'I was just taking the rubbish out.' Betty wiped her hands nervously across her apron – back and forth, back and forth – leaving clumpy dust streaks behind.

'It's almost five thirty and there is nothing prepared for dinner.'

'I took some prawns out of the freezer, just like you asked me to.' Betty gestured to the plastic bowl filled with fish in icy water.

'And you've cleaned them? Deveined them like I showed you?'

'Yes.' It was a process Betty detested; poking the edge of her pinky into the gray-white flesh, getting a hold of the worm-like vein and carefully maneuvering it out with minimal damage. After she was done, her hands would be littered with fish insides and smelled like something terrible.

'Good.' Pooja closed her eyes, scratchy from sleep. Then, as if she had just remembered, she said, 'Leena is at her friend's house and Mr Kohli will be out tonight. It's just Jai and myself.' She stared down at the bucket of prawns. 'Since it's only two of us, we'll have something simple – sausages and eggs. Do we have baked beans?'

'I'll check the cupboard.' Betty was angry, having spent close to an hour cleaning the prawns. She wouldn't have minded so much if Mrs Kohli had given even a moment's notice to the time she had spent but the woman was moving out of the kitchen without a care. She called after her, 'Mrs Kohli? A cousin of mine has suddenly become unwell and has asked that I go and stay with her for a week.'

Pooja didn't pause for reflection. 'I can't possibly allow you to go for so long. What will happen to the work that needs to be done?'

You're here, aren't you? Isn't this your house?

Betty's silence was full of so many unsaid things.

'It's important I go. She's all alone.'

Pooja listened with impatience, resentful of being cornered in such a manner. *She's probably lying. They all do. If it's not malaria, it's pneumonia – if it's not pneumonia, it's an aunt who has died five times already.* 'What's her name?' she asked.

'Esther Kipligat.'

'Where does she live?'

'South C.'

'What's wrong with her?'

'She has pneumonia.' It was the first affliction that came to Esther's mind and she realized that the man had not told her what was wrong with her cousin.

Pooja cocked her lip. 'What was her name again?'

'Esther.'

It may or may not have been the same name as before, but Pooja couldn't remember. She sighed, disturbed by her dream and the small tickle of anxiety it had left festering. She wanted to lie down again.

'I'll allow you two days, but that's it. I need you back by Friday because we're having guests over.'

Betty was overcome by a surge of irritation. She wanted to shout. To let the woman know that this was only a job and not her whole life. *You don't own me*, she wanted to say.

Instead, a soft and helpless, 'Thank you.'

31

'So we meet once again.'

Jai looked up from his books, keeping his fingers tight on the page as it struggled, wanting to rise in the gust of wind blowing through the open cafeteria.

'Hi,' he greeted Steven Kimani.

The man slid onto the bench opposite him, his palms pressed down, elbows bent back so that he seemed, at any moment, ready to take off again.

'How's your arm? It looked like you hurt yourself badly.'

'It's starting to heal.' Jai rolled up his sleeve, showing the bandage. 'I wasn't able to thank you. You saved me from a big injury.'

'Comrade Power, right?' Saying it, Jai recalled a small bit of the excitement he had felt, chanting the phrase within a crowd of other voices. It sounded conventional and a little cheesy now, but he held the memory of how powerful it could be.

'Exactly so,' Steven nodded. 'Exactly so.'

Jai's eyes trailed down to his textbook, not reading but allowing the words to blur together, become ant-like images. Steven watched the students who milled in the open corridors, pausing against classroom doors to discuss weekend plans, to flirt and catch up.

'What must it be like to live your life so ignorantly?' Steven wondered out loud. His face turned hard, bitterly disappointed. 'Most of the students here accept whatever injustice comes their way. They will complain about it for a few days and then they'll simply accept it. This is how the government is, they say. This is Kenya. What can we do about it?' Jai looked up and met his questioning gaze. 'Why does no one believe in fighting for anything any more? We are so satisfied with being lazy.'

'I can't understand it either.' Jai felt a tug of affection for this man, their common frustrations tethering them to one another.

'You're different, I can see that. That's why I've come to find you.'

'What do you mean?'

'I want you to join the Student Union, of course. We desperately need more members like you.' Steven leaned forward, his fingertips hovering at the edge of Jai's textbook.

Jai had derived great satisfaction in the protest, the kind he had not been able to find in all his hours spent at the library or discussing his new ideas with Michael – and every time he thought about the canister propelling toward Steven, he felt a lightning pulse of adrenaline jerk his blood, making him light-headed.

But Michael had been quiet and reserved ever since that day, having made it known that he didn't approve of the violence and messiness that had arisen from the riots. He had told Jai, 'They weren't there to fight for the students. They were just there to fight.'

Steven broke into his thoughts. 'You're hesitating because you are an Indian, is it not? You're worried people won't take you seriously. They won't accept you as one of them.'

'Many Indo-Kenyans have that problem,' Jai acknowledged. 'But it's never been one of mine.'

'Because you care. I can see that in you – you care about Kenya, about this university. About *us. Kenya ni yetu, sindiyo?*' He rose, thumping his closed fist down on the table thoughtfully. 'The next meeting is on Friday after classes. Bring your friend if you want.'

After Steven had left, Jai reopened his book. He began to skim the pages but his mind kept wandering to the student protest, to the passion and eagerness in Steven's voice – flattered that he had been sought out. He contemplated how he would convince Michael to join him and finally snapped the textbook shut in frustration, because every time he caught onto a spark of an idea, he searched within it and came up blank.

On Friday evening, the campus was empty. Most students had returned to their dorms or gone into town to celebrate the weekend and fast-approaching Christmas holidays. Jai walked quickly down the corridor, throwing anxious glances at Michael.

'Thank you for coming with me.'

'It's only because I don't trust the guy.'

'You're just hesitant because of what happened at the protest,' Jai tried to reassure him. 'Sometimes it gets violent, even if no one wants it to, Mike.'

'He was enjoying it,' Michael insisted. 'He had been waiting for it. He's not like us.'

'Just go in there with an open mind.'

The lecture hall had peeling carpets and was built on a slight slope. Out of the hundred blue chairs packed into the room, only the first two rows on the left side were occupied. Steven was nowhere to be seen.

'We're so glad you could make it.' Ivy came up to greet them and gestured behind her. 'As you can see, we are always looking for new members.'

'Where's Steven?' Jai asked.

'He'll be here soon. Please have a seat.'

Ivy was the only woman in the room and the rest of the men cast curious glances toward Jai, whispering in Swahili. It had been his experience that most of them assumed he couldn't speak the language, hoped that he wouldn't because it justified their dislike. *What is he doing here? Does he think this is the Hilton Hotel?* They followed him with their stares as he sat down.

Usually, he would have answered with a funny one-liner in Swahili or a joke, but today he was preoccupied with what Steven had planned and so he said nothing.

Eventually, the discussion turned to the protest.

'Anthony was arrested,' one man said.

'That's the second time now.'

'If he's not careful, one day he might never come back out.'

The first man spoke up. 'Steven wasn't happy about it. That's why he called this meeting.'

Jai didn't have to wonder too long about what they meant because the space outside was soon filled with fast approaching footsteps and the door swung open.

'*Pole, pole.*' Steven strode to the podium with an armload of papers that he threw onto the table behind him. Ivy was there to prevent them from scattering onto the floor. 'I was in a meeting with the dean of the university, informing him that we are planning another protest.'

'What's this one for now?' Michael spoke up.

Steven glanced up from the first row of men. 'Ah, Jai. I see you've brought your friend.'

'What will you be protesting this time?' Michael stood. 'Ivy told us that we were protesting about school fees last time because a source told you that the government was planning a fee increment.'

'That's correct.' Steven held both sides of the podium, his fists tightening – 'such a contrast to Michael's cool assuredness, Jai's friend showing no sense of strain in his demeanor as he stood almost lazily with hands slung in his pockets.

'And yet never once did anyone else hear about it. Only you.'

'What's your point?'

'Why the second protest?' Michael's question was insistent. 'Another source telling you about another increase in fees?'

'Can you sit down? I'm the one conducting the meeting.' Steven looked toward Jai as he said this.

Jai tugged Michael's shirt sleeve. 'Can you hear him out at least?'

Reluctantly, Michael returned to his seat as Steven continued. 'As you all know, Anthony was injured and detained during the protest. He was taken to the police headquarters, where he remained for two days until I could persuade them to give him bail.' Steven paused with a dramatic breath. 'When he came out, that was when I saw how badly hurt he was and not from the protest either. He had some broken ribs and other injuries, which he informed me he got while in the jail cell.'

'It's the police!' someone shouted from the front row. 'They want to kill us all.'

'They want to silence us,' agreed Steven. 'They are working for men much more powerful than we can imagine. These men want to take all the money for themselves and build holiday houses and drive Range Rovers and send their children to fancy overseas schools. And who has to pay for all of this?'

'Us!' they shouted in unison. 'It is us who have to pay.'

'Whether it's with our money or our health or our lives, we are the ones paying.' A long, deliberate silence to let his words sink in. Then, in a hard tone, 'I'm sick of it.'

'What do we do?' someone called out.

'Ivy and I are in the process of planning another protest. Anthony will not have suffered in vain. We will make it clear to the public, to the dean of the school and the president that we will not back down. We will always fight for our rights. We will always fight for one of our own.' He turned to Jai and said, 'I want you to lead this protest with me.'

The energy that had been rising, warming the room, became icy. All heads turned in Jai's direction. Ivy dropped her clipboard, bent down to retrieve it and asked, her voice shaking slightly, 'What about me?'

'We must give everyone their chance to shine,' Steven told her.

Someone else protested, 'He's not even a Kenyan. He's just a *muhindi*.'

Buzzing with excitement from Steven's invitation, Jai interrupted, 'I was born in Nairobi. I've lived here my whole life.' He turned toward the man who had spoken but was met with the back of a head. 'I'm just as Kenyan as you are.'

'You may speak Swahili fluently and have a Kenyan friend,' Ivy swept her hand toward Michael, her cheery disposition gone, 'but we all know what kind of Kenyan you really are.'

'Which is what?'

'A member of the elite group who are so out of touch with being Kenyan, it's ridiculous. You probably live in Karen or Runda and went to British private school – the kind all rich kids go to. The kind of Kenyan who doesn't know what it's like to take a *matatu* until you grow up and decide to be wild with your friends and take one to town, just to see what it would feel like.'

Such accusations failed to anger him, though they always pinched slightly. 'Since when does one's social standing determine their Kenyanness? Are you saying that someone who lives in Kibera or

Mathare slums is more Kenyan than you, simply because you belong to a middle-class family?'

Another man came quickly to Ivy's defense. 'Let me tell you, there is no such thing as an Indian Kenyan. Kenya is a *black* country, even if you have lived here your whole life, you aren't Kenyan. We should have kicked you out back in the seventies, like they did in Uganda.'

Steven held up his hand. 'I've made my decision.'

'If he's helping you with the protest, I won't come,' said the man.

'Neither will I.' Ivy crossed her arms, her ultimatum heavy in the air.

Though he was ready to argue his point further, Jai sat back and said, 'I'll be glad to help.'

'We haven't discussed it yet,' Michael said to him.

'You aren't joined at the hip,' Steven said to him. 'Come if you want, or don't.'

'I have to show them they're wrong about me,' Jai told Michael in a low voice.

'This guy is using you for your skin color,' Michael warned him. 'He'll get more exposure, people will take notice. He thinks the media will listen to you because you have a fancy accent and an expensive education. He's using your differences to his advantage, so how is that any better than these guys here?' When Jai refused to answer, Michael slid out from his chair. 'I won't help.' They looked at each other for a long moment and when Jai didn't make a move to stand up, Michael turned and strode out of the lecture hall.

They watched him leave, the door swinging in his absence, and Steven looked out at the sullen faces in front of him. 'Anyone else want to follow? Or are you going to respect my decision?'

When no one spoke, rustling uncomfortably in their seats, Steven nodded firmly at Jai. 'Good. Let's get to work.'

32

Betty paused at the gated entrance to Victoria Courts, clutching a small bag of clothes and wondering what she was doing there. She didn't even know Esther Kipligat, couldn't be certain that it was her cousin. She remembered the name, the skin blackened by scars from a bout of chicken pox. She had been ten years old when Esther's family had come to visit them upcountry, in Busia.

Betty hadn't thought about that small town in Kenya's Western Province in over five years and was uncertain of the truth of the vivid image that came to her mind. It held the essence of a border town, aggressive, trade-driven, dirty and bustling with bicycle taxis that were the main mode of transportation. She remembered how she would straddle the metal platform just below the cyclist's seat, wrapping her head in a scarf to protect her hair; the way she knew everyone on her work route and would have her hand up in a permanent wave.

All this reminiscing brought up the memory of a particular incident when Esther had come to visit. They were sitting outside the salon her mother used to work at, soaked in the scent of peroxide and watching the large, cylindrical tankers line up on the highway, waiting to cross into Uganda.

'What if we jumped on one?' Esther had said to her. 'If we go right now and climb one of those ladders? We could cross the border without anyone noticing. Our parents would look for us for a little while but then they would give up. It would be like we never existed.'

Betty had thought her cousin so strange then, frail and spirit-like, talking about disappearing. So she perhaps wasn't that surprised when Esther's husband had appeared on the Kohlis' doorstep asking for help. What she wasn't sure about was why he had come looking for her.

'I'm glad you've come.' The man approached the gate; he walked in short, wide steps, his dark brow already glinting in the heat. As if reading her mind, he said, 'You're the only family Esther has here and she refuses to go upcountry to see her mother.'

'I only have two days.' As she followed the man into the main building, which smelled of wet cement, Betty was suddenly glad that Mrs Kohli had refused to give her a week. They went up a single flight of red terracotta stairs and the man pushed open his door.

'Esther!' The man jostled Betty through the door. 'Your cousin is here.'

'You're a police officer.' She was surprised, noticing his blue uniform – the black walkie-talkie attached to his belt, the calf-high army boots.

'Yes.'

She had been terrified of him when he had come to see her – had thought him a thief – and found it amusing that he was part of the security force, but kept her smile to herself for he didn't look like a man who appreciated being laughed at.

'If you haven't had breakfast, there is bread in the kitchen. I hope you aren't one of those relatives who thinks visiting someone's house must include eating all their food.' He glared at her. 'Things cost money.'

'I understand.'

After he had left, she sat alone in the quiet of the bright kitchen, drumming her fingers on the old table and keenly watching the half-eaten loaf of white bread that sat uncovered on the counter. There was a host of fruit flies swarming above it as they made their way to the blackened bananas, left to rot in the sunlight. It explained the smell, ripe and pungent like moist earth. She rose to open a window. Paused and listened for footsteps. She wondered if she should go up and check on her cousin. Instead, she broke off a piece of hard bread and sat back down.

Eventually, Esther came in dragging her feet. She wore a white nightgown and upon seeing her, Betty was sure the man had tricked her. This woman could not be the same girl she had met all those years ago. She was large, even larger than her husband, and walked with a slow sway, a raspy continuous breath escaping her throat.

'Hello, Esther. Do you remember me? I'm your cousin, Betty.'

The woman didn't reply, moving toward the cupboards. She was too short to be able to look into the cabinet so she searched with her outstretched fingers, banging into jars and plates until she found what she was looking for, dragging it out with a satisfied '*Ah*.'

Picking up a glass from the sink, she came to sit beside Betty and placed the bottle of cheap whiskey between them. Without looking up, Esther asked, '*David ni wapi?*'

Shocked at the sight of the alcohol, Betty's first thought was to remove it from the table. 'He's gone to work.'

The woman reached for the glass, poured a generous amount of the tepid, yellow liquid and, after a large gulp, she pulled her lips back. '*Aah*.' Finally registering Betty, she said, '*Wewe ni nani?*'

'I'm Betty. Your cousin – I've come to visit,' she said, shouting, as if talking to a small child.

'That man.' Esther sat straight, her large legs knocking into the table. 'Where is he?'

'I told you, he's gone to work.'

'I hope he never comes back,' Esther whispered, sliding down low as if to hide under the table. She gestured for Betty to come closer. 'Sometimes, he doesn't come home for days and I'm happy. But then, all of a sudden, he's here, demanding, ugly, reminding me of everything.' Her tone was airy, as if the words were too weighty, pressing down on her tongue and suffocating her. 'He thinks I don't know what he did. He thinks he has me fooled but really, I'm the one who fooled him!' Esther forgot about her glass and picked up the bottle instead, wrapping her mouth around it, wincing at its hardness. 'I'm the one who fooled him,' she repeated, rising.

Every movement she made was a laborious and painful process. She had to hold onto the table, press her weight down into her arms as she pushed herself up. 'How else could I have afforded to stay in my house? Who would have taken me in after what happened to David?'

She started to sway out of the room.

Betty called after her, 'I don't understand. What happened to your husband?'

Esther was near the sitting room now. She paused, bottle cradled between her breasts as she collapsed against the door frame. She stared blankly into the air as she suckled the whiskey. Then she said again, in the kind of hopeful voice that belonged to children and mad people, '*David ni wapi?*'

The day passed in such a way: intermittent waves of lucidity followed by longer, more bizarre moments of madness. Esther asked after David repeatedly, puffing about the house with the alcohol tucked under her arm.

'Where is he? Where is he?' Her question filled the house, darkening it. 'Soon at ten o'clock, they will call to tell me that he is dead. He will be hanging above the desk. I will start crying.' She looked at Betty, as if preparing her. 'I won't stop.'

'Esther, it's two o'clock now and your husband is fine.' Betty watched the clock on the wall, willing its thin, black hands to move faster. Already, she missed her small room at the Kohlis' residence; its concrete coolness in the middle of the green heat of the garden. In this empty house, which seemed even smaller with its erratic occupant, Betty missed her home and made up her mind that as soon as the police officer was back, she would leave and never return.

She made lunch for them with whatever ingredients she could find – *ugali* and some black-eyed beans – and because she didn't believe in wasting food, she used the over-ripe bananas to make *mtori*, though the recipe called for green ones.

After they had eaten, Betty tried to speak to Esther once more and when the woman reached for her whiskey, Betty pried it away. 'I'll make us some tea.'

There was no milk, so Betty steeped the *Ketepa* tea leaves in a pot of boiling water before heaping three teaspoons of sugar in each cup and placing one in front of Esther. 'It will make you feel better.'

They sipped for several minutes, pausing to blow on and then slurp the hot liquid.

'What do you do all day?' asked Betty.

The tea and banana stew having soaked up some of Esther's alcohol, she spoke more steadily than she had all day. 'I wait for David,' she said.

'Don't you get bored? How can you afford not to work?'

'David promised me my own hair salon a long time ago. I can weave braids like a mermaid.' A crooked smile turned into a scowl. 'But he's gone now.'

Betty patted her hand in comfort. 'He only went to the police station. He'll be back this evening.'

At that, Esther scoffed. 'If you think that's David then David isn't who you think he is.' She looked away and continued her tiny sips. Betty was trying to work out what her cousin had meant when Esther said, 'Do you remember when I came to visit you in Busia?'

A leap in Betty's throat; so the woman knew her after all. She was immediately overcome by a sense of comfort, a pooling of familial love in her belly. All day she had been planning to leave the house and now, she didn't want to move from the old chair.

'I was thinking about that this morning,' Betty smiled.

'And I told you I wanted to disappear.'

'You did.'

Esther asked eagerly, 'Do they still have those cargo trains?'

'I haven't been back there in a long time.'

'Perhaps I should visit again. If they're still there, I'll climb that ladder and strap myself to the very top. I will go far away from here.'

'What about your husband?' Betty asked. 'You can't just leave him.'

'That man is a monster.' Esther scratched into the wood of the table with a fork left over from lunch. 'Thanks to him I no longer have a place to call home.'

The man didn't come home that evening. Betty waited by the living room window all night, watching out for any indication of movement: a shadow, slight footsteps, a voice. Without alcohol in her system, Esther slept soundly and the whole house shrunk and rose in rhythm with her snores. It sealed itself up in loneliness, creaked and whimpered in the wind.

Betty must have fallen asleep in the chair only to be woken up at around four o'clock in the morning, disturbed by the thrashing of drums upstairs and the misty morning glaze upon her cheeks. She heard the sound of the door and quickly stood, straightening out her skirt and clearing her throat of sleep. The police officer was creeping in, hat to his chest. When he saw her, he jumped back like a startled elephant.

'*Eh-he*, are you trying to kill me?'

'You didn't come home last night,' Betty accused.

'And you sound just like your cousin.' He brought his four fingers together at a point, moving them up and down against his thumb, indicating the motion of talking. '*Kelele, kelele*,' he mocked, going up the stairs, unbothered if he woke Esther. 'I have to get a change of clothes. I won't be coming home again tonight.'

'Who is David?' she called after him.

Having pondered over her lunchtime conversation with Esther, it became clear that David wasn't this man standing in front of her. This man was the monster Esther had referred to. And yet, Betty found it difficult to be afraid of him – as round and almost pretty as he was.

The man halted, mid-step. His lips were drawn and white. 'How did you hear of him?' He descended the stairs toward her.

'Esther says she's waiting for him. She said something about a phone call that was coming to say he's dead.'

'He is dead.' The man sagged against the wall, as if in telling her, he was hearing it for the first time as well. 'David is dead.'

'Who was he?' Betty came closer to him. 'Perhaps if I know, I can help your wife get better.'

'My wife?' His eyebrows creased. 'Ah, yes. I'll tell you who David was.' He seemed to shake himself out of a stupor. His mannerisms became rude once again. 'He was my partner and friend. We worked together for two years in the police force.' A jaw stuck out, back teeth grinding together. 'I helped him out – I pushed him forward in his career and let mine come second. I invited him into my home, he drank my whiskey and ate my food and one day, I came home to find—' He chewed down hard on the inside of his lip. 'I came home to find him in bed with my wife!' He yelped the first half of the sentence and then calmed himself to a whisper. 'I told him to get out, that I never wanted to see him again. I said that I was going to ask for a transfer and take Esther far away from him.'

'What happened?' Betty didn't realize she was clutching her chest, feeling faint.

He looked so sad then, so vulnerable, and if he had been her brother or cousin, she would have reached out to comfort him. 'The next day we received a phone call in the morning. They told us that David had hanged himself at the front desk of the station.' The hat dropped from his hand, rolled across the floor. 'I suppose he couldn't live with what he had done.' The policeman grabbed Betty's hands, clinging onto them. 'Esther blames herself but really we both know it's my fault. It's all my fault and I don't know how I'm supposed to carry on, to be the same after all that.'

He drew her closer and his breath was aflame with alcohol and cigarettes. She tried not to flinch away.

He begged, 'If you can tell me how, perhaps I can go back. Perhaps I will remember...'

'I'm so sorry for the both of you.' She extracted her hands from his too-tight grasp. 'I'll do whatever it is I can to help relieve you of this burden.'

Her words snapped him out of his trance. He wiped his face with his sleeve, composed himself, and when he spoke he sounded like the man she had first met. 'Yes, Esther is your burden now because you are family.' He thundered up the stairs. 'You tell her to stay away from me, you hear? I've had enough of that woman. All she does is carry around ghosts and I don't want to be reminded, is that clear? I don't want to be reminded of any of it.'

33

'*Eh-ma!*' Pooja clutched her head, digging her fingernails into the soft flesh of her temples. 'No, no, you stupid girl!'

Leena tugged at her hair, the short strands escaping her grasp easily. She looked down at her empty hand, momentarily surprised. 'You don't like it?'

'Like it?' screeched Pooja. 'What makes you think I would want my daughter to look like a little boy?'

'You're being overdramatic, Ma.' Leena went to the mirror, turned her head left and right. Slanted up her chin and cast her gaze downward, under wavering lids.

'The first time you cut it, I said, *Okay, it's not so bad, it's liveable, not too short but no shorter*! And now…' Pooja gestured at her daughter with a scowl of disgust. '*Uh-ruh-ruh.* Who will marry you now, when you are looking like that?'

Leena's black hair, so enviously full, had been thinned down to wispy layers and grazed the bottom of her pointed chin, swept to the right in a long wave. Leena pushed up the bob and then, worried the continuous fussing would ruin it, patted it back down again.

'It's fashionable, which is why you don't like it,' she told her mother. 'Besides, when I go to England—'

'Just because you're going abroad for studies doesn't mean you have to change yourself.'

Leena was in her last year of high school and, along with most of her classmates, was looking at universities in England to continue her education. On this, Pooja supported her whole-heartedly – had wanted Jai to do the same thing four years earlier but the boy had been adamant about staying in Nairobi.

'But you're so clever!' Pooja had exclaimed in dismay. 'No one will know that. They'll think you weren't accepted into any schools in England, that you settled for second rate. No one goes to the universities here.'

'No one *you* know goes to the universities here,' he had corrected her.

'Exactly my point. Why attend Nairobi University when you have an opportunity to go abroad?'

'I don't want to waste three years of my life in a country I'll never return to after I'm done studying. I want to be here, to grow here. Besides, University of Nairobi is a reputable school.'

'I don't care what kind of school it is,' Pooja had protested. 'It'll never be as good as the schools in England. Here, all they do is go on strike for this thing or that, and all the classes are taught by *kharias!*' She drew the last word into a wail and grabbed her son's arm imploringly. 'Please, Jai. Now is not the time for your big ideas.'

'I've already received admission. If you aren't going to support me then I'll get a job and pay for it myself.'

'What has happened to you? To be so disobedient to the people who raised you, who feed and house you – where would you be without us?'

But of course, it would not have been right to turn her back on her son and so she had asked for what she always did in such situations with Jai: a compromise. 'You do your first degree here, *okay,*' she said. 'But then I want you to go and study in the UK for your Masters. You must do that, Jai. These things matter.'

'Matter when? When I'm looking for a wife?'

'All my friends' children are getting such degrees.' Pooja ignored his jibe. 'In a few years time, it will be the normal thing.'

All she was able to think of was how people would whisper about her son, how differently they would perceive him now. He would be viewed as less than the other men in their community, less educated and desirable – too old-fashioned.

Leena, on the other hand, was itching to go. University of Birmingham, Cardiff University, LSE, Nottingham University – the brochures of these places littered her room and she would spend hours losing herself in their glossy dreams, examining with dim longing the spacious lecture halls and the promises of romances waiting to be had. Nairobi was already far behind her.

'I want to go to Manchester,' she had told her parents.

Pooja pulled a face. She knew that one.

'Full of racists,' a woman from the compound had told her; her son had just returned from his fresher year there and had asked her, the first day back, to buy him some bleaching cream.

'They call me a curry muncher, Mum!' he had wailed. 'If I could just look more like them, things might be a bit easier for me…' he went on, drowning in his homesickness and inadequacy, clinging to her like a child.

'Forget that,' another woman had interjected. 'Do you know what our children get up to in those cities? Nightclubs, bars, lining up in their *short-short* skirts and high heels. They drink and smoke, forget how to respect their elders, forget everything we have taught them!' Suddenly caught out, the woman hurried to add, 'Not *my* Shivani, of course, but she knows girls like that.'

So Pooja had crossed Manchester University off her daughter's list. 'Don't you trick me, young lady,' she warned, wagging her finger. 'I've heard all the stories about Freshing Week.'

'It's Fresher's Week, Ma.'

'Freshing, Fresher's, same, same. You'll go anywhere you want in London – LSE, King's College, City University – but you'll stay with your uncle and that's the only way you will go.' Pooja had been adamant and the girl relented, so unlike her fighting brother.

Pooja wanted to make sure that her daughter wouldn't get up to any silly mischief over there. No *gorah* boyfriends or back tattoos, coming home and sneaking cigarettes in the garden because she had gone wild over her freedom. Liberty was over-rated, Pooja had decided long ago. Much better to live simply, in an orderly fashion, otherwise things became too messy, impossible to sort through, and it was easy to get lost and never find your way out.

Idly playing with the uneven edges of Leena's haircut, trying to capture the sleek strands, she said, 'You don't have to worry about this. It'll grow out in time. No harm done.'

Pooja settled back on the couch, watching her daughter fiddle and pout in the mirror. Such a lovely looking girl – petite and dramatically featured, the adolescent awkwardness almost completely faded out.

'Keep your shoulders down, stand up straight,' she reminded Leena and watched as the girl pulled herself up.

Pooja closed her eyes contentedly. It was silly to concern oneself with such things. Overall, she was extremely satisfied with how her daughter's life had turned out. It was exactly the way she had planned it.

*

Across town, in the petrol-filled atmosphere of an overcrowded garage, a *matatu* glistened with a fresh coat of fuchsia paint. Soon it would dry and Michael used these few moments to sit down – hold his heavy head between his hands.

He had been commissioned to do the artwork on the bus but he was distracted. He hadn't thought about her in many months, and even now it wasn't the image of the twelve-year-old girl who occupied the crevices of his mind but rather the strictly structured, filled-out version that had fallen out of Jai's school bag last week. Picking it up, Michael had wondered how seven years had passed since he had seen her.

He liked the way she looked in the photo. Unlike most of the Indian girls he came across on campus, her hair didn't fall into the dip of her back, or wasn't twisted around in a thick plait; it was much shorter, skimming her shoulders and making her seem too modern, as if she belonged someplace else. He grinned, remembering the day she had adamantly refused to come out and play after her mother had forced almond oil into her scalp.

In Jai's picture, she had been wearing a white T-shirt and it made her hair appear darker, gleaming almost blue in some parts. She had tucked it behind her ear so that whoever had taken the picture had captured the glint of a gold stud, the sudden protrusion of a cheekbone – a knifelike structure that had not been there when he had known her. Though she was different, he discovered within her expression the same hot-headedness and determination of the young girl so long ago and he missed her with such intensity, everything else dulled in comparison.

He had only a few seconds to trail his hand over the image before Jai had returned from the bathroom and he quickly stuck it back into the rucksack's front pocket. Michael had hidden his face in his textbook, a vain attempt to push her from his mind.

Yet her loveliness had carved a permanent home in his every thought so that whenever he shut his eyes, there she was – chin in palm, one shoulder bare and exposed.

A voice came up behind him. 'Don't tell me you're still thinking about that bitch.'

Without moving, Michael said, 'Don't talk about her that way, Jackie.'

'What shall I call her then? Racist? Cruel? A betrayer?' She had come to stand beside him.

'Stop it,' he said, more seriously. 'She's none of those things and you don't even know her.'

'And you think you do?' Jackie retorted. 'You spent two months with her almost seven years ago.'

'You're right – we were just children. I don't even think of those days any more.'

It was the truth. In the past seven years, though she had passed through his mind occasionally when he came across something to remind him of that perpetual summer, he hadn't been consumed by her memory. But after having seen that photo, being jolted by the reminder that she did in fact exist and had grown to be so exactly how he had pictured, she clung to him and he couldn't shake her.

'What do you want, Jackie?' he said, changing the subject.

'I need some *doh*. There's a concert at Carnivore and all my friends are going but I'm broke.'

'Shouldn't you be studying for exams?'

'Please, Mike.'

He slipped off the stool and went back to the bus, tested the pink paint. 'What about your mother?'

'She's been gone since Tuesday. It's the usual story. The guy is back in her life and, as always, she takes off running like no one else matters.'

'I'm sorry, Jackie,' he said, glad he had decided to stay in Nairobi despite his mother moving to Eldoret in the last year of his high school.

'Your grandmother's cousin, Mama Itanya, says she cannot look after the house any longer,' Angela had told him. 'She needs someone to come and work the shamba with her.' They had shared a look of understanding. 'I'm tired of this place and I want to leave.' Being dismissed from the Kohlis house had hurt Angela more than she cared to share. 'I'm tired of working every day of the week and I want something that's my own.'

'I got accepted into Nairobi University and I want to go.'

Angela had been overjoyed. 'Eldoret isn't that far,' she assured him. 'We can visit each other all the time. And someone needs to look after Jackie.'

With his cousin watching him eagerly, Michael pulled out five hundred shillings. It was difficult to part with the money, because paying school fees, and for food and more than his share of rent, was proving almost impossible. But she looked so eager that he couldn't refuse her.

'Thank you, thank you!' She pushed the notes quickly into the back pocket of her glued-on jeans and then turned back to the *matatu*, which he had begun working on once more. 'What are you supposed to be designing?'

'A new American girl-group called Destiny's Child.' He brought out the spray-paint gun. 'The driver said they're all true African women and I have to portray them as such, which to him means their boobs hanging tastefully out with asses the size of a politician's holiday house.'

Jackie giggled. 'All the men will be fighting to ride in it.' She climbed into the bus, even though he kept asking her not to. 'It's even got disco lights and a TV!'

Recently, due to a boom in the *matatu* industry, many of the nine-seater vans that had been used in the tourism sector were being bought by investors and converted into PSVs. The owners then hired artists to do the designing; these requests were often cultural or political, carrying some social satire, and it was the chance to take part in these traveling stories that had drawn Michael to his current job. He had not signed up to design the exaggerated curves on singers and movie stars and it annoyed him today more than ever.

Jackie was about to leave but detecting a mild sorrow in his face, she stopped. 'What's the matter, *cuzo*?'

Seeing Leena's face so unexpectedly had affected him more than he would have liked. He felt the memory of her pulsing in his gut, filling him with a desperate need to see her again. 'I feel like I should be doing something – not this. Something important.'

Jackie put her arm around his waist, leaning her head against his shoulder. 'This is only temporary, Mike. Just to get you through school.'

'But Jai and I, we had all these plans.' His voice tapered.

'All your life, you've been living in that boy's shadow,' Jackie said.

'That's not his fault.'

'I never said it was.' She suddenly seemed very wise and he grinned ruefully at her. 'You don't have to wait for him, you know,' she said. 'He's your friend but you can't put everything on hold while he's doing what he wants. You also matter.'

'I don't know where to start.'

Jackie gestured to the bus. 'You have great talent, *cuzo*. Where else to begin but there?'

34

Steven was a mini celebrity on campus. He couldn't walk ten minutes without being stopped for a high-five, a small chat from someone asking his advice or just an awe-struck student, claiming to have seen him on the KTN nine o'clock news.

'You're my inspiration,' they would tell him gravely.

'My woman is in love with you, *jama*! Tell me your tricks, Stevie.'

'How does one go about joining the protests? It looks like fun,' said a girl twisting her dreads around her finger.

'It's not supposed to be fun,' Steven would reply, as serious as ever. 'Our future is not a game.'

And she had apologized profusely, more infatuated with him than before.

'Don't you get tired of it? These people never leave you alone,' Jai asked him once.

'I'm their leader. They voted for me, put their trust in me.' Steven said it in that deceivingly patient way he had – one always felt slightly disparaged afterward. 'They look up to me, have granted me the humble responsibility of giving them answers. Wouldn't it be insulting if I were to say that I was tired of them?' It was posed as a question but the tilt of Steven's head was arrogant.

'Steven!' Ivy was moving quickly toward them, clutching the straps of her backpack, her glasses having fallen half-way down her nose.

'What is it?' Steven didn't hide his annoyance at having been interrupted.

Despite threatening to leave the union in the last meeting, Ivy had stayed on, though Steven had grown deaf to her hopeful quips and suggestions, sometimes even taking an idea she had put forward and presenting it as his own. Without waiting for a reply he turned to Jai and said, with clicking, urgent fingers, 'Grab a marker and get this poster done. The background can be a picture of Anthony...'

'Anthony has returned to campus,' Ivy told them. 'He wants to meet with you.'

'When?' he asked, his voice sharp with sudden attentiveness.

'This morning.'

'And you waited until afternoon to tell me?'

'I'm sorry, Steven.'

'Just tell me where he is.'

'In his dorm room. You remember the number—'

Steven waved her away. 'Let's go and meet him,' he said to Jai.

'I have a class right now. Perhaps you should take Ivy with you.'

A rigid silence. 'If you aren't serious about this, I'll find someone else to help me.'

A discomfort settling in his stomach, Jai said, 'I suppose I can miss one class.'

As they left, Jai heard the whisper, sharp and malicious, directed at Ivy. 'Get your act together, woman. You're becoming useless.'

To a person meeting him for the first time, Anthony wrongfully evoked an overwhelming sense of pity. Hard boned and slightly tremulous, he had a too-thin face crowded by gigantic features – the kind one found on a helpless animal. A swollen eye and freshly bruised upper lip were souvenirs from his recent stay in jail, and he had pupils so large that when Jai looked into them he was met with a liquescent, almost hypnotic darkness.

Anthony was sitting on the floor as they entered the room, leaning against the back of his single bed, in the process of lighting a joint. He looked up with a sibilant puff as the two boys squinted through the muddy cloud. 'Close the door behind you.'

The room was small and overcrowded. The only space not littered with clothes, books and cans of food was the desk facing the wall. It remained empty and pristine, as if it had just recently been polished.

Unlike most of the people Jai had recently met, Anthony did not rise to quickly shake their hands, did not release a string of silly flatteries expressing his gratitude at Steven's visit. Instead, he shut his eyes and disappeared into his own pleasure.

Jai sat at the desk while Steven remained standing. He appeared so different then, the usual rigidity of his stance collapsing, eyes darting and a mouth that moved in frozen, silent words as if it wasn't just a place to sit that he was searching for. He seemed paralyzed in the middle of the room until Anthony opened his eyes and said, 'There's a space on the bed over there,' and, finally released, Steven sank down gratefully.

Anthony offered the joint to Jai and he accepted, closing the tip of his mouth around it and understanding that his initial pity was unwarranted. There was nothing sorrowful about this man.

'What's your name?' he asked Jai in Swahili and it was refreshing to meet someone who expected Jai to adjust to him and not the other way around.

'Jai. I've just joined the Student Union.' He handed back the joint.

'That's good news.' Anthony nodded his approval, took another drag. Steven motioned for the joint but was ignored. 'We need strong people like you.' Anthony stuck his arms out from the elbows, imitating a chicken. 'Not like this guy over here, short like a little girl.' He gestured at Steven.

Jai and Anthony chuckled and Steven's face flushed with embarrassment. He reached over and snatched the joint. 'That's not funny, Tony.'

'I told you not to call me that.'

Chastised, Steven retreated into silence.

'He has no sense of humor,' Anthony told Jai. 'Even when the students voted me in to be chairman of the union, he was so upset I had to hand it over to him. What do I need a position like that for anyway?'

'Is that true?'

Steven refused to answer Jai's question, hiding himself behind a growing marijuana haze. 'We're planning another protest,' he told Anthony. 'They shouldn't have done that to you,' he added, indicating the fresh injuries.

The man wasn't impressed by the smooth words, the eyes burrowed in concern. 'If you want a fight, Steven, then be man enough to say you want one. Don't pretend this is for me.' Anthony stretched over for his joint and said to Jai, 'Did you know Steven here wants to be a politician? *Kama* those fat men in striped suits with the big briefcases and fancy cars.' He laughed throatily. 'He is enjoying all of this attention – KBC, KTV, people are just beginning to know who you are, *sindiyo*?'

'Are you going to join us or not?' Steven's voice had reached a whine.

'I've never said no to a good fight before.' Anthony struggled to his feet. 'When is your next meeting?'

'Two days from now.'

'*Sawa.* See you then.' They were at the door when Anthony said, 'I want to talk to Jai alone.'

Steven's hand hovered at the knob as if trying to force Jai out of the room with him, but it was impossible to be intimidated by him any longer.

'Don't be too long, we have work to do,' he glowered.

'I didn't know he wanted to be a politician,' Jai started, but Anthony raised a finger to his lips.

He whispered, 'I bet that little rat is trying to listen in on what we are saying.' Then back in a normal voice, 'Now that you've joined the Union, I want to show you something.' He pulled out a sheet of lined paper that was creased from constantly folding and unfolding. 'Read it out loud, please.'

Jai cleared his throat, began.

> We labor together in search for
> Knowledge and truth.
> We bless and honor Thee, we are the pinnacle of
> Excellence in knowledge,
> Knowledge to serve our mother land (*Oh, Kenya*),
> Knowledge to serve all mankind.
>
> Be not engulfed by pride, let excellence prevail.
> May we all shun the pitfall of being the ivory tower.
>
> With sacrifice and dedication, our problems
>   we will overcome.
> We are the fountain of knowledge we create and hold the
> Vision.

> God gives us grace to serve, and the future for us is bright,
> And the children
> Shall drink from the fountain of knowledge, knowledge
> Shall surely set us free (*beyond the stars*)
> Knowledge shall
> Surely set them free.

His voice disappeared as he folded the paper back up and placed it delicately on the desk.

'That's beautiful. Where did you find it?'

'I wrote it.'

At Jai's expression, Anthony laughed, forcing Jai to quickly rearrange his face. 'I didn't mean to be insulting.'

'The university is looking for a school anthem. I want to submit this and I was hoping to get your opinion.'

There was a special feeling that came with being requested into this man's private life. 'You write wonderfully,' Jai encouraged.

'My parents spent most of their money sending me to school. They sacrificed everything so that one day I could be standing here, in front of you.' He looked at Jai gravely. 'Life has not been easy but when I look at this, I am reminded that it has all counted for something. I wrote it for my sister, Enna, so that she will also know how important education is.'

'Speaking of.' Jai checked his watch. 'I have to go because my next class will be starting soon.'

'Of course.' Anthony didn't look up as Jai turned to leave – he was gazing at the poem, his hand hovering above it. 'You must be very careful of Steven.' At the warning, Jai stopped at the door. Anthony's eyes rose slowly. 'You and I might be fighting for a cause we believe in but Steven is only fighting for himself. Do you understand the difference?'

Jai thought of Michael – perhaps he had been right about Steven all along. He paused, not wanting to leave just yet. 'See you at the meeting?'

'Ah, yes.' Anthony got up and slipped into his chair, the sunlight falling in from the window behind him, entrapping him in gold-flecked dust. 'See you then.'

His hands were spread lovingly over the smooth desk, traveling in wide, thoughtful circles. His eyes were closed, the shadow of a smile hovering on his lips. It was an image that stayed close to Jai the whole day, many hours after he had left the dorm room and made his way down the long, lonely corridor.

35

On a shady street corner, beneath the stretching, yellow bones of an acacia tree, Jai stood with Steven three days later in front of a KTN news anchor, who was saying, 'Here we are on the usually busy Uhuru Highway. Today, however, as you can see behind me, it is completely empty.' The man gestured at the road that was devoid of all cars, motorists having chosen to take diversions rather than risk being stuck in the middle of the strike. 'Once again, the students of Nairobi University are protesting, but this time, it is not about school fees. It is not about the administration. Today, they are fighting for something much more important. They are fighting for one of their own.' Here, the camera turned toward Steven. 'We are talking to Steven Kimani, the chairperson of NUSU. Please tell us why you are here today.'

Steven looked seriously into the camera. He was a handsome man, with an arresting face and pleasing lines, but looking upon him from the sidelines, Jai could see the pretense in every practiced smile, every somber hand to the chest. 'As the nation knows, the students of the university have been protesting the proposed increase in school fees. We made it clear from the very beginning that we wanted peaceful demonstrations. That we did not wish to use any violence but simply to speak up, to begin conversations…'

Jai turned, tried to find Anthony in the crowd and admitted to himself that he was also hoping to see Michael. Steven continued speaking.

'However, as usual, the police did not heed our request for peace. They came to attack us with many weapons – guns, tear gas, flares – and we, being bare handed, had to of course use whatever was within our reach – rocks, sticks – because one always has the right to defend oneself.' The presenter was nodding enthusiastically with every word. 'As you also know, one of our most important members, Anthony, was unlawfully detained, after being badly injured in the strike.' Steven pointed to himself. 'I, the chairperson, went personally to collect him from Chiromo police station. They didn't allow me to see him for at least three hours and even then to set bail was a troublesome process.'

Jai left him mid-sentence, wandering into the crowd, which was as upbeat as last time – a normal gathering of people, enjoying the excuse not to spend the day locked up in the libraries or lecture rooms.

'I see Steven is lapping up his time in front of the camera.' Anthony was limping toward him.

'It should be you up there, talking to them.' As Jai spoke, he was jostled and pushed by the students flocking to them. They wore big smiles and greeted Anthony warmly.

'*Sasa*, bro?'

'Good to see you. They almost got you in there, didn't they?'

Anthony clapped hands, backs and the shoulders of everyone who came up to greet him; he knew and cared for each one personally and they stayed for long moments at his side, always reluctant to move on. As he engaged them in conversation, Jai turned to see that the cameraman was no longer filming. Instead, he was smoking and talking amongst a group of students while Steven was huddled behind the acacia and conversing with the TV presenter in a rapid manner, constantly stretching his neck out from behind the pale bark to see if anyone had noticed them. He shook the presenter's hand firmly before emerging – hands in his pockets as he ambled toward their group.

On his way, someone handed him the megaphone and he called through it for people to join him. 'Anthony would like to say a few words.'

As Anthony began reciting his poem, Jai's eyes were drawn back to the tree. He noticed with surprise, and some unease, that the TV presenter was accompanied by a police officer.

Once Anthony had finished, Steven led the crowd down the street, chanting, '*Cooom-rade POWER!*' and Jai found something ridiculous about the mantra that had once seemed so thrilling and romantic to him. They were just words now, powerless and empty, and when he shouted them, his throat went dry.

'Are you alright?' Anthony came to walk beside him.

'I thought I saw—'

'I want you both to walk in the front with me.' Steven inserted himself between the two of them and pushed Anthony out ahead, beyond Jai's reach.

The violence erupted quickly. They hadn't been marching for more than twenty minutes before the first flare shot up into the air, bridging the short distance between the police officers and students, landing less than a meter away from their front line. As the crowd behind them pushed forward eagerly at the provocation, Jai said urgently to Anthony, 'Stay close to me. I can help you if anything happens.'

They had a clear view of the police, huddled in front of their cars and minivans, and he saw one pull out a tear-gas canister.

His eyes and skin stung at the memory but he pushed away his fear.

'*Cooom-rade POWER! Cooom-rade POWER!*'

How much he wished they would stop repeating that mundane chant; it was beginning to irk him so he was glad when someone close to him took up a line of Anthony's poem instead. 'We labor together in search for / Knowledge and truth.'

The repetitious chant fed into the crowd so that it found its feet at last, bursting forward. The police officers – in helmets and bullet-proof vests – shoved at each other while hanging back. '*Enda! Enda! Come on, go!*' They had shields and guns but there was something imposing about the protest, a quiet strength, led not by Steven but by Anthony, limping yet steadfast, with Jai close to him and them shouting together, 'We labor together in search for / Knowledge and truth.'

Another tear-gas canister swallowed up some students in its breathless, horror-filled panic. It spread quickly into the crowd behind Jai, breaking it off in many small directions and as the students ran, they scooped up rocks from the roadside, throwing them at will so that even the pedestrians passing had to cower behind trees and cars to avoid being hit.

While Steven joined in the violence, Anthony stayed quiet, marching ever forward. He repeated his poem to himself, helping people up off the road after they had been hit by the tear gas, wiping their eyes with the frayed ends of his jacket. If he came upon someone who was ready to launch a stone or pull up a signpost, Anthony would catch his wrist and say, 'Think first. What is the point? How will they understand what you are trying to say when you are saying it like an animal?'

During the chaos, Jai glimpsed Steven isolated from the group. At a distance, it looked like he was getting into a tussle with a policeman. Their heads were bent close together, Steven's hands on the officer's shoulders, the cop grasping his elbows. But then suddenly and simultaneously, they pulled away from each other and Steven threw himself back into the crowd, his fist raised above his head. Jai could hear him, the fury in his voice, 'You cannot condemn us unheard!' and the policeman was heading in Jai's direction, but when he searched about him he could not find Anthony.

He shouted out his name but it was lost in the thousands of other voices, and he pushed through the crowd roughly, blinking away the residues of tear gas. 'Anthony! We have to leave,' he called out, a heavy feeling in his chest – not knowing why they must go, only knowing that they must.

When he finally came to an opening, he spotted a police truck and a familiar limp. He began running, shouting in Swahili, 'Leave him alone!' When he reached the officers, he tried to pry them away from Anthony, asking, 'What are you doing?'

One of them kept his tight hold of Anthony, who had gone with them so peacefully that no one had noticed. The officer said to Jai, 'You must leave this place. It is becoming dangerous.'

'He's done nothing wrong. Let him go.'

'Disturbing the peace is something very wrong. He must learn his lesson.'

'What about everyone else? Aren't you going to arrest me as well?'

'And have your *mzee* get me fired?' the cop scoffed. '*Enda*, go!' He shook his baton in Jai's face, just beneath his chin. He had leaned in so close, their noses were almost pressed together and Jai recognized him as the policeman talking to Steven earlier. He tried to reach around him in panic, more certain than ever that something was wrong.

'Anthony!' he shouted but was cut off as the policeman's baton made direct contact with his gut. His breath halted mid-way and his knees hit the tarmac, legs folding beneath him. There followed a heavy kick with an army boot to the same place, right at the navel.

The policeman brought down the baton in a swift swing, right in the center of Jai's shoulder blades so that he collapsed forward. 'Now you've learned your lesson.'

They had loaded Anthony into the van but before the door slid shut, Jai heard him call out, 'If you don't mind, perhaps you can come and get me from the station...' before the car sped away and Jai was left coughing up a cloud of spiraling dust.

When he finally regained his breath and sat up, he saw Steven standing not two meters away from him.

'They took Anthony,' Jai called to him. 'We have to do something.'

The short man watched the shadow of the van slowly fade and silently turned around to rejoin the group of students. His body blended into theirs, his voice camouflaged within their sounds until Jai could no longer distinguish him and he fell back onto the hot ground, blinded by the sun.

He couldn't be sure how long he staggered the deserted roads in town, the side streets tarred and gleaming in the heat, the midday sun cracking his skin. Nairobi had never seemed more cruel, indifferent to the pounding ache that refused to leave his temples or the sharp stabbing in his side. When he finally found a taxi, Jai's throat was so parched that the words choked him and came out in gasps.

'Chiromo police station.'

He borrowed the driver's mobile phone to call his father, handing it back with a fifty shilling note.

When Raj arrived at the police station, he found his son in a furious debate with one of the officers sitting at the desk.

'You can't hold him without cause!' Jai was shouting. 'I'll pay the bail if it's a matter of money – I'll give you however much you want.'

Raj forced his son to be still. 'What happened to you?'

'These guys beat me up.'

The policeman cowered under Raj's stare. 'Not me, *mzee*. I've been sitting behind this desk all day long.'

'They have my friend in there. They took him during the protests – only him,' Jai said, clinging to Raj's forearms, reminding him how young his son still was. 'Something is not right, Dad. I have to get him out.'

'What's the reason for holding the boy?'

'Disturbance of peace. He was being violent and it was either shoot or arrest him.'

Jai's protestations were becoming weaker as the throbbing in his head turned to a steady pain. 'I was there the whole time and he never did anything like that.'

'I'll pay the bail for him.'

'Sorry, *mzee*, I can't help you this time. The court date will be set tomorrow and then you can come and fetch him if you wish, *sawa*?'

'Not *sawa*.' Jai slammed his fist down on the desk and winced.

Raj held his son back. 'There's nothing we can do for him now. I promise we'll come back first thing tomorrow. We have to get you to a doctor.'

Jai ignored his concerns. 'I can't just leave him here.'

'Jai?'

A worried voice from the door and Raj saw a short, light-skinned man moving forward into the station, sweat stains butterflying out from his armpits.

A flash before Raj's eyes – he stumbled back in shock as his son reached out and grabbed the man's collar and said, 'Hey, you little shit, what are you up to?'

The man held up his hands in surrender. 'I've come to fetch Anthony. What happened to you?'

'Don't pretend like you didn't see me lying there when they took Anthony away.' The room was spinning and Jai's anxiety was making it more and more difficult to stand. The floors began to slope and slide, the desk pulled away from him. He leaned against his father's steady weight.

'You should go home now.' Steven's voice sounded far away – 'I will get Anthony out – don't trouble yourself, everything will be okay' – before the world split apart beneath his feet.

Jai hid a grimace as Leena accidentally brushed up against him. His stomach was badly injured and even the slightest movement sent a ripple effect of hot pain through his body and set his head and teeth ringing. He lay with his neck tilted upward, catching tiny hiccups of air.

'I don't understand why you had to play soccer with those *kharias*,' Pooja muttered, eyes glued to the television set glumly. 'They only know how to be rough – of course they would hurt you.'

'How many times do I have to tell you not to call them that?' Jai snapped, his pain making him quick to anger.

She shook her head at her husband. 'They injure him until he cannot even breathe and still he defends them. This is all your doing.'

Raj knew that he should tell her that he had taken their son to MP Shah Hospital earlier that afternoon, that Jai had suffered many bruises and a mild concussion, but he had promised his silence and so instead kept his gaze fixed away from Pooja.

She turned up the volume. 'Look, it's another strike. What did I tell you about that university?'

But her words turned insubstantial, never reaching Jai. He was so focused on the images flashing on the news, waiting impatiently for the moment when the camera zoomed in on two presenters, smiling inanely, oblivious to his agitation.

'Sit back, Jai. You need to relax,' Pooja was saying but he waved her words away, keeping upright and clutching his abdomen. A tight, sick feeling built in his chest, an aching sweat in his palms when he saw a picture of Anthony marching in the crowd. His bowels went loose from fear, a low groan as he fell to his knees.

He heard the presenter's girlish, high voice. *It is with deep regret and sadness that we report a student of Nairobi University has died during today's protest which took place on Uhuru Highway.* Jai struggled to string her words together but they were too far away to grasp. *Anthony was a third-year university student and he was arrested today for inciting violence at a protest which many students say was meant to be peaceful.*

He heard his name being called. 'What's the matter with him?' Pooja's concern swallowed by the roar of the TV.

'Oh!' His sister's astonished voice and Pooja turned back to the news to see a young man talking into the camera and beside him was her son. The man was saying: *We made it clear from the very beginning that we wanted peaceful demonstrations. That we did not want to use any violence but simply speak up, to begin conversations...*

Watching it took Jai back to that morning when everything had made sense. When his head didn't hurt and his stomach wasn't in pieces – when he wasn't exhausted by guilt and sorrow.

Pooja was in an uproar. 'What are you doing on TV? What are you doing over there with those people?'

'Stop asking me so many questions.' The carpet dug into his skin as he collapsed against the couch, his sister's cool fingers at his neck. Their steadiness anchored him for a little while, the room around him temporarily stilled.

The presenter was now saying: *It has been reported that the young student committed suicide whilst being held at Chiromo police station earlier this afternoon.*

This time, a current shot of Steven standing outside the doors of the station, surrounded by a horde of somber-looking students. Ivy was beside him, holding his hand.

Steven was saying, 'Anthony was arrested once again this afternoon, put in the central police cells and now they are reporting that he has taken his own life by passing an electric wire over his neck. They are saying that he strangled himself.' He looked straight out, at Jai. Gravely, hand to chest, 'Please know that we will not stop seeking justice for him. We want the police commissioner to order a full inquiry into his death and we won't rest until those responsible are held accountable for their actions.'

Raj flicked off the TV, sending the room into a stunned silence. He knelt down beside his son but Jai brushed him away. 'I told you we should have stayed. We could have saved him but now he's dead.'

'It's not your fault. You need to rest.'

'What was my son doing on TV?' Pooja kept demanding. 'What has happened? Why is he like this?'

She was ignored by everyone in the room as Raj asked Leena, 'Help me with your brother.'

Arms slung over strained necks, slow and careful footsteps led him up the stairs into the soothing darkness of his room. His father went to get a sleeping pill while his sister stayed beside him, touching his face and asking repeatedly, 'You're going to be okay, you will be okay, won't you?'

Raj re-entered the room, forcing his son into a sitting position and putting a small white pill in his hand. 'It'll make you feel better.'

'I have to go and find Steven. He planned all of this. I knew it and I didn't stop him.'

'Tomorrow,' said Raj, pushing the medicine between his tightly shut lips. 'You have to sleep now.'

As the medication began taking effect, he heard them leaving – dulled footsteps and muted concerns as the world began to unravel, become loose and inconsistent. He spotted a shadow at his door, hovering, and called out, 'Anthony?' and in a flash of lucidity, recognized the hurried gait, the straight back. 'Oh, Ma,' catching the sob as it came up but even that was too hard and he released it with a despairing grunt.

The back of her hand on his cheek, brushing away his hair – weathered lips to his feverish forehead. 'It's okay, *beta*, just close your eyes. I'm right here beside you,' and he did as she said, surrendering to her even, tender strokes, suspended somewhere in childish happiness before tumbling, spiraling, speeding head first into a waiting nightmare.

Steven was stacking his folders, rolling up the banners and posters from the protests when Jai went to see him the next day. He was alone in the sloped-wall lecture room, behind him a large, green blackboard that had recently been wiped clean. The smell of chalk-dust was heavy in the air.

'I thought I might see you here.' He stopped what he was doing when he saw Jai come down the aisles between the seats. 'How are you feeling?'

'What happened to Anthony?' Jai stopped at the front of the room, the podium between him and Steven. He held onto it for support, still feeling the effects from the day before.

'Surely you must have watched the news.'

'I want the truth.'

'I'm afraid I don't understand.'

Jai leaned forward. 'I saw you speaking to that policeman and the reporter yesterday before the protests.'

Steven shrugged, collecting up his papers in a yellow manila folder, sliding it into his satchel. 'That happens. I'm the chairman – I have to give statements on behalf of all the students.'

'You planned the whole thing to get some media attention.' Jai's neck gave a violent shake, anger rushing out of him, unstoppable. 'You had them take Anthony away – you had him killed so that you would have another cause to fight for, another excuse to be on television.'

Steven's voice remained calm, a half-smile upon his thin lips. 'But you saw me yesterday at Chiromo station. I was coming to help him.'

'You wanted to make sure they got rid of him. He knew what you were up to and you didn't like that.' Jai had an urge to reach out and grab the man, shake the ugly confession from him. 'You also knew it was the perfect way to get camera crews out to your protests, to make a name for yourself.'

'I'm very sorry you have misunderstood me in this way,' Steven said. 'I thought you wanted to help this cause but I can see I was very wrong.'

Jai's fist hit the podium. 'I saw you talking to the journalist and that cop, and then during the riots they came straight for Anthony. No one else – they arrested him on the spot even though we both know he didn't believe in violence.'

'Just because you met him once doesn't mean you knew him.' Steven's usual velvet-like disposition turned sour.

'You saw them put him in a van. You could have saved him then but you didn't.'

'There were other people who needed me. I couldn't leave them alone – Anthony would have understood that.' Steven came around the podium to stand beside him. He put a hand on Jai's shoulder as if they were friends sharing a secret. 'In every war there are casualties.'

Jai pushed his hand away. 'Don't talk to me like I'm one of those idiots who follow you around campus,' he warned. 'You had Anthony killed for your own reasons, not for a greater good. And even a greater good doesn't justify his death.'

The smile lingered on Steven's face even as he said, 'Please do not come back for any more meetings. You are no longer welcome.'

Jai could have tackled the man, thrown him to the ground and inflicted upon him the pain he deserved. But instead, he collapsed into a chair as Steven left, drained of energy, his body sore and bruised. Through the thin walls he could hear lecture hall doors slamming open as the last class of the day finished. People hurried down the hallway outside, calling out and laughing at one another, as if today was just an ordinary day – as if one of them, the best of them, had not just been lost. It was worse than anything – that careless, uninhibited sound of life moving on.

PART FOUR

2003

36

It was too early in the morning for such nonsense and Jeffery spat out the tobacco he was chewing in irritation. It sprayed thickly at the corner of the vandalized wall.

'Fucking guys.' He stamped his feet against the wet cold. 'Fucking, fucking guys.'

There had been a heavy downpour the night before, which had lasted well into the early hours of the morning, and now the streets were flooded with rainwater – tepid, brownish streams that disrupted day-to-day activities. But the wall of this public toilet, in the direct eyeline of the main road, was protected by a wide shade of trees so that despite the storm it had remained dry and resolute, shouting out its truth.

It was a simple graffiti – one that would require only a single layer of fresh paint to cover up – but Jeffery refused to look at it because the words burned holes into his eyes and caused him to shrink away in terrible shame.

THE LEADERS WE HAVE	THE LEADERS WE WANT
Unreliable	Visionary
Inconsistent	Patriotic
Mean	Intelligent

Buffoons	Women
Inconsiderate	In touch with the people
Slow	Competent
Lazy	Honest
Greedy	Reliable
Vultures	Men

His eyes moved to the right side of the wall, down toward the corner where the slogan had been scrawled. *Kenya ni yetu.*

'Who are these guys?' he wondered out loud to the police officer beside him. 'I've seen their words on three different graffiti walls now. One in Westlands, in Parklands near the police station and now, here.' The muscles of his face rolled into tight knots of aggravation. 'I don't want to waste my time with these things.'

The writing on the wall angered him because it dragged up a memory rusty with disuse, one he thought he had rid himself of. He stared dazedly at the left side of the list, the words forming like clots in his chest, and he loosened his shirt collar.

'What shall we do now, *mzee?*' the officer beside him asked.

'Call someone from the city council.' Jeffery made his way back to his white Toyota, pushing away congealed mud and resisting the temptation to smear it across the wall, hiding the words away until someone could get to it. He couldn't bear the idea of so many people seeing the words. 'Tell them to come straight away. *Mafalas,*' he muttered to himself as he swung wildly on to the main road, cutting through cars and ignoring their protests. 'Just wait until I catch them. I'll teach them a lesson they'll never forget.'

The drive back to the police station was excruciatingly long and he wished he had taken the other police officer with him. The radio didn't work and in the silence his remorse was free to sit in the passenger seat and grow fat.

To contain his own guilt was easy. There were countless spaces, tiny secret pockets within him in which he could hide it, shut it away so he would never have to think of it again. But to have someone else recognize it, display it for the entire country to see, was another matter altogether. He felt exposed; a big-bellied fraud, which was why, as he stormed past his secretary, he snapped, 'Why are you looking at me like that?'

'That boy is here to see you again.' She kept her voice hushed, inaudible to the rest of the office, adding, 'I tried to send him away, to do what you told me—' as Jeffery slammed out the sound of her apologies with a kick to his door.

He came around his desk and sank into his chair with a growl. 'What have I told you about visiting me in my office?' His eyes jerked up, the hair on his neck rising. 'What happened to you?'

The boy stank – his whole office filled with his dampness, like wet garbage. Nick had moved the extra chair to the corner of the room, where he huddled into himself behind the door.

'All I know is that I woke up this morning on the bank of Nairobi River with no idea how I got there.'

Jeffery rolled his eyes. 'If you're stupid enough to become so inebriated, that's none of my concern.'

'It was those men.' Nick spoke in a rush. 'They want money. They want more money all the time and I don't have any to give them.'

A fresh bruise was breaking out on his cheek – a blooming, purple pain. Jeffery noticed how the boy had changed in a few short months – he was bony and gray-skinned, with a nervous habit of twisting his head from side to side, continually checking his surroundings. Ducking down at the slightest sound.

Jeffery clenched the edge of his desk. 'You're becoming very problematic, *kijana*.'

'They know who you are.' The confession came like a gust – a pulse of blood from a severed artery no longer able to hold itself together – thick and fast.

'Say again?' Jeffery cocked an eyebrow, as if intimidation could force the truth to change.

'They know that I'm working for you and they said they want you to help. If you don't—' Nick wrung his fingers desperately, flapped his wrists up and down.

'If I don't, then what?'

'They'll make you.' Unable to sit any longer, Nick rose, his eyes running to every corner of the room.

'Get out,' Jeffery commanded. 'I don't want you to come back here.'

At the door, Nick turned. '*Mzee*, you must understand. Killing to these men means nothing.'

'You just worry about yourself.' Jeffery waved him out. But before he left, the policeman barked, 'Don't forget – Wednesday at Aqua Bar. I'm expecting something.'

'Yes.'

'And I don't care if they took all you had, find a way to get some more. I'm not in the business of feeling sorry for anyone.'

Tucked away within a high-roofed, airy studio, off a busy street packed with jacaranda trees and Chinese restaurants, Michael was painting. Running along the fresh white walls, pitched up against window frames, there were numerous photographs and artwork, all of which were unfinished, most abandoned almost as soon as they were started. Littered across the floor were his tools: a second-hand easel with a loose leg, different-sized paintbrushes and empty cans of spray paint. He sat amid the clutter, lost in the startling clearness of his mind.

He took photographs for a living, sprayed walls for the love of his country. But his paintings were personal. How soothing it was to turn himself over to the thread-like strokes of the brush, the cheerfulness of color and shapes and various patterns – to discover a cohesiveness in ideas without edges and boundaries.

The sound of a key turning in the lock broke him out of this spell and he stood quickly, dragging the painting to the farthest corner and facing it against the wall. As Jai stepped into the room, Michael turned around guiltily.

'I thought you were in class.'

'The seminar ended early,' his friend said, adding sadly, 'Someone from the city council is already there, painting it over.'

'We expected that,' Michael reminded him. 'It was in a very public spot. Politicians pass there every morning.'

'It was only up there for three hours.'

Michael grinned. 'That tells you how effective it was.'

'How's that?'

'No one ever bothers to cover up lies. It's the truth they're all running from.'

Jai looked around the room. He noticed the photograph sitting against the desk. 'That's new.'

They stared together at the young lion yawning, the tiny, bronze hairs of his mane bristling and curious.

'I got a contract with a travel agency,' Michael replied. 'I went to the National Park a few days ago and found this guy.'

After having worked with *matatu* owners for several months, Michael had been drawn to art and its various forms, so when Jai bought him a camera for his birthday, he quickly went about collecting as much life as he could: the legless beggar on the street who walked on his arms, balls of inflexible muscle sweating in the sun; the young girl selling red peanuts so that she could afford her school textbooks; two lovers leaning against a bus post, caught up beneath the silver threat of clouds. Like Jai, Michael was often frustrated with the impermanence of graffiti, which had caused him to gravitate toward photographs and the reliability of them, yet there had been something that kept tugging him back to blank spaces in dark corners, waiting to be filled. He had taken Jackie's advice and begun his own form of quiet protestation, starting off in toilets and isolated places such as the kiosks in Kibera slums. It was only when he and Jai began working together that everything had changed.

Michael couldn't be sure of who had suggested doing the first one – perhaps it had suggested itself. They were sitting at the university bar, listening to the conversation happening between some students beside them.

'I can't even afford *unga* any more,' one of them was saying. 'It's a hundred bob now! A hundred shillings for one packet of flour. *Aki!* How are we supposed to survive this way?' The girl gulped her drink. 'We elect a new government and they promise us all kinds of things. Free education, affordable housing, lower cost of the essentials. But it's all bullshit. They come to us for support and when we get them into State House, they forget about us.'

'Why don't you do something about it?' Jai had asked.

'Excuse me?' The wine glass coming down from her mouth, puckered in annoyance.

'If you believe so passionately in your rights, why aren't you doing anything to protect them?'

'Was I talking to you?' she snapped.

Jai held his hand out. 'My name's Jai.'

'You could be my father for all I care,' she growled and turned back to her friend.

'Maybe if you were more proactive, you wouldn't feel so power-less.' Jai was unperturbed by her irritation.

'And what exactly do you think I should do?' She swung her body back around so that she was sideways on the chair, arching her neck to talk to him. 'Some of us don't have the time to do whatever we want. We have to work – nothing comes free to us.'

He brushed aside her taunt. 'There are lots of things you can do. You can write an article and submit it to a newspaper. You can organize a protest. You can vote.' He leaned in closer and asked, 'Do you vote?'

'That's none of your business,' she said, burying her words in her wine glass.

'Right.' He sat back and crossed his legs, Michael's kicks falling on deaf shins. 'And then you wonder why you are being stepped on.'

Michael paid hastily for their beers and once outside, instead of heading back toward campus as they had planned, their feet found another direction. Jai walked fast, breathing out stiff clouds of air. 'Silly girl.'

Michael forced him to slow down. 'I know what you were trying to do in there but you don't have to be so forceful.'

'She was an idiot.'

'You can't belittle people that way. If you think they should know something, then educate them. Follow your own advice and do something.'

Jai started to move again, faster and more excited. 'You're right. Let's go.'

A few hours later, they stood in a deserted alleyway with spray paint residue on their fingertips and clothes and a hastily scrawled message that they could hardly decipher under the yellow shards of a broken street light above them.

It was a picture of a fat politician, a briefcase stuffed with money in his hand, a chain around his neck. At the other end of this chain was the young woman from the bar, dragging him down the steps of Parliament. Beneath the picture, Jai had written:

MY VOICE. MY VOTE. OUR FUTURE.

As they squinted to survey their work, admitting that they needed practice, Jai said, 'We should wear gloves next time.'

'And plan it out better and bring a torch,' replied Michael.

They always worked with simple designs and most often in black. It was difficult, with just the two of them, to find time to do something intricate, starting off in deserted areas but then moving to more public spaces as they became more skilled, where they could be sure to get a wider audience. They did it once a week, on Saturday evenings, because it was easy for Jai to leave the house without Pooja questioning him and the cops were usually preoccupied with drunk misdemeanors so they were less likely to be caught.

It was Michael who had the idea for a slogan.

'I think it's important to put our mark,' he told Jai. 'Let people know that they're not alone – that someone is out there fighting for them.' And so they had come up with the slogan *Kenya Ni Yetu*.

'Kenya is ours. It's perfect.'

It had been close to a year since they had made their first graffiti design and had finally decided to place it in the most visible spot they could think of – the wall of a public toilet on Koinange Street, facing the street, where most politicians drove by on their way to the office. That was why Michael wasn't surprised when Jai told him their graffiti was already being made to disappear.

He told his friend, 'This country is built upon lies and cheats and to uncover it could mean the collapse of everything we know.'

Jai sat against the windowsill, extending his legs outward. 'So why do we do it?'

Michael looked past his friend, at the cloudless sky, the metallic skyline of the city just visible in the distance. 'Because this country is beautiful and full of life,' he answered. 'And who will fight for it, if not us?'

37

She went there most evenings now, reaching South C shortly after nine o'clock in the evening, down the ill-lit street, where she knew Esther would be waiting for her by the window – a large and anxious shadow pacing behind the muslin curtain.

Betty was aware that her cousin watched her come through the gate, had calculated the exact number of footsteps it took for her to reach the front door, because it always stood open when she arrived and then she was gathered up into Esther's soft folds of fat – silky skin that smelled of a nostalgic mix of Johnson's baby powder and Vaseline.

'I was starting to wonder how I would pass the evening alone…' Every day, Esther was surprised and unable to hide her relief when she saw her cousin. Always greeting her with the same pleading gratitude.

'Don't hold me so tightly.' Betty would extract the woman's hands from her own, taking her usual seat at the small table. 'Come and sit down. I've missed you,' she said to Esther, as if talking to a child, careful singing – full of love.

Tea was boiling on the stove, the low bubbling over a blue flame warming the kitchen, and Betty thanked her cousin for the sweet cup of tea, blowing on it unhurriedly in an effort to rid herself of the chill outside.

Esther sat with her own mug. She had given up drinking alcohol and, slowly, had begun to resemble the girl Betty remembered. Her body was no longer grossly bloated but now charmingly overweight. She looked at the world as if she recognized it once more, though the dullness in her eyes remained. It was only when Betty came through the door that the cloud of sadness lifted and Esther would stamp her feet in impatient excitement, speaking in rapid tones as if she had collected all her thoughts throughout the day, storing them for this moment.

'Did you know the maid in Flat 6 is having an affair with the askari? I saw him go in when the lady of the house wasn't there... How can *unga* be so expensive these days? I thought Maggie from the kiosk was surely cheating me but it really is a hundred bob... Do you like my new braids? I got a woman to come home and do them for me...'

She never left the house, despite the constant encouragement from Betty, who would come in early on Saturdays to cheerless, cold rooms and she would go about opening all the curtains and windows, saying, 'Really, cousin, how can you live this way?'

'I don't want to leave David alone,' she would tell Betty, refusing to step outside. 'What if something happens? What if Jeffery comes back?'

Betty would take her cousin's hand, rubbing the glossy skin with her fingers, in a soothing, circular motion. 'You know David isn't here any more.'

'It's not my fault you aren't looking properly – that you can't see him. I don't want that man to get to him again.'

And Betty would persist, 'What happened, why won't you tell me?' But Esther remained determinedly silent.

'What does it matter what happened? He's gone and that's it.'

But that evening, her outline flared by the brass glow of the kerosene lamp, Esther said, 'Today would have been his birthday.'

Not wanting to jolt her cousin out of her daze, Betty put the cup down carefully. 'Who?' she asked, though she already knew. Her curiosity about David had been growing ever since she had had the conversation with Jeffery on the steps, his face swallowed in darkness. How defeated he had sounded, talking about that man, how heavy and broken.

'David would have been forty today.' Esther tapped her index finger nervously on the table, *taptaptaptap*, until its legs shook and Betty had to reach out and stop her. 'We always had a cake,' she continued. 'I used to wake up early to bake one, stick up some balloons and he would bring his policeman friends back here.' She was concentrating hard on the memory, trying to bring it into focus. 'I would always get so angry with him. I used to ask, *Why can't it just be the two of us? Why do you have to bring all of those men?*' She looked up at Betty. 'But he always owed someone something.'

'What do you mean?'

'He wasn't a bad man.' Esther almost begged her to believe it. 'He just did bad things sometimes. I used to tell him to stop but once you start down such a path, it becomes difficult to turn back.'

Paraffin oil leaked into the air, phenyl-like and sweet, transporting Betty back to their childhood days, when she thought Esther so queer and ghost-like, and her skin tightened in shivers.

'What did he used to do?'

'What else do policemen do here?' Esther cocked her eyebrow. 'He stole from everybody he could and then blamed the government, as if we have no control over our actions. As if the injustice done to us gives us the right to treat others so poorly.' The creased skin of her closed eyelids trembled. 'Still, I loved him very much and he didn't deserve what happened to him.'

Confusion tugged at Betty's mind. 'I don't understand. Jeffery said you were having an affair with David. So how come you spent every birthday with him? Where was Jeffery?'

At this, Esther began to laugh. She howled until she was clutching her stomach and doubling over, grasping at air. 'Oh! Oh! Oh!' she mumbled between hysterical waves. 'Oh, that man! That man has no shame.' Her laughter suddenly died and her face fell into an ugly hardness. 'No respect, even for the dead. I said that David did bad things but that he wasn't a bad man. But Jeffery is different. He can do anything.' She tapped Betty's skin, *taptaptap.* 'But then again, I'm living with the man who killed my husband so I suppose you should ask me, what else did I expect?'

The words were knocked out of her. 'Wha—'

'It's this country that does it to you.' Esther ignored her cousin's reaction. 'It teases you with a mirage of beauty so that you believe all things are possible. It tempts but cannot give you anything. You see people suffocating under piles of money while you're struggling to put even one meal on the table. There are mansions constructed from the finest materials, so unnecessarily extravagant for the two people living in it, while somewhere in Kibera, seven people share an impermanent shack the size of this kitchen – so how can you not be angry? When there is all this unfairness around us, how can we blame our men for going mad?'

Pooja flitted about the house, checking all the rooms, ensuring the paintings were perfectly aligned against the walls and the fridge was fully stocked: cheese, grapes, hot sauce – all of her daughter's favorite things. She called out as she went, 'Is no one going to help me? Why must I do all these things myself?' her sharp voice reaching the high ceilings and traveling to all the upstairs bedrooms so that Jai came out on to the landing.

When she saw him, she demanded, 'Does no one but me care that your sister is coming home today?' wiping away the smudges on a decorative mirror with her *chuni*. 'Where is Betty?'

'I'm here, I've arrived.' A hurried voice, the sound of the back door closing as Betty rushed in.

'You're always late these days,' retorted Pooja, unamused. 'Even though I told you there is a lot of work to do today.'

'There was such a big jam on Waiyaki Way,' Betty tried to explain. 'I left as early as I could but the traffic refused to move.'

'You have a room here.' Pooja gestured in the general direction of the outhouse. 'I don't understand why you would sleep elsewhere.'

It was not often that Betty stayed at Esther's, but last night they had talked until the pale hours of the morning, undisturbed because Jeffery never came home. By the time she had jolted from the bed, Esther snoring loudly beside her, it was already nine o'clock, an hour past the time Pooja was expecting her.

'My cousin is very unwell,' she lied.

'One day it's your cousin, the next your aunt.' Pooja waved her arm snidely in the air. 'You can do whatever you want, Betty, just don't treat me like I'm stupid, okay?'

Jai came down the stairs quickly. 'Just tell us what you need to be done.'

'Everything,' Pooja snapped, walking rapidly away into the kitchen. 'That's why I told her eight o'clock – we have to make sure everything is perfect.'

It was a strange sensation, flying back into a place she had left only a year before. Although everything seemed familiar, it was also joltingly different. Here, the streets smelled of burning garbage and flowers, as they always had, while close to her uncle's house in Stanmore, it was the spices of kebab shops and the stink of beer from the pub across the street.

The British way of life had fascinated her. She had learned much about it from observing out of her bedroom window the simple goings-on of the Drunken Goose across the road, the quaint bar that played seventies British rock music. The patrons would sing along, their voices reaching her as she blew bored steam-circle onto the glass. How tempted she had been on some nights to climb out of the window and join them.

She had been astonished and envious of their lives, for here young people could do whatever they wanted. Women smoked with strange men and then left the bar with them, waving goodbye to friends who barely acknowledged them going. People drank until they were forced to throw up in trash cans, bushes or even right on the street and yet still, no one whispered. No one pointed. They were not worried that they might run into a cousin, a family friend, who upon seeing them would immediately report the misdemeanors to a parent. That is what had impressed her about life in Britain; one never had to worry about suffering through any shame for having fun.

People roamed the streets at two o'clock in the morning, never checking over their shoulders to ensure they were safe. Leena never realized how deeply the concept of fear and suspiciousness had been engrained in her until she watched those people; she had never resented her lack of freedom to do certain things because she had never known how simple and easy it could be to do them.

This country was not made up of real worries, she concluded from all her watchings. Yes, people were concerned about how much money they had to spend, about bills and jobs and heartbreaks, but it is a different thing altogether to be burdened with the fear of your life. To wake up to stories about a woman being strangled by her housemaid, or a friend of your parents who was shot point-blank on his way out of the office because someone had spotted a briefcase in his hand. Back home, you were forced to keep yourself tightly hidden away, behind the locked doors of houses and cars; you spoke to those who were like you, people you knew, and ignored strangers, just in case.

London was boring in a lovely, comforting way and now that she had become used to that, she found it frightful coming out of the arrivals building in Nairobi – assaulted in every way by the noise, the colors and the rushing bodies, mindless of her presence.

And then there were arms going around her waist and she yelped with fear until she caught a whiff of the mint gum on his breath, the warm air of his laughter at the nape of her neck. And he was saying, 'Come on, monkey. It's only me.'

And the gateless house in Stanmore was forgotten, the Drunken Goose only a funny story and London nothing but a place that wasn't home.

38

The two men had been watching him for a while now, hunched so closely over the small bar table that their elbows were tip to tip, the tops of their shoes touching. They sat to the left of him, slowly sipping their Tuskers. That was what had made Jeffery suspicious. No grown man spent that long drinking a single beer unless he was waiting for something.

'*Ingine?*' Marlyn's voice offering him another drink. He dragged his eyes away from the men.

Lowering his voice, he asked, 'Who are those guys?'

'They've never been in here before.'

Dressed casually in cotton shirts and white sneakers, they were unremarkable, nothing startling about their behavior, and yet Jeffery couldn't shake the prickling disquiet disturbing the hairs on his neck. *Stupid boy. Coming into my office and scaring me for no good reason. Now it's four o'clock and he's not even here yet.*

He had called Nick three times already but there was no answer. He sat sipping his watery drink and listening to the drone of the standard Safaricom message, insensitive to his growing frustration – *Mteja hapatikani kwa sasa* – telling him what he already knew: the boy was unreachable.

'Something the matter, *mzee*?'

He had been so focused on phoning Nick that Jeffery hadn't noticed the two men approaching his table, blocking him on either side.

'Can't you see I'm busy?' he snapped.

'Who are you trying to call?' The man leaning in on him had sagging jowls, countless lines bracketing his mouth. His voice was rich, the kind that would lend itself nicely to TV or radio. If he hadn't looked so menacing, he might have been pleasant.

'Do I know you?' Jeffery let his eyes wander the bar, as if in boredom, but he was anxiously looking to see if there was anyone else in the room. Marlyn was at the back and he was the only customer. The man swung his body onto the stool beside him.

'Unfortunately, Nick is unable to pick up his phone at this time.'

'Why?' Jeffery's voice shuddered.

'The boy became greedy. We had a deal and he thought he could outsmart me. When I found out he had been stealing from me, I asked for my money back.' The man shrugged at the simplicity of his actions. 'If he had done so, perhaps he would have only lost a finger or an eye, but sadly…'

Panicked, Jeffery dialed Nick's number again. 'What have you done to him?'

Fingers pinched into the soft dent of his collarbone, collapsing him forward. 'Let's say he won't be answering his phone any more, *sawa*? However, he still owes me money and I have come to collect it.'

'From who?' Jeffery asked. The man pressed down harder into his shoulder and Jeffery struggled to remain upright. 'I'm not the boy's father. Why would I pay you?'

'We know he was working for you.'

Jeffery remained adamant. 'You have the wrong man.'

'And yet here you are, calling-calling him for almost two hours now.' The man released Jeffery and he fell backward against the wall.

'I know he comes here every Wednesday with a package for you.' The man stood, indicating with a tilt of his head to his companion that he was ready to leave. 'Two hundred thousand – that's how much he owes me.'

'Get it from someplace else.' Jeffery feigned bravado but as he raised his glass to his lips, the liquid splashed against the sides, spilling over, and he quickly put it down.

The man said, 'If it's not here on Wednesday, two weeks from now, I shall come to South C and collect it myself.'

Jeffery's chest caved with the realization that they knew where he lived. After they left, he snapped his fingers and whistled for Marlyn. She came running as he shouted, 'What's the matter with you, woman? Get me a drink!' snatching it from her as soon as she brought it and gulping it down.

His head spinning unpleasantly, Jeffery dialed Nick's number again. 'Pick up, pick up, *mafala*!' But there was no answer for the rest of the day.

Her presence changed the nature of the household. When he stepped in that evening, he was greeted by a bell-like laugh and tea cups hitting the wooden table and, for a split second, Jeffery didn't feel so lonely. On the rare occasion he did come home while Esther was still awake, they hid from each other and the rooms remained silent and gloomy. But nowadays, the house was more cared for, its surfaces and corners polished and glowing, its furniture and floors shining with the pleasure of use.

He hadn't paid attention to the sound of Betty until now, light and simple. He was touched by the way she brushed Esther's hair from her forehead, checking to make sure her tea was always warm. Watching them, Jeffery hesitated to enter the kitchen, but he had spent most of the day drinking and was in need of water. Slinking in, he hoped to sneak out with minimum fuss, but when Betty looked up he couldn't stop the 'Hello' that slipped from his dry mouth.

Esther's back tightened at the greeting, her fingers clutching Betty's as they glanced meaningfully at each other. Humiliation set his cheeks alight when he realized, in that one look, that Betty had been told the truth about David.

'Hello.' Her voice was timid and he wanted to reassure her, *I'm not going to hurt you*, but he had spent so many years now being malicious that he had forgotten how to speak gently. 'I've just come to spend some time with Esther,' she explained.

He took a sip of water – 'Very good,' nodding enthusiastically and staring at the back of the woman who was supposed to be his wife, thinking how she was still a complete stranger to him. It was in times of such self-awareness that he ached for his mother, the comfort of that unlit shack, the late-night noise of people drinking, living and loving. Even the stench of human waste had a special quality about it because it felt like home.

'I'll be in the next room,' he told them gruffly, taking his glass, a chair tucked under his arm.

Once settled at the open window, Jeffery watched the long-legged mosquitos dance in, their thin wings iridescent in the blue glow of the television. He pricked his ears in the hope that he might be able to eavesdrop on the women.

'I don't know why he's home today,' Esther was saying. 'I was really hoping he would stay out.'

Jeffery had stopped feeling insulted by such things. After all he had done to her, how could he blame her for feeling that way? But when Betty said, 'He looks like the most evil man I've ever seen,' even the pinpricks of itchy poison from the greedy mosquitoes weren't enough to distract him from the truth.

As they continued speaking, Jeffery tried to settle his mind. He had spent most of the afternoon drowning his anxiety in the buttery skin of Marlyn, wishing he could hide out in that motel for the rest of his life.

Nick had been discovered that evening, a broken and bent heap lost in a garbage dump near Nairobi River. There was a gunshot through his chest, but Jeffery could see that prior to that he had been severely beaten. Hoisting up his trouser legs, Jeffery had crouched to adjust the boy's crooked glasses, overcome by a horrible and unexpected remorse even though he thought he would be used to death by now.

As they wrapped Nick in a polythene bag and slid him into an ambulance, Jeffery knew with certainty that there was nothing stopping those men from killing him, and he had returned to the bar, hoping to find the solution somewhere in his alcohol-soaked, numbed brain. Yet even now, the answer had not come to him, until he heard Betty say, 'I'm sorry, Esther. I must get going – Mrs Kohli wants me back at the house early tomorrow so I'll take the late bus tonight.'

He sat up so suddenly that the glass almost tumbled from his knee. He had forgotten all about that house, its marble pillars and modern, brick roofs. The three cars in the wide driveway. An idea was coming to him, still taking shape, as Betty passed him on her way to the door and said to him, he felt almost out of fear, 'Goodbye.'

The chair crashed to the floor as he rose. 'Wait, please. I'll drop you.'

'I'll be alright.' Her expression told him that she would rather face the crushing blackness of night and all its possible horrors than sit in a car with him for twenty minutes.

'It's the least I could do, given the good care you have shown my wife. Come on, I don't mind one bit.' He didn't give her another chance to protest.

She was turning back to Esther for help, but by then he had already swung the door open and herded her firmly out.

They didn't talk for the first few minutes of the drive but he hardly noticed because night-time in Nairobi was full of noise. The thrum of Westlands bars, street vendors desperately haggling for one last sell, the thousands of crickets like chirping pinpoints in the dark. He turned up the volume on the radio and glanced at her from the corner of his eye.

She was pressed close to the door, her hand lightly wrapped around the handle as if she were preparing to jump out.

He asked, 'Do you enjoy working for your employers?'

It took her a moment to answer. 'Why?'

'I'm only wondering,' he replied, swerving to miss a *matatu* speeding on the wrong side of the road. 'You know, I wanted to be a policeman all my life. Now that I am one—' He clucked his tongue. 'Well, that's a different story.'

'I won't stay a housemaid forever.' She was offended. 'I'm planning on starting my own beauty salon.'

This time when he looked at her, he saw that she was much younger than him. 'How old are you?'

'Thirty next month.'

'Yes, you have time.' He nodded his approval. 'It's a very good dream but takes a lot of money.'

'I'm saving up.' She was curt, didn't want to reveal herself to him.

'And what do your employers do?' He kept his tone neutral.

'They own a business. A furniture store.'

The information sparked the first hope he had had since those two men had come to visit him at the bar. Without thinking, he murmured, 'They must be very rich.'

She said sharply, 'Why are you asking me all these questions?'

They had reached the house and Jeffery didn't answer as they rolled down the paved hill, where he pulled to a grinding halt outside the gate. As Betty climbed out, Jeffery spoke, staring up at the rise and fall of the impressive home.

'It doesn't make you angry?'

She paused, one leg still in the car, her eyes craned downward. 'What?'

'That this isn't even their country and yet they get to enjoy every part of it while we're the ones made to suffer.' He thought of his mother again, chewed down on his lip.

In the close confines of the car, the only sound the humming of insects in the blackness beyond, his words stung her with something she had always known but never wanted to consider before. For a moment, she forgot how frightened she was of him and said, 'You're right. It's not fair at all.'

They shared a look, a feeling, and it was the closest he had felt to anyone in a long time. 'See you tomorrow.' His voice turned husky, the house blurred and forgotten behind him.

She knocked on the gate and whispered through the gap for the askari to let her in. She paused at the step, turning to wave.

It hurt him, that simple gesture – almost like an acute rip in his gut. But then she disappeared and he looked up once again at the house. And he had to smile because it was going to be his way out – and Betty was going to help him.

39

The large manila paper was spread across the desk as Jai and Michael discussed their latest graffiti. They had spent a week completing it, an image of a young girl dying in her mother's arms while all around them wealthy politicians sat in a gilded restaurant, fat-bellied and fat-pocketed. Although the woman's hand was reaching out for help, they ignored her, lost in their gluttony. Beneath it, it read:

PEOPLE BEFORE PROFIT

'I'm not sure about this one,' Michael said to Jai. 'It's very intricate and there's a lot to draw. How will we get it done in under an hour?' Nudging his friend in the side. 'Are you listening to me?'

Jai shook himself out of a thought. 'Sorry, I was distracted.'

'I don't think we can get this done in under an hour,' Michael repeated, pointing out the details he thought they could do without and, again, Jai's mind wandered.

Leena had been home for two weeks now and, although he was happy to have her back, he was troubled by the fact that ever since she had landed, she had been edgy and critical of everything around her. She was ungrounded, perturbed, and when he asked her what was wrong, she said, 'It's difficult to explain since you've never been out of Nairobi.'

He tried not to feel insulted by her tone when she said, 'I'm strangely disappointed.'

'About what?'

She thought of her small room in Stanmore, all those handsome British men and a life scattered through with brief romances and said, 'When I was away, I would be so homesick, I think I made up memories of this place. But now that I'm back, I find that it's not really that rosy. I feel a pull to go back there, but while I was in London I wanted to return home. It's like I'm in some kind of suspended reality.'

Jai spoke as he always did about this topic, forcefully. 'Everyone we know has this idea in their mind that they need to leave here and see the world – it doesn't matter what they'll find, they're just sure it'll be better.' He looked out into the rolling, gray horizon, thick with fast-approaching thunder clouds. He could smell it rising from the baked earth, moist and dirt-like. 'I could never bear to leave this place.'

'Jai the savior.' She had said it with a smile but there was an old bitterness in her words.

He told Michael all of this. His friend had stopped looking at the drawing, fixed on Jai's words instead. His every muscle was unmoving, trying to grasp what Jai was saying. Though all he could comprehend, all that rung through his mind, was that she was back.

It was rare that he remembered Leena. It was only when he saw children playing a game of marbles or caught the lemon scent of another woman's hair that he would indulge in a moment of nostalgia – sink into the comfort of a well-worn recollection and laugh to himself. How he used to wash his underarms in the sink or linger on the veranda, waiting to catch a glimpse of her, because the leap in his chest and the swimming in his head made him feel more alive than anything else ever had. And that is what this news did to him: made him dizzy with sick excitement as he realized just how empty Nairobi had been without her.

He forced steady words out. 'Everyone changes, you can't stop that. It's normal to feel distant for the first couple of weeks.'

'I guess you're right.' Jai turned back to the drawing and said, 'You're also right about this drawing. It could definitely do with some cutting.'

It was Michael's turn to be distracted. He was full of something: a dusky evening and a bougainvillea bark lit with gold. A magenta flower sliding from his fingers to behind her small ear and a gaze, however small, still shared. Weighed down and thrilling.

He shook himself free and tried to ignore it; that was the disturbing thing about memories. They have a way of growing, even when there is nothing left to feed them. Beautiful things but dangerous – waiting for the right moment, the most inconvenient time, to spring up and surprise you with something that can never be true.

He was alone on Saturday night when it happened. He hadn't planned on ending up there; he'd left Jackie in the apartment to go for a long walk because the house had been too constricting for his looming thoughts.

It was a hot and uncomfortable evening – a reflection of his own feelings. *Stifling. Inescapable.* The idea of her refused to leave him, even after he had exited the building and moved rapidly down the road. He dashed across the street, avoiding men transporting cartons of water in large-wheeled carts hoisted upon their shoulders, slowing down traffic.

At first, it had been enjoyable to think of her. To recall the games they had played, the first time he had ever listened to music from a Walkman. To cycle hands free on a bicycle he had borrowed from a man in the park and let his memories catch up.

Knowing that Leena was in the same city kept him constantly

nervous; he worried and hoped that he might run into her on the street, though he knew how impossible such a scenario was. Even if he did, would they recognize each other? Even worse, if they recognized each other, would she even care? He recalled the inconsiderate way in which he and his mother had been dismissed from the Kohlis' house. He had been sent from the apartment block without even the opportunity to say goodbye, but it hadn't mattered because she had been so caught up in moving houses, in the prospect of her fancy, new life, that she had immediately forgotten the old one and everyone in it.

A few weeks later, when Jai had come to visit him, he told Michael that Leena hadn't come along because everyone in the family agreed it was best she make her own friends. The loss had been agonizing, a constant somersaulting in his stomach so affecting that he felt it even now, pulsating slightly.

'You're only sixteen,' Jackie had said to him back then as he sat sullenly by the window. 'What can you possibly know about love?'

Ever since Jai told him Leena was back, Michael had been spending early mornings in his Lavington studio, trying to pin down his feelings, but found that they ran too deep and refused to surface. They were reluctant to reveal themselves. For what would happen if they were nothing but emotions he had expanded on his own, developed into things that weren't real but just some sunny-day boyhood recollections and nothing more?

He had needed space to think, which was why he found himself climbing the short green gates of Aga Khan Primary School, leaping into the deserted parking lot. He stilled himself, listening for any guards, and when he was certain he was alone, he took off in search of a canvas.

As always, he carried a can of spray paint with him when he left the house and now, finding a small wall at the back of the building, amid parked school buses, he shook it open.

He had no idea of what he wanted to say until he wrote it, didn't know who he was angry with until mid-way, when he stopped and exhaled an understanding '*Oh.*'

Before him was an outline of a woman – slim in face, narrow in shoulders and with a hard, unrelenting brow. Worry and age had sprung up in lines around her mouth and the corners of her eyes but she had retained a youthful attractiveness, hardly having aged a day since he last saw her. She guarded something behind her: a girl who was trying to peer over her mother's shoulder. Before them stood a boy and it was this boy he colored in, flushed at the thought of having something so personal and inerasable displayed in public. On impulse, he leaned into the mother's face, scrawled on top of her eyes and over where her mouth should be:

IF ONLY CLOSED MINDS
CAME WITH CLOSED MOUTHS.

The can dropped from his hand and he sagged against the wall. He missed her terribly, felt the brunt of her indifference even now, years later, but more than that, it was Pooja he was livid with. She had seen them on the evening of her anniversary party, when he had pushed the flower into Leena's hair – and though he hadn't been able to make out the exact features of her face, he had known from the stiffness of her pose how distressed it had made her. Michael had watched in dismay as she crushed the bougainvillea in her daughter's hair, throwing the flattened and colorless petals onto the steps.

When she fired his mother, Michael had pretended not to know the real reason because he hadn't wanted Angela to be right. He had ignored her warnings and lied to himself that the differences between the Kohlis and them didn't matter – and then had been appalled to find that they were the only things that did. He knew that, in her own way, Pooja had been afraid of him. She had packed up and shifted their entire lives in three weeks because she didn't want Michael to be a part of them any more. Michael had the sudden urge to call Jai; he would ask him where he was and he would go and see Leena.

He stood to take the mobile phone out of his pocket when he heard a voice.

'That's a nice drawing, *kijana*.'

He turned slowly, an arm raised to shut out the blaze of the torch. He said, 'It's not a drawing, officer. It's art.'

A few minutes before this, Jeffery had received a phone call from one of the security guards at the Parklands Mosque. He had noticed some suspicious activity – a young man jumping over the gates of Aga Khan Primary School.

'So go and check it out yourself,' Jeffery had snapped. 'What are you calling me for?'

'We don't know if he's armed, sir,' the guard had said. 'And I don't have a weapon.'

Jeffery had slammed down the phone. The police station was empty – it was still too early for drunks and thieves and Jeffery was bored, so he decided to take a walk.

The night was warm and usually he would have enjoyed the sticky way it clung to him but he was jumpy. After discovering Nick's body in the river, and knowing that the two men were familiar with where he lived, and surely where he worked, he felt nervous and exposed, and half-way to the school he almost turned back.

But now, standing before the young man, Jeffery was glad he had come. He shone the torch on the drawing and recognized almost immediately the handiwork. He moved the spotlight down to the bottom right-hand corner – saw the slogan there.

'You've decided to become more risky?' He shifted the light back to the young man's face, enjoyed putting him at the mercy of the unrelenting torch.

'I don't know what you're talking about.'

The boy stayed leaning against the wall, seemingly unbothered. He was composed and well dressed, unlike many others Jeffery had to deal with. Perhaps he was the rich, rebellious kind, with a father who was a successful criminal lawyer or a gynecologist. It would make sense because the boy talked to him loudly and with confidence, such mannerisms that were reserved for those with money.

'I recognize your handwriting. And that saying, *Kenya ni yetu*, just like the other ones…' He waved his hand in the air, as if thinking, though the words had never left him. He stretched his lips back in an effort to frighten the boy. 'Very clever but it's still not allowed.'

'I was out for a walk when I came upon this. I was reading it when you surprised me.'

Jeffery snatched the boy's hand up and held it under the light. He raised his eyebrows at the telltale ink stains on his palm. 'Let's go.'

'Where are you taking me?'

'Don't mind that. Just follow.'

'I'd rather not.'

'It's not a request,' Jeffery growled, pulling out his gun.

The boy raised his hands, infuriatingly at ease. 'I didn't know it was a crime to walk in this city.'

'You're on private property and it's illegal to draw on the walls.'

'It's art,' repeated the boy, 'and you don't know that I did it.'

'I don't have time for your silly debating.' Jeffery swung his gun in the direction of the gate. 'Let's get moving to the police station.'

He shoved the boy ahead of him, forcing him down the loose gravel parking lot. They left behind them the still-fresh story, consumed by the darkness and splitting apart slowly, dissolving in the hot rain that had just begun to fall.

No one came in or out of the station. The flimsy *mabati* door swung in the sudden wind, the chill of the thunderstorm roaring in. The boy sat in handcuffs, looking about as if bored.

'Do you know that the defacement of public buildings is an offense?' Jeffery asked finally.

Usually, he wouldn't have brought the boy back here. He would have bribed him for five thousand shillings or more and left him at the school – would have gone to get himself some fried chicken and chips. But he had wanted to see the boy in the light, the person who had attacked him personally with every drawing, the one who had publicly revealed his shame.

'Everyone has a right to voice their opinions,' the boy told him.

'Then do it at home on a piece of paper that they can hang in one of those fancy galleries,' Jeffery said. 'You can't ruin the image of our city just because you have an opinion. Do you think you're the only one living here?'

'I think I'm the only one with a working brain who lives here.' He was suddenly visibly upset. 'Just because someone has more money than you, or is a different color, doesn't mean they should treat you badly.'

The unexpected confession surprised them both. Jeffery said, 'In that regard, I must agree with you.'

The metal cuffs clanged against the edge of the table as the boy sat back. 'Can I go now?'

Jeffery was busy with his own thoughts. He was irrationally driven to seek this boy's approval, as if it would lessen his disgrace, which the drawings had solidified and made painfully real. He asked, a childish glint in his eye, 'Do you want to make some money?'

'Doesn't everyone?'

'Yes.' Perhaps this boy was more similar to him than he had imagined. 'Suppose I have a way of helping you make some fast *doh*.'

The boy continued to stare at him and Jeffery took this as a positive sign to continue. He told the boy of his dilemma. With Nick gone, he was alone and it couldn't hurt to have someone young and strong on his side – and the boy seemed much more astute than Nick had ever been. When he finished recounting his plan, Jeffery crossed his arms over his chest and smirked, so certain in the lure of greed that when the boy asked, 'You want me to rob a house?' Jeffery nodded pleasantly.

'Exactly so. I will give you your fair share, of course.' He was salivating in excitement, felt it wet the corners of his mouth and dabbed there with the heel of his hand. 'The house is in—'

'I don't want to know.' The boy held up his handcuffed wrists. 'An officer of the law who has just arrested me for defacing public property is now asking for my help to steal from someone else.' The boy laughed and it was rude and snide. 'Put me in a cell or let me go, but I won't help you to rob from my fellow Kenyans.' Then he remarked, 'It's because of people like you that I'm forced to draw, as you call it, on walls.'

Being reprimanded by someone half his age and in his office!

'Have it your way.' Jeffery was enraged and grabbed the boy so forcefully that the table was pushed aside. 'I wanted to give you a chance but if you would rather wait in a jail cell until someone comes looking for you, then please allow me to escort you there.'

Jeffery heaved open the metal doors behind the front desk, the persistent *clang!* of it ringing in his ears, and he shoved the boy hard, sending him stumbling head first into the pitch-black corridor ahead.

40

Sunday morning stillness filled the Kohlis' house. All Betty could hear as she let herself in was the high *weeho* of the black-pied crows perched on the eaves and a toilet flushing upstairs. She locked the back door behind her and went into the kitchen, staring in annoyance at the pile of dishes waiting by the sink.

The family had eaten dinner late yesterday, after Betty had already left. She saw that no one had bothered to rinse them before stacking them messily and now there was a thick stream of black ants marching from the window frame to the plate rims, picking at crumbs of white rice and goat curry.

She had woken up edgy and irritable; the slight hole in her cardigan kept snagging on her earring and she had tugged until it had finally ripped. Looking up from the ruined sweater to the palatial house, she thought of the Kohlis, snug in their beds while she was forced to rise at seven o'clock to prepare their breakfast and clean the house.

She pushed the dishes into the sink with a forceful swipe of her arm, watched the ants panic at this sudden disturbance. She turned on the tap and let the steady stream of water fall over the plates and experienced a mean thrill at the vicious assault.

Jeffery's voice refused to leave her as she pulled out two pink papayas from the fridge and an apple, skinning them according to

Pooja's preference. His words settled heavily in the crook of her brain, spreading like a dull and unforgiving headache. As she went about chopping the fruit, the tightness in her temples grew until she had to pause and cling to the edge of the counter to steady herself.

'Are you alright?'

Leena was watching her from the doorway.

'Yes. Everything is okay.' Betty had to put the knife down because it refused to stay still. Then, hating that she felt compelled to ask, she said, 'Can I make you some tea?'

'Would you bring it upstairs for me? There's something I want to show you.'

'Okay.' Betty was curt, turning back to her work. The knife sliced easily through the pulpy flesh of the fruit and she wiped away black seeds and a stringy mess, dividing them into neat cubes. As she went to boil the water for tea, she wondered if it had ever crossed the girl's mind to do it herself.

She found Leena rifling through her closet, her room turned upside down with strewn clothes, old picture albums and high-school love letters, written in blushed secrecy.

'I have your tea.'

'Just put it on the table.' Her voice was muffled behind the door.

As Betty placed it down, she took the opportunity to scan her surroundings while the girl was distracted. She noted the abundance of items – a computer open at the desk, a mobile phone occasionally beeping on the bedside table and a music device, blue and shiny, in Leena's back pocket. Things that were beyond Betty's comprehension and desire – she had never cared about possessing them. But in her present state of mind, she grew resentful once more of everything that came so easily to this young girl and for all the distant dreams she was working toward. 'Why did you need me?' she asked, trying to keep the hardness from her voice.

Leena came to sit on her bed, a box in her lap. 'I have some things you might be able to use.' She slid off the cover and tilted it toward Betty. There were necklaces and earrings caught in a heap of multicolored beads, one or two lipsticks and an oblong crimson perfume bottle that had never been touched. To Betty, they seemed sorely precious lying in a cushion of torn blue velvet and she thought that perhaps, after all, her anger had been unjustified.

'These are just some old things I don't want any more – if you won't take them, I'll throw them out.'

Insulted, Betty drew her hand back. To think that she was being given things deemed worthless made her feel pitiful. She should have said no but something pulled her to the dark-red bottle, a shimmer of gold coming through and its intricate, twisted top. She had never owned a perfume and found it impossible now to refuse. Clutching the box tightly to her chest, she muttered a 'Thank you so much,' before fleeing downstairs.

In the concrete dimness, Betty ran her hand over the flat glass pendants of the necklaces, held up beaded earrings to her lobes and let them fall coolly against her neck. She sprayed the perfume on her wrists and the lily scent took over everything in her small room – settled into the few pieces of decor she had – picture frames and a potted plant, a blue-and-white checkered bedspread that acted as her door. The rectangular bottle, with its tremendous, sharp corners, was easily the most expensive thing she owned, besides the old radio that hardly worked any more.

Her throat raw with disappointment, the rims of her eyes burning, she had the sudden desire to sleep – a deep, insensible, week-long hiatus – and she lifted her feet into the tangled sheets, holding her wrist firmly to her nose. And then, her mind and body rapidly gathering self-pity, Betty began to cry.

She remained stony and mute for the rest of the day, even at Esther's table later in the evening. She had gone through her work with such aggrieved distraction that she had broken two plates and a mug, pulling the handle right off as she was washing the dishes.

The Kohlis' house, it seemed to Betty, had kept itself cleverly apart from her, enshrouded in an invisible veil that she hadn't noticed until it was tangled about her, choking and tight. Now she saw the uncouth extravagance, the irrelevance of so many of its spaces. The nooks in the walls, where Pooja insisted on keeping fresh flowers in massive, tubular vases, the 'mess' room constructed especially to store dirty shoes and clothes and Raj's cricket kit – larger than the one Betty slept in. There were lavish paintings on every blank wall, a small yet impressive chandelier fracturing the dining table into mirrors of light. All these items had always seemed excessive to her, altogether silly, but that day they were terrible, jeering things that hounded her.

'There's something wrong with Jeffery.' Betty was tugged back to Esther's smiling face – her cheeks ballooning out in a laugh. 'You should have seen him last night. He pushed the dining table across the door and watched out of the window until morning. I don't know who he was expecting but he was frightened.'

Betty tried to bring her attention back to her cousin. 'You should be careful.'

'I'm past the point of worrying in my life. I'm just here to wait for whatever comes.'

'I'm tired of you talking that way.' Betty's composure finally gave way and Esther was an easy target. 'Stop squandering your time, gossiping about maids having affairs and complaining about the price of *unga*. You must start living again.'

Esther remained unperturbed. 'I can't live without David. That's my punishment.'

'No one is punishing you except yourself.'

'You're wrong.' Esther cupped a palm around her mouth, as if sharing a secret, though they were alone in the house. 'Look at Jeffery. Something terrible has happened to him. He can't sit still, can't eat – he won't even drink his whiskey. That's what happens when you do bad things, Betty. Bad things start happening to you.' Esther straightened out her floral-patterned gown, patted down the lace collar in satisfaction. 'Remember that. The devil will always bite you back.'

There were questions resting between them, impregnating the already overheated spaces of Jeffery's car and Betty had to roll down the window.

'Esther is safe in the house, isn't she?' She asked because it seemed to be the only concern acceptable to address. She wanted to tell him about her day, how much his words had disrupted her simple world, had altered something inside of her so that she couldn't look at the Kohlis the same way.

Jeffery glanced at her sideways, her profile unclear in the darkness threaded through with dim street lights. There was something he liked very much about this woman. She was modest and didn't carry the burdens he did, or perhaps she only carried them better, but he was finding it difficult to bring up his prospective plan with her. So he was glad she spoke first. 'Why would you ask that?'

'She told me that you're worried about something. That you stayed up all night with the dining table blocking your door, waiting for someone.'

347

His jowls loosened, his cheeks relaxing into a downward smile. 'I didn't know she noticed such things. That she cared.'

A quick correction. 'Actually she was pleased about it.' Betty was upset that he had caused this permanent shift inside her, this twisting and turning of all evil things such as jealousy and hatred and bitterness.

Hardening, Jeffery glowered. 'And she wonders why I spend so much time outside of the house.'

'Perhaps it's because you murdered her husband.'

It came as a swift relief, to hear her say it. Now that his secret was finally exposed, he was glad to have this chance to explain himself to her.

'Things weren't as straightforward as Esther claims they were. Whatever happened to David is not what I wanted.' His eyes locked on the road, a glittering, tarmac point ahead. 'I was stupid and greedy. Even now, I can't say that I've learned my lesson. Money is extremely important to me.'

'It's not everything.'

'Yet without it, what is the standard of life?'

He wanted to recount to Betty the story of his mother. He felt such an urgent desire to speak about it with her, overcome with the need that she understand what had happened to him. 'I used to be a good person.'

The grave humiliation in his voice startled her. She said, 'It's not too late to go back.'

'There comes a point when change becomes impossible.'

'Maybe you just don't want to,' she retorted.

The contemplative silence that followed was interrupted by the occasional brushing sound of his tires and the wind knocking tirelessly across the windows. 'Perhaps you're right.'

He pulled up at the gate, watched her climb out with his fists tightened against the steering wheel. Then, terrified he would lose her, he knocked wildly on the passenger window. When she spun around he waved and, when she returned the gesture, he quickly smiled with what seemed an inkling of his old self.

He drove the twenty minutes home in contemplative leisure, forearm draped over his open window and soft music between his ears, all the while the jasmine-scented breeze filtering through, cool and invigorating, bringing him a much-needed peace.

They cornered him the next day in the Aqua Bar bathroom. He was there to tell Marlyn that he would not be seeing her any more. But as he came through the main door, a spring in his step after so many sluggish years, the two men accosted him, grabbing him by the underarms and dragging him to the toilets.

One stood guard at the door and every time someone tried to enter he shook his head and said, 'Not working. Come back later.'

The other man stood facing Jeffery, the white daylight streaming through the windows. 'Do you have it?'

'It's not yet Wednesday,' he had protested weakly.

'Wednesday is tomorrow so either you have it or you don't.'

'Just give me an extra week,' a bursting plea.

'I need it now.' The man loomed over him, profuse, vine-like muscles traveling out from under the collar of his shirt.

'I can't get it for you by tomorrow.' The confession came in a flood of terror and then there was nothing but hot, white pain. It was a flash of cold first, the sensation of splashing yourself with icy water but then it stayed too long and began a fire beneath his flesh. Broken bones, a fractured mirror in front of him – he felt something sticky against his gums and worried that he had lost a tooth. The hand on his neck was drawing his head back again.

'Wait – please,' he said, falling to his knees and clutching the man's trousers. He was dizzy and thought he might vomit onto the cracked floor. 'No more.'

'Are you going to get it for me?'

The blood from his forehead seeped into his eyes and everything turned a watery pink. His head drooped forward, so heavy he thought it might explode as he tried to nod a yes. The man caught it in its downward trajectory and forced it upward.

'You better otherwise I'll be coming to your house.' He dropped Jeffery's chin and with nothing holding him up, he collapsed to the floor, twisted legs beneath him. He struggled to keep his eyes open, his mind understanding. 'I've seen your wife and the mistress you keep.' A deep belly laugh. 'Two women in the same house – what a lucky *mzee* you are.'

'Don't hurt them.' His fingers grappled with the man's shoelaces and he received a swift kick in the abdomen. He doubled over, the breath suspended in his lungs before squeezing forth. 'I'll get it for you, just don't harm them.'

'I'll give you one more week, *sawa*? No more chances after that.' The man straightened out his shirt, wiped at a spot of blood on his cuff and told his companion amicably, 'I need a beer.'

The next thing Jeffery was aware of was Marlyn turning him over on his back, shouting for help, the ends of her weave turning clumpy with his blood. 'Wake up, Jeffery, wake up.' But he wasn't listening to her, didn't care for her rising panic because all he was thinking of was every wrong choice he had ever made and how, if he had been different, he would have allowed himself to fall in love with the quiet yet headstrong housemaid – how everything he had ever been greedy for was now worn out and foul and all those things he had abandoned only aching, incurable regrets.

*

By the time he arrived home, Esther was already asleep and Betty was standing by the front door, fastening the buttons of her cardigan. At the sound of his key, she flitted quickly to the wall. A shiver in her stomach gathered into a shortness of breath – she clutched tightly to the pleats of her skirt.

In the weak moonlight, his movements were only sounds – laborious and painfully slow – and when he reached for the light her hand flew to her mouth in a horrified gasp.

'What happened to you?'

A face purple as a raisin, raw cheeks that broke into minuscule eruptions of blood as he grimaced at her. 'Nothing. Why are you here?' Curt and abrupt once again with no sign of the man Betty had glimpsed in the car. He had been drinking; she could tell from the way he repeatedly smacked his lips together and squinted, concentrating intently on putting one foot in front of the other.

She tucked her purse under her arm and said stiffly, as she shoved by him, 'I was just leaving.'

He stepped in front of her and flicked the door latch. Caught up in a twist of elbows and grasping fingers, she noticed the tremble of his long eyelashes, how lovely the full curl of his mouth was – traces of a past handsomeness – and she wished she had known him then. He asked, 'Please, won't you help me?'

'What happened to you?' she repeated, once she had assisted him in staggering to a kitchen chair.

Ignoring her persistence, he said, 'First get me some Dettol and a painkiller.' He poked at his cheek and groaned. 'Everything hurts, even my insides.'

He told her where to find the items – the small, plastic bottle of antiseptic, some cotton swabs and two small white pills. She handed him the tablets with a glass of water.

After he had swallowed them she scooted closer to him and grasped lightly at his chin. With the sting of ethanol in her nose, her eyes watering, Betty dabbed slowly at his torn cheek. Jeffery winced, struggled away, but she held him firmly.

'Are you going to tell me what happened?'

'Isn't it obvious?' The irritated sarcasm again and she stilled her hand, the cotton swab hovering. Their eyes met – hers were stern and made him smile. Softer, he said, 'Two men attacked me at a bar.'

'Why?'

His face stung at the memory but he was enjoying the light sureness of her fingertips, the bitter tea-breath that reminded him of his old life. He didn't know how to say it to her. No doubt there were enough possessions in that Runda house to get him the two hundred thousand he needed but he didn't want to face her reaction. He couldn't ever remember being this intimate with someone, grazing the delicate edges of familiarity with a stranger, and he was reluctant for it to end. But time was running out.

'I owe them money.'

She had withdrawn her hand to pour some more Dettol onto a cotton ball and when she dabbed again, her actions were lighter and disappointed. 'What for?'

'I made some deals that went wrong.' He trapped her hand as it left his face, pressed his thumb to the fleshiest part of it and felt the unwavering beat of her heart. He brought his mouth close to her palm, almost touching. 'I was a good man, you know,' he told her. 'And I can be good again.'

'I believe you.' Her hand itched, struggled to push itself closer to him, and when he took her elbows, pulling her downward, she let her mouth fall open slightly, felt the sweet sting of his breath, just before he said, 'But there's something I must do first.'

She pulled away slightly. 'What is it?'

He arranged the words on his tongue, prepared them carefully, but when they came out they were cleaving blades. 'Betty, I need your help getting into the Kohlis' house.'

His request sent horrified vibrations through her mind and she began to laugh hysterically. 'What are you talking about?'

'I need two hundred thousand shillings by next Wednesday and if I don't get it by then, they're going to kill me.' He thought it necessary to add, 'Then, they're going to come for you and Esther.'

For a long moment, the earth became a vacuum, trapping her inside its rushing stillness. Then she felt a touch, hard and worried, on her knee and everything burst into movement once more, sending her into a sickening turmoil. She shut her eyes tight and whispered, 'You used me.'

He reached out two fingers and held lightly to the hem of her skirt. 'I'm protecting you.'

She slapped his hand away. 'You told them who I was so that I would have no choice but to help you get into that house.'

It stung him that she could so easily think of him that way, cut him to the quick. 'I would never do that to you.'

She stumbled up with a face dark and shiny with tears. Spat at him, 'Even if they were going to kill me, I would never help you do something like that.'

'I don't have any other option.' He held on to her cardigan, tangled it between his hands and they struggled, ridiculous and wide-eyed. 'I promise you no one will get hurt – we can do it when they're all out of the house. There are ways, Betty.'

'And when they find that things are missing? When I lose my job? What then?'

'You'll come and live with me.' He said it as if it were a decided thing and at her look of incredulity he whispered, more questioningly, 'I want to look after you.'

His words wrapped around her – she had wanted him to say it for a while, she knew that now. But his words had come at the wrong time, in the most impossible scenario. She fumbled for her purse at the door, struggled with the strap. 'Tell Esther I said goodbye.' Her indignation was interrupted by hiccupped sobs, a face creased with sorrow as she retreated out of the door. 'Tell her I'm sorry, but I won't be coming back.'

41

Michael had only been in there for a few hours, but even days later the cold stayed with him, seeped into his bones. The moist stench of human feces that had littered the walls and floors of the tiny communal lavatory, and the *shuka*-draped, aging villager with sharp knees who huddled close to him for warmth, had all disappeared from his mind. He couldn't remember if there had been six cells or twelve and whether or not there had been any women, tourists or *muhindis*.

But he hadn't been able to get rid of the chill, to forget how his hands and feet ached with cold – the kind that was dull and difficult to precisely locate. The muscles along his shoulders and back had cramped so painfully that every movement he made stuck half-way.

When the policeman came to get him, calling several times from the door, Michael had been unable to respond; he had been grinding his teeth so hard, his mouth was numb.

'*Kijana*, do you want to stay here until God himself comes to get you?'

It had been a sensation like floating, or walking on a very high carpet with electricity beneath his feet, springing up in a host of pins and needles as he limped forward. When he reached the doorway, the police officer shoved him forward, slamming the door and the protesting villager behind him.

'What can I do for you, officer?' Back at the small table, Michael feigned a carefreeness he no longer felt. The policeman hadn't allowed him a phone call and he was acutely aware that no one knew where he was.

'I want to know why you refused to help me.'

He was a dark-skinned man with ripe cheeks and a face that could have been sweetly handsome.

'How did you expect me to agree?' Michael asked.

'Are we not the same, you and I? Do we not know the same sufferings, the same injustices?' His hands swept across the table in urgent gestures and he said, 'When I was very young, around your age, my mother died.'

'I'm sorry for your loss.' It seemed odd that this stranger who he had just met, who had arrested and jailed him, should now choose to share something so personal, and his foot tapped nervously on the ground.

The man didn't look up from the table. 'She died because other people here live too large. Because some of us have to make do with nothing while they, the real thieves, hide out in their huge mansions or escape for a little while overseas.' His voice trailed, lost in the crevices of old pain. 'My mother didn't even have one sip of good water available to her. This country failed her and that is why she is gone.'

'I don't understand how robbing a house is going to make what happened to your mother right. You're an officer of the law – you should know better than anyone how wrong that is.'

'Yet if I don't get that money, I will die also.' The officer's eyes came up, sightless and black. 'If what happened to my mother taught me anything, it's that to survive we must be selfish. No one else is going to look after you.'

'If that's the case, if we refuse to look after our country and instead steal from and kill each other, what does that mean for the future of Kenya? Things cannot just change by themselves. We have to accept responsibility for that.'

'I used to sound just like you.' The policeman gave a derisive snort of laughter. 'But one day you will see that while you were busy thinking pretty thoughts about everyone else, they were pushing you down to get to the top.' He stopped to contemplate his words. 'I love this country but I must accept it for what it is. A place where thieves are celebrated and good men die unremarkable deaths.'

Nothing could be heard but the sleepy, second-hand clock overhead and the crickets outside, which meant that the policeman's words rang unimpeded. Michael was slightly frightened of them and asked, 'Can I go now or do you want to put me back in the cell?'

The policeman scraped back his chair legs tiredly. 'You may go.'

As Michael collected up his things quickly, slinging his satchel over his shoulder and going for the door, the policeman stopped him. 'You must remember what I said.' His voice lagged with defeat. 'One day, the same thing will happen to you and you will say, *Oh, Jeffery,*' a finger pointed at himself, 'that's my name. *Jeffery was right. I have spent my whole life doing the right thing, only to have the wrong thing done to me.*'

When he told Jai what had happened, his friend laughed incredulously.

'You were arrested by a cop who then tried to convince you to help him rob a house?'

'That's right.'

Jai ran frustrated fingers through his hair. 'That makes absolutely no sense. Do you know what Leena would say about all of this?'

The name jerked tiredly inside of him – he felt exhausted now when he thought of her. 'What?'

'She's picked up a habit of saying "*only in Kenya*" and then she rolls her eyes and expects me to understand what that means.'

'How is she?' Despite himself, Michael asked and found that, as he waited for the answer, the cop and the jail cell were forgotten and, temporarily, so was the cold.

'She's come down with the flu so she's been in bed for the last couple of days.' What Jai said next made Michael snap to quick attention. 'She's leaving next week.'

Michael looked toward the large storage cupboard, shut tightly with a steel padlock. A few days before he had been arrested he had begun a sketch, and even after an entire afternoon it remained rough lines and jagged dips, not enough yet for anyone but him to know what it was. The morning after he had been arrested, instead of heading home, he had come here to finish it. A nude woman lying on her side, the dip of her curves leading to the sweeping up-rise of her thighs, dark hair thrown over her shoulder.

She lay over a box, her back to him, guarding his cowardly secret and all the insecurities he had thought himself immune to. Those he had been too afraid to say out loud because he was terrified of being rejected or being made to feel inferior, afraid of what Jai might say, that he wouldn't approve and that the reason would be identical to Pooja's: that Michael wasn't good enough.

He thought about what the policeman had said to him; the reason his words had frightened Michael was that because, in some way, they were true. Pulling his eyes away from the cupboard, filled with the determined hope and resolution of his youth, he said to Jai, 'I want to see her.'

He did not want to die an unremarkable death.

42

She had prepared dinner for him. He came through the kitchen at nine o'clock and reeled from the new scent. The house had smelled like this when David was alive and Jeffery would come to visit them. Standing now at the alcove, he collected up the sourness of burned *ugali*.

Esther was sitting at the table, gray smoke making its slow yet steady rise from the pot. He dropped his coat and rushed by her, dragging the bread off the heat and saying, 'Are you trying to burn this house down?'

'I made you something to eat.' Her voice was flat, uncaring. 'If you haven't eaten already at the bar.' This was her greatest weapon against him: talking past him and treating him as if he were nothing but a nuisance.

The kitchen was descending into a light layer of choking smog and he was forced to open the window. A brown moth, attracted by the lights, fluttered in and settled on the kerosene lamp, warming itself.

Jeffery stared down at the mess in the pot. It was runny and blackened but he spooned it onto a plate and added a large helping of the beef stew. Seized by the oddity of the situation, he went and sat by Esther. In an attempt to thank her, he scooped up the *ugali* with his thumb and forefinger but it was too watery and refused to stick. He settled for a fork and eating the beef stew on its own.

'Thank you,' he said gruffly, between bites.

Her eyes were fixed on a spot on the wall behind him, somewhere above his head, and when he turned to follow her gaze, she said, 'I want to go and see Betty.'

Jeffery kept his face turned, his breath ragged. It had been three days, seventy-two long hours, since he had last seen Betty. 'I'm afraid that's not possible. Remember I said that she's very busy this month and won't be able to come here as often.'

'Take me to her workplace then. You know where it is.'

He had forgotten what a headstrong woman she could be. He recalled a night, some years ago, after the three of them had eaten dinner at this very table, while the two men were relaxing and David had said, 'I have the police commissioner calling me now, investigating our office for corrupt activities. He's asking for our logs, receipts.' He had turned desperately to his whiskey. 'What will I do?'

His wife had regarded him unsympathetically. 'If you choose to lie down with dogs,' she had said, 'you must be prepared to wake up with fleas.'

How different she had been then – with her stinging words and laughing ways. Now her life was made up of small, meaningless activities – pacing her room, cleaning the stove, watching the wall, which she did with the staring, blank eyes of a dying fish.

He said to her, feeling guilty for countless reasons, 'You know I can't do that, Esther. What would her employers think?'

Finally, her eyes came down from the spot on the wall. They were shining with mischief, treating him as an accomplice. 'She told me that on Sundays, they all go to the temple. They're gone in the morning and don't come back until two.'

Esther couldn't have known the value of her words; how they invigorated him with new hope, settling the turning in his stomach. But it was diluted by something else: a worry for Betty, the fear of pushing her even further away from him.

'It's too risky for her,' he heard himself say from someplace else.

Esther's patience evaporated fast. 'You do so many wrong things, every day, every hour! Why can't you do this one thing for me?'

He thought about the house again: the massive driveway and carved red-wood door; the quiet, waiting richness promised within. There was a hard pressure on his hands and Esther's gripping, pleading words. 'Please, Jeffery. We'll go in and out, straight away. No one will even know we were there.'

That Saturday evening, he scanned the dim club for Marlyn in annoyance. All he required in order to wait was a drink and a chair, but neither seemed available.

His usual table had been pushed against the wall to make room for a dance floor, where the music throbbed in his ears and the crowd was terribly young and rowdy – already his shoes clung to the floor, sticky with spilled alcohol. Jeffery slipped out onto the narrow patio, where it was possible to see most of Westlands in one swooping gaze. It was an overcast night, the stars hidden within spreading gray clouds, and he settled on a wicker chair, glad for the quiet. When a waitress came to take his order, he had shouted after her, 'Tell Marlyn to come quickly! I want to see her.'

He had come because he needed a break from the press of his unrelenting thoughts, because he craved the blinding oblivion of a drink and because he had a feeling the two men would be here. When the whiskey was placed in front of him, he caught the waitress's bony wrist.

'Where is she?'

'She's busy with customers.'

Marlyn had never made him wait before and her absence made his grip on the world slowly slip. Everything about him was collapsing into turmoil and he needed to steady himself again, feel in charge once more; the temptation and promise of the Kohli house grew and became potent.

'Spending my money?'

Today it was a relief to hear the gritty voice. Jeffery sipped thinly at his drink and said, 'Please sit down and celebrate with me.'

It was only him tonight, the man who had slammed his face into the bathroom mirror, and as he settled in the chair, tossing his jacket back, Jeffery glimpsed the metallic flash of a gun.

'What is there to be merry about? I can only assume you have my cash.'

'I don't.' He held his hand up to keep the man from interrupting. He was afraid that any disruption might cause him to falter, cause his decision to crumble. 'But I have a plan on how we can get it together.'

'What are you talking about, you crazy *mzee.*' The man leaned forward to grab the lapels of Jeffery's jacket. 'I already told you, I want my money by Wednesday.'

'And I can get you that tomorrow plus much more.'

He was released with a shove. The man ran greedy fingers over the armrests. 'Keep talking.'

The keen interest on his face shone out under the white city lights, loosening some of the tension forming in Jeffery's temples. He said, 'We'll have to do it tomorrow and it'll have to be together. I have it all planned out.'

43

Pooja sat at her dresser, brushing out her hair furiously. 'I don't understand why you won't come,' she said to her daughter. 'It's just a small flu.'

Leena rolled over in her mother's bed, burying herself deeper into the covers and away from Pooja's annoyance. From beneath this weighty, protective cloud, she heard her brother say, 'She has a fever, Ma, and a throat that's so sore she can hardly speak. She won't be able to talk to any boys, so what's the point?' His voice was light and teasing.

'That's not why I want her to come.'

Jai was rifling through Raj's closet, searching for a tie. 'You want her to get married. Everyone knows that.'

'So what if I do?' Pooja spoke through a mouth held open in a wide oval, applying a generous coat of dark lipstick. 'I got married when I was her age and look how happy I am.'

'Things are different now, Ma. People don't get married at twenty-one any more.'

'The younger you are, the earlier you can start a family of your own.' Swatting away groans from her children with a sunny tinkling of gold bangles on her wrist, Pooja continued, 'So spoiled, you children are today. You think that all there is to life is studying and going out with your friends. You have no worries. When I was your age, I was thinking of my future, of *your* future,' and she was out of the room, shouting for Betty to find her shoes.

Jai stood at the full-length mirror and knotted his tie slowly, the silk cool in his fingers. He watched his sister, beneath the covers, and was glad that his mother had left them alone. Leena was going to London in two days and he knew that tonight would be the only possible time for Michael to meet with her. The tie kept slipping from his grasp, refusing to sit properly.

'This evening I want us to go for a drink.' He said it in a rushed whisper, guilty for going behind his mother's back, of breaking that long-ago promise.

The blanket came down, her hair everywhere. 'I'm sick.'

'Can't you have one drink with your brother?' Finally, the tie tightened, perfectly shaped. 'A friend of mine is going to be joining us and I think you'd be interested in meeting him.'

'Not you too.' She threw herself dramatically back onto the pillows.

He ran tidying fingers through his hair. 'I saved you with Ma today, so you owe me.'

She conceded. 'Knowing her, I would be at the temple today and married by tomorrow.'

He said goodbye and she listened to his footsteps rush down the stairs, her mother shouting something to Betty about dinner before the door closed and the echoes of voices receded, the house falling into a calming and much welcomed stillness.

Betty listened at the bottom of the stairs for the girl but she couldn't hear a sound. Usually, Betty waited eagerly for Sundays, when she would be alone for three hours, free to do whatever she wanted.

Sometimes, she watched TV, always a colorful Bollywood movie with a woman draped in a sequined sari, surrounded by yellow daffodils or atop a snowy mountain, leaning her face up to a romantic, dark-haired man – both of them lamenting about their impossible love.

It felt deliciously redemptive, after all those hours spent working, to put her feet up on the same couch they had, to touch her mouth to the rim of Pooja's favorite cup and forget herself in the bright and foreign sounds of the movie.

But today, she knew that even if Leena had gone with them, she wouldn't have continued with her normal routine because everything around her was changed and nothing felt the same. She missed her cousin and the warm smallness of the kitchen – how close, in that raised one-bedroomed apartment, the sky had seemed, shot through with stars. *And how much I miss him.*

She had been appalled when Jeffery had asked her to help him rob the Kohlis, his face intently close to hers and muddling her emotions. How foolish she had been leaving the house so abruptly that night, promising never to return when all she had wanted was for him to stop her.

These thoughts caused a twisting, pinching regret within her and she was so busy fighting it that she didn't hear the knocking, loud raps on the metal gate, and she followed them out, her rubber sandals slapping on the carbro driveway.

'Betty, Betty. It's me. Please open the gate.'

Her insides fell weak with pleasure. In retrospect, the real reason why he was there should have crossed her mind but she had been vain and flattered, thinking he had come to make things right. She had trusted him and so, without any questions, Betty twisted the key in the lock and opened the gate.

*

Earlier in the day, they had waited, half-perched upon the curb beside a row of kiosks just outside the turning into the Kohlis' street. Jeffery watched anxiously out of the window while his two companions fussed with their teabag-like pouches full of fine grain tobacco. He watched as they dipped the brown flakes between their lower teeth and gums, occasionally rolling it with their fingers to keep the leaves in place.

When the silver station wagon passed them close to eleven o'clock, Jeffery was certain it was Betty's employers – the decorative mirrors on the woman's outfit reflecting the sunlight and disturbing his eyes, the two men dressed in suits. The time coincided with the information Esther had given him, so he told the man to drive.

That morning, he had left Esther at home, prying away her strong grip. 'You promised you would take me today. How can you say that you're too busy?' Her words trapping him. 'All these nights you've spent with your whores, I've never said anything. But after all the things you've done to me…'

It was the first time either of them had mentioned what had really happened.

Esther was at the bottom of the steps, clutching her handbag. After so many months, she was out of her nightgown and in a long-sleeved white blouse and printed skirt. 'You owe me this.'

'Maybe next week,' and he had stalked away, shutting out her collapsing face with a firm slam of the door.

Now, his bowels loosened uncomfortably with fear and beads of nervous sweat broke out underneath his shirt. But it was too late to turn back and he focused instead on consoling himself. *I'll convince Betty once I am inside. We'll take what we need and then leave.*

So he had pointed out the gate to the men and climbed out of the car when they reached it, rapping loudly and calling out her name.

'Betty, Betty. It's me. Please open the gate.'

He knocked and called, rolled his fingers into a fist and pounded. His voice began strong, then cracked into a blubber. He worried that she had gone out, that she didn't want to see him, but then he heard her slapped and hurried footsteps and nodded quickly to the men behind him.

She didn't hesitate, pulling the gate open in welcome, her smile unexpectedly bright. 'I was hoping you would come—' Her words faltered when she noticed the pro-box rumbling behind him. 'Who is that?'

He opened his mouth to explain but one man had already burst from the car, quick on his feet and with such blurred movements that one minute they were facing each other and the next, Betty was pressed up to the gate with a gun to the back of her head.

'Don't scream,' the man warned her. 'Open the gate.'

She was so distraught that the keys trembled within her fingers, missing the lock, and on the man's command she handed them to Jeffery, who ignored her pleas.

The white pro-box lurched into the driveway and the man pocketed the gun and told Betty, 'You come with us but a single sound from you and I'll tie you up.'

'No need to do that, she'll co-operate,' Jeffery rushed to intervene, leaning down to Betty's ear. 'Just do as they say and no one will get hurt.'

Her voice was thick, the words struggling through. 'Jeffery, what have you done?'

'They would have killed me and then come after you.' He took her hands, pressing them close. 'I'm doing this for all of us.'

'But the girl is inside.' Turning to his companions and grabbing one of them, she said, 'There's a girl inside – she's sick. If you leave now, I won't tell anyone you were here. Come back next week and I'll help you.'

Betty was slapped across the mouth, her head snapping back, and Jeffery felt it, a twin sting in his cheek.

'Go back?' They laughed and held their bellies. Jeffery shrunk closer to Betty as they were both commanded to move. '*Twende*.' They threw a black balaclava at Jeffery, instructed him to put it on as they slid behind similar masks – stiff, weaved cotton that burned his skin in the heat.

She met them on the stairs, four silent bodies creeping slowly upward. Upon seeing them, she was blinded by the ridiculous thought that her pajama shorts were too revealing and she wished she had put on some trousers.

The men before her seemed equally bewildered. As if, just as she had found herself unknowingly revealed on the staircase, they were equally shocked to be there, with guns in their hands and struggling on the slippery, hardwood steps. For a surreal, distant moment, she thought Pooja might have given her too much cough syrup, causing her to hallucinate, but then the man's gruff voice lurched her back to reality.

'Turn around, back upstairs.' He threw the gun in her direction and she screamed, ducking behind her arm.

'Shut up!' Panicked, one of them yelled, 'If you make a sound, we'll shoot.' Something cold was pressed into her hair and her skin broke open in fear. She imagined blood, crushed bones and her body sprawled on the stairs – her family finding her that way, exposed and shameful. 'Let's go.' His breath came at her rolled in scents of coffee and tobacco, her own voice from an unclear fog: *You can take whatever you want. Just don't hurt me.*

The gun moved from her temple to right between her eyebrows and its largeness startled her – a clunky, new pressure point in the center of her forehead. The man addressed Betty. 'Show him where the jewelry is, hurry up.'

Passing her, Betty's fingers grasped hers – cold and tight – and Leena muttered, 'It's all in the third cupboard drawer. She keeps the key under her mattress,' and then she was alone – between two surprisingly relaxed-looking men.

'Where's the money?' one asked.

Leena gripped the handrail, the floor sloping beneath her. 'What money?'

'Don't play games. Your father must keep money in the house – all you *muhindis* do.'

For the first time, she felt her fear as if it were a real, inescapable thing. She had been taught: *If they come into your house, give them whatever they want and they'll leave. They won't hurt you.* But she didn't know if her father kept money in the house and, if he did, where it would be. The rim of the gun dug an imprint into her temple and a sob cracked in her throat. 'Please, don't.'

The gun was removed slowly, his fingers, thick as anything, around her neck and forcing her eyes upward. 'Where's your bedroom?'

Disgust swelling in her chest, puncturing her eyes with tears. 'No.'

'Your bedroom,' he repeated. 'Or I'll shoot.'

She thought it would have been better to die because nothing could be worse than being taken prisoner in your own home, surrounded by things that once made you feel safe. It was bizarre to have her head angled in the direction of her bedside table, where her favorite Winnie-the-Pooh teddy bear sat, having been passed down from Jai, while the man unbuckled his belt above her. He pinned her down, his knee on her chest, but as he went to undress, it lifted slightly and she took the opportunity to kick out. Her heel hit him squarely in the abdomen so that he doubled over and she scrambled up to leave.

He got to her before she reached the door, slamming into her so hard that her head met the wall and the air congealed into small, multi-colored spots and her body collapsed unresponsively. He dragged her back down to the marble floor.

'Fucking *muhindi*,' he snarled in her ear. 'You think you can just come here and take everything from us without giving anything back?'

Slapping hands, struggling fingers as he tugged down her shorts. She dug into his skin with her nails, welded her thighs together and spat into his eye. 'I'd rather die than have you do this to me.'

A punch to her mouth, the iron taste of blood. She almost choked on it and had to release her grip on him to spit it out. Before she could turn back, he had pushed her legs apart. A sharp angry pain, thick fingers pressing down on her stomach, clutching her shirt so she couldn't get away. His wet breath moistening her face, suffocating her, until she went slack.

44

Three bodies swallowed in darkness, unmoving and bound by a terrible silence. When Esther reached out to flick on the kerosene lamp, Betty stopped her.

'Don't. I can't bear to look at him.'

His grasp was blind in the night. 'Betty, just listen to me.'

'Did they kill her?'

'No.'

'Did they rape her?' The sounds refused to leave her ears – shrill cries that ripped her arms and neck out in goosebumps, even now.

Softly, 'Yes.'

'Ohh.' A trailing, wraith-like moan, reminding him of the ghost women his mother had once warned him about, haunting the edges of Mombasa town. Damaged and lost, left to their sufferings – Betty seemed like one now with the helpless *ohh*, the constant shaking of her head. 'No, no, it's not true. No, no.'

'I'm so sorry.' He would have comforted her if he could but everything of hers was pulled tightly away from him, shrunk back in horror.

She spat, 'You're a coward and nothing but a petty thief and I wish I had never met you.'

'And a murderer,' Esther chimed in, wrapping her arm around her cousin and drawing her further away.

'I did it for you,' he protested weakly.

'Don't say that.' Her voice was a hard warning.

'It's not my fault and I did it so that you—'

To see her rise in such a tremendous state, a woman he had come to love for her unshakeable calmness, made him wince and lean back. 'Today, you went into a house that wasn't yours and you stole a woman's wedding jewelry, violated her memories. Because of you, a young girl's life was ruined.'

He wanted to put his fists in his ears. 'I didn't rape her.'

'No one would have if you hadn't brought them to the house.'

'It's not true,' he mumbled, his conviction weaker this time.

'And you did it all to save your own life.'

'I could never have known it would turn out this way.'

'And then you handcuffed me and put me in the trunk of your car. Brought me here and for what?' she scoffed. 'You think I want to be here? That I want to stay under the same roof as someone as vile as you?' Spit gleamed at the corners of her mouth. 'You should have shot me instead.'

Esther rose. 'It's been a very difficult day. Why don't you come with me?'

He listened to the two women go upstairs – the soothing hushes of one and the unstoppable cries of the other. How the roles had reversed today and how much he had damaged Betty. He searched desperately for some solace. *She has nowhere to go now – she has to stay here and eventually, maybe months or a year from now, she might forgive me.*

He nursed his whiskey, thinking back to his conversation in the car with the men.

'You didn't have to hurt her,' Jeffery had said.

'No,' one of them had agreed. 'But I wanted to.'

And huddled over in the darkness of the kitchen, engulfed by the cool camphor of a now-lit kerosene lamp, Jeffery understood exactly what the man had meant.

45

For days after the incident, the world took on a watery shapelessness. Emptiness blocked her mind – black shadows and the dirt-stench of wet tobacco, the cherub cheeks of her Winnie-the-Pooh teddy bear. After she was released from the hospital, she had to throw the toy away because she couldn't look at it without being sick, haunted by the dead-bead eyes that held an infinite reflection of that moment. It had angered her that she couldn't keep something that had once meant so much to her, that she had been forced out of her room and into Jai's. Every morning she awoke to find that her body had receded a little further from her, her eyes growing so heavy with shame that she could no longer look at people when they addressed her.

Men scared her. She hated the women, especially when they said, 'It's not your fault. It's them – those dirty, dirty *kharias*,' because they didn't understand that shifting the blame didn't change the fact that it had happened, only made it more real. She was broken and damaged now and not in the mysterious, romantic kind of way, but rather in the way that made people uncomfortable and nervous. Pooja's words were all that filled her head in those next few months. *Who was going to marry her now?*

She insisted that they keep the lights on permanently in the garden and she watched out of the window, tracking every sound and shape.

'You need to get away from there now,' her father would say.

'Leena, eat something. You must stay strong.' The pinched voice of her mother.

'You're safe with us. Nothing is going to hurt you any more.' Her brother's protective reassurings.

Their words made her feel like a stranger. For how could they possibly begin to understand what had happened to her and where could she start to explain it? After the rape, conversations became merry-go-rounds.

'You know, it's normal to feel that way after what happened.'

'You should rest. You've been through something terrible.'

'He's a horrible man and he shouldn't have done that to you.'

'Done what, Ma?' It was a week after the incident when her frustrations finally broke through, over flakes of dried toast crusted with strawberry jam.

Pooja had stopped talking, her hands clutching desperately at her *chuni*.

Leena's voice was loud and unwavering as she repeated, 'What did he do, Ma?'

Her mother had shifted in her chair, tapping, smoothing, fussing with the tablecloth. 'Come on, eat something.'

'Not until you say it.'

'I know you're angry, sweetheart.'

'Just say it.' Leena gripped the edge of the island, furiously batting away her trepidation.

'He hurt you—'

'He raped me.'

Tears sprung to Pooja's eyes and Leena scraped back her stool, appalled that she had been waiting for that exact reaction.

'That's what happened so let's not hide from it.' Leena had thrown down her fork and fled to the bathroom, where she had kneeled over the toilet just in time.

She heard the three of them talking in the living room one evening, thinking she was asleep.

'Of course Betty was involved in this,' Pooja was saying. 'You give and give to these people and they just take advantage whenever they can.'

'You don't know for sure that she was, Ma,' Jai had interrupted.

'Who else could have let those men in? Led them straight to my jewelry?' Her voice had cracked. 'To my daughter?'

Raj's always-steady voice. 'It'll be okay. She can take the next year off university and we will get her the help she needs.'

Though Leena came into the room quietly, they all heard her and turned with their cheeks aflame from having been caught planning her life without her. 'Classes start in two weeks and I want to go back.'

'I don't think that's a good idea,' her brother interjected.

She was more adamant than they had ever seen her. 'It's what I need to get better. Don't you want that for me?'

'Of course we do,' whispered Pooja, distraught.

'Then let me go. I can't stay here any more.' She looked out into the fast-approaching night, thought of all the things it concealed within its inky shade and said, with contempt in her voice, 'It's the ugliest place in the world.'

46

In the small border town of Busia, two women and one suitcase hitched a ride with a driver of one of the cylindrical oil tankers waiting on the busy highway to cross into Uganda. It had two-and-a-half seats upfront and Betty was pressed between her cousin and a man who smelled of drying paint and grease. Packed in so tightly, the artificial dust of the air conditioning smearing her face, she felt especially suffocated after the five-hour-long bus ride from Nairobi – during which she had spent the majority of her time hiding her sorrow from Esther.

With a splitting heart, Betty had watched as the city she loved fell away behind her, its large houses, tall buildings and purposeful people folding into dirt-red roads scattered through with cheap motels, kiosks and barefoot children playing. Past the lush green coffee-growing town of Meru, which sat up in the northern slopes of Mount Kenya, and winding through the narrow lanes up toward the Great Rift Valley. They had stopped at the viewpoint there and were given a five-minute break to stretch their legs.

While Esther had gone straight to one of the curio shops to talk to the selling women, in the hope of receiving a hot cup of tea and something to eat, Betty had stayed at the observation point, her hands upon the flimsy, zebra-patterned barrier, watching out.

It was a gray morning and the fickle weather had hidden the low hills of Mount Longonot but still allowed her an impressive view of the valley below. Looking upon the dipping crater, she had felt so insignificant in the midst of so much history and had quickly retreated, wondering what she was doing so far away from home.

Once back on the bus, she had consoled herself by admitting that she would have never been able to live with Jeffery, after all that he had done, but that didn't mean she didn't feel a sickening plunge every time she thought of him coming home to their note on the kitchen table – so cruelly evasive. Esther had insisted on being the one to write it, a manic grin upon her face, the bumpy pink tip of her tongue peering out between her lips, saying, 'You cannot imagine how long I have been waiting for this very day, cousin.'

Betty had agreed to Esther's plan because after the incident at the Kohlis' house, Nairobi had changed overnight. It became dirty to her, and her mistakes followed her around like spiteful ghosts, haunting everything she did. She knew that if she wanted to be happy again, she would have to leave its busyness – its chaos and wonder – behind.

'Can I climb the ladder and sit on top of this tank?' Esther asked the driver and her voice, childishly silly, broke through Betty's thoughts.

'Are you crazy, *Mama*?' the man shook his head. 'You'll fall right off.'

Esther patted the torn seat, stuck her finger into a hole where sponge stuffing was springing out. Greenish-gray flecks littered her skirt as she picked at it. 'This will have to do, then.'

Just before they crossed over the border, Betty allowed herself to think of Jeffery one last time, to wonder what he was doing. She felt an expanding sense of loss in leaving him behind because she knew that in another life, which wasn't his, things between them would have been different. She wondered if he would search for her and it gave her a small pleasure to think that perhaps he might, if only for a little while. As if she could read her cousin's mind, Esther rolled down the window.

'Wave goodbye to Kenya, Betty. Soon we will cross that border and he won't be able to hurt us any longer.'

The truck jerked forward, the strong vibrations of its engines rising up and spreading through the bottom of her seat and although she was tempted to look back, she couldn't bear to. She tried to reassure herself that, soon, it would be over. That in a few minutes she would be in a new country and beginning a fresh life and everything that she loved, had been comforted and injured by, would become nothing but fading beauties, half-formed images that she would eventually have trouble knowing. In a little while, she comforted herself, it would be like none of it had ever existed at all.

He had come home to a dark and cool house, the promise of rain lingering, and failed to see the note waiting for him on the kitchen table. He called out for them, listening within the creaking house for their sounds.

'Betty? Esther?' He had gone quickly up the stairs and pushed open the bedroom door – 'Where is everyone?' – before coming to a startled, dismayed halt.

The cupboard doors swung aggressively in the wind coming through a forgotten window and he rushed to it, catching it between movements. All of Esther's belongings – her bible, the old pictures she kept of David, the tub of Vaseline she used every evening on her skin – were gone.

In a confused tumble of thoughts, Jeffery tried to recall if Betty had any other family or friends she might have gone to; he struggled to remember where exactly upcountry her home was, but he had largely ignored her in those early days and so his mind stayed blank, stiff with dread.

He tore away the remainders of the room, left them scattered over the floor as he tripped downstairs once more and came to a stumbling stop right at the chair, blinking down at the open-faced piece of paper.

Jeffery,

We've climbed the ladder and you will never find us.

He squinted down at the writing, the incoherent ramblings of a mad woman – Esther, no doubt. What ladder? His first, clenching thought was that they had jumped out of the window and that the ladder was an implication that they had climbed up into heaven. He dashed to the window and, panting, leaned out. Spotless tarmac pavement. He was almost disappointed.

What ladder? He slumped down on a chair, whiskey and glass in hand, automatically pouring out a neat, amber shot. Time had once again turned on him. One minute, he had had three women and in the next, he was alone with a tricky note and empty cupboards. *You will never find us.* What ladder? *You will never find us.* He threw the sentences around in his mind but they only became more jumbled, more idiotic, and he knew that had been the point of writing it that way. Esther may have gone but she still wanted him to suffer.

He crumpled the letter and pushed it into his glass, which was still a quarter full of whiskey. The alcohol flooded the paper, its stiffness slowly collapsing until their secret taunts were nothing but smoky ribbons of ink, escaping the note and staining his drink black.

PART FIVE

2007

47

It's too late in the year for jacarandas but they line the highways and small side streets in full bloom anyway, their fallen flowers creating a glossy, periwinkle carpet. The five-lobe petals make quiet *pop-popping* sounds as tires speed over them, bursting apart and releasing their honey stickiness into the air. It seems ill-mannered to Michael that such brightness should exist while the country is falling apart at its seams, a violet taunt of all the things they could have had and all the things they chose instead.

Earlier that week, a woman and her two-year-old daughter were found dead in Tana River county beside a watering hole. In that baking corner of Kenya, they had been hacked to death with a *panga* and Michael thinks of the pictures he had been sent there to take to accompany a newspaper article. He had captured the shot from the waist down – his own effort to give her one last dignity. She had been holding her daughter's hand, a small girl with unusually clean feet because she was being carried when they were struck.

At first, the killings hardly garnered any attention. Ethnic violence was rife in that former coast province where conflict over water and farmland was high. But then, a few weeks later, eleven more people were dead, an inkling of a more serious, wider issue.

Such is the method of crude politics, the article that went with the picture had read. *Ensure that your tribe is in the majority – so that in Tana River Delta, this violent competition to ensure that their main man gets governorship looks an awful lot like ethnic cleansing.*

It is death more than anything that reminds him of his own weakness when it comes to Leena. Perhaps it is the intensity of emotion it brings with it or the jarring reminder that one day, his chances with her will run out.

'You need to leave it alone now, *cuzo*,' Jackie had said after catching him with the painting. She had pushed it back behind the many others, ensuring that it was wrapped tightly away, and led him from it. 'There are some things we have to move on from otherwise we will waste away from wanting them so badly.'

Nairobi is a sly town. It is so small that run-ins with people one is trying to avoid are a common occurrence, yet it is segmented enough to keep two searching individuals apart. It has been almost three weeks since Michael last saw Leena at the police station and he is restless and irritable, though unsurprised.

The city was designed to keep people apart, European from African, African from Asian, Asian from European. Each group had been assigned their selective pockets and even though, after independence, those boundaries had grown more precarious, that feeling of division had been hard, if not impossible, to shake.

So when they stumble across each other at a bar one Saturday night, it is confusing for both of them. He isn't sure which one of them is in the wrong place and she knows his face but is having some difficulty recalling where she last saw it.

'You're here,' is all he manages to say.

'I am.' She has been drinking and he is handsome in a comforting way, so she smiles and leans against the cushioned wall outside the bar. When he looks beyond her into the low intensity, blue-lit space, he sees a group of people watching them. They are perched on cream chairs and whisper to each other without taking their eyes off him. Michael realizes that he is the one who is out of place.

'Your friends are worrying about you.'

She follows his gaze, satisfied with herself. 'Let them.'

They laugh softly together until the shared pleasure is used up. She is exactly how he remembers yet not the same at all. The round face and amber eyes, the misplaced dimple that is like a dent in her cheekbone, the wide stretch of smile with its narrow fleet of teeth. Her hair is long once more, falling in a steady wave over a single shoulder. Seeing Leena in the flesh makes him grow tired of the image he heaves around – he wants to know her this way, this real way, and understands that once he leaves this place, the memories he has of her will no longer be enough.

'That's where I know you from.' She snaps her painted nails and takes a sip of her drink. When she speaks again, her words are fueled by vodka. He thrills in it, for how grown up she has become. 'It was at the police station.'

His mouth runs dry and he looks around for a waitress. As he does so, she leans in, so small that she is forced to stand on her tiptoes.

She winks and he realizes that she is teasing him. 'You're the one who did all the art.'

'Don't say it too loudly – you never know who is listening.'

'I've been thinking about you.' It spills from her mouth after another sip of her drink.

The words take him aback, warm him with pleasure though he should have expected it – she has always been so bold. It infuses him with the same confidence.

'Actually, we met before the police station.'

Parallel lines of confusion appear around her mouth. 'But I've just got back from London.'

Placing her drained glass on an empty table, she shoots her eyes uncertainly back toward her friends, who are gesturing her over. He catches her wrist lightly, a throb of blood beneath his thumb. 'It's me – Michael.'

He watches with some amusement the stages her expression passes through. A pulse of familiarity, doubt, remembering, and then she laughs – a girlish, short tinkle. 'It really is you.'

It is difficult to decipher what she is thinking; her eyes are charcoal, darkened by the poor lighting. He cannot tell if she is glad to see him or just enjoying the unexpected resurfacing of her past.

'How come you never told me who you were at the police station?'

He grins wryly. 'Being in the position I was in, can you blame me?'

She wants to hug him, feels an insistent, rope-like tug drawing her forward. 'It's not at all like the boy I remember to get into such trouble.'

Michael straightens out his ribbed sweater, more gray now than black, and is suddenly overly conscious. 'It's been a very long time since then.'

Agreeing with him, she asks about his mother. 'She took such good care of us when we were younger.'

'She lives in Eldoret now,' he tells her. 'We have a house there.'

'What about you?' The old habit in her hands has stirred and they move animatedly along with her words. He is glad to see that there are some parts of her that have remained unchanged.

'I'm a photographer.'

The impressed glint in her eye churns his stomach with pleasure. But then he asks about her and her answers are vague and her body stiffens, shrinks away. She has picked up her empty glass and is playing with it idly. Her lack of willing responses means that they run out of conversation quickly and she looks back at her group – they are calling out for her once more.

'I should go,' she finally tells him.

Cursing his weakness, Michael says, 'It was wonderful to see you.'

She is watching him with that old, keen expression. Her mouth puckers slightly as it always used to when she was concentrating hard on a problem. 'Maybe I can give you my phone number?'

He smiles.

She had always been the braver one.

The early part of the next week passes in a mild, thrumming panic. Somehow, the bar napkin she scrawled her number on keeps finding its way back to his unfolding fingers until he has it memorized – is even able to pick out an individual digit and know where in the order it belongs.

Michael is tempted to call Jai and tell him what happened, for he could use some advice, but a larger part of him wants to keep this between the two of them. When they were younger, he had never known Leena outside of his friendship with Jai and seeing her last Saturday – the maroon lips and short, dark dress – he wants it to be different this time.

Playing with the keys on his phone, he dials her number and as soon as he presses the call button, ends it. Every time he punches it in, he is seized by the memory of four nights ago. Maybe she had woken up the next morning kicking herself for giving in to him. Perhaps she had been glad, relieved even, that he had not yet called – or after all these days, she might have forgotten him altogether.

'Give me that.' The phone is snatched from his hand.

He lunges at Jackie but she is too quick for him, backing away with his mobile. 'What are you doing?' he protests weakly.

She presses the redial button and waits for it to ring. 'Can't hang up now, *cuzo*.'

Michael clears his throat, practices *hello-ing*, all the while ignoring his cousin's smirk.

'Hello?' Her phone voice is different. She sounds older and unlike herself, words clipped with a British accent.

Goaded on by the fact that she might hang up if he remains mute for too long, he says, 'Hi, this is Michael,' and squeezes his eyes shut painfully against the formality of his tone.

He concentrates on the growing silence at the other end, his palms aching with anticipation. Glares at Jackie.

'You called.' Leena sounds surprised, but with the drumming between his ears Michael cannot tell if she is pleased or not.

'I was wondering if you wanted to have coffee with me.' Straight to the point because he has already waited too long for this moment.

When she replies, she sounds unsure and distracted, wrestling a million different responses. It is a swallowed-up whisper when she says, 'How about lunch tomorrow?'

'That sounds perfect,' he says calmly, struggling to hide the smile in his voice.

'Where shall we go?'

And he stops smiling because that is an entirely different problem. He tries to suggest something he thinks she will like. 'How about Java House?'

'I was thinking of that new shopping center – Junction Mall. I heard they have some pretty good restaurants there.'

He tries not to see it as a bad omen; even in the simplest of things, their differences arise, clashing and struggling to find middle ground.

'It's a little out of the way for me,' he admits. 'I don't have a car.' Then, ears filled with static silence, Michael wonders if he should have lied and said it was in the garage, but reminds himself that he has nothing to be ashamed of. 'How about Diamond Plaza?'

'Too many Indians.'

'What's wrong with that?' he challenges.

'They stare a lot and it makes me uncomfortable.'

He laughs, remembering the watchful gazes of the sari-clad women in the compound, wing-tipped with black kohl. Leena joins him, timidly at first, but then really laughing, just like he remembers how she used to. He can picture her sitting at her desk or on the couch, upright with her hands fussed in her hair or pinching her top lip.

Her voice is worried when she asks, 'How will we ever decide?'

'We'll manage,' he replies, and wonders if they are still talking about coffee shops.

Eventually, they settle for a non-descript café called Khawa downtown, nestled between an optometrist's store and a Hooters, so hidden that most people pass it by. It has shredded, twine chairs that poke mercilessly through their clothes, and linoleum floors – the whole place stinks of cold cheese pies, refried chips and Peptang tomato sauce.

'This place is perfect,' she says.

He looks around. 'Because it's empty?'

'I like my privacy.' She fiddles with the corner of the menu – a single sheet of old paper that has recently been laminated.

Pooja hates it when she comes to town, *full of thieves, no place for a young girl like you*, and it is the first time Leena has come alone. She feels vulnerable, exposed, and it doesn't help that Michael is watching her so carefully, that his eyes are warmer and browner than she expected, his lips impressively bowed. He seems so free and unbroken, unlike her. She chuckles to think of what her mother would say if she could see her now.

'Is something funny?' he asks. It is the thing she remembers most about him – his ability to be so straightforward without crossing into the obnoxious. An honesty she rarely encounters.

'I was thinking how unexpected it is that we're here together.'

He puts the menu down. 'After you moved, I kept waiting for you to visit me. It's silly, I know, even after Jai told me that you wanted to make your own friends, I just kept on waiting.' His skin darkens with embarrassment.

Eyebrows knotting. 'You kept in touch with Jai after we left the compound?'

'He came over every Saturday. I thought you knew that.'

It comes to them almost simultaneously. Michael registers the knowledge with a sinking anger, a surprised pang that his friend could have done that to him. Leena rolls her eyes playfully and the careless gesture makes him feel worse.

'That's my mother for you.' Leena tosses her hair back with a silly laugh. 'Always meddling.'

She couldn't have known what it meant to him and he tries not to be offended that she can brush it away so lightly. Grabbing hold of his finger, she tugs it. She is emboldened, knowing how unlikely it is that she will run into anyone she knows in this innocuous, brown café. 'Serious as always,' she teases.

'Some things never change,' he tells her and hopes she understands what he means.

In the breezy afternoon, amid car fumes and the oily stench of deep-fried chicken, she almost does. But then she pulls away from him and turns silently back to her menu.

48

In the days leading up to the elections, Pooja makes sure that the cupboards in her kitchen are fully stocked, barrels of drinking water stored away in her pantry and emergency supplies inventoried. Many of her friends and most of the foreign families who live in Runda have left, catching flights to safer places as is the norm during the election period, and the suburb is quiet and still, a reflection of the entire country. Anxious and waiting.

She had wanted to leave for London. Unlike her husband, as an East Indian residing in Nairobi, Pooja often feels as if she inhabits a liminal state. She has lived here her whole life and yet it doesn't seem permanent. She tries to empathize with Kenyans but finds it impossible to identify with being Kenyan. She loves this country, its lushness and ease, but it has never felt like home. No matter what Raj chooses to believe, she knows that there remains an impenetrable buffer between Indians and native Kenyans – a wall that she is constantly aware of and doesn't mind because it protects her.

She is distracted from these worries by the compressed sounds of her daughter's whispers. Setting down a can of tuna, Pooja shuffles closer to the corridor so that she can hear the girl better. But still, it is impossible to understand the rushed words spoken under half-breaths.

An old uneasiness tickles her chest. For the past week, her daughter has been acting strangely, even more so than when she first arrived. Leena is constantly distracted and keeps to her room and when Pooja puts her ear to the whitewashed wood, she hears surges of laughter and low conversations, carrying on for over an hour.

'Who are you talking to?' She bursts out of the kitchen but her daughter is already putting the phone back in her purse.

'No one.' She reaches over Pooja's head to take the car keys from the hook near the door.

'Where are you going?' Pooja tries to convince herself that the prick of fear is unwarranted but she cannot shake the feeling that something is being kept from her.

'Out.'

Again, Leena is stopped by her mother's protestations. 'Out where?'

'You can't be serious.'

'I'm very serious.'

Leena softens her voice. 'I'm going to meet some friends.'

'Which ones?' It hadn't started out as an interrogation but the way her daughter is standing, one sandal-clad foot out of the door, her ponytail roped around her wrist, Pooja knows she is hiding something.

'What does it matter?'

'The situation here is not very good at the moment. I want to make sure you're safe.'

'Kiran.' Leena throws her hands up in exasperation. 'I'm going for a coffee with her. Are you happy now?'

Pooja follows her daughter out onto the steps of the main entrance. Her anxiety is a dead weight at the back of her neck, springing her nerves into frantic energy. She waits until the car has fully reversed out of the closing gate before she hurries back into the kitchen, picks up the phone and dials Kiran's number.

He leans casually against the metal gate of Parklands Sports Club with the heels of his feet pushed out. Concentrating hard on something, he trails his toe over the ground, making a shape. Michael hasn't yet spotted her, he's so engrossed in his drawing, and she slows to a crawl. She wonders, not for the first time, nor for the tenth, what she is doing here.

He is attractive and interesting, a refreshing change from her usual friends, with the same assuredness she remembers from when they were children. Watching Michael, her mind becomes a series of images – arms thrown out, a bike beneath her, his voice calling out her name as she tripped over the curb. But the pleasure she gains from these memories is spotted, thinned by an unspoken resistance between them, and although he doesn't seem affected by it, she is.

She had thought that perhaps it might have something to do with what happened four years ago; after all, that would make sense. It would be understandable, a suitable excuse. But the more she ponders and the closer she watches him, the more she comes to realize that it is something that runs much deeper than that one problem. She was never taught to love someone like him.

Closer now, the hum of her engine audible, Michael approaches the passenger side and she glances about her, thinking how reckless it is that they're meeting here. She could run into anyone at any moment.

'What are you looking at?' He slides into the car, sounding as if he knows her thoughts.

'Nothing.' She does a quick U-turn and they are back on the main street. 'Where do you want to go?'

'Any place where there aren't too many Indians, right?' His voice is light but slightly frigid and she looks at him, feeling guilty and small-minded.

'Michael—'

'It doesn't matter.' He waves it away – the stiffness that suddenly settles between them. 'I know a good place.'

He can't be sure if he takes her there just to poke some fun at her. They arrive at a kiosk-style nyama choma restaurant in Hurlingham, tucked behind a garden center. The fern-colored shade of the Tiger Palms and the moisture thickening the air creates a damp, rainforest-like heat.

Here the tables are made from recycled barrels and the beer is warm and costs a hundred bob. The toilets are in an outdoor shed – nothing but narrow holes in the ground. She holds tightly to his elbow as they make their muddy, uneven way to the door.

'It looks interesting.' She is being polite, sensing that she upset him in the car.

'They definitely have the best nyama choma in town.'

Before she sits, she discreetly wipes at the seat of the plastic chair and he laughs away her apology when she catches him watching her.

'There's no reason to be sorry.' He gives her a kind look, signaling for the waiter. 'I've always found you charmingly sweet.'

She flushes to think of how he must have seen her those many years ago, a scrawny, sulky girl disturbing their games.

'I was a nuisance back then.' She tugs the straight edges of her hair.

He takes her fingers, bringing her hand down. 'Quite the opposite.'

What sneaky desire his words spark in her – a weakening of her muscles and bones, collapsing her inward. She doesn't know anyone else who speaks in that manner, so unafraid of his feelings, as if he can't understand the point of secrecy.

'I'm sorry for what I said before – about not wanting to go to Diamond Plaza because there are too many Indians there. I didn't mean it that way.'

'Yes you did.' There is no malice in his voice.

She chuckles at the old familiarity they share. 'Okay, I did.'

When he leans forward to scoop up some meat, she notices the lovely shape of his hands – the handsome dip of the palm and how it occasionally rubs at his stubbled cheek. The light running of veins just below his skin, dark forearms extending outward from casually rolled-up shirt sleeves. *To think he was the boy I once wished away from our lives.*

'Why does the thought of people seeing us together make you uncomfortable?' His voice pulls her back to him.

'Because the people I know are incapable of minding their own business. You remember – they'll talk about me.'

He sits back and crosses his arms over his chest. 'Do you think you're doing something wrong?'

She pauses to contemplate with a sip of tepid Tusker beer before telling him the story of Simran; how, when she was an eighteen-year-old girl, she had seen a woman only a few years older get kicked shamefully out of her house in the bitter hours of a cold morning for kissing a man who wasn't Indian. 'My mother agreed with Simran's parents. She didn't think that there was anything wrong with sending one's daughter packing in the middle of the night. So can you imagine what will happen when she finds out about us?'

He looks back, unimpressed. 'You haven't answered my question.'

She stammers, unsure. 'I just did.'

'I asked if you think what we're doing is wrong,' he says. 'You've only told me your mother's opinion.' Before she has a chance to speak, he continues. 'You don't want to go anywhere too public, don't want to talk to me too loudly, just in case people notice and talk about you only because you think you're doing something wrong.' He straightens up in his chair and gestures the waiter over, indicating for the bill. The cheerful disposition he had only moments ago has disappeared.

He reaches into the back pocket of his jeans to pull out his wallet. She offers to pay but he refuses and she sits in confused silence, feeling caught out. Most of the food remains uneaten.

When they reach the car, he lingers. 'I'm going to walk.'

'I don't mind dropping you off.'

He takes her hand and she is momentarily distracted by how pleasant it is – dry and smooth and when she looks down, she recalls that clean and constant palm.

'I really like you,' he tells her in a tone of dead seriousness. He is so much more grown up than the other boys she knows, doesn't look like he wastes time on anything as childish as going to bars and gossiping. He sounds like he knows the world and understands it in a way that is only possible when you pay attention. 'But I'm not in the habit of being ashamed of myself and I don't want to be with someone who is embarrassed of me.'

He stops her protestations by placing two fingers on her mouth and it makes her remember three emerald peas, sheets of newspaper beneath her feet and a red plastic bucket in the middle of their circle. A boy flying through the market, his back solid beneath her.

'You need to think about some things, Leena,' he tells her as he throws his jacket over his shoulder, moving toward the gate. 'Before you decide whether or not you want to see me again.'

49

He sits at home alone most nights now with nothing but the sad drumming above him, old and tired as well. Sometimes he holds the remnants of their note in his hand, reading and rereading what is left of it in the hope that one day he will know what ladder Betty climbed and will be able to find her. For the most part, however, he leaves the smudged paper beside his bottle of whiskey and it flutters teasingly in the evening breeze. Oftentimes, he is tempted to let it be carried away. Perhaps then he can let her go.

He had planned on leaving Nairobi – to travel somewhere upcountry, almost two hundred feet above sea level, where the vices of the city would not follow. He didn't know where to, just somewhere that wasn't filled with ghosts, both dead and alive. But with the elections less than a month away, he had been told that his services were needed. *To ensure that peace is kept.* He scoffs at the idea – whether or not it was would not be up to him.

There are traces of violence starting up though it's hardly a cause for concern because it's what happens every election period. Luos fighting Mkambas fighting Kalenjins and everyone fighting the Kikuyus. *The Jews of Kenya.* A fellow police officer had told him just yesterday, 'Ever since Jomo took his place as our first president, they have all been rubbing our noses in their pre-eminence. These

Kikuyus are obnoxious, loud, thrusting and everywhere – they need to be taught a lesson.'

Jeffery had always kept away from politics. When he was younger, it had been too dirty and disturbing for him. Kenyan politicians were a strange breed, their heads full of water and more indecisive and easily swayed than the most uneducated man in the country. Men here did not go into politics for a love of Kenya and its people – it was for the high salaries, the holiday villas and private jets.

It is humorous to think of the relentless campaigning, all of them coming in with such grand promises. Better housing. Lower food prices. Land relocation – 'Vote for me and I will be for all Kenyans and not just my tribe – it's time we unite.' Never mentioning that for the past fifty years, the ruling elite had always been determined to hype ethnic differences to cover up its more suspicious activities. These promises were then dusted out of State House as soon as the new president entered the sprawling, three-hundred-acre property with its high gates and beautifully crafted gardens.

Jeffery has time to reflect on such things now. Soon after Betty and Esther left, Marlyn did too, coming to him in tears and a makeup-less face. She had looked more alluring that day than he had ever known her to be, handing him back the very first necklace he had bought her.

'When I wear this, I remember you as you used to be. Perhaps it will give you the same comfort.'

She had kissed him on the cheek, keeping the trembling tips of her fingers close to his mouth.

'Why are you doing this?' He had held tightly to the flesh of her arms.

'Because you aren't the man I fell in love with.'

After she had left, he sat with the jewelry set in his lap, watching his reflection within its shiny, gold-plated surface and found that Marlyn had been right. He was hidden within the grooves of the fake crystals, the chipped and dulled rhinestone setting – a shy young man staring into the silky display window of an Indian clothing store. He had snapped the case shut and put it away, never looking at it again.

Now he turns up the radio, grateful for its presence because it drowns out the stillness of the house, and listens to the presenter.

'Most Kenyans are still hoping for a peaceful election, a fair one.'

Since they have never had either, it is not a question of whether it will become violent but rather *how violent* it will become.

That is the problem with Kenyans, Jeffery concludes. They are foolish, hopeful dreamers. Trample on a Kenyan with fake promises and flatteries and he will rise up and run straight back, hungry for your boot. Yes, he may for a time protest and speak out, but eventually he will return to his life, nonplussed, consoled by family and friends. *What can we do, how much can we say – our lives don't matter but they are ours, carry on, carry on, this is the way the world has always been.*

50

Pooja is waiting in the doorway for her daughter, so anxious that her eyes have become slightly unfocused, her thick plait coming apart.

'Where were you?' she demands.

Lost in her musings, Leena steps into the house and snaps, 'I told you, I was with Kiran.'

'Don't lie to me. I called her after you left – she didn't know what I was talking about when I asked if she was meeting you for coffee.'

'You're checking up on me?' Leena drops the car keys on the counter and pushes past her mother. She wants to be alone, to wallow in the unexpected disappointments of the day.

'Don't walk away from me!' Pooja hurries after her. 'Tell me where you went.'

'It's none of your business.'

For a moment, Pooja forgets which child she is speaking to. There is so much fight in the girl's words.

'I won't be angry with you,' she says in an effort to placate.

'It's not about you being upset, Ma.' Leena recalls his last words to her, accusing her of not having her own thoughts and she feels childish and unworthy of him. 'It's about you treating me like I'm twelve years old. Leena do this, Leena do that – Leena, you can only go to this university and be friends with these people.'

The two women look at each other, caught up in the difficult truth of their relationship. Leena is gripping the banister while Pooja clutches her *chuni* desperately to her chest, wondering where her daughter could have possibly gone to make her come up with such wild nonsense.

'It's only because I'm concerned for your safety. This city can be dangerous or have you forgotten everything that has happened?' She grabs Leena's wrist to stop her from going up the stairs. 'Have you forgotten what they did to you?'

The air tightens between them.

Pooja's desperation has loosened her tongue and she is instantly regretful. Her carefully constructed world is coming undone and she grapples with its aging strands, anxious to knot it back together, however roughly.

She watches her daughter struggle with the words but then Leena's face snaps back into stubborn determinedness.

'Your husband doesn't listen to you. Your son does whatever he wants and I have been placating you my whole life. I'm sick of it.' Leena marches up the stairs, energized and speaking rapidly. 'In case you haven't noticed, I'm an adult and I can do and think as I please.'

Slow, deliberate clapping at the entrance of her room. She keeps her eyes fixed on the ceiling, weighed down by gloom and unable to move from her position on the bed.

'My little monkey is all grown up.' Jai slides into the desk chair, rolling it toward her with a smooth flick of his heels. She flips onto her side, the fluttering in her chest slightly released now that she has him to distract her from the afternoon's events: the sure, yet airy touch of Michael's fingertips, the unrelenting directness of his gaze.

Leena pulls a face. 'I really upset her.'

'It was the truth and someone had to say it.'

Alight once more with indignation, she sits up. 'Even while I was living in London, she was always calling, always checking up on me. She never gave me a chance to grow up on my own.'

'Where is all this coming from?' Jai asks.

She wonders if she should tell him, if he has already been told. 'Michael.'

The spinning chair stops. Jai's back is turned to her and softly, as if he has been expecting it, he says, 'I see.'

'How come you never told me you were still friends with him?' She grabs hold of the chair, forces it around.

'Ma made me promise not to.'

'Since when do you listen to what she says?'

Jai thinks back to that day – of how quickly the panic had descended upon his mother. He had never seen her that way before, chin quivering and a bloodless face. It was as if there had been something of utter importance at stake – something that, at his young age, he had been unable to comprehend.

'I was only trying to protect you.' Jai struggles to understand the rapid burning in his chest – the idea that the two of them have met without him makes his stomach churn. He hasn't spoken to Michael in over a month, though he has tried calling him many times. He is so used to being the center of Michael and Leena's relationship that now, having been made inconsequential, he feels perturbed.

Leena continues talking. 'I was so embarrassed to be seen with him and when he asked me why, I had nothing to say except that my mother told me to be.' She hugs a pillow, brings her knees up the way she used to when she was a child with a problem too big to solve. 'She would never forgive me for this. You heard what she said.'

Pooja's careless statement had jolted her but less than she expected. It was the first time the incident had been mentioned since Leena came back from London and it was almost a relief to hear it, a mighty exhalation as the tense energy surrounding her return finally cracked; and, to everyone's surprise, she didn't break with it.

'I think you should do what you feel is right.'

It still pinches, that old adage which has evaded her ever since she was young. Something that comes so easily to Michael and Jai holds a mountain of uncertainty for her.

Leena picks anxiously at the blanket. 'There are so many things to consider. It's not as simple as you make it out to be.'

She thinks of all the things that being with him will mean. Facing her mother's tornado-like disapproval, the questions and gossip from the community – subjecting not only herself but her family to suspicious scrutiny.

Her mind travels back to the way the women at the old compound turned so readily from Mrs Laljee when they caught a hint of her son's indiscretions, the cruel taunts and ugly, black words locking them away from their neighbors. A nervousness butterflies in her stomach when she thinks of how her friends might view Michael, of the relationships she might jeopardize by taking a chance on him.

When she speaks again, her voice is far-off and regretful. 'He looked so disappointed in me.'

Jai stands. 'I should go and calm Ma down.'

She stops him at the door with a question. 'Do you think I should see him again?'

Jai fights his selfish instincts and attempts a reassuring smile. 'I think he sounds good for you.'

The sound of his slow footsteps fades out as she drops back down onto the bed, lost in the confused tumble of her thoughts.

51

The two men have returned, lurking beneath his window. They pace the small patch of garden, blackening it with tobacco spit. They are discussing something in low tones, an occasional rising laugh as they lean against the wall, happy to wait.

It has been a long time since Jeffery has seen them. Following the incident at the Kohlis' house, there had been a long, drawn-out inquiry and the father and brother of the girl had been frequent visitors to Parklands police station.

Jeffery can still recall the determined *slap-slap* of the older man's leather slippers, his cotton *kurta* carrying whiffs of sandalwood. His ears still ring with the patient growl of the man's voice, despite his obvious distress.

'I don't care about my wife's jewelry. I just want you to catch the criminals who hurt my daughter.'

For several weeks, he sat in a plastic chair in the corner of the room, politely shifting back and forth to make space whenever the station became overcrowded, constantly tightening the white shawl around his shoulders. But despite the persistent chill, he had refused to leave, filling in numerous police reports, requesting abstracts for insurance companies – asking and answering countless questions pertaining to that day, a common thread running through all of them: Betty.

'I don't want to make any hasty accusations,' the man was careful with his words. 'But there was no sign of forced entry and she disappeared with them. I haven't seen her since.'

With a tightening gut, Jeffery had listened through the closed door of his office. The Kohli men had brought in a photocopy of Betty's ID and it sat on his desk, atop a pile of other papers, and he had spent many hours trying to decipher her life from it.

She would be turning thirty later this year and she was not originally from Nairobi. Her traditional Kalenjin name, Cherop, told him that she had been born during the heavy rains and it made sense to him because of how clean she was, stripped and washed of anything ugly. In the poorly taken photograph, he searched for her short-lashed, dark eyes and the gathered mouth, but the blotched ink had made her featureless and it could have been anyone.

It had been a long time since Jeffery had experienced such a level of guilt, a selfless, all-consuming sorrow that left him constantly listless. Just as Esther had done following David's death, he found a permanent spot beside the living room window, letting the night air freeze his thoughts. His mind was haunted by the upheaval he had forced into Betty's life; he had sought out her help and then made her into a thief, an accomplice to the most horrific crime. It was in those still, quiet moments that Jeffery understood why she had run from him, though it did little to soothe the permanent sore just above his breastbone, growing more acute every day.

He had made certain that the Kohlis' case remained at the bottom of an endless pile of similar complaints, hiding out in his office, oftentimes calling in sick – terrified and sure that if he met those two Indian men, faced by their impressive size and flashing eyes, he would confess everything.

Three months of constant anxiety, hounded by those two tobacco-chewing fellows – *If we hear you've snitched on us* – until finally, the station grew quiet and empty once more.

Jeffery was told, 'His wife came in yesterday and begged him to stop. She told him that they had to move on, that this investigation would amount to nothing.' A smirk and chuckle from the reporting officer. 'She called me a useless *kharia*.'

After that, the two goons left him alone and Jeffery's life had fallen into a peaceful, if imperfect, rhythm: work, a steaming roadside chapati for lunch, two whiskeys in the evening then falling asleep on the uncomfortable, hardback chair.

But now, those heavy boots scuffing the grass flat, the whistles alerting him to their presence, promises to disrupt it all. He shut his eyes, hoping they might leave.

'*Weh! Mzee*, let us in.'

Jeffery presses himself closer to the wall. *Go away – can't you see what damage you have already done?*

'Do you want me to tell your neighbors what kind of man you really are?'

Rushing to the windowsill and looking downward he hisses at them, 'What do you want this time?'

'We have a business proposition.' Stained smiles, two bellies quivering with malicious joy, their sounds carrying forever up into an impossibly bright and cloudless afternoon.

They drain most of the whiskey before beginning. One settles in Jeffery's chair, the other moves slowly about the plain living room. He kicks the pot of a houseplant and the crisp, dead leaves come loose. He runs a thick finger down the dusty TV screen and holds up his hand, unimpressed.

'I see your women have gone.'

Jeffery doesn't answer, staring longingly at the last golden sip of his drink. The man continues.

'As you know, the elections are taking place next week.'

'So what?' He resents their presence here – the way they have settled in, trampling carelessly over his losses. Unlike Jeffery, they carry with ease the responsibility of what they did, almost proudly, and they are as eerily cheerful as he remembers.

'We have come for your assistance, what else?'

'You gave me your word that you would leave me alone.'

The man draws his lips back over his teeth. 'Things have changed unexpectedly. We need to destroy a station.'

A blink of confusion. 'My police station?'

The seated man examines his fingernails, chews on a torn piece of hard skin while looking up at Jeffery. 'A polling station. The one in Kibera to be exact.'

At this information, Jeffery's body shudders involuntarily and he strides over to the table to escape it, taking up his bottle of whiskey. His mind is already shrinking with fear, their words cutting uneasily into his stomach. He holds the alcohol for a long time to his mouth, even after it has all been drained. *If I stay still long enough, perhaps they will leave.*

But they watch him lazily, entertained by his erratic behavior, and as he removes the drink from his mouth with a steaming gasp, they laugh. His head swimming, Jeffery mutters, 'You're asking me to affect the outcome of a presidential election.'

They remain mute as he pants absurdly, his tongue burning with alcohol and dread. When Jeffery speaks again, the heat in his mouth turns to bile, sour as vomit. 'I won't do it.'

A threatening creak of his old floors as the black army boots of the standing man approach, the mirth vanished from his face. 'Perhaps you have forgotten what we are capable of doing to you.'

'Kill me then, I don't care.' The words are overdramatic, momentarily thrilling him but then he instantly regrets saying them.

'If you refuse me, I will drag you to that poll station myself and burn you with it.'

Jeffery begins to whimper. 'It's so wrong— I can't do it.'

The men are pitiless. They smile inanely as the police officer throws his head violently from side to side. 'Then find someone else to do it for you, *sindiyo*?' The standing man gestures for his companion to rise. 'Like that boy – what was his name?'

Remembering the muddy rush of Nairobi River, the twisted glasses. *Nick.*

Jeffery tries again. 'We had an agreement – I got you the money you wanted and you promised never to disturb me again.'

'There are some things that are also beyond our control.' One of them shrugged, leaning in close to Jeffery. 'I don't care how you manage, just get it done, *sawa*?'

They pat his back heavily and turn to leave, the door swinging shut on their terrible mockery just as Jeffery collapses forward on his knees, bringing the empty bottle crashing down with him – a thousand mocking shards of his reflection; broken, unfixable little pieces.

52

Two days since he last saw her, Leena sends him a text message asking him to meet her at Diamond Plaza. And at lunchtime too – their busiest time of day. She has a point to prove and he chuckles at this stubbornness, thinking that it is the part he likes most about her.

The shopping center is within walking distance from his apartment and he sets off, wanting to prolong the moment of contemplative happiness. The mall has been aptly nicknamed 'Little India' because it is made up of a multitude of small, overstocked and mostly East-Asian shops – tailors and dressmakers, clothing and material retailers and dozens of stores selling Indian knick-knacks. Recently, other stalls have appeared carrying cheaply priced mobile phones, iPods and other counterfeit goods. The scent of resin peppers the air and small copper bells tinkle outside the various temple shops.

Leena is already seated within the galvanized metal shade of the outdoor food court, sipping on a mug of sugar-cane juice. Squeezing the tip of the straw between her teeth, she waves away a host of waiters, pleading in broken Swahili for them to leave her alone.

'There are a lot of people here today.' He reaches her, shoos away the insistent waiters and their countless, similar menus. The formica tables are full of businessmen sneaking a quick barbequed lunch, loud families on outings and jostling tourists, cameras hung about their necks and shopping bags at their feet.

They hold each other's gaze until she breaks away with a nervous sigh. 'I wanted to apologize.'

'That's not why I came.'

'I know but I was wrong and I see that now.' A deep scarlet rises up her neck, her throat constricting into a twin pair of hard ridges. But when she speaks, she sounds sure. 'I want to give this a try.'

'It's not going to be easy,' he warns, distracted by the light layer of green foam that has stuck to her lip from the juice. He rubs his thumb along it, collecting up the moistness of her mouth. For a moment he thinks he has been too bold but then she smiles.

'I know.'

He hesitates but has to ask. 'Your mother—'

Her eyes jump open, a translucent ocher in the sunlight. 'Actually, do you mind if we keep this between us for now?'

'I told you, I don't want any secrets.' A rush of disappointment shifts him away from her.

'I just want to enjoy this for a little while without having to explain it to anyone.' Annoyance dashes across her face. 'Can't you understand that?'

In the distance, he can make out the rolling, high notes of a Hindi love song escaping the open windows of a parked car. The buzz of chatter overwhelms it as a sudden horde of shoppers enter the food court and already Michael feels the prick of their gaze, people struggling to make sense of the two of them sitting across from each other, fingertips grazing. The sneaky looks and loud whispers are a rude distraction upon their private moment and he catches her hand as it moves away. 'Okay. We'll do it your way.'

He runs his thumb slowly up and down the inside of her palm in deliberate, secret circles. When he eventually pulls away, she feels the absence of him acutely – a throbbing, sweet hum just below her skin.

The country is stirring with the beginnings of trouble, its corners already unraveled, but they don't pay attention to it because they are too busy coming together.

Before meeting Michael, if someone had asked her to describe Nairobi, she would have struggled with the answer. Her replies had always been vague and run through with an air of fiction. Sweeping red-night skies and daylight robberies. Thin-faced street children compelling you to save them; dusty game drives through yellowing, flat savannah. Things that, though sincere, were the least true things about her city.

Back then, she couldn't have told of the huge, open flea markets such as Gikomba, where gumboots were required to move through the muddy terrain and where one had to arrive in the frigid hours of the morning to beat the rush. She wouldn't have been able to describe the unique yet ordinary pockets – the kind one found elsewhere in the world – such as Arboretum Park with its green trails and park benches frequented by joggers and couples looking to steal a romantic moment; the modern, silver-peaked skyline that would not stop growing.

All those intricate details that made Nairobi less of an enigma and more of a capital city in its own right, she knows them now and they give her home town roots and a firmness in her mind so that for the first time, Leena feels as if she belongs to it and it belongs to her.

She tells him this, leaning against a crooked street light and tilting her mouth up to catch the vanilla streams escaping her ice-cream cone. Michael takes it from her and throws it in the dustbin.

The first time his mouth comes down, it's quick – the brush of a question – before leaving. She tries to talk but once again his lips cover hers, firmer this time, a pressing claim, and he takes her by the waist, drawing her impossibly close.

'I'll buy you another ice cream,' he says afterward.

She steps back, fingers hovering at her startled mouth. 'Can we go somewhere quieter? We need to talk.'

In the middle of the afternoon, the apartment block and street around it are tranquil. Not a sound except for their footsteps moving upward, fingers linked. She trails behind him, distracted and overcome by a familiar, dizzying breathlessness whenever her thoughts come too close to what happened that day. Once inside, he leads her to the couch where she pulls her legs up into a soft, lumpy corner, hands busy in her lap. Michael places himself a few spaces away and waits.

Head dipped down, her lips move wordlessly. Talking about what happened isn't the problem. It's trying to explain how it has changed her. Every time she begins, she is met by a veiled uncertainty – shadows seeping into the edges of her thoughts and obscuring them.

Jai has already told Michael about what happened but hearing it from her is painful. He feels it – a rallying anger in his gut – compelled forward just in time to catch her as she falls back, head tucked beneath his chin.

'I wish I had seen his face because right now, he could be anyone.'

It is easier to talk while supported by the steadiness of his body, the assured pitch of his breath calming her. To confess the anxiety that had extended beyond the man who raped her to others who reminded her of him. To admit that every time one of them brushed against her, approached too near, spoke to her, she recalled the violent rush of his fingers, taking away what was rightfully hers, the accusations he spat so readily, as if she carried within her every injustice of the past.

'For the longest time, I didn't want anyone to look at me, let alone touch me. Until just now, outside that ice-cream parlor.'

He kisses her face – all those hollow, sharply formed crevices – and holds her for a long time after that.

53

'It's dirty business, what's happening up at Tana River.' Raj is talking more to the television than he is to his family.

'Most of our friends have left for the month. We should think of doing the same – perhaps visit your mother in Toronto or go to London. I haven't seen Amandeep in a while.' Pooja is worried, unnerved by how isolated their street has become, as exposed as it is to the main road. One never knew who could be sneaking in to climb over her neighbors' gates, taking advantage of their prolonged absences – the idea causes her to shiver theatrically.

'We can't just leave.' Raj's eyes never stray from the graphic images on the news.

At dawn that morning, a village in Tana River Delta belonging to the semi-nomadic Orma tribe was attacked by Pokomo farmers armed with spears and AK-47 rifles, reigniting an age-old rivalry between the two groups.

Even though the pictures have been blurred out, Pooja can still make out the horrific damage: burned, grass-thatched huts split open and blackened like rotting teeth. A small boy, shot from behind, lies unmoving in the blood-clumped dirt. He is still wearing his school backpack, ribbed blue socks pulled up to his knees. Pooja looks away, thinking of her own children.

Her anger at her husband burns stronger than ever, fills her ears with a buzzing heat as she listens to the villager being interviewed on KTN. *These politicians are setting us up, taking advantage of the long-standing conflict between our two groups – do they think we don't know who is funding and perpetrating this violence? I'm lucky no one saw me – I jumped out of my back window and escaped through the swamp.*

Pooja says, this time more aggressively, 'Look at the situation. Why shouldn't we go when everyone else is doing it?'

'What kind of Kenyans would we be if we just ran away when it was convenient?'

'You and your morals.' His love for this country is a selfish streak within Raj that Pooja has never been able to reconcile with, such insensibility from an otherwise practical man.

Raj thinks of Pinto, disrespectfully hidden away in his toilet. 'I'm going to cast my vote at the end of this week.'

Jai speaks up. 'There has been some upheaval in the Rift Valley area. I might have to go there for a few days.'

Pooja shakes her head emphatically, still perturbed by what she has seen. 'You're going to stay here with all of us, in case something happens.'

'It's for work, Ma.' Just like his father, Jai doesn't even look at her.

'I don't care. Let those *kharias* solve their own problems.'

Today, her words have a poisonous bite. Perhaps it is the knowledge, as Jai watches the nine o'clock news – the murders, the buying of votes, politicians ready to promise anything just as long as it gets them into State House – that certain things are beyond his reach. It is the slow muting of an impossible childhood hope. He might spend his lifetime fighting and never see any progress at all.

He wants to talk to Michael but his friend hasn't spoken to him in a few weeks, no matter how many times Jai calls. He cannot help but feel that it's all his mother's fault. It had started when she had sent Angela from their lives for nothing more than a hunch, a silly worry. She had spent so much time trying to keep everyone in her control, heeding to certain black-and-white rules of behavior that were as outdated as they were outlandish, simply to fit in with the community, that she was blind to the fact that the world was moving forward without her.

'When are you going to stop calling them *kharias*?' Jai rises. 'How many times do I have to ask you not to? You don't pay attention to a word anyone says and yet you expect the whole world to listen to you.'

Pooja's face contorts into shameful arcs; windmill eyes and a mouth dropped open into a tiny *o*. 'Show your mother some respect.'

'Why should I when you have no respect for me?' he challenges, going for the door and finally understanding the cause of his anger. It is the building tension that is stretching this city tight – Jai feels it, ropelike, in his own body – unfurling, ripping, racing headlong toward breaking point.

She has been instructed to stay at home but instead, at ten o'clock that night, Leena is still sitting at Mercury Lounge in a hard, red booth. The dim light falls in thin bars across the faces of her friends, making them appear villainous and not quite real. She eyes the door-less nook leading out into the open-air patio, feels a pull toward its chilly relief but then Michael rests his hand on her thigh – a firm anchor instantly calming her.

'I think it's so cute that you two are together.'

The cigarette-filled air has dried out her eyes and makes it difficult to see anything properly but Leena detects a finger pointing out of the darkness at the two of them. The voice is high-pitched and has an annoying tendency to elongate every word.

'Thanks.' As always, Michael is open and generous with his smile but Leena cannot help the frown that pushes her bottom lip upward, creasing her chin.

At the beginning of the evening, the tension at the table had been palpable, though well hidden. The conversation had been stilted and formal, her friends' eyes permanently stuck on their drinks. It had reminded Leena of the first time Michael had played cricket at the compound; the group dynamic had shifted, becoming uncomfortably fluid and difficult to navigate.

But now, two rounds later, released by the alcohol and dark ambience, her friends lean forward eagerly to inspect Michael. They wear silly, scary smiles and are accepting – encouraging even – of their new relationship, and Leena isn't sure which of these two conflicting attitudes makes her feel worse.

'Good for you,' someone told her when Michael had gone to the bathroom. 'We're not stuck in our parents' generation any more.'

'Nairobi is becoming so cosmopolitan, we have no choice but to accept each other's differences if we want to move forward.' The words are directed at Michael. 'It's a shame we still have all this nonsense about tribalism.' Whiskey tilts and glints orange as a glass is placed to a speaking mouth. 'Are you worried about the possible aftermath of these elections?'

Leena sits upright, involuntarily gripping Michael's fingers. 'What do you mean?'

Michael speaks slowly, as relaxed as always, his nail tracing slow lines in her skin. 'There have been a few instances of tribal-based riots outside of the city recently with people saying that the only way Kibaki will be re-elected is through a rigged election. And if that happens, they are threatening that it will be us Kikuyu who will pay the price.'

'But it's just talk, right?' She has forgotten about the people sitting around them; it's only his face – calm and seeming to smile even in its stillness – that she sees. 'You aren't really going to be in any danger if he is re-elected?'

'Maybe not.'

The whiskey-slurred voice of one of her friends reaches her, slightly muffled. 'All you Africans are quite well educated now...'

They both ignore the careless insinuation as she shifts closer to him, resting her head on the back of the booth so that he feels the quickness of her breath. In a small voice, she says, 'I don't want anything to happen to you,' and then, his chest expands outward in delight when, right in front of all those watchful eyes, Leena leans forward and kisses him softly on the mouth.

54

The name has changed but everything else in the bar has remained the same. There is still the pervasive beer stink hanging in the air, though the floral chairs are faded now, lacking shine – much like Marlyn herself.

'What are you doing here?' She approaches him wearily, perched at his old table.

The bar is the only point of contact between him and those men and he has come to dissuade them, to beg them to leave him alone. 'I wanted a drink.' His next words surprise him with their truthfulness. 'And to see you.'

A sigh – a glint of pleasure quickly hidden away. 'One drink and then you must leave.'

But the whiskey is not helping today. If anything, it makes everything seem more dire. Sinking into a relaxed mood he is able to think more cleary, to understand better, what it is those men are asking of him.

Kibera slums is the constituency of the opposing electoral candidate. Jeffery knows that, on voting day, the line-up at that poll station will be over a kilometer long. People will wait all day, some up to twelve hours, to drop their ballots into the color-coded boxes, leaving with a sense of accomplishment, a shared hope. His hands tremble when he thinks of what he will be destroying, and David's words, that long-ago warning he never heeded, come back to him. *The line has to be drawn somewhere. If it wasn't, imagine all the things we could do to each other.*

When he next looks up, wanting another drink, he sees Marlyn speaking to a young man. His back is turned to Jeffery but there is something familiar about the straight, drawn-back shoulders, the casual way he leans against the bar despite the urgency of the conversation.

'She's staying at different men's houses, going from place to place with no direction. You need to start thinking about your daughter's future. I can't do it all.'

Marlyn puts a placating hand on his upper arm. 'You're right. I'll do better from now on.'

Jeffery feels sorry for her. Worry and age have overtaken her beauty completely. The impressive fullness of her hips has sunk into boniness; the shine has seeped from her skin. He remembers when it was lustrous with shea butter and sweet promises, *Mar-Lynne the mermaid*, all color and sensual brightness.

He is still watching her when the man turns, almost misses him. Their eyes catch – a spark of recognition and a slow grin from her companion, arrogant and superior. The man pushes open the door and leaves.

Jeffery calls Marlyn over. 'Come here, now.'

She rushes to him with a full glass. 'I'm sorry about what I said before. Here, have another drink.'

Waving away her apologies, he asks, 'Who is that?'

'It's nothing to be jealous of,' she teases, stroking his chest.

'I'm being serious, Lynne.'

Her hand drops dully to her side. Black irises inky with disappointment. 'He's my nephew.'

'I've arrested him on several occasions.'

She laughs at this, a strong snort that shows off her large, pearl teeth. 'You have the wrong boy.'

'I've caught him for vandalism numerous times now.' Jeffery's mind is working fast, an idea forming and unforming as soon as he has a grasp of it.

'It's impossible,' she protests, suddenly worried. She recognizes the tightening grip on her wrist, those lips pulled back in a snarl.

'What's his name?' Twisting her arm until her lips go pale and dry.

She gives a sharp breath, the leaping hope of his impromptu return quickly gone. 'Michael.'

Jeffery has been to this apartment building several times before, when he foolishly believed he was in love with Marlyn. He would watch as she was dropped at the gate, always as the sun was rising and always by a different man, stumbling over loose gravel in matchstick heels. How tempted he had been then to chase those cars and shoot the driver between the eyes, but all he had been able to muster was a growling grimace, undetectable in the busy night.

The building looks more rundown during the daytime – broken windows displayed like missing teeth, packed washing lines resembling a bazaar strung from one balcony to another. He is about to climb out of the car when he hears voices – as sunny as the day outside and in the sing-song manner reserved for new lovers.

Marlyn's nephew is standing with a woman at the main entrance, pressing her up against the door frame, his mouth caught up in her neck. She makes a move to leave and is pulled back – he kisses her again through her protesting laughter.

'Do you really have to go?' he is asking.

'It's getting late.'

'Where did you tell her you were this time?'

The girl reaches up to smooth his brow, taking her time when she puts her mouth against his. 'I'll see you tomorrow.'

When the boy finally releases her and she approaches the parking lot, Jeffery shrinks into his seat. As she comes closer, the world sharpens bizarrely. He knows that face. Though today the features are softer, touched by happiness, he remembers when they were seized with fear, recoiling with disgust. The small body stumbling up the stairs, full of fight. How still she had been when they had left, pink pajama shorts at her ankles.

Now she looks at Jeffery as she passes his car. He smiles, filled with wretchedness as she returns his grin jovially, jumping into her vehicle that is parked just beside his. After she has left he spends several seconds collecting his breath, watching the boy as he does so.

Michael remains at the doorway, his face and body arched in the direction she has gone. When he hears the policeman's footsteps, his smile fades fast.

'Are you following me?'

'We have to talk.'

'I have nothing to say to you.' Michael retreats into the building, about to close the door.

In a voice that has not been used in a very long time, Jeffery says, 'She's pretty, is she not, the Kohli girl?'

For the first time since he has known him, Jeffery catches fear on the boy's face. He grins, forces himself into the cool, cement shade of the building. 'Perhaps we should go upstairs.'

Pooja is keeping a silent vigil over her daughter's comings and goings. She has trained her sharp ears to block out any sounds that are not the clip of high heels, the stuttered creak of a door hinge – Leena's noises as she navigates the darkness of the house, occasionally stumbling into a standing vase or tripping up the stairs. At these times, Pooja feels very far away from her daughter, as if a foreign house guest is tiptoeing about her home, politely secretive and preferring to keep out of everyone's way.

The exact knowledge of her daughter's whereabouts is beginning to accumulate in Pooja's mind, though she is not yet ready to face it fully. It has provided her comfort to believe her daughter's fibs about coffees with Kiran and late-afternoon shopping errands that turn into dinner and drinks with some old high-school friends – and Pooja has been careful not to ask too many questions, satisfied with the practiced information her daughter feeds her. But after what she heard at the temple today, the truth refuses to leave her alone, ticking mercilessly at the center of all her thoughts.

A woman had cornered her in the *langar* earlier, while Pooja had been busy with a pot simmering with eggplant curry, steaming her skin in the aroma of bay leaves and black seeds.

'Is it true?' A whisper almost lost in all the commotion.

'Is what true?' Pooja had been busy frowning down at her cooking, upset because the vegetable was too soft, falling apart at even the most experienced touch of her wooden spoon.

'What everyone is saying about Leena.'

The broken eggplant forgotten, Pooja turned to the woman sharply, her breath caught at the base of her thin throat. 'Who is saying what?'

The woman appeared uncomfortable but simultaneously pleased with the power she now had. 'Perhaps I shouldn't have said anything.'

'Just spit it out!' It came out as a desperate yelp, which Pooja gathered back quickly and rearranged into a more concerned murmur. 'With things the way they are at the moment, we need to keep a close eye on our children, *na*?'

Nodding her consent, the woman leaned in so as to make sure no one overheard. 'Someone saw her at Diamond Plaza a couple of weekends ago with a boy.'

A distressed ringing began between Pooja's ears. 'So what? It was probably one of her old school friends.'

'He was an African.'

The information was a quick bullet, halting everything around her, even the blood in her veins. She was certain the sound had carried above the steel clang of pots, whispering into people's ears, and she felt the pressure of their snide disapproval. It was so heavy that she dropped the spoon into the curry and mumbled, 'I just remembered, I have to pick up Raj's blood-pressure medication from the chemist today…' and she hurried out, her *chuni* wrapped protectively over her face, tears stinging her cheeks.

Now she sits in the sloping darkness of the kitchen and waits for her daughter to creep in. She hears the *cling* of the car keys hitting the countertop and asks, 'Where were you?'

Leena jumps back with a surprised yelp. 'You scared me, Ma.' She looks flushed and pleased, her eyes jumping with a smile.

Pooja finds her happiness disrespectful and her voice turns hard. She sits facing the window, away from her daughter. 'I want to know where you went and with whom. No lies this time.'

'I told you, I met up with some friends.'

After playing along with the farce for so many days now, Pooja is tired. 'It was Michael, wasn't it?' She speaks the name quickly – almost wanting her daughter not to hear it.

But to her dismay, Leena's shoulders collapse downward in relief. Grabbing her mother's hand, she says, 'I wanted to tell you, Ma. I really did.'

A barking laugh springs from Pooja's throat as she yanks her hand away, twisting her *chuni* around her palm. The objects in the kitchen begin to vibrate around her – infected by some manic energy – and try as she might, she cannot get them to quieten down.

'Do you know someone saw you together at Diamond Plaza? Do you know that we have become the joke of the temple?' She doesn't realize she is shouting, her voice lost in her own panic. 'You will not see that boy again.'

'I don't have to listen to this,' Leena says, but her mother's fingers pinch her elbow tightly, keeping her rooted in place.

'This is not just about you sneaking around any more – it concerns all of us. It's about our family's reputation.'

'Tomorrow people will be talking about someone else.'

'People will not forget this,' her mother warns. 'And what happens when you learn that I am right? That no matter how much you like this boy now, such a relationship is not practical here. It won't last.' Pooja takes a shuddering breath. 'This thing between you will inevitably fall apart and you won't be the only one who has to deal with the consequences.'

Leena shrinks against the darkness and when she speaks, her voice is hollow. 'I think I'm falling in love with him.'

Pooja cannot bear to look at her daughter. Instead, she fixes her eyes on the cold, half-moon traveling in and out of the night clouds. She is soothed by its hard exterior, its unwavering shape.

'Feelings are like visitors, Leena,' she says, drawing her *chuni* around her shoulders. 'They never stay with us for long.'

The next time Michael opens his door, it is to a different Kohli.

He moves behind Jai to close the door, deliberating his next words. There is a specific reason why he has called his friend over but there are more important things to discuss first.

'How come you never told me Leena was back?'

Jai's head gives a slight shake of regret. 'I planned on it. I wanted to tell her about you too but when she got back from London, she was different. All jumpy and fragile – terrified of this place.'

'I would never hurt her.'

After a moment, Jai speaks. 'Ever since we were children, she always believed that I was the one who was protecting her, keeping her safe.' He thinks back to those moments when Michael had stood in front of his sister, guarding her body with his own; the way he had always so readily leaped to her defense, whether she had been right or wrong. 'But we both know it wasn't me.'

'I love her.'

'I've known that for a very long time.'

In a rush of gratitude, Michael slumps down on the couch beside Jai. Once again, his stomach grows heavy with fear when he thinks of the policeman's visit. He cannot understand how or when things became so complicated, only that they did. He thinks of the cop striding out of the front door, pleased with himself and with what he had threatened Michael into.

'I need your help,' he says and tells his friend everything.

There is something about the hush of that night, the unusual calmness, which takes them back to the first wall they painted on. Their earlier graffiti has long been covered up but they can still recall the fast excitement, the fear and determination as they worked – their breath twin fogs in the night.

It is a Wednesday evening and there is hardly a footfall around them so they take their time, lost in their own reflections, interrupted only by the occasional whisper. The villagers in Tana River Delta remain heavy in the forefront of their minds, a stinging reminder of how easy it is to dismiss lives in some parts of Kenya, treating people as pawns for political gain – training them to become systematic enemies so that neighbors raided each other's houses, teachers killed their students, the youth turned on their elders.

After it is completed, the two of them step back to observe their work. Forty-seven hands joined together – a representation of the forty-seven tribes of Kenya – fingers intertwined. Within the unbreakable oval of their union, Michael has written:

PEACE IS ONLY POSSIBLE WHEN WE COME TOGETHER

Jai asks his friend, 'Do you think this made a difference? All those hurried nights, you going to jail – do you think it was worth it?'

Michael stands with his hands in his pockets and his reply is as composed as always. 'Whether one person or a hundred see it, we did our part. That's what matters.'

As they make their way to Michael's apartment, the stars blinking at their backs and a smell that lingers like an ache in Jai's chest – smoke and dust, the honey-sweetness of flowers – he thinks of how this is his favorite kind of evening. It has an endless quality about it, the kind that allows you to know yourself completely, even for a short time.

They are on the main road, surrounded by *matatu* noises and the leering whistles of touts. A cyclist speeds by, narrowly missing them and ringing his small bell in irritation, echoing far into the obscure darkness. Tired street vendors pack up, taking a momentary rest for a steaming plate of *githeri*, which they buy off the old woman who sits by the roadside with her *jiko* and small radio. They talk together briefly before the men drop their dirty dishes in a bucket of soapy water and leave for the night. A young woman leans into a car window; she is smiling a painted smile and adjusting the shortness of her dress. Her eyes dart about before she disappears behind the tinted windows.

It stuns him because life in Nairobi is so raw, a series of short and poignant moments that, standing on the curb and watching life pass, acknowledge him like an old friend. Jai finds it impossible that anyone could ever wish to be any other place but here.

55

The city is restless and, tired of waiting, rouses early on voting day. Before dawn, eager Kenyans blow whistles and trumpet-like vuvuzelas, calling for people to rise from the warmth of their beds. Raj wakes his son at five o'clock, the stars waning figures in a bluing sky.

'I want to get a headstart.'

They leave Pooja and Leena at home, slow breathing bumps beneath bedsheets, and drive to the closest polling station in Muthaiga. By the time they arrive, a pink chill has hardened the air and the wind disturbs Jai's unbrushed hair.

'Looks like everyone had the same idea as us,' he says.

The voting is taking place in the suburb's main police station, temporarily transformed into a frenzied market of people. The absence of signs and officials means that they wait in shifty, confused lines – bickering and shoving, eager to cast their ballots. The two Kohli men walk the entire vicinity before spotting the main desk, hiding within a narrow, cool corridor. While Raj shows their IDs and Voter Cards, Jai returns to the waiting crowd.

'The main desk is this way,' he calls out. 'You need a number first.'

There are six different stations, separated into alphabetical order according to surnames. Yet still they must wait four hours before dropping their ballots into the color-coded containers. Breath held, folded paper forced into too-thin slits of the boxes, and when Jai exits the dark room he is met with dazzling, late-morning sunlight.

People are growing impatient, disturbed by the heat, their voices rising as they begin to argue with officials and each other. Somewhere, a cheeky voter is caught trying to skip the line, causing a chaotic disruption as people turn on him.

'I've been waiting here since early morning – are you the future president, you think you are so special?'

'These Kikuyu think they can get away with anything.'

The man is jostled, kicked and tugged by the collar to the end of the queue where, reprimanded, he stands baffled and wearing a shamefaced grin.

An elderly woman wrapped in a shawl lightly touches the man's arm and says in a voice loud enough for Jai to overhear, 'It's okay to wait because we are making history. If you want to do something good, you must be patient.'

These are the words Jai carries home with him and that dissipate slightly the nervous fear that springs up whenever he thinks of the long day still ahead, the predicament that Michael and ultimately his sister have found themselves in – the unsettling clench of not knowing what is yet to come.

The phone vibrates noisily, skipping over the table with a flashing blue screen. The name appears in bold, black letters and Michael turns the mobile over so that he can no longer see the display.

The apartment is empty. He has sent Jackie and his aunt to stay with his mother in Eldoret. 'Things are uncertain here. No one is sure what will happen,' he had told them.

'What about you, *cuzo*?' Jackie had been a wide-eyed child, clinging to his wrists. 'Aren't you going to join us?'

'I'll see you very soon,' he had promised.

With the glare of the late-afternoon sun in his eyes, Michael moves slowly through the rooms of his home. He notices the things he has forgotten to look at: the permanent indentation of the living-room carpet from where his mattress used to lie; the bathroom door with its constantly squeaking, loose hinge; the wine stain on the couch where his aunt, after a working night, had fallen asleep with a glass between her fingers.

He puts his hand to the rough upholstery, cracking now with age. It is also where Leena had trusted him with her secret: where twelve long years had stretched out and disappeared between them, rising in a new and much more urgent way.

These are the stories of his life, neglected and left to fade, and he wishes he could take them with him. Misunderstood, they will be nothing but a nuisance to the next occupants, things to be fixed, because only he can see their magic.

He is pulled from these musings by a loud rapping – quick and hard knocks on the door – and instinctively, he presses closer to the wall. He checks his watch. It is just past four thirty; the policeman is early. Then he hears her voice and his muscles weaken with relief.

'I'm glad you're here,' he starts, pulling open the door, but the expression on her face stops him. It is stiff and annoyed and she stalks into the apartment with hurried words.

'It's such a disaster – my mother has found out about us.' Leena throws herself onto the couch. 'What am I going to do?'

Her panic is abrasive, setting his already racing heart pounding even faster. He closes the door and goes to her.

'At least now we don't have to hide.' Then Michael remembers that he has not yet told her about the policeman's visit. Perhaps now he will be able to convince her to go with him – a leaping, painful hope in his throat turning to stone as soon as she speaks.

'This is the worst thing that could have happened. Everyone at the temple is laughing and talking about me. I told you, I didn't want to have to explain this to anyone.'

She is so caught up in her own worries that she doesn't even notice the emptiness of her surroundings. Gone are the bed, the *sufurias*, the portable drawers of vegetables – even the *jiko* was packed up in a cardboard box and taken to Eldoret. Only the couch and threadbare carpet remain.

'Just tell me what you want to do.' For the first time, Michael is angry with her – feels a pang of irritation at her childish selfishness.

She asks, 'What if there comes a point when we can't cheat ourselves about how different we are from each other?'

'The only difference between you and me is that I'm not constantly questioning this relationship.' He is cold; he thinks of all the things he has agreed to do and how oblivious she remains – caught up in silly anxieties that hold no real importance.

'It's not so black and white, Mike,' she protests.

'And it never will be. You just have to figure out if this is worth the risk.'

Having dispelled some of her anxiety, she finally recognizes that he is not his usual, patient self. His eyes keep wandering up to the clock, his fingers fidgeting over his stubble; he looks like he hasn't shaved or slept in a few days.

'Is everything okay?' she asks, feeling the inklings of alarm.

He says, 'Actually, it's getting quite late.'

'My parents are expecting me home for dinner.' She wants to reassure him of her feelings but something holds her back. As she glances around, she notices the absence of all the luxuries she is used to, seeing the frayed couch and the old-fashioned floorboards, and is reminded of her own home, so spacious and full, tucked into an expensive, modern suburb, and she feels the truth of her mother's words pinching her stomach.

When her eyes fall back on him, he gives her a long and hard stare. 'Then you should leave.'

As Leena walks by him, the sunlight a tangle of topaz in her hair, he wonders if this will be the last time he sees her. He is tempted to stop and tell her what is happening but before he can, she is reaching up to kiss his rigid cheek.

'You mean a lot to me but there are other people I have to think of as well. Please just be patient.'

His chest deflates sharply, disappointment gnawing at him as she walks away; he is angry at how easily she can do it.

After she leaves, it takes him a long time to get dressed and he does so sitting on the edge of the couch, his legs heavy. He has to skip some of the button holes because of the tremor in his fingers; his khaki trousers snag and he pulls so hard that the seam tears. When he pauses, he notices that the shaking in his hands has become worse, has traveled up to his chest and shoulders.

The phone rings again. This time he picks up without hesitation.

Jeffery slips his mobile phone back into his breast pocket, holds up his empty glass and shakes it at the bartender.

'*Ingine*,' he calls out and then, because he is feeling slightly unanchored, promises himself that it will be the last one. It is almost five o'clock – in less than two hours, it will be dark. The streets outside remain empty. Most people have either stayed at home or shut their businesses early. 'Turn on the television!' he shouts in the direction of the bar, wishing that it was Marlyn here to serve him. But she had left for Eldoret that morning, promising him that she would not be returning to Nairobi, and the way she had looked at him, so neutrally, as if he no longer mattered to her, Jeffery believed it.

A staticky flicker, a silver buzz of promise before the screen falls blank again. 'It's not working,' he is told. 'Go home, even your companions have left.'

'Who is in the lead?' Jeffery speaks to the shadows, detects a slight, gray movement as the bartender wipes down the shelves.

'It's still too early to tell, *mzee*. Why worry?'

He thinks of Betty, hopes that she is safe wherever she is. He is used to the dull bellyache her memory gives him – is beginning to understand that it will stay with him forever. 'Do you think it's going to be alright?' His voice has shrunk into a pleading whisper. 'Do you think we're all going to be fine?'

'God gave us this country. He will keep it safe.'

Jeffery slides off the bar stool and pushes away his glass. The two men had left over half an hour ago, after listening to his plan with unamused scowls. They had not been happy when he told them that it would be necessary, after all, for them to be present in Kibera.

'I thought we told you to take care of it.'

'I'll do the most important part but you must bring the equipment. I have some last-minute things to work out before I can join you.'

And they had threatened and growled at him but had eventually agreed as he knew they would, because they were bound to another person the way he was to them, someone who had compelled them into action, leaving them little room for choice.

Now, Jeffery moves toward the door, finding the speed in his feet at last. There are still many things to be done and the sky is fading quickly.

56

A voice springs up in the darkness. 'Do you think she'll hate me when she finds out?'

'You're only trying to protect her, Mike.'

It has been almost an hour and the waiting is worse than anything. With no distractions, Michael cannot stop the thoughts that hound him. Ice-cream parlors and black silk hair – her warm laughter against his mouth. How close they came to the end.

'I won't be able to stay here after this,' he tells his friend. 'Not for a while, at least.'

'Where will you go?'

'My mother needs some help with the *shamba* in Eldoret and Jackie is already there.'

'If you tell her the truth, maybe she'll wait for you.'

Michael shakes his head. He is tired of putting his life on hold. 'That's not fair to either of us.'

Kibera is asleep. For those residents who have televisions, they remain glued to the news, filling their houses with anxious neighbors, packed tightly within mud walls, and the two friends sit outside the polling station undisturbed. The dim, yellowing moon reveals the outline of a primary school, flat and boxy with countless pillars along thin corridors. On the wall closest to them, the times tables from one to twelve have been printed out in childish colors. It reminds Michael of his old school in Eldoret, sitting in an L-shape around a concrete playground.

'They don't even care about what will happen to the children afterward.'

Before Jai can say anything, the air drags with heavy footsteps, labored breathing and then a pause. One man spits into a mountain of garbage, *thwack*, disturbing the stillness. Jai tenses up and it dawns on Michael how difficult this will be.

'You better go,' he tells Jai. 'They can't know that you're here.'

A few meters from where they sit, a thicket of bush runs the boundary of the school, cutting it off from the rest of the houses, and Jai heads that way now, disappearing from view with a loud rustle. After several seconds, the silence resettles and Michael is alone.

'Who are you talking to, *kijana*?' The voice behind him is rough and smoke-filled, approaching from the shadows.

Michael doesn't turn around. A part of him is compelled to look upon the men who hurt her but there is a sick tightening in his gut and he finds himself paralyzed, able only to stare straight ahead.

'Let's get this over with.'

'Where is Jeffery?' The bulky figure comes closer, disturbs the thick night.

'He stayed at home.'

They chuckle disapprovingly together, standing fully in front of him now, twin bald heads gleaming in the poor light.

'And he has sent you to do his dirty work.'

Their dark faces creep with smiles. Their movements are unhurried, as if they don't mind being here, as if it never occurred to them that something might go wrong. One takes a tobacco leaf and pushes it underneath his red-stained tongue.

'Didn't you make him your scapegoat?' Michael asks.

Their smiles catch. Unlike Nick, eager and nervous to please, this one is hard-faced and refuses to hide his contempt, spitting out his words.

'Don't talk of things you know nothing of,' the chewing one tells him. 'You're only a boy.'

Last week, after Jeffery had forced his way into the apartment, Michael had listened to his story with disbelief – a mounting rage that had set the room spinning. *They were going to kill me. I didn't know they would do such a thing – you have no idea what they are capable of. You must help me. They know where she lives so you have to do exactly as I say.*

Being sneered at now by the two of them, one sending a spray of pink spittle to the ground, Michael is tempted to tell them everything he knows. Instead, he concentrates on the wet semi-circle in the mud and swallows down the truth.

'Have you got everything?' he asks, sliding off the small wall.

One of them taps the backpack on his shoulder. 'We told Jeffery to take care of it. I still don't know why I'm here.'

'It was short notice and I couldn't get the kerosene in time.'

With a disapproving grunt, the man says to his companion, 'I told you the *jama* was useless.'

Michael heads toward the school. 'One of the classrooms on the ground floor should get the job done.' He holds his voice tight, hoping they won't sense how it wavers. He is overcome by a crippling doubt, convinced that he has been tricked – cornered in this faraway place by a wily policeman. Then he remembers Jai crouching behind the bushes and his nervousness slows.

There is a night watchman who has been instructed to guard the building but Jeffery has already bribed him for his silence and as he sees the three approaching figures, he turns down the corner and heads away from the building.

He has left the main door slightly open and they enter unimpeded. Their footsteps echo through the bare corridor – long sounds petering out behind Michael as he forces his feet forward, toward the last classroom. He thinks he hears the scrape of table legs, hushed voices and pauses to glance back at the men. They are relaxed, conversing pleasantly, and when they see him watching, one scowls.

'We don't have all night, *kijana*.'

The classroom has not been cleaned up from the day. The wooden desks are littered with pencils and scraps of paper, empty ballot slips and an ink case, used to mark the fingernail of each voter. Along the far wall, taped-up cardboard boxes, full of votes, are piled haphazardly upon each other. Tomorrow, they will be transported to the main center to be counted but for tonight, they sit exposed and neglected, as if their contents are unnecessary.

A large stock cupboard sits at the back of the room and creaks slightly in the wind, looking ready to tip over. Michael's skin breaks open in an anxious sweat as the backpack is kicked toward him.

'Get moving.'

He takes his time unzipping it. An overhead clock ticks inanely, mocking him with every second passed. The kerosene has been poured into a one-liter, plastic container of cooking oil and as he picks it up from the bag, Michael asks, 'Are you sure you want me to do this? It's not too late to stop.'

They were meant to stand aside and let him do it but now that they are here, the two men have grown impatient and begin to reshuffle the furniture, shoving the desks together in a cluster behind the cardboard boxes.

'Stop talking and give it to me.' When one of them gestures for the kerosene, Michael hesitates. 'Hurry up! You're taking too long.' An annoyed shout and, reluctantly, the container exchanges hands.

As the man begins to unscrew it, Michael's ankles tense up. His shoulders clench, ready to tackle him. But he is distracted by the loud noise of cupboard doors slamming open. With a loud yelp, four policemen spring out of the stock closet.

Wild eyes, a heaving chest – the two men are astounded to see Jeffery rushing toward them, gun pointed and face set in such determination; they fall immediately to their knees before him. The cooking oil container is kicked away, unopened.

Jeffery shouts, 'Stay on the floor – you are under arrest for attempting to tamper with votes.'

Michael follows their cue, spreading himself out onto the floor and shutting his eyes tight as a gun is pressed firmly to the back of his head.

57

In the pale lavender morning, the two men walk slowly along the gravel pathway of Parklands police station. Jeffery pauses at the edge of the parking lot, extending his hand outward. Michael shakes it with a firm warning.

'Remember your promise.'

'Those men will be in jail for a very long time – they have many things to pay for, as do I.' Jeffery's face is marred by an exhausted sorrow but the previous night has rid him of a certain weight and his steps are lighter, his voice moving with a friendly skip.

When Michael says to him, 'I should go, I don't want to miss my bus,' the police officer scuffs his toe bleakly in the dirt and hovers in front of the boy, reluctant to let him leave.

'What happened to your friend?' he inquires, secretly glad that he didn't have to face the *muhindi* boy.

'He had to go home.'

Once he was sure that Michael was in no danger, Jai had left the police station, apologetic and explaining that it was an emergency. 'You know I wouldn't go if it wasn't important,' he had called over his shoulder, hurrying out of the *mabati* door.

Jeffery says now, 'It's a good idea to leave Nairobi, for the present time at least. Those men have many connections and you must keep yourself safe.' He feels a strange tie to this boy and is sorry to see him go. After a quick pause, he asks, 'That girl – is she going with you?'

'I haven't told her I'm going.'

Jeffery is surprised by the dull thud in the boy's words. 'You fight for many important things so why give up now, at this most crucial time?'

It is Michael's turn to fix his gaze upon the dusty ground, to rub his toe in a frustrated circle. 'There is only so much fighting I can do alone. At some point, she will have to join in.' It is easy to be truthful with the policeman, who, despite everything, is still a stranger to him.

'It's unfortunate that some of us have to lose so much in order to learn what is worth keeping,' the officer acknowledges.

Attempting to change the subject, Michael asks, 'Where will you go now?'

Jeffery glances back at the station – gray and unwelcoming, brimming with ghosts. He will not miss it. 'I'm going home.'

'Kibera is not safe at the moment.'

The police officer is taking small steps away from Michael, a new smile tugging the edges of his lips; it is not mean nor grimacing but sparks a sweetness in his dark eyes. When he speaks, however, his voice is grave. 'It seems I have spent a lifetime avoiding my true duties. If things are to come crashing down now, I want to be there to catch them.'

The bus station in Nairobi is the busiest place in the city. The uncertainty from the elections has infected people with a restlessness and most feel unable to stay in the capital city, needing to be upcountry with family and loved ones.

He sees the orange and blue colors of the Eldoret Express, with its dusty tires and heavy load; already people are squeezed in against the windows and the bags that do not fit at the bottom of the bus are strapped insecurely to a rack at the top or piled up on passengers' laps. Michael has not taken the bus since he was fifteen years old, clutching his favorite satchel throughout the bumpy ride. Back then, he hadn't known what to expect when he reached the capital and he recalls the student he had met on the bus, how she had warned him of the city's lure – its ability to snatch up and keep you.

Stepping off the bus into this very station those many years ago, he had felt cheated by her, but today, he understands what she had been trying to tell him. He wonders what he will do without all the noise and cheerful busyness – the shivering promise that runs through Nairobi like a current.

He is so preoccupied by these worries, lost amid jostling bodies packed tightly about him as they fight to embark first, that they almost miss each other. It is only because he pauses to catch one last glimpse of the city that he spots her, a distant figure enshrouded by morning light, a protective hand over her eyes. A gust of wind disturbs the hem of her dress and she catches onto it. By the time he reaches her, the breeze has settled and the air is expectantly still.

When she speaks, he drops his bag at her feet with collapsing, relieved shoulders. It is everything he wants – all his memories in an urgent, sweet claim.

'Ever since we were children, I have loved you in some way. You took away everything that ever frightened me and now it's my turn to keep you safe.'

They stand before each other, barely touching. When her fingertips brush his skin, he is reminded of what he loves most about Nairobi. As he brings his mouth down to meet hers, he feels it again – the possibility of all things – beating slowly in his chest.

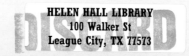